Praise for
BLACK MOUNTAIN

"Isaiah Coleridge [is] an intimidating presence . . . a big bruiser who likes nothing better than a good fight."
—*The New York Times Book Review*

"Things get downright hallucinatory as [Coleridge] proceeds toward a climax that seems as much Bram Stoker as Lawrence Block. [A] supportive librarian-girlfriend and a loyal partner-in-arms give the P.I. the emotional backup he needs to return (no doubt) for further bizarre adventures at 'the mysterious intersection of coincidence and fate.'"
—*The Wall Street Journal*

"Barron's second novel featuring retired mob strongman Isaiah Coleridge is as nasty as a cornered pit viper—and its plot is about as sinuous. . . . Barron peppers the text with literary references and philosophical reflections that provide rich counterpoint to the violent bashing and bloodletting. Fans of hardboiled crime fiction and wiseguy vernacular will be well satisfied."
—*Publishers Weekly*

"Like a lyricist, Laird Barron excels at manipulating the tones and cadence of language."
—*Associated Press*

"There's an atmosphere in these novels that rivals the darkest episodes of *True Detective*. Barron's prose bites you like a cornered animal. . . . Do you enjoy crime novels? Are you fascinated by investigators hunting down creepy serial killers? Do you like your noir dosed with existential horror? Then stop reading this review and go pick up a copy of Laird Barron's *Black Mountain*."

—*San Antonio Current*

Praise for
BLOOD STANDARD

"The action is fast-paced, the characters well drawn, the settings vivid and the hardboiled prose quirky in the manner of a writer who cut his teeth on horror and poetry."

—Associated Press

"Laird Barron has so much fun with this character, who admires Humphrey Bogart's take on Sam Spade and tosses off one-liners that bring the spirit of Dashiell Hammett into the twenty-first century."

—*Raleigh News & Observer*

"Massive, scarred Isaiah is a thug's thug, but he's also a well-read student of mythology. He's indifferent to stab wounds and generates righteous mayhem in his quest. Fans of violent crime fiction will love this one and will be eager to hear more from Isaiah."

—*Booklist* (starred review)

BLACK MOUNTAIN

LAIRD BARRON

G. P. PUTNAM'S SONS | NEW YORK

PUTNAM
—EST. 1838—
G. P. PUTNAM'S SONS
Publishers Since 1838
An imprint of Penguin Random House LLC
penguinrandomhouse.com

Copyright © 2019 by Laird Barron
Excerpt from *Worse Angels* copyright © 2020 by Laird Barron
Penguin supports copyright. Copyright fuels creativity, encourages diverse voices, promotes free speech, and creates a vibrant culture. Thank you for buying an authorized edition of this book and for complying with copyright laws by not reproducing, scanning, or distributing any part of it in any form without permission. You are supporting writers and allowing Penguin to continue to publish books for every reader.

The Library of Congress has catalogued the G. P. Putnam's Sons hardcover edition as follows:

Names: Barron, Laird, author.
Title: Black mountain / Laird Barron.
Description: New York : G. P. Putnam's Sons, [2019]
Identifiers: LCCN 2018013263| ISBN 9780735212893 (hardcover) |
ISBN 9780735212909 (ebook)
Subjects: | GSAFD: Noir fiction.
Classification: LCC PS3602.A83725 B57 2019 | DDC 813/.6—dc23
LC record available at https://lccn.loc.gov/2018013263

First G. P. Putnam's Sons hardcover edition / May 2019
First G. P. Putnam's Sons premium edition / April 2020
G. P. Putnam's Sons premium edition ISBN: 9780735217461

Printed in the United States of America
1   3   5   7   9   10   8   6   4   2

A little bird lit down on Henry Lee

—"HENRY LEE," P. J. HARVEY, NICK CAVE AND THE BAD SEEDS

Stranger: I wear no mask.
Camilla: No mask? No mask!

—*THE KING IN YELLOW*, ROBERT W. CHAMBERS

The Nightmare Life-in-Death was she,
Who thicks man's blood with cold.

—*RIME OF THE ANCIENT MARINER*, SAMUEL TAYLOR COLERIDGE

ACKNOWLEDGMENTS

Many thanks to my editor, Sara Minnich; publicists Karen Fink and Carolyn Darr; copy editor Anthony Davis; and the entire Putnam team; my agents, Janet Reid and Pouya Shahbazian; Yves Tourigny and his tireless efforts to collate my bibliography; and James McAlear for his expertise in matters of violence. Special thanks to Jessica Maciag for her love and support, and to my aunt, Timbi Porter, who always believed in me.

For Jessica M

BLACK MOUNTAIN

PART I

A LITTLE BIRD LIT DOWN

CHAPTER ONE

One lonesome winter, many years ago, I went hunting in the mountains with Gene Kavanaugh, a grand-master hitman emeritus. Sinister constellations blazed above our camp on the edge of a plateau scaled with ice. The stars are always cold and jagged as smashed glass in the winter in Alaska. Thin air seared my lungs if I inhaled too deeply. Nearby, a herd of caribou rested under the mist of its collected breath.

We weren't there for them.

Gene alternated between drinking from the neck of a bottle and playing bars on the harmonica he carried on a leather string around his neck. The tuneless tune was halting and eerie as the one Charles Bronson made famous in *Once Upon a Time in the West*.

God lit a candle and then made us. He was afraid of being alone in the dark. Gene tossed aside the empty whiskey bottle and lurched upright. He swayed, one boot in the embers of the fire, and spread his arms to embrace the dreadful star field. *What big teeth. Oh, my*

4   **LAIRD BARRON**

terrible soul. That's my reflection, out there, blown up god-sized. And look, there's yours, Isaiah. The Death's Head Nebula and its nephew. A man doesn't apprehend heaven in his gaze; he beholds a chasm. For he gazes not upward, but downward; deep into a cold, black rift strung along its jaws with tiny, dying lights.

The old man didn't rant *when* he drank; he only became louder and waxed ebullient. My participation wasn't required. I preoccupied myself with cleaning and reloading my .308 Winchester. The rifle was fairly new to me, acquired from a private dealer in Anchorage. I hadn't shot anyone with it yet.

His canvas pant leg caught fire; a single licking red flame. He glanced down and his eyes trapped the flame and glowed red as twin portals into hell. He snickered, unzipped, and urinated on his pant leg and the ashes, until steam rose and clouded his silhouette.

Disquieted, I uncapped the lens cover on my rifle and peered through the scope, panning west across wind-blown swale. I could've read a book by the cascading illumination of the stars. Eventually, I spotted the faint glow of a gasoline lantern. The light emanated from a neighboring camp tucked into the base of the drumlin ridge. Distance blurred the details. Even so, there would be three men huddled around a portable stove. Caribou hunters a long, long way from civilization.

Earlier that week, Gene and I shared a few drinks with the party of caribou hunters at the roadhouse. I didn't memorize their names, only the essentials. Two were Chicago boys. Bluff and hearty types who held their liquor, yet were soft as city people often are—expensive outdoor gear, decent haircuts, subtle cologne. One was a lefty who wore thick glasses that would surely steam over as he exhaled in the cold. The other's nose and ears were flat. A boxer's telltale badges of pugnacious courage. He breathed through his mouth and it was evident he'd long passed his prime. Both swilled beer and puffed on stogies. They identified themselves as construction workers with vacation days to burn. No better place than Alaska.

Might have been a cover story, or maybe they were on the level—Gene hadn't divulged the contents of the contract dossier. It didn't matter what occupation the pair listed on their W-2s, because it *was* a fact the boys were affiliated with the Outfit. Two lost lambs who'd gotten on the wrong side of somebody powerful and didn't even know it.

The third individual dressed and acted like a last-frontier version of the Marlboro Man. He operated as a local guide for greenhorn tourists. Zero connection to the secret lives of his clients. Hard luck for him. Another sad but true fact? Every day, people disappear without a trace in the Alaska wilderness. Nature cares not a fig for innocence or fairness.

Now, darkness and cold gathered around us. Civilized lands and the warmth of the roadhouse might as well have existed on another planet. By setting foot in this primeval vale, we'd detached ourselves from human laws and customs. The meat grinder that is fate growled into motion.

Gene had a keen nose. He scented my worry.

Relax, killer, he said. *We'll dust 'em in the morning. I need some shut-eye.*

A storm roared out of the far north and settled over the valley. Dawn brought screaming winds and drifted snow. We were buried in our tent for forty-eight hours. Visibility reduced to mere yards. When the weather broke, the other party had vanished. Gene and I strapped on snowshoes and backtracked to the roadhouse. Bastard of a slog. I slumped at the bar, rubbing my numb hands together, while he phoned Anchorage with the bad news.

I recall sipping bitter black coffee and how sweet it tasted. A monstrous black wolf's head snarled at me from its mount over the bar. The wolf disdained my temporary escape from the clutches of the wild.

It whispered, *Next time. Next time, two-legged bitch. Next time will be different.*

Almost spoiled my wonderful coffee. My mother believed in the Māori death god, Whiro, a god of darkness not dissimilar to the horned and fanged iterations of Satan. I have long held that if Whiro, or something like Whiro, exists, he's the Lord of the Wilderness—a *genius loci*, vast and immovable as a mountain. His malignance imbues the feral beasts, the trees, and the creeping ice. His evil voice is the wind crying among branches that begs men to step off the path and wander to their destruction. I felt Whiro's gaze through the dead eyes of the wolf's head.

Gene returned and ordered a shot of bourbon.

Good thing we lost those guys in the whiteout. He gulped his booze. *Get a load of this: the bosses changed their fuck-*

ing minds. It's off. Believe that? Off. Don't worry none—we still get paid our commission. You get the commission if they call it. We always get paid—plug that into your memory banks.

The Chicago duo and their guide straggled in near sunset, windburned and shaken, but very much alive. Those guys were overjoyed to have survived their ordeal. They bought rounds for the bar and paid our dinner tab. We parted ways with mutual backslapping and jocular fare-thee-wells.

Damn, life is a kick, ain't it? Gene said as he drove home along the slippery highway. *I'm sure those humps recognized me. Guy in the glasses is sharper than he lets on. When we parted at the door, we had us a moment. I saw the fear in his eyes.* The truck shifted queasily as the highway descended in a series of switchbacks. Nothing except a gulf of treetops and mist on the passenger side. *Yeah, he knew. He knew he'd shaken hands with the Reaper.*

I asked if that presented a problem.

Problem? No problem. What do I care? He'll have a story to tell his buddies in Chi-Town. He gave Mr. Death the slip. None a them will believe him. Gene's smirk softened and became inscrutable. *Besides, this road is a terminal accident waiting to happen if your brakes aren't one hundred percent.* He shimmied the wheel to emphasize his point and the truck fishtailed lazily before he got it under control by tapping first the accelerator, then the brakes. *Man, I hope that wasn't a puddle of brake fluid I saw under their car. That would be terrible.*

The truck swayed and I white-knuckled my armrest.

You were over getting drinks and they told me a story about their last hunt, Gene said. His expression had flattened into a naked skull. I had never seen him like that before. *A bummer, according to our Chicago pals. They hiked into the woods for nothing. Couldn't find a sign of moose or any other big game. They got bored, you see, and shot a mama grouse out of her nest with a bear gun. Mama grouse exploded. Nothin' but feathers, the guy said and giggled. Real knee-slapper, ain't it? Tell you what, I didn't like that story very much.*

Gene masked a smoldering anger that always threatened to roar into an inferno. He contained his rage by putting a lid over it, like snuffing a pan fire. This tactic didn't actually kill the flames; it only disguised his emotion. He clicked his tongue when he was dangerously pissed.

He'd smile, click his tongue, and wag his finger. *You shouldn't be rude with me, friend. Easy there, chum. Cool it, amigo. You should take care, pal.* He said that while imagining the offender's face crunching under his boot. He'd told me the same in exactly those terms.

Reflecting upon our adventures, I recalled that Gene had indeed performed the tongue-clicking, finger-wagging routine during supper.

I never heard about the Chicago boys again.

GO FORWARD TWENTY YEARS. Forward through fog and blood. The youthful me lay dead and buried, at least in the metaphysical sense.

Gene K's influence marked my past. I wouldn't think of him for months and then he'd be everywhere I turned. His merry fatalism preyed upon my mind a lot lately. Because it's the smallest details that eventually catch you. It's the minutiae that destroys you.

CHAPTER TWO

I was admiring a velvet tapestry that depicted a Botticelli-lush nude pursued by satyrs through jungles of the night when the trailer door flew off its hinges and two men burst in.

Goon the First—broad-shouldered and bearded—choked up on an aluminum bat, likely dented from the last skull it had crushed. He wore a plaid coat. Let's call him Beardo.

Goon the Second was a family-sized version of the first, except shaven of face and head and buffed to a high gloss. Wifebeater T-shirt, jeans, and combat boots. My man had worn the right foot apparel, at least. He dragged a three-clawed boat anchor by a chain. Not a heavy-duty boat anchor; more the type you might find on a skiff. Wouldn't have cared to get smacked with it, in any event. Let's call him Mr. Skinhead.

He co-owned a welding shop and acted as a captain of the local Aryan gang, Sons of the Iron Knife—animals who represented the weakest link in the scumbag food chain. Still, they *were* organized, mean, and numerous as flies on a pile of horseshit. Being half Māori, I wasn't popular with the Iron Knife for obvious reasons. There were less obvious reasons too; I'll save that story for another time. Suffice to say, normally I tried to steer clear. Today was different. Today was unavoidable.

I recognized Mr. Skinhead since I made a point to keep tabs on Hudson Valley scum the way a kid collects cards of ballplayers. He was also the guy I'd waited for all morning on behalf of my rightfully nervous client. Let's call my client Mr. Realtor. The trailer was his semi-secret bachelor pad situated on an otherwise vacant lot near the Kingston city limits. He'd tricked it out with mood lights, shag carpet, glass coffee tables and shelving, a selection of crass paintings and tapestries, and a plush, heart-shaped bed in the back. Tacky didn't cover it. Smelled kind of nice, though.

Why were we gathered in this love nest? Ah, for among the oldest reasons in existence—caveman jealousy. Mr. Realtor had perpetrated a sleazy affair with Mr. Skinhead's wife. Alas, somebody let the cat out of the bag, as gossipy gangbangers are inclined to do. Mr. Skinhead craved vengeance for his slighted manhood.

I'd hoped to greet one opponent. In close quarters, such as the living room of the double-wide, I could handle three amateurs without resorting to a gun. Probably. There were only two, though. Reasonable odds. Unless five more apes waited in the wings. In that scenario, someone, or several someones, would get shot, stabbed, and/or set afire.

"Hi, guys." I'd stuffed weapons into every pocket and up my sleeves. My empty hands set them slightly at ease.

"You ain't the ratfuck I'm here to beat." Mr. Skinhead ran the chain through his fingers.

"Correct," I said. "The rat couldn't be with us . . . today. I'm an entirely different animal."

Mr. Skinhead gave me a slow once-over. My worst scars don't show when I'm wearing a suit. Can't hide them all, though; the visible nicks gave him pause.

His eyes narrowed instead of widening.

"Wait a sec—I know you. You're that guy. The lunatic. Coleridge."

"What?" Beardo said. "Who?"

"Charmed." I cracked my knuckles.

SO, A QUICK ASIDE ABOUT MR. REALTOR, the man who'd hired me to run interference. He operated a thriving real estate company and owned a spread near Port Ewen. Drove last year's model Jag, often accessorized by a hottie in the passenger seat. His well-tanned likeness winked from a billboard on Route 9W, and he flashed an irritatingly glamorous smile in frequent television spots.

Mr. Realtor fancied himself the Second Coming of Lothario. Clean-cut and pretty as a Ken doll, so why not? Problem is, Lotharios risk getting run over by karma. Can't say everybody who knew Mr. Realtor loved him, but they *knew* him. Business is a contact sport. Some of these folks, the ones lacking warm and fuzzy feelings, expressed violent desires, and that's where I came in.

The story so far: Mr. Skinhead (counseled by his cheating wife) had approached Mr. Realtor about the possibility of laundering money via a real estate scheme. My client didn't use those exact words, but I got the drift. A few days ago, Mrs. Skinhead alerted Mr. Realtor to the unsettling news that her husband was on to their affair and plotting to even the score when their paths crossed again. Mr. Skinhead didn't know that Mr. Realtor had been tipped off to this fact.

The realtor's plan was straightforward—feigning blissful ignorance, he'd call a meeting to go over particulars regarding the scam. I'd be on the scene in his stead. After I beat some sense into the angry husband, Mr. Realtor would enter from the wings and break the news that he'd recorded their "business" conversations. Essentially, forgive the affair and nobody would go to jail on a Federal money-laundering beef.

Aside from abetting infidelity and extortion, I calculated it would be a cut-and-dried job. Maybe a 3 or 4 on the risk scale if cuckolded hubby packed a gun. Silly me.

WERE THIS A NICE, SIMPLE HIT, I would've jumped out of a broom closet with a shotgun blazing. *Boom, boom,* account closed. Sadly, I'd sworn off hitting. For the most part. The straight and narrow is a rocky row to hoe.

Assessing a foe, I imagine a triangle over his knees and groin. I visualize a line that divides his face from the bridge of the nose to the chin. Strike under the jaw with sufficient force, you'll shatter the mandible and possibly dislocate vertebrae in the neck. Perhaps he'll sever his tongue and strangle on blood. Strike the nose hard, temporary blindness results. Clap an ear, he'll go deaf. Clap both ears simultaneously and the subsequent rupture might cause death. Punch the throat or sternum, you take away his air. Possibly more. One can never tell. The human body is a paradox—nearly indestructible, yet infinitely fragile.

I made a last-ditch, albeit disingenuous, attempt to reason with my visitors.

"Be advised, I'm here to parlay. This doesn't need to get ugly." Yes, yes it did.

Mr. Skinhead sneered.

"'Parlay'? Only thing I want is to see you bleed." It signified nothing more than the bark of a dog; he hoped to distract me by the meagerest fraction and give his comrade an opportunity to get in some work.

Dream on. I watched Beardo make his play before it ever began.

Any given fight has a multitude of variables, but is usually governed by the principle of the path of least resistance. Most bullyboys simply aren't creative. Ninety percent of the time, a lug cradling a baseball bat is going to unleash if he thinks he has room.

Beardo swung at my head like he intended to belt a homer over the Green Monster. I stepped forward as he rotated his shoulders and caught the barrel of the bat with my left hand and his left wrist with my right. The contact, although partially arrested, jolted my brain. He was strong. Under no circumstance the manner of brute you'd want to pit your manliness against in an honorable contest. I dragged my heel down his shin and stomped his instep. He would've screamed—because imagine the edge of a dull ax scraping bark from a tree trunk—except as the shock of pain rolled over him, I cranked the bat as if wrenching the wheel of an out-of-control car. His left shoulder separated and he lost his grip and I yanked him toward me, off-balance, then shoved in a whipsaw action. Beardo ate aluminum. He keeled backward and went down.

The entire struggle lasted under three and a half seconds.

Mr. Skinhead reacted adroitly once his partner dropped. He pitched the anchor underhand at my head and missed by a gnat's hair. A window tinkled behind me. I could guess what came next and slid sideways as he heaved on the chain and the anchor recoiled. Metal grazed my arm, ripping suit fabric and gashing me deep. The blaze of pain cost me a second and I was late setting my feet to receive the inevitable rush.

He released the chain, lowered his head, and bulldozed into me. My ribs bent inward as far as they could, and a smidgeon farther.

Heavy, muscular, and frenzied with rage and fear, Mr. Skinhead's tackle was no joke. He clamped my shoulders and carried me to the floor. Falling, I tucked my knees into my chest and straightened them the instant we landed. It's a judo technique called *Tomoe nage*. My dad taught me a half-assed version of the traditional throw in grade school. He called it the monkey flip. The way it's supposed to work is you drive your heels into your opponent's midsection, jackknifing, and he's lifted and flung away in a sort of forward somersault like a drunken Superman. I'm no martial artist, and, remember, cramped quarters. My head bounced off the floor, and that screwed my timing as well. Instead of a graceful somersault, Mr. Skinhead crashed through the ceiling, hung there for a moment in a tangle of trailer innards, then fell on his hands onto the carpet, right leg caught in the hole so that he dangled vertically. I rolled, stood, and after a few seconds of gloating at his predicament, front-kicked him in the belly. Less than full power. Forceful enough that he ripped free, rebounded from a wall, and face-planted on a coffee table. The table collapsed beneath him in a bed of shattered glass.

I gave the man kudos for sheer belligerence. Mr. Skinhead struggled to his hands and knees. Jags of glass stuck out of his face. You can picture the bloody mess. He went for a gun in his waistband. I slapped it away as he pulled the trigger and the bullet holed one of those funky tapestries.

My expression must have spoken volumes.

"Aw, shit," he said.

I looped the anchor chain around his neck and dragged him through the front door, down two cinder-block steps, and onto the gravel lawn. *Bump, bumpety-bump.* His head bounced satisfyingly. He choked and groaned until I kicked him in the gut again.

Waiting for him to recover, I sat on a cinder block and examined my injuries. Yet another suit ruined and a chunk of flesh sacrificed to the death gods. Blood streamed from my cuff and over my knuckles. More blood trickled from a knot on the back of my head. My left hand already swelled where the bat had jammed my fingers. Sharp jolts of pain in sync with my pulse indicated I'd broken, or re-broken, a bone. Similar deal with my rib cage where it had absorbed the brunt of Mr. Skinhead's battering-ram tackle. It hurt to breathe, which meant bruised or cracked ribs. Goody. I thought about kicking him again. Too much effort.

Mr. Skinhead curled tight. He dry-heaved and finally regained the strength to open his eyes.

"Does it hurt more getting whupped by a darkie?" I said. "Is it a Nazi demerit? Will you have to make up a story to tell your pals?"

He asked if his buddy was dead or alive and I said alive.

"Hope you got your fee in advance," he said.

Indeed, I had collected a modest retainer, balance due after the job depending upon what exigencies arose.

"Say again?"

He wheezed laughter.

"Dude—why'd you hire on with a scumbag? He's a crook, which you know. He's bangin' my wife, which you must also know. Why'd you take his side in this?"

"You can hardly blame the lady—I wouldn't fuck an Aryan scuzzball either." I dialed my client and went directly to voice mail.

Mr. Skinhead sighed dramatically.

"Had a feeling that slimeball was in the wind. I didn't come here to retrieve my woman. I come here to retrieve a shitpot of money. Too late now. Those two are in Mexico for sure."

I asked him what was so funny. Turns out, absolutely nothing.

YES, MR. REALTOR had already skipped town. I admit my surprise; the guy had sunk roots in Ulster County. What I didn't know until my chat with Mr. Skinhead was that he and Mr. Realtor were in cahoots to perpetrate a land development swindle.

My client had played me hard. While I dealt with the angry husband/business partner, Mr. Realtor and the skinhead's wife disappeared to parts unknown carrying matching luggage jammed with cash.

Whoops, as the kids say.

Luckily for me, and unluckily for him, Mr. Skinhead's entrepreneurial wheelings and dealings weren't sanctioned by the gang. Worse—for him anyway—he'd "borrowed" a stomach-churning quantity of capital from the Iron Knife treasury—i.e., the dough Mr. Realtor had carried away.

After an earnest heart-to-heart, Mr. Skinhead and I agreed to let bygones be bygones and never ever speak of the incident.

I packed him and Beardo into my truck and ferried them to the ER at Kingston General. A security guard surveyed the mess and asked what happened. I said the first guy ran into a door and the second guy tried to help him. Then I casually split for home.

Forget supper—I gulped a shot or three of sour mash and fell unconscious in my chair, blood still dripping down my arm and onto the floor in a puddle.

That marked the close of my second summer in exile.

CHAPTER THREE

The headless corpse of a small-time criminal named Harold Lee surfaced on the Ashokan Reservoir. Page 2 of the local paper featured a black-and-white photo of a body bag near tall reeds. The water looked cold. Mystified cops compared notes in the background. Setting aside the luridness of the composition, it seemed nothing more than another sad example of "Live by the sword, get your head lopped by the sword."

I'd met Lee (inevitable, since we traveled in the same crooked circles) at one bar or another. Average height and build. Handsome in a distinguished dad fashion, with blue eyes and a square jaw; black hair going silver, although he usually covered it with a hat. Dapper fellow—his wardrobe might have been best described as on-a-budget sharp. He favored Rat Pack knockoff suits. Lee bought me a round, or maybe I treated him. We weren't friends. We weren't anything, really.

I flipped to the funnies, wincing at the tenderness in my hand—I'd recently removed the homemade splint. The whack to my dome gifted me with headaches now and again. I didn't heal so quickly anymore and feared the time of reading glasses and arthritis pills loomed nigh.

A wiseguy named Marion Curtis rang and told me to meet him around 7 p.m. for drinks at the Green Goddess, a hole-in-the-wall in Rosendale. He hung up before I could say I was busy washing my hair.

I kept it casual—leather jacket, white T-shirt, jeans, and my favorite steel-toed Doc Martens. Oxblood, laced tight. I holstered a .38 snub against the flat of my back and climbed into the pickup.

The Rondout Valley is country mouse to the hilt if you're accustomed to NYC or even Albany. Dregs of an alkaline-orange sunset filtered through a tunnel of dying leaves. Rolling past secluded cemeteries, a boondocks VFW hall, and clapboard houses shuttered tight against the onrushing dark, I pondered the tête-à-tête with Curtis. What *does* an ex-hitter such as myself say to a mob captain who refuses to accept you've gone semi-straight? The drive afforded me a few minutes to rehearse polite demurrals.

One wouldn't find the Green Goddess by thumbing through the phone book. Essentially, a modern-day speak-easy, its clientele made the list by invitation or referral. Instead of illicit hooch and dancing girls, Green Goddess dealt in *illicit information* and dancing girls. The water-hole of choice among the discerning effete and criminals.

The club occupied the basement of a former church that had undergone several conversions since its Gothic Revival heyday. Fronted by an antique store, the alley side was modeled upon a grotesque architectural phase of offbeat nightclubs, circa 1920s France. Ivy screened crumbling brick walls. Windows were blacked out. A six-step descent brought patrons to the arched threshold of a heavy door, also slathered in black paint. Three gargoyles leered from atop the lintel.

Legend had it, the gargoyles originally warded an English cathedral. Some ne'er-do-well pried Huey, Dewey, and Louie free and smuggled the trio to America on a steam freighter. Lore further claimed bootleggers had used a tunnel beneath the Green Goddess to access hidey-holes among the caverns of Widow Jane Mine in nearby Joppenbergh Mountain. Wind didn't moan through the shafts—those were the cries of the restless dead.

My kind of gin mill.

A bouncer slid aside the security grate at my knock.

"Let me in by the hair on your chinny chin chin," I said.

He wasn't impressed. I grudgingly recited the password of the evening (*We make this world our hell*) and he threw the bolt. Hinges squealed like the front door to a haunted mansion in a Universal monster flick. The bouncer even bore a passing resemblance to a young Vincent Price.

"Welcome to the Goddess." His disdainful glance implied that I'd undershot "casual dress" by a mile or so.

"Much obliged, Vince." I stepped past him into the belly of the whale.

THE SHADOWY DEN smelled of anise and cigarettes. Low, ribbed-beam ceiling and velvet upholstery. Electric candelabras. Tough to nail what the designers were going for—hipster decadent? At any rate, Oscar Wilde would've detested the cedar paneling.

Card tables were occupied by the well-heeled set. Not too many bohemians among the dinner jackets and party dresses. However, I spotted two plainclothes cops of my (unfortunate) acquaintance, a mob fixer, and a gigolo gone stag for the evening. A man in Roaring Twenties' gangster attire serenaded the audience from a dais under the lonely blue icicle of a spotlight.

"Absinthe?" I slid in across from Curtis at his corner booth. "I'm told it maketh the heart grow fonder."

"Oh, Jesus, Coleridge." He stirred his drink. Two empties indicated he'd gotten a running start. "Try one on for size. Lady might agree with you." The bags under his eyes weren't convincing.

"Didn't that hooch kill Poe?"

"Didn't help. Poe died of rabies anyway."

I ordered a double whiskey neat from the server who'd made a beeline at my host's nod.

Curtis wore one of his trademark suits—tonight, a Caruso butterfly. Had somebody sworn he presided over Sunday gangsters' barbecue in formalwear, I would've believed them. Slick, graying hair, neatly manicured nails, pancake makeup, a hint of eyeliner, and a pat of Clive Christian's 1872 in the unlikely case his Rolex required complementing. At a glance, one might write him off as a pretty, slightly soft, middle-aged executive. Big mistake—he served as the red right hand of Eddy Deluca, don of the Albany Syndicate. Curtis knew where heaps of bodies were buried because he'd shoveled the dirt.

"Thanks for showin'." He extended me the courtesy of implying I'd much of a choice. Less than a year ago, he'd provided material aid in disposing of my worst enemy, an Outfit button man named Vitale Night. "How's your girl?"

"Meg is annoyed I'm boozing with you instead of rubbing her feet after a long day. And yours?"

"Same. I slipped the pool boy a twenty to massage her bunions." He plucked a Nat Sherman from an ashtray and dragged. "Wish somebody would rub mine, for once."

"This modern era is bedeviled by inequity between the sexes," I said. "Foot rubs are a one-way street."

"Speakin' of the street, word out there is, you're a busy man. Got dirty laundry? Call in Isaiah Coleridge. He gets the tough stains out."

"Sounds dramatic. I mostly stick to the legit."

"Sure, pal. Although 'mostly' leaves a wide streak of gray to navigate."

"It does indeed."

Curtis smiled with all his teeth.

"Music to my ears. Means you'll have no problem doin' me a favor." He didn't add that it also wouldn't be a problem because I owed him big. The tab always comes nigh with the mob and there's no past-due notice. Except this was worse than I'd reckoned on. "You recently, uh, accepted a job for a realtor in Kingston. Tuned up a couple of guys who were doing business with a shady realtor. Yeah, your expression says you know of whom I speak."

He shook his head to forestall my commentary. "Don't sweat it. It's a teeny bit complicated because we have a minor interest in what those fellas were doing. See, one of the guys you thrashed worked for me, undercover-like. He was supposed to let the deal unfold and then do the good ol' double cross. Now our boy's listenin' to his bones knit and the ringleader is in the wind. I ain't mad. I know your character. You'll wanna square accounts."

Tempting as it was to make with eloquent excuses, I waited for the other shoe. That was easy; I could see him winding up to smack me with his size ten.

"Catch today's *Gazette*?" he said.

My mind's eye did a smash cut to the story about the dead goon in the Ashokan.

"I may have skimmed it." The joke didn't land. "What's the noise?"

"Harold Lee got clipped. Horrible, absolutely horrible. Remember Harry? Tight with the Kingston crowd. Mr. Nothin' Personal."

"Alas, I knew him. Although not well." My drink arrived and we clinked glasses. "To Harry 'Nothin' Personal' Lee." Harry always reflexively apologized before he put the hurt on some hapless piker. "Here lies a man who knew how to twist an arm."

"*Salud*. My crew swore by the fella. Real pro, not a yahoo. That end a the racket is crawlin' with yahoos."

"You're telling me."

According to the stat line, the recently departed Lee had done a contract or two in his impetuous youth and decided it wasn't his cup of tea. He specialized in strong-

arm collection; Louisville Slugger or a lead pipe, pick
your poison. Mild gambler, moderate drinker, no dope.
Leaned on debtors exactly hard enough to do the job.
Perfect for loan sharks who wanted a rent-a-thug to handle the light work.

Curtis said, "They dumped Harry in the reservoir.
Washed up day before yesterday. Buddy a mine with the
Kingston PD puts the body at close to a week in the drink.
Real half-assed disposal effort. Wallet and cash weren't
touched." He lowered his voice. "Report doesn't state the
cause of death. His body was mutilated, though. Some
bastard sawed his head and hands off."

"As in . . . ?" I made a slicing motion.

"As in, decapitated with a serrated knife. A big one—
Green River or Bowie."

"Goddamn."

"Exactly my reaction," he said. "Animals runnin'
wild." Curtis operated with cool precision. In his mind,
unorganized crime constituted a plague. While the Mafia
might be savage, it imposed order upon chaos, much as
the Romans brought law and culture to the "barbarian"
hordes. He had me pegged as one of the good savages,
and I let it ride.

"The killer absconded with the hands and head?"

"Hell if I know. All I heard is, they haven't recovered
'em."

"But you have your suspicions."

"Oodles and oodles of 'em. Suspicions are free as air."
He dabbed his mouth with a napkin. "I want you to look
into this on the Q.T."

"Where's your faith in the police?" I nodded toward the off-duty detectives. The frumpy couple might've passed for man and wife if I hadn't known the score. We crossed paths now and again. I could testify that the dishwater blonde threw a mean hook. "I'm *certain* Kingston's finest will bust ass to solve the death of a career felon."

We shared a chuckle.

He said, "The pigs keep wrigglin' from under my thumb. Can't get a solid day's labor out a them. I fear this demands an independent investigation."

"You must have what, a dozen foot soldiers bucking for a promotion? Round up a posse of goons and see justice done, Old West style."

"No can do." His blunt rejoinder contained a multitude of implications, none pleasing.

"No? What does that mean?"

"Means no. Means I require a fuckin' consultant and you're bustin' my balls here. Ain't you a detective? I got a card that says you are."

"Unlike flattery, mockery will get you nowhere."

Problem was, he indeed carried my spiffy new business card.

Acquiring a New York State PI license was a snap. Not only had I picked an opportune moment to be thrown out of the Outfit, what with the Russian mob tightening its grip on Alaska, apparently years of criminal activity on behalf of the Outfit hadn't left more than a minor blemish or two on my permanent record.

A retired investigator in Alaska recalled me fondly. The former gumshoe vouched for my investigative experience and dummied up the relevant papers. I aced the exam and paid the fee. A few short weeks later, presto. Snazzy photo ID in hand, I joined the hallowed ranks of private dicks alongside the Continental Op, Mike Hammer, Spenser, et al. This lent me supreme authority to snoop and an excuse to pack heat on the regular.

While Coleridge Investigations wouldn't be taking on too many traditional cases, it provided a plausible shopfront for my more esoteric enterprises. If I caught the occasional gig tailing a cheating spouse or pocketed five hundred a day to track a runaway teen, fine and dandy. That said, tackling a murder investigation on behalf of the New York mob hadn't figured into my wildest plans.

I tried another tack.

"Leg breaker gets iced, and you give a damn because . . . ?"

"Compelling interests in Kingston. Harry wasn't quite family, so I can't overreact. But, I gotta go through the motions. It's a matter of perception. Leave it at that."

"La Cosa Nostra moves in mysterious ways, blah, blah. How it usually unfolds: I get a name and I hunt the person. Very straightforward. This is tricky. As in, actual detective work. I understand you want to play it close to the vest, but you have to throw me a rope."

"Fair point," Curtis said. "Harry isn't the first of our affiliates who've kicked in a similar manner. Second-story pro Ray Anderson took a shiv two years ago. Serrated knife right through his guts. Key word: *serrated*. Went down late at night near the waterfront. Drunk pack of fraternity brothers interrupted the proceedings. The attacker melted into the woodwork. Anderson died at Kingston General without regaining consciousness. He'd done jobs for us since George Bush, Senior, ran the White House, so we interviewed the wife."

"I'm guessing she couldn't help crack the case."

"Anderson's wife said he spent his last night on earth doing the town with an acquaintance. She didn't catch the friend's name. Figured he might be in the life, for obvious reasons. I let it slide. Shit happens, yeah? Now Lee receives the same treatment, with a side of mutilation. Enough to make a fellow wonder."

Two similar murders didn't necessarily indicate a pattern. Two dead independent contractors who'd done business for the local mob? Well, as Curtis had said, it was enough to make a man wonder.

"Is there a direct connection between Lee and the thief?"

"Did they know each other? Sure, sure. Everybody knows everybody and everybody pulls a job or two together. Were they die-hard buddies?" He spread his hands and shrugged.

"A former colleague with a vendetta could have done them both."

"Possible. Here's where you come in, like a cadaver dog. You can navigate the underworld. People will tell you what they'd never dream of telling a cop. Regular rules don't apply."

"More important, I'm unaffiliated." Code for "I could tread where he dared not." Best of all, if I went too far, it was my problem, not his.

"Bingo. You've got scruples, but not too many of 'em."

"I'm not interested in bloodshed." Saying it didn't make it so. My relationship with violence was ever-evolving. No use burdening my mobster pal with undue nuance.

He feigned innocence.

"Bloodshed? *Moi?* Who said anything about bloodshed?"

"This isn't about Vitale Night?"

"Ah, because you snuffed Mr. Quick Draw, maybe I think you got a special talent for icing button men? No, it ain't like that."

"Carrying water for wiseguys tends to lead down a dark path."

"Ask around. It'll ease my mind. Mayhem is strictly optional."

"Ask around, okay?"

"Be your mean self while you're asking."

"That's the only self I have." I drained my whiskey. Couldn't think of a polite way out before I reached the bottom of the glass. "I'll shake the tree. Be swell if you could point me toward a likely candidate. Any disgruntled former employees in particular you like for this?"

"Traditionally, we fit malcontents with concrete galoshes. Tends to have a discouraging effect."

"Sure does. Back in Alaska, I chaired the Outfit's Department of Union Grievances."

"Interview Lee's housemate. Kid named Nic Royal. He moved in earlier this year—Harry was showin' him the ropes. Another tough-as-nails bouncer, rent-a-thug.

Cover the bases. Royal even looks at you cross-eyed, I wanna know."

"Cops say it's always the spouse."

"Call me *directly* if you find somethin'." His emphasis on *directly* didn't escape my notice. He pushed a fat envelope across the table. "Your retainer plus the police report, the contents of Lee's wallet, and a list of notable acquaintances. Get you started on the right foot."

It chilled me that Curtis had obtained physical evidence from a major crime. Forget the long arm of the law—the Deluca Family's reach was frightening. I'd almost forgotten the power of the Family.

"None of my associates are to hear a whisper," he said. "Fat Frank, Bobby the Whip, none of them. As for the cops"—he nodded at the plainclothes pair. "They come across anything pertinent, I'll pass along the news. Got it?"

I didn't get it, not even close, and that worried me plenty.

CHAPTER FOUR

Lunar moths battered the porch light at Meg's.

My girl split a modest two-bedroom house in Tillson with her son, Devlin, and a seldom seen roommate. Her librarian's salary didn't cover many frills after student loan payments, babysitting fees, and all the rest.

We weren't married, might never be, and that curtailed my role as a provider. I brought groceries once or twice a week and took her and the boy to dinner as often as she'd permit. Difficult to help Megara Shaw—she was as stubborn as any person I'd met. The merest whiff of being kept by a man was anathema to her sensibilities.

I let myself in and sneaked around the darkened interior, trying not to trip over scattered toys. School night meant Devlin had already gone down for the count. Occasionally, when the world piled trouble on my shoulders and life grew ever more byzantine, I felt a melancholy pang for mac and cheese dinners and a first grader's curfew.

Devlin's room was painted purple and yellow. Glow-in-the-dark stars formed the Big and Little Dippers across the ceiling. Superhero posters; a wooden footlocker with toys jamming the lid open. One dared not venture inside while barefoot for dread of a Lego- or action-figure-related injury.

Meg sat in the kitchen, organizing bills by the lonely glow of a porcelain lamp. She'd loosed her dark hair and slipped on a pair of drugstore reading glasses. I'd told her they looked sharp. She hated the glasses, never mind my opinion. Minerva lay at her feet, motionless as a stone, eyes burning holes into my soul.

Over the past year and change since her rescue, my mongrel had evolved from a scrawny, terrified puppy to a confident watchdog bolstered by pearly white fangs and seventy pounds of muscle. An associate of mine had begun training her as a protection dog to properly channel her instincts. Minerva ranged Hawk Mountain Farm (where I currently hung my homburg) or camped with Meg and Devlin when I wandered afield on business. A kid should grow up with dogs. Judging by Minerva's sweet, implacable protectiveness, I had a hunch she loved them best.

The dog rose and pawed my knee until she received her quota of pats.

I rummaged in the cabinet, retrieved a bottle of California red, and poured half a glass. I set the glass near Meg's left hand and kissed the nape of her neck. Then I leaned against the sink and watched her for a few minutes. She sighed and stared into the distance. She got that thousand-yard stare when visualizing her recently estranged husband, Mackenzie.

"Is he late with the child support?" I said.

She sipped and grimaced.

"Child support is discontinued."

I didn't do the gallant thing and offer to brace the ex or tide her over with cash. She would've punched me in the balls. Instead, while she drank her wine and fumed in radioactive silence, I kept my trap shut and waited.

She raised her glass and I refilled it.

"The ex took a job in Nicaragua," she said. "His aunt owns a construction company. He sent me a note and that's all it said. *Jettin' to Central America, see ya when I see ya.* Broke the lease on his apartment. Didn't leave a forwarding address. I don't think we'll hear from him anytime soon."

I wanted to say sorry. I couldn't muster the hypocrisy.

Meg stood and rinsed her glass. She gripped my belt and towed me toward the bedroom. Sleek and wiry, she possessed the outsized power of a serious athlete. Her robe came undone and we toppled onto her bed.

"Please don't hurt me," I said half seriously.

Her vulpine smile promised nothing.

"WOULD YOU KILL HIM IF I ASKED?"

Once upon a time, I might've lain in bed and smoked a cigarette. Now, I stared at the ceiling and regretted my temperance. Our shoulders and thighs touched, sealed with cooling sweat.

"Kill whom?" I said.

"You know."

I knew, indeed. The dastardly deadbeat ex-husband had pissed her off royally.

"Would you . . . take a contract?" she said.

"Technically, *you* take out the contract. I fulfill the contract."

"Okay, smartass. Answer the question."

It seemed I'd spent the entire night dodging rhetorical gambits.

"I'd decline."

"Why?"

"Besides that I'm retired? A chick driving a 1997 Passat can't afford my rates."

She caressed my belly.

"You aren't retirement age. So . . . could I finagle a friend discount?"

"Pro bono is an option." I turned my head to regard her in the near darkness. Doubtless, this rendered my expression suitably sphinxlike. "This what you want? Are you certain?"

"Smile. I'm putting you on." When I didn't respond, she stiffened. "Can't you see I've had a rough day and I'm joking?"

I gazed at her, and let the mask slip a fraction, let her feel a whisper of the winter wind that blows through my heart of hearts.

"Isaiah," she said. "Tell me you understand I'm kidding."

"Do you want it to look like an accident? Dead easy to slip off a roof. Or would you prefer an example to be made? The Outfit goes gaga over examples. A sander can buff a man's skin from his bones. Earplugs and a raincoat are recommended for that menu item."

"Should I be afraid? Is that what you're hinting at?"

"Of me? No. I'm your willing slave."

"Why are you acting like this? For the third time— I'm joking."

"Many a truth is told in jest."

"Many a jest is told in jest, jerk."

It hit me not too long after that. Her ex received custody of Devlin every other Saturday. The realization flowed through my blood, cold and dark.

"Did Mac . . . Did he tell Devlin?"

Her breathing slowed.

"They were supposed to tour the Wild Acres Animal Sanctuary over in High Falls. The only things Dev loves as much as his superheroes are wolves. It was kinda rough explaining why his daddy left without a good-bye. He didn't cry, didn't ask any questions. He was coloring in his book. Said, 'Okay,' and kept coloring. Hasn't mentioned it since."

I wanted to communicate to her that we're humans; we learn to accept whatever indignity, whatever intolerable condition. She didn't need me to state the obvious. I did the only thing I could, and that was to hold her hand as it got later and later.

PHANTOM DENIZENS of my subconscious swooped in for their periodic torments. They spirited me back to

Alaska for a nightmare about my old mentor, Gene K, and my father, Mervin. My long-dead dog, Achilles, was there too.

Gene passed away during a blizzard in the Wrangell Mountains in '08. No such luck in regard to my estranged father. He'd retired early from the Air Force and currently moonlighted as an asset for one government intelligence agency or another. To my knowledge, the men hadn't met in the real world.

Dreams are like that, though. Murky distortions of reality. Rarely, they're a wiretap on the cosmic phone line— an early warning of some hell headed one's way. This was such an instance, although I wouldn't put one and two together for a while.

The four of us bunkered in Gene's cabin in the depths of a blizzard. Besieged by the forces of evil, was my impression of our circumstances. Frost rimed the interior walls. Floorboards groaned as we lurched from window to window with our rifles. I'd reverted to early childhood. The weapon felt heavy.

Figures skulked among the trees that surrounded the cabin.

Gene hunched, gaunt and feral as a starving wolf. His own totem animal made flesh. Dad's silver hair hung lank over his red-rimmed eyes. I must not have looked any better, because he glanced at me mournfully. The real Mervin Coleridge would have sooner gnawed his arm off than display a glimmer of sentimentality.

Dream logic being what it is, I knew the civilized world

had succumbed to darkness. Everyone we'd ever loved was dead. We were dead too; just spending the last of the bullets.

Gene said, *Don't worry, killer. We're gonna make it.* He'd always been a smooth liar.

Dad said, *Love and loyalty are the two most powerful forces in the universe. They won't save you in the end. Nobody is saved.*

The cabin dimmed as snowdrifts blotted the winter sun. My companions became silhouettes, then disappeared except for their agonized breathing. I crouched, blind, cold, and afraid. Achilles began to bark.

Nightmare Dad was correct. We still hadn't made it when dawn's light beamed through the curtains and woke me from the death dream and into the present.

CHAPTER FIVE

I drove home to Hawk Mountain Farm. My agenda: a three-mile jog over hill and dale followed by a scalding shower. The jog was more of a stagger; my cracked ribs and bruised spleen were on the mend, but drawing deep breaths required real willpower. Better every day; that and *You should see the other guys!* were mild consolation.

Established in the '60s, Hawk Mountain Farm proper was a tranquil collection of antiquated structures at the end of a winding private dirt road amid the hills north of New Paltz. A raggedy association of white-haired refugees from the days of Timothy Leary and peak counter-culturism, tenanted shacks and lean-tos scattered across several hundred wooded acres.

The languid pace and cast of eccentric local characters soothed me. Minerva loved to race through the fields and into the surrounding woods. Her doggy joy counted for much as well. We dwelt in a snug cabin—bedroom, bath-room, and kitchenette. The well-stocked fridge, DVD player, shelf loaded with books, and a stereo satisfied my basic survival requirements. The dog received a steady supply of kibble and steak bones. Neither of us required any more in regard to material comfort.

After the run, I put on a decent suit and searched for my dear friend Lionel Robard. When not playing Iolaus to my Hercules on one mission or another, he worked as a roustabout and bunked in a cabin near my own.

The farm—or rehabilitated hippie commune, as Lionel saw it—belonged to the Walkers, an elderly couple who hosted symposiums on a multitude of esoteric subjects and provided life-coaching services to wealthy rubes. Incidentally, the couple rescued stray animals—and the occasional stray human, as I could attest. My former boss with the Outfit, Mr. Apollo, pulled strings to land me a bed at the farm when I departed Alaska as an exile.

Shortly after my arrival in New York, the Walkers' teenage granddaughter, Reba, had gone missing under a cloud of mystery. Signs pointed to her relationship with local gangbangers as the cause. I went looking for the girl and found her. Too late.

Perhaps that singular failure is why I still hadn't moved on—in every sense of the word. Guilt is a burden that begins as a grain of sand and ultimately becomes a boulder you push up an endless hill. In any event, the segue from my previous life of adventure and routine bloodshed to that of a rustic detective required an adjustment.

Lionel had assisted my search for the Walker girl. Our failure hit him hard, although he was the type to conceal such pain. Prior to his role as a farmhand, he served multiple deployments in Afghanistan and Iraq with the Marine Corps Force Reconnaissance.

My own difficulties with acclimating to a relatively normal existence paled next to his. Reintegration to civilian life proved a challenge. Lionel said if his existence were dramatized as a cable network Movie of the Week, he'd weep whenever a car backfired and ultimately find salvation in honest country labor and the love of a good woman. He spent his days in the field, bucking hay and mending fences, and his nights down at the Golden Eel, running up a tab. Consorting with a bevy of loose women hadn't moved him along the path to redemption either.

He emerged from the barn as I approached.

"I have a job opportunity for you," I said.

Minerva, who'd ridden home shotgun, barked and trotted over to him. Lionel didn't own a dog. That didn't fool Minerva.

"Already got a job." His hands were skinned from repairing the tractor. Cold-eyed and lean, he'd let his blond crew cut grow shaggy, although he covered it in a dusty safari hat that snapped on the side. He knelt to scratch Minerva's ears.

"Yeah, yeah," I said. "I promise this will be even more fun than shoveling shit. Are you and your car available early tomorrow morning?"

"Chauffeuring you is frequently hazardous."

"Understood—this will be no exception. Name your reasonable price."

Lionel gambled heavily. Football, basketball, boxing,

ponies—you name it. Lucky streaks were the reason he owned a restored 1975 Monte Carlo and an arsenal to rival the collections of gun nuts and militiamen everywhere. More common losing streaks, alongside a ferocious booze addiction, were also the primary source of his perpetual impoverishment. He quite literally could not afford to refuse my offer.

He said, "My day rate is gas money, two packs of cigs, and a bottle of hundred-proof bourbon."

"Sold. I'll buy you some clothes too. Twill Dickies and a safari hat? For the love of God."

"It's a safari *adventure* hat. Nobody cares how I dress. I'm merely the wheelman. You're the face."

"A face ideally suited to hand modeling."

"Draw to your strengths, brother. Why don't we get started today?"

"I want to lay the groundwork, make a few calls. And I've got other fish to fry. Phone has rung off the hook lately. People are desperate."

"Damsel in distress? Kitten up a tree?"

"The owner of the Deadfall Gymnasium has a problem that requires a delicate touch."

"Makes sense. You're renowned for your delicacy."

THE DAY I'D formally established myself as a private detective, I rented an office. It is an immutable law that a bona fide private detective must acquire a bolt-hole to hang his homburg and .38, preferably shepherded by a buxom girl Friday. A beautiful receptionist might get me into more trouble than I could handle, so I opted to keep the overhead low, for the moment.

I'd chosen a building two blocks north of Main Street in Stone Ridge, a hamlet between New Paltz and Kingston. Stone Ridge used to be a province of Greater Rosendale; rock quarry country a few miles southwest of the Ashokan Spillway. Now it was a bedroom community bordered by farmland.

A tourist could hit every highlight in a five-minute cruise, end to end, along the main drag: Emmanuel's, a boutique shopping center in the west; Davenport Farms, a market warehouse for local agriculture in the east; and a string of banks, restaurants, and assorted shops between. You'd pass stands of big trees and historical homes dating to the Colonial era, and frequently glimpse those green mountains to the north. The hamlet charmed me instantly. Rural, yet central to my activities in the Mid-Hudson Valley.

In a twist of fate, that shady realtor who skipped to Mexico with the Aryan blood money and left me holding the bag? Indeed, he's the man who originally showed me the property and that's how we came to have further, less fortunate dealings.

The Elton Cooper Building, a stone-and-plaster job slapped together in 1938, occupied its own lot. Lynn's Fortune Shop sat across the quiet lane adjacent to an abandoned garage. The proprietor read palms and peddled occult knickknacks. She smoked ganja on the front porch. Residential houses were scattered farther back amid copses of elm, maple, and old-growth sycamore. A stream curved through the woods to Stone Ridge Pond. Raccoons pillaged trash cans and deer grazed on lawns. That was the neighborhood.

The ground-level neighbor had recently departed New York City. He ran an art gallery. Second floor was me and a recording studio down the hall. The studio operated about as frequently as I did, which is to say not very. I had not met the owner. The interior aesthetic clinched the deal. From the frosted-glass entrance that read COLERIDGE INVESTIGATIONS to a reception area and rear space for my private office, the atmosphere reeked of film noir.

A tall, skinny window overlooked Atwood Street. Dingy black leather furniture smelled like it had traveled through time directly from the 1950s. My nook featured a desk, sofa, Diebold safe, and a closet. The safe held my passport, several hundred bucks, and a Colt .45 auto a former client had forked over in lieu of cash. I don't care for automatics and stashed the piece in there until I decided what to do with it.

I moseyed in after lunch and dialed a handwritten number on the reverse of an FBI-issued card. Virginia area code. I rested my shoes on the desk and waited.

"Bellow speaking," Special Agent Ezra Bellow said. Kids screamed joyfully in the background.

"There's an edge to your voice," I said. "Children underfoot?"

"These little motherfuckers are everywhere," he said in the hushed tone of an eyewitness reporting an in-progress murder to 911. "Family barbecue and I'm in charge of the inferno. What can I do for you, Coleridge?"

We'd first crossed paths (and swords) while I searched for Reba Walker. Bellow and I forged a wary friendship despite the case's tragic ending. Several years my senior, African American, widower, conservative in dress and philosophy, albeit not a total stick-in-the-mud. A by-the-book G-man willing to read between the lines in the service of justice.

"I'm looking into a murder most foul," I said.

"Who's the client?"

"Marion Curtis." I smiled grimly to envision Curtis's reaction were he to ever guess an ex-contractor such as myself was on cordial terms with a Fed. The revelation would likely shorten my life expectancy by a minute or two.

"I see. The victim?"

"Guy with a toe tag was a rent-a-thug named Harold Lee of Kingston."

I heard him pull away from the phone and yell at the kids to stop doing whatever they were doing.

"Two minutes," he said to me and hung up. Ninety seconds later, he rang. No human background noises. "Take it from the top." In character, icy and official.

"Hold on. Where are you? Where in the house?"

"The study in a wing-back chair. Staring into a full glass of vodka, because whatever you've got on your mind is bound to give me a headache. I actually started hitting the sauce this morning. A miracle I restrained myself this long. The extended family landed three days ago. Brother, sister, a cousin, and their entire brood. My nerves are shot."

"Please accept my sympathies. I'm trying to picture

the scene. Do you happen to be wearing an apron and a chef's hat?"

"Affirmative," he said after a long pause.

"That's adorable," I said.

He exhaled heavily.

"You say Marion Curtis is bankrolling your investigation. Deluca Family henchman, Lord of the Underworld, Curtis?"

"That would be him."

"Are you in or are you out? Gimme a scorecard." Bellow had perused the FBI file on my preceding career as a suspected hitter. Didn't seem to hold it against me much.

"Out, definitely out. I'm not contracting."

"It would not be in your best interest to advertise, even if you *were* back on the job. In short, what's a poor Fed to believe?"

"Relax, I'm a changed man," I said. "Besides, were it otherwise, I'd lie my ass off to save us both the trouble. But I'm not on the job. Cross my heart. This is an old-fashioned PI case."

"Except, your client is a mob captain. Worst of the worst, some folks in D.C. might argue."

"Let's not be judgmental."

"I'll do my best. What favor do you want that I am going to officially refuse?"

"I'm wondering if Lee's murder has pinged the Bureau's radar. It may be connected to a similar killing that took place two years ago." I consulted my records. "A thief named Ray Anderson. Both gentlemen did piecework for the Deluca Family. Both got the wrong end of a big knife."

"Better lay the entire scenario on me."

So, I did.

Bellow didn't speak for a while after I wrapped the good-parts version of my adventures thus far. Glass clinked and I heard him swallow a presumably copious measure of vodka.

"Hmm," he said. "This doesn't bode well."

"Which aspect?"

"Every aspect. Pros getting shived and/or decapitated is troubling. Curtis's involvement is troubling. Him involving *you* is extra-troubling. You don't need me to say it's healthier to avoid Chinese court dramas as a lowly peasant."

"I don't."

"Haven't heard news regarding your stiffs. I've been far afield this month. Coulda missed the latest office gossip. The M.O. is familiar . . ." More clinking. "I'll run it up the flagpole. Be a day or two."

"Thanks," I said. "Good luck with not murdering the children."

"Counting the minutes until they apparate back to their lairs. Try to avoid getting pushed into a woodchipper."

CHAPTER SIX

A man who operates in my sphere should always have several irons in the fire. Paying an evening visit to Burt Plantagenet was such an iron.

Burt P owned the Deadfall, a gym in west Kingston catering to professional boxers and mixed martial artists and those in training for the pros. A rude structure made of brick and sheet metal, the Deadfall had been a neighborhood fixture going on forty years. It squatted two blocks from the Hudson between a Catskills charter company and a pizza shop. Weeds grew in pavement cracks. Street signs were tagged with gang argot.

Nevertheless, once he pulled the chain on the steel roll-up door, the interior radiated pure George Reeves goodness. A knuckle-dragger's paradise of heavy bags, striking dummies, boxing rings, and Olympic barbells. Bleach, sweat, and adrenaline. Curled-up-at-the-edges posters of Charles Atlas and Muhammad Ali glared like old gods down upon their supplicants. Classical inspiration for a spanking new hernia or a fat lip.

Burt P proved true to type of a character in his line.
Bluff and jocular. Arms thick as moose haunches. He
dressed in a stained shirt with the gym logo and a V-neck
that revealed entirely too much dead-white chest hair. He
rolled his sweats up to the knee because his calves were
simply that enormous. The man possessed a solid-gold
reputation among the fighting community. He paid his
protection and didn't hassle the camps if they fell behind
on the rent, didn't get mired in politics or infighting,
and prohibited illegal activity on the premises. Patrons
knew where they stood.

We ate a pizza in his office that overlooked the main
floor. The walls were patterned with receipts and award
certificates and photos of celebrity fighters. I didn't recognize anybody except for a Puerto Rican welterweight
boxer who'd left the game when I was in college.

Shoptalk ensued. Business remained steady, although
he'd widened his advertising and that attracted a certain
casual element to the gym. He referred to this element as
"asshole yuppies." I wondered aloud what I could do for
him that his protectors, the Deluca Family, couldn't.

"Not what they can't do." Burt P's voice rasped from
an eon of chain-smoking. "It's what they won't. I ain't in
any rackets. Mind my p's and q's and Mr. D's boys lay off
my shop. Muscle costs extra. I won't let myself in for that."

"Smart man. Mob will eat you alive." I took a bite of
pizza to illustrate the point.

"Tryin' to teach your elders to suck eggs, sonny. You
come recommended. Albany says nice things. Dino the
Ax's nephew is who sold me, though."

"Charles Bachelor. Swell kid." Not really.

Chuck was an ex-con, a hard case I'd put in traction at the request of Marion Curtis. Arcane mob politics. Chuck and I had patched it up since. Granted, he'd limp for the rest of his days, and I heard damp weather gave him pains. His essential nastiness remained intact. Nastiness has its uses. As does gratitude. I could've stomped his spine instead of his knee.

"He trained in here for a while before he went away," Burt said. "I agreed as a favor to his uncle. Great jaw, decent hands. Might a done somethin' if he'd stuck with it. You smashed his leg. He won't say why. Although, I can guess a hundred and one reasons."

"Men will disagree."

"Chuck usually gets the better of it. Anyway, he vouches for you. Says you throw him some work now that he's benched."

"Seems fair. I snuffed his burgeoning career as a hood and, ostensibly, his shot at the title."

"Beats an ice pick in the ear," he said. "Chuck's a maniac and no secret. His uncle's the sole reason he isn't in a pine box already. The way Jesus stands between mankind and God's wrath, Dino shields that boy from old gangsters with long knives and short tempers."

"Dino the Ax attends Plantagenet family dinners?"

"I opened my doors in 1977. I know everybody in this town. Dino and me were in the Army together. 'Nam."

"Small world. My dad flew jets over there."

Mervin, my father, graduated from the Air Force Academy with honors. After he'd spent a few years in the cockpit, the brass assigned him to AFISRA—Air Force Intelligence, Surveillance, and Reconnaissance Agency. Perfect job for a man who relished puzzles and excelled at underhanded bullshit. I didn't say any of this. It might have ruined the bonding moment Burt and I were sharing.

"Don't have much in common with Dino anymore," Burt said. "We honor our families. Do anything for blood." He inhaled, steeling himself. "Which brings us to the reason I called you. My granddaughter, Aubrey, is in love. Her boyfriend is true-blue. There's a problem."

"Yes, there's a problem," I said. "She's in love. On a scale of one to ten, how complicated is the situation?"

He rubbed his jaw.

"Romeo and Juliet. On a scale of one to ten. Opposite-sides-of-the-tracks affair. A river of bad blood divides our families. There's a jealous suitor who set her cap on the boy. Gangster wannabe, and she's backed by a rough element. Naturally, the boyfriend's daddy prefers the wannabe."

"The road to true love never did run smooth."

"This road's got potholes that'd sink a tank. See that bruiser when you came in? Musclehead in tights?"

The brute had given me the stink eye on my way into the gym. A regular Mr. Beefcake. The type who made sure the entire world saw and heard him.

"He came around outta the blue a few weeks ago," Burt P said. "Brought some pals along. They aren't with any fight camps. Then again, quite a few of my customers just come here to lift. Still, I have a sneakin' suspicion he and his posse are here to keep an eye on me and send a message if I step over the line."

"Your granddaughter's rival has juice."

"Dunno about juice. Her family is into shady crap. That's what I know."

"Throw the brute and his crew out on their asses," I said.

"The Deadfall is Switzerland. Musclehead and his boys pay their fees and they ain't done nothin' except make me nervous."

"Kick them to the curb anyway."

"Might come to that. I'm biding my time. Got a lot to lose on my end. So, whaddya think? Will you take it on?"

"Well, Burt, I don't know."

"They're stalking Aubrey. Crank calls, threats—"

"Terrible. This might be a job for the cops."

"—and one of 'em killed her cat—"

"Killed her cat?" I straightened in my seat.

"Uh, yeah. Strangled her and stuffed her in the mailbox."

"I see. Tell me your woes."

CHAPTER SEVEN

At last, Burt P concluded his tale worthy of a Viking saga.

"Oh, boy," I said. "You have a pillowcase stuffed with hundred-dollar bills? Because this will be expensive."

"I can get my paws on whatever you want. Long as you can fix my problem."

I rubbed my temples. The demons would not be exorcised.

"Where can I find your granddaughter? Like to chat with the girl, take her measure and whatnot."

Burt P proposed dinner at his house. I demurred, citing a previous engagement. I wished to observe Aubrey from afar, perhaps speak with her friends and associates before introducing myself officially.

He recited the details and I jotted them down.

"Big fella, lemme grab some cash outta the safe for your retainer . . ."

I took the hint and went downstairs to loiter.

A throng of gym rats encircled the heavily muscled guy

doing bench presses. By heavily muscled, I mean he could've stood in for a heavyweight pro wrestler. Mr. Beefcake screamed every time he heaved the bar off his chest. To be fair, he was probably pushing sufficient weight to win a regional competition.

An hour or so of tossing around barbells had brought his blood to a high simmer. Blond, tan, middle-aged alpha male ready to dominate any potential new rival. His singlet was blazoned with AMERICAN AS APPLE PIE.

Meanwhile, I'm built along the lines of a middle linebacker during the NFL off-season. A shade over six-foot and deceptively soft if you don't recognize the warning signs. Neither too small nor too big—the exact size and shape to tempt a three-hundred-pound bully spoiling for a challenge.

One possibly insolent smirk from me and it was on.

He lumbered over, his coterie in tow. The younger guys postured like runway models and felt up their own chiseled biceps. Unlike their fearless leader, none had stained his workout duds with a drop of sweat.

"Where you lift?" Mr. Beefcake looked me over. "Or, you one of those fellas who don't need to pump iron? Your people are naturally strong."

"My people?" I said.

"Islanders are beasts even before they ever step into a gym. Can't argue with genetics." Behind him, a youngish fellow wearing a sweatband let his tongue loll and briefly pantomimed a haka.

"And a bunch of us are killers before we ever set foot in a dojo; alcoholics before we ever belly up to a bar, am I right?" I let Mr. Beefcake stew for a moment, then winked.

"Relax, Goldilocks. I cut Neanderthals slack. You are correct—I *did* inherit brawn from my ancestors in New Zealand. I'm a baby compared to my mother's kin. Those details notwithstanding, my brutishness and violent impulses derive from the English side of the family tree."

His blank stare indicated that much of the nuance was lost in translation to caveman-ese. One of his groupies chuckled. That did it.

"Punk, you wanna be careful how you talk." Mr. Beefcake sidled closer. To impress me with his bigness, presumably. His forehead was dented. So were his tightly clenched fists.

"I'm. Speaking. As. Slowly. As. Possible," I said. He paled and I raised my hands to forestall an ill-advised haymaker. "Easy, easy. You're the butchest hombre in this gym, I take it?"

"Baddest motherfucker on the floor right now," he said. His jaw bunched and relaxed like he was chewing a bag of ten-penny nails.

"On any other day, that might be a winning answer. Let's test the theory."

"You come in here off the street and talk trash? You ain't got shoes, you ain't got gloves, or tape. This a joke?"

"Burt, my cash, please."

Burt P had come down the stairs and watched as the scene unfolded. He placed a small paper sack in my hand. I removed a thousand dollars, counted it where the increasingly fascinated crowd could see, and gave it to Burt to hold. The remainder went into my jacket pocket. I removed the jacket and shoulder holster rig, unbuttoned my collar, and rolled up my sleeves. Eyebrows rose at the sight of the revolver.

"Choose your routine," I said to Mr. Beefcake. "Name the weight. Grand prize goes to whoever moves the most iron. Two-to-one says it'll be lil' ol' me."

He couldn't decide whether or not to be nervous. He studied my arms and chest. Wrong way to judge a man's power, but whatever.

"How much you bench?" he said. A yokel's even less reliable gauge of a man's strength.

"God only knows. I don't lie on my back to lift weights."

"Deadlift?" a stocky guy in a NY RANGERS T-shirt said. "You'll smoke him, bro." The others nodded approvingly.

"Dumbbell deadlift," Mr. Beefcake announced to a chorus of reverential murmurs. "The 275s." He clapped and chalk flew. "Yeah, baby. The 275s."

Ninety-nine percent of gyms on the planet don't stock anything remotely that enormous. Burt P represented the old school; practically Jurassic.

The tribe scraped together the ante and passed it along to the bemused Burt P. Wads of cold, hard cash imbued the proceedings with a sacred air. Smiles vanished. A pair of strapping minions lugged the dumbbells to a mat. These dumbbells were fossils of the days of strongmen in tights and bearskin capes; behemoth hunks of primordial iron, hacked from a mountain's spine, black finish chipped over the decades to natural gray, the shade of death. Their metal bore the fingerprints of gods and titans.

"Well?" My nemesis seemed disappointed that I hadn't fainted away.

"Be my guest." I leaned against a rack and began to regulate my breathing. "You're already in a lather."

"Show him how it's done," the guy in the Rangers shirt said.

Mr. Beefcake enacted an elaborate preening display—belt cinch, neck roll, arm shake, chest flex, and bullish hyperventilation. He abruptly squatted, snagged the weights, rocked to and fro, and stood with a shout that must have terrified bats in the rafters. Nice clean form. Second and third lifts went as smoothly. Fourth pass, he struggled; face red and veiny, barbarian roar more of a groan. Five hundred and fifty pounds is no joke. Fifth pass was a close thing. He cheated the sixth. He failed the seventh try and collapsed onto a bench, huffing and puffing. His buddies surrounded him, hooting in appreciation. They slapped his back and doused him with bottled water.

Gradually the crew settled. Every gaze beamed in my direction.

"Dude won't clear the mat," Rangers Shirt stage-whispered to his comrades. A few dollars more changed hands.

I stepped into position and relaxed. My mind drained . . .

. . . It refilled with bloody light as I bent, seized the handles, and straightened. My freshly healed left hand merely twinged. The weights levitated, hollow as papier-mâché. On the seventh pass, I bucked the dumbbells over my thighs and hips and onto my chest, tilted slightly backward for maximum leverage, exhaled, and gorilla-pressed them overhead without dipping my knees. I held the pose, reveling in the onlookers' expressions of horror and awe, and then slowly lowered the dumbbells. The only difficult part was disguising the brief tremor in my legs. As I said, 550 pounds is no joke.

The reddish light dissipated and I returned to myself, mortal again.

"Mother Mary, Jesus on crutches," Burt P said. "That's circus-strongman shit right there."

"You can't do that," Mr. Beefcake said, dazed.

"I got it on film." A punk in the back waved his cell phone. Doubtless, the video would be posted on the internet within the hour.

"It ain't possible. Dude cheated. No other way." Mr. Beefcake wagged his head, stupefied. He cast about for support. None was forthcoming. His homies shuffled their feet and scrutinized interesting details in the water-stained walls. His appeal to the gods of physics was a cry in the dark. "Not possible. Not friggin' possible."

"You're not wrong," I said. I didn't explain to him about my gift of the hideous red light. Didn't explain I could summon its terrible strength the way berserkers of old fell into a blood rage and lighted their hair on fire. "A wise man taught me that the universe is inexplicable. Its rules are merely suggestions." I retrieved my gun and coat and smiled into their slack faces. "Should any of you have the misfortune to meet me again under less friendly circumstances, don't say you weren't warned."

Nobody uttered a word as I gathered my winnings from Burt P and departed. Easiest dough I'd made in a while. Damned satisfying as well. Feats of strength for fun and profit tickle me pink. Delivering narcissistic creeps their comeuppance? Gravy.

I committed their faces to memory, hopeful there'd be a later.

ONE THING LED TO ANOTHER and I didn't slouch home until well past the witching hour. I skipped the bourbon nightcap and settled for checking my cell phone messages before sleep.

Agent Bellow had left a doozy.

"Head for the hills," he said, deadly serious. "The calls are coming from inside the house." He paused and then chuckled. "Seriously, your day just got worse than you know. Hit me back tomorrow. You might have stepped in it, my friend. Been digging and came across a name . . . A blast from the past. The Croatoan. You heard of him all the way up in Alaska, I'm sure. Sleep on that and we'll talk soon."

I sat clutching the phone. The feeling in my guts was the sensation you get when you take a step and instead of solid earth there's a void waiting.

Minerva lazed near my feet. She raised her head and growled softly at the window. Nothing out there but dreaming farm animals and fungal darkness. For the moment, the universe balanced perfectly on the edge of a hunting knife. All possibilities existed. Minerva growled again. We both knew something was on its way.

"Oh, shit is right." I retraced my steps to the pantry and took down a bottle.

CHAPTER EIGHT

None of us spring into existence from Jupiter's forehead, wholly formed and ready for battle. Not even guys like me. I survived nearly two decades as a contract hitter for the Outfit thanks to instinct and adaptability, and also with a little help from my friends.

As one man sharpens another, a dyed-in-the-wool professional badass is bound to owe his or her success to a mentor.

Gene "Ace of Spades" Kavanaugh was mine.

Piss on the dogma of scientists and philosophers, he said. *The universe is inexplicable. Its rules are merely suggestions. Could be a hologram; could be an insect's dream.*

Like me, Gene wasn't Italian, so could never be made. Among the top five dangerous humans I've ever met, and mildly eccentric. That's a mouthful. He'd guzzle a fifth of single-malt and lie in a snowbank for hours to gaze at the Northern Lights undulating across the stars.

Gene read Jack London and Itzhak Bentov. He quoted Robert Service's and esteemed Alex Jeffers's antisocial tendencies. Odds were, he'd hidden a Unabomber-worthy manifesto under the floorboards. He lamented he'd never x'd out a national politician of either major party.

Twenty-two years gone by, Gene K took this green-as-grass lad under his wing. I could not have asked for better tutelage in the fine art of murder. The secret—he didn't teach me new and esoteric methods of killing; he taught me perspective.

Remember, nothing is solid, nothing is real. Everything you think you see is upside down and four feet off-center. Death awaits, down in the hole at the heart of it all. Try to drag a few sonsabitches with you on the way down. Now, where did my whiskey go?

Don't get the impression Gene spouted wisdom like some sort of Westernized stunt double of a Shaolin monk or Buddhist Zen master. No, Lee Van Cleef's hardest, baddest mercenary gunslinger on a bender and muttering imprecations against the encroaching cosmic gloaming is closer to the image I carry. Like Angel Eyes himself, Gene always followed a job through.

HOW DID WE MEET? The death gods smiled upon us.

Gene K, grizzled and avuncularly evil, had fulfilled myriad contracts, survived a dozen Syndicate purges and twice that many gang wars. He hung up his guns and retired to the wilderness of Copper Valley, Alaska. In a moment of mock candor, he explained he'd walked away from the job because of arthritis in his trigger finger. *Shot so many fuckers I can barely pick my nose.* And grinned.

Unquestionably, Gene's former Outfit paymasters were aware of his location. These were the types of guys who hated loose ends. Be that as it may, the bosses quietly weighed the pros and cons and decided against messing with him. Cutting bait seemed wisest, considering their man's lengthy history of ultraviolence, his longevity despite terrible odds, and a marked relish for petty vengeance. Take a run at the Ace of Spades and miss, there'd be a river of blood raging in the mean streets of Anchorage and Chicago. None of the bigwigs were eager to get blown to smithereens in a car bomb. None of the old bastards wanted an anthrax Christmas card either.

Upon divining this legend's existence, my life ambition instantly revolved around meeting the infamous Mr. Gene K.

As a baby ronin in the feudal era might seek to apprentice himself to a surly, gray-bearded swordmaster, I hiked the mountain path to his shack and begged for wisdom. Ah, a young man's blissful optimism. I gave him my sob story: the previous autumn, my debut gig cost me a good dog and nearly my own life. Clearly, I required finishing school.

Gene eventually succumbed to my winning ways. Instead of shooting me in the face per his customary habit of greeting trespassers, he poured a tall glass of Kentucky bourbon and broke it down like this:

Bounty hunters, cops, and loan sharks have it far tougher than assassins do. Hitting is cake. Folks watch too many crime flicks. See, here's how it is for contracts. No hand-to-hand in an alleyway. No shoot-outs. Not to say these things never occur, but such scenarios are rare and indicate either a failure of planning or extraordinary circumstances. Sometimes a hitter will make it too personal and get in close when it's unnecessary. Psychos do it like that. A man who'd prefer to live into his dotage best make a practice of avoiding such occurrences.

The Syndicate decides to x your eyes, it will transpire while you sit in traffic or at a diner booth. Double tap to the back of the dome. Car bomb. Sniper from an overpass. Cyanide in your coffee. Your plane experiences a mechanical failure. The car brakes give up the ghost at an inopportune moment. You slip in the shower or allegedly slit your wrists or O.D. while getting your fix. No fuss, no escape.

I accepted this as gospel. Two decades and numerous brushes with the Reaper taught me that even geniuses nod. His exceptions and rare birds proved less rare than he preached. Some killers won't cut your throat unless they can gaze into your eyes as the claret flows.

I WINTERED WITH GENE, learning the do's and don'ts of our venerable tradecraft. He took me into town for unscheduled R & R. Being an impatient jackass, I asked why, and he said, *Wax on, wax off. Get in the truck, numbnuts.*

His uniform consisted of a red-and-black plaid coat, canvas pants, leather gloves, and Sorel boots. Drove a flatbed truck with country music blaring. Chewed tobacco and wore bifocals to scan the Sports Section during his monthly buzz at the barbershop. Central Casting

may as well have dialed up a generic rural, middle-aged
uncle.

Gene was laconic and taciturn in private, unless he'd
gotten into the liquor. His accent was unadulterated Yan-
kee drawl. Watching him slip on a mask and perform in
public spooked and impressed me. In plain light on the
street, he didn't resemble anybody special. Prematurely silver, barrel-chested, and affable. His features were mutable,
forgettable. In near darkness, as we sipped bourbon by the
fireplace, I sometimes glimpsed the *real* him taking shape
in the shadows. Can't say it was a comfortable sensation.

None of the locals ever guessed that in his salad days
he'd worn a conservative business suit and stabbed people in the spine with the casual aplomb of a man spearing
cherry tomatoes. They never realized he was armed to
the teeth or that he stashed an AR-15 behind the bench
seat of his truck. His home arsenal included fragmenta-
tion grenades, claymore mines, a .50 caliber sniper rifle,
and an array of poisons. He called the mini stockpile his
Break Glass in Case of Emergency Kit.

Locals were fond of Gene. His social camouflage paid
dividends in that regard. Clerks at the general store and gas
station smiled as they rang him up. The tavern rowdies
greeted his entrance with a cheer. He tossed darts and wagered on football. Won some, lost some—good-natured
stuff. He rambled at length, and loudly. Politics, the
weather, or whatever seemed topical. Kibitzing was another
arrow in his quiver. His example taught me that a smooth
operator adheres to the "When in Rome" code of behavior.

Then he taught me something else regarding predatory coloration.

New Year's Day, we braved a snowstorm and trekked into town to watch the Orange Bowl on the tavern's widescreen. Several punks on vacation from the city had the same idea—drunk, aggressive frat bros who whooped and cursed and spilled their beers while the bartender and server observed with unmistakable anxiety. Tavern regulars glared with dull resentment at the invaders.

Gene waited until the king of the bros left to take a piss and casually plopped himself in the guy's seat. I didn't register what had transpired until the bro returned and stood next to Gene and fixed his attention on the game. Gene drank the dude's beer too, smirking blandly. The bros knew he was there among them, but they ignored him. For some reason, the whole scene roiled my stomach.

Slogging home through a headwind and drifted snow, I asked how he pulled off that bit of psychological jujitsu.

An elk should get wind of your scent and continue grazing. A man should stare through you and step around without registering your presence. The trick isn't to become invisible like a fucking ninja; the trick is to become part of the scenery.

Late that night, I awakened to Gene stumbling around the cabin, sloppy drunk, hair wild, long johns flapping, rifle in hand. He was on his way back down the hill to find those fraternity brothers and show them his other side. I distracted him with an untapped bottle of liquor.

Gene held on to a grudge like grim death to a pauper.

———

HE SAID, *Isaiah, if you should ever drop your luck and pick up a horse turd, you'll know because you'll come across someone like me on a night trail. Run. No shame in living to bushwhack another day.*

Job opportunities with the Outfit brought Gene K to Alaska. The inimical spirit of the land attracted him. He chose to die there, alone in the wilderness. The death gods graced me with his friendship, if a pair of wolves can be rightly called friends.

Spring thawed our mountain retreat. Scant green and loads of slush and mud. The bright morning, I returned to civilization. He clasped my hand and gave me the rarest of smiles—one of the real ones he hoarded like gold.

Embarrassed to admit, I was suspicious that Apollo sent you, an expendable kid, on a suicide mission. The reason I didn't snuff you the day you knocked on my door? Them rabies tags hanging around your neck. I had a dog when I was young. Good dog.

His parting gift to me, besides his sterling advice? A ballistic vest, custom-designed for my height and weight, give or take a few pounds. Extremely old-school and too heavy for military deployment, yet ideal for brief and deadly excursions. Unlike the majority of contemporary Kevlar vests, this beast was lined with ceramic plates and designed to retard a spectrum of kinetic-force impacts, including bullets and slower-piercing weapons, such as knives and arrowheads. Impossible to fit under a suit; I could wear it with bulky outdoor jackets and pullovers and

for short durations. It went into a closet with similar trea-
sured, albeit impractical toys; namely, a gothic battle-ax,
an authentic clay-forged katana, and an iron breastplate
modeled on the Late Roman Republic centurion model.

We embraced like father and son and I walked down
into the trees. Once screened by spruce branches, I glanced
back and saw him on the porch; a small, somehow wan
figure, pallid and diminished. I turned and kept on and
lost sight of him forever.

Ironically, the Outfit boss in Anchorage, Mr. Apollo,
had indeed encouraged me to put a round through Gene's
brain—if, and only if, the opportunity presented itself.
Mr. Apollo promised to make the hit more than worth
my while. I lived with Gene for an autumn and a winter;
there were plenty of chances to punch his ticket. Man's
got to sleep. Man's got to obey the call of nature.

I'd had my chances. I *didn't* have the balls.

CHAPTER NINE

The late-night message from Agent Bellow wormed into my brain and stirred the sediment. Memories of Gene K, blue-collar philosophizer and avuncular assassin, haunted me as I tossed and turned over that other relic of the dark ages of mob warfare, the Croatoan. Small wonder. Both Gene and the Croatoan were of a generation. Both men harbored love for a violent profession. It's a grim truth, we're all headed across the threshold to the other side. These men swam through rivers of blood to get there.

That's where the comparison broke down.

The Croatoan represented a bogeyman, especially among East Coast mobsters. A mysterious freelancer, true identity known by a select few, who conducted wholesale slaughter on behalf of the Family (and other nefarious bidders) since the latter 1970s. Older mafiosos speculated that he'd done three hundred and fifty hits. A fantastical, impossible total. Others argued that the number was far higher—four hundred or four hundred and fifty. All agreed the killings were done with extreme prejudice.

When the Croatoan didn't cause his victims to evaporate, he scattered their fleshly pieces to hell and gone. A renowned torturer, he'd allegedly filmed several of his interrogations on VHS and circulated the cassettes as a method of striking fear into the hearts of would-be enemies. Mission accomplished. He was seldom referenced in polite conversation. However, when liquor flowed and tongues loosened, a hush ensued and bystanders crossed themselves.

Gene attested to meeting him in Buffalo in '86 on the occasion of a major intrafamily whacking. A regular mob party. Five wiseguys were shredded in a blaze of machine-gun fire and buried in a mass grave. Gene flew in special from Chicago. He missed his connection and arrived after three Carlucci Family foot soldiers and another independent contractor had finished their wetwork. The crew celebrated with a few drinks at a neighborhood bar called Scottie's.

Carlucci's boys were festive, whooping and kibitzing and annoying the locals. The other shooter, a quiet man dressed to blend, introduced himself as Joe. Gene knew that was a fake name. *Everybody* went by fake names or monikers. He suspected the stranger's identity from the jump. Rumors had floated for days that the don planned to bring in a real heavy. This caliber of hitter could've handled the job solo, no sweat, but the don wanted to ensure his young pups got a taste of blood at scant risk to themselves.

I asked my mentor what sort of impression the Croatoan made.

Gene had shrugged. *I dunno, killer. He was a guy. He drank Yuengling Porter and smoked . . . Benson and Hedges, I recall. Here's the deal, though: I knew three or four contractors who did work with "Joe," and a few more who made the brag, but I got no way of verifying.*

They all said the same thing. The Croatoan had a trick; leastwise, that's what wiseguys muttered. Hypnotism—the fancy shit stage magicians use, not the tepid stuff where quacks talk you out of smoking. A hitter in Boston said it was a voice modulator that fucks with your mind. Somebody else swore it was the eyes, the way a snake freezes its prey. I dunno. The Croatoan could paralyze a whole carload of mooks and whack them at his leisure. Nuts, right? It's what I heard. Others claimed he wore a mask, a nylon stocking. Not nylon, something else, and it warped his face when he pulled it loose.

Since "Joe" and I were parked at the bar, killing an hour or two, I bit the bullet and asked him how he managed crowds. Figured he'd bullshit me and he did. Looked me in the eye and said he knew words of power. One word could blind a man or cause his brain to leak from his ears. There were other words that caused worse effects.

"Don't make me raise my voice," Joe said. He grinned to prove it was a joke and we drank another round.

Years later, I talked to a mechanic who'd seen the Croatoan in action. A standup guy too. We cut our teeth together in Chicago before he moved to Philly. My friend said he and the Croatoan took down a Russian crew all by their lonesome. Odessa wannabes; dangerous all the same. No shit, the Croatoan told him to stay a step or two behind him on his flank where it was safe. He had a device, something he'd tested for the military in 'Nam. Then he fit his hand over his mouth, like you do with a harmonica, and . . . I dunno, screamed, or howled. Boom. *The Russian gangsters dropped. My friend ran over and capped 'em while they writhed on the ground.* "Shooting gallery," *he said.*

I pestered my colleague to tell me everything about the Croatoan. My friend says, "He's a guy, Gene. Nothin' special. I tell you what—I see him, I'm walkin' the opposite direction. He's so ordinary, he scares me shitless."

AT DAWN, while the coffeepot perked, I placed a call to my FBI friend. I had a feeling he'd be stone-cold awake.

Agent Bellow, in full-bore G-man mode, jumped in without a hello.

"Get a pen and write this down. Brother, oh brother, you hit the jackpot. I'm friendly with a couple of agents assigned to a case that may involve whoever did in your loan shark associates. You ready?"

"Ready," I said.

"The murders of Harold Lee and Raymond Anderson fit an M.O. of a suspected serial killer active along the corridor between New York and Danbury, and west into Mount Pocono, for the past eleven or twelve years. Seventeen working girls and drifters have gone missing during that period. The eight recovered bodies exhibited a variety of wounds—decapitation with a serrated blade chief among these. The corpses are frequently, albeit not always, disposed of in lakes or rivers."

"You mentioned the Croatoan in your message."

"My friends' theory is that the Tri-State Killer and the Croatoan are one and the same. At a minimum, the murderers share methods. Execution via serrated blade is a common denominator. Main difference is the tri-state killings target a high percentage of women with decapitation as a preferred method. The Croatoan hits male criminals almost exclusively and his methods run the gamut, *including* decapitation."

"Bit of a racist moniker," I said. "He's probably not even a Native American, much less a Croatoan."

"File a complaint with your pals in the mob," Bellow said. "They groomed the asshole. Whacking wiseguys is well and good. Should earn you a tax credit. Whacking civilians is a whole next-level kind of problem. If our theory is sound, he began moonlighting as a serial killer. The Family owns that garbage."

I didn't remind him that *pals* was a strong word. This wasn't badminton; I didn't need to score points. The explanation I'd heard about the Croatoan nickname concerned some college-educated wiseguy's fascination with the Lost Colony of Roanoke legend. Since the hitter disappeared a heap of people from Florida to Maine—*boom*, he was the Croatoan. Considering his body count and grisly methods of dispatch, what began as a bit of clever wordplay wasn't amusing anymore.

"Touché!" I said. "Any leads?"

I heard Bellow shuffle papers.

He said, "Yes, there's a guy my colleagues like for this. Beginning in 1976, the chief suspect is one Morris Oestryke of Deering, Michigan; DOB, 1951. Only child. Father not in the picture. Mother died of cancer in 1969. No other close relatives, no sweetheart. Played football in school; average grades. Served 1969 through 1973 as a red-blooded Army volunteer. Two tours in Vietnam. Made staff sergeant. Humdrum, wouldn't you agree?"

"Not really the potboiler," I said.

"Hold on to your hat. Except for notation of rank promotion, Oestryke has next to no record between his Army induction and the day he showed up at a vocational school, post 'Nam. His military records are largely redacted on authority of the Department of Defense. Upon his discharge, he slipped beneath the radar for several years. We have no idea where he lived or what he did.

"In early '78, after he came into view again, he relocated to Albany, attended Smithfield Technical College, and eventually toiled a route for a refrigeration company. Repairs and installations, then promoted into sales. Married in latter 1978; three children. Oestryke died in 1987. Factory explosion. Three casualties, no identifiable remains. Widow collects a wad of life insurance dough and moves on. Cops don't give it a second glance."

"Extra-crispy convenient," I said. "We're going to reach the part where you reveal why you suspect Oestryke worked for the mob between Freon runs . . . ?"

"Okay, before his untimely obliteration, Oestryke maintains his cover as working-class family man. Meanwhile, out in the world, the Croatoan is whacking people left, right, and center. Gradually, this activity slows. Sight-ings of the hitter become rare, then stop. Word among the wiseguys is, he's either retired or kicked the bucket. Either way, the recent slayings of Anderson and Lee notwith-standing, the Croatoan hasn't accepted a contract or shown his face in gangland since 2006. The tri-state mur-ders begin around that time."

"When was the last-known murder that fits the tri-state profile?"

"Roughly thirty-six months," Bellow said. "That doesn't mean he isn't piling corpses up somewhere for us to find later."

"Try this on," I said. "Oestryke survives the explosion and changes his identity. Eventually, he retires from hit-ting. He still has a taste for blood. By no degree is this dude a regular contractor. More of a rogue tiger. Dusting prostitutes and vagrants satisfies those old familiar urges."

"Why didn't we think of that?" Bellow said. "Shut up and let me finish my story. Behold the big reveal: five years ago, forensics unearths a partial print match from a cold case murder—Teamster boss got assassinated in Philadel-phia, 1993. Wiseguy scuttlebutt indicates the Croatoan did the hit. No reason for the Bureau to be skeptical; Teamsters and mobsters go together like peanut butter and jelly.

"CSI initially lifted the print from the hilt of a Ka-Bar knife dropped at the murder scene. Serrated, wouldn't you know. Evidence packet was misplaced. The Teamster boss gets his wake and the world turns. The FBI doesn't forget, but it doesn't lose much sleep dwelling on lost causes. Years go by. A zealous intern recovers the evidence during an annual inventory sweep and a supervisor initiates a new review."

"The print belonged to Oestryke, which outed him as the Croatoan," I said. "He made a mistake. It happens, sooner or later."

"Ding-ding."

Bellow quickly and succinctly laid out the rest of it:

Way, way back in '74, before the Croatoan whetted a blade, Oestryke, freshly discharged from the service, got pinched for a minor beef with a couple of hard cases at a bar. He brandished a knife and the cops hauled his ass in. Released him the next morning and dropped all charges. Local DA had a soft spot for veterans. That was the moment he vanished from the grid and didn't resurface until 1978.

Voilà, that incident eventually connected him to the slaying of the Philadelphia Teamster boss in '93. As Oestryke was allegedly six years dead at that date, the FBI forensic department became rather intrigued, to say the least. Furthermore, nothing in Oestryke's background explained why he'd transitioned from a regular guy to a hitman-cum-serial-killer. He represented a right-angled pivot on the spectrum of aberrant psychology.

"Wouldn't the Army have fingerprinted him when he enlisted?" I said.

"Noncriminal records prior to 2000 aren't in the database," Bellow said. "Your tax dollars really go to Christ-

mas parties and stripper slush funds. We're supremely
fortunate a civilian agency tripped him."

He went on to reiterate that the Croatoan didn't exactly
amount to a Bureau priority. The aforementioned long-
suffering field agents drew the short straw and whittled
away at the case in their spare moments. Chatted up every
man jack who ever knew Oestryke—colleagues, family,
and mafiosos alike. A time line of his movements between
the latter 1960s and 1987 was charted alongside eyewitness accounts, crime scene reports, and known activities of
the Croatoan and the more recent tri-state slayings.

"The emergent picture is compelling, albeit inconclusive," Bellow said.

Assuming Oestryke survived the explosion, I asked if
Bellow had any clue what identity he assumed next.

"None. Legend goes, only select Family muckety-
mucks knew the Croatoan's real name. Capos handled
him the way we manage our own undercover agents. The
whole double-life charade: limited chain of command;
need-to-know basis. Sources claim the hitter communi-
cated almost exclusively through dead drops. The old
capos who were aware of his true identity have long since
crossed over to the afterlife. Even so, a man has to ask
himself how much Curtis knows and if he ever availed
himself of Oestryke's services."

The notion that Curtis might function on a collegial
basis with a guy like the Croatoan didn't surprise me,
which is not to say I welcomed the development. Best to
arm myself with more data before cracking open that
potential can of worms.

"It gets weirder," Bellow went on. "My colleagues use the word *stymied* to describe their progress. Support is sluggish, to put it politely. Reports are dropped into a black hole. Essentially, they've run into a brick wall. And it has less to do with the evidence than it does the bureaucracy."

"Think they're being waved off the case?"

He hesitated.

"A bunch of paperwork is missing or redacted. More DoD interference. Smells like a parallel investigation running farther up the food chain. The agents won't comment further. Either because they're in the dark, or because they're smart. Whichever, the case is in suspended animation. Part of the reason I'm letting you in. Maybe a bull in a china shop is the cure."

"Interdepartmental cooperation would ruin a perfectly acceptable cliché," I said. "What if—and this is pure speculation—what if the DoD or the CIA was directly involved somehow? We know the government ran shady ops during Vietnam. Suppose Oestryke was an asset? It would explain the weird discrepancies in his background and why FBI brass is hiding intel and freezing its own investigation."

"I'll never know. That's one rabbit hole I'm not hopping into this close to retirement."

"Understood. Any chance I could get ahold of a photograph of Mr. Oestryke? And—this might sound morbid—do you have a copy of any snuff tapes the Croatoan made?"

Dead silence stretched for a few seconds and I knew

the next thing he said would either be a half-truth or a full-blown lie.

"Mobsters are as paranoid as Cub Scouts gathered around a campfire," he said. "Those tapes are a myth. Not much scares professional hard cases. They spin bullshit stories to get under each other's skin. Even if the damned tapes existed, why would you want to screen them anyway?"

"I'm morbid. What about Oestryke's photos . . . ?"

"You've got email. Military headshot and another from his company profile. Shitty and dated, obviously. Passed along some of our data as well. Be sure to lose it when you're finished."

"Hey, Agent B, I'm a detective. Totally legitimate for us to collaborate."

"I'd rather not push that line of reasoning in front of an inquest committee."

"You've done a manly deed; take the rest of the day."

"Fat chance. The kids are already climbing the chandeliers. Mind sharing your plans?"

"Back to shaking trees," I said. "Indulge me in one more question. Where does a man like Oestryke go to ground? Is he hiding in plain sight—a kooky resident at a trailer park or apartment complex?" I thought of Gene K and how he spent his golden years in the woods. "A bunker?"

"If this investigation were really a thing and not a façade? And if I were assigned? I'd map all the murders and disappearances attributed to Oestryke. The Catskills region would be bloody with red pins. This is a man who moved in mob circles for thirty years. He associated with monied scumbags of all ethnicities. As predators grow long in the tooth, they remain closer to familiar hunting grounds. He's lurking somewhere in the Jewish Alps among those abandoned resorts and bungalow colonies. Mark it down."

"The Jewish Alps?"

"For Pete's sake, Coleridge—didn't you ever watch *Dirty Dancing*? The Jewish Alps, also known as the Borscht Belt after the Eastern European immigrants who put down roots in the hills and the Jewish entertainers who did the resort circuit. During the '60s, come summer, daddies parked their families at these full-service resorts and worked in the city during the week. They'd visit the family Friday nights through Sunday afternoon, then trudge back to NYC or Albany, or wherever. My wife, God rest her, and her parents did that routine when she was a young girl. The culture dried up and blew away. Atlantic City and cheap air travel killed it."

"Taking that theory further," I said, "does Oestryke have a support network, or what's left of one?"

"I have a feeling we'll never know," Bellow said. "The creep will pull a Zodiac Killer on us and simply vanish." He hesitated before continuing in as sober a tone as I'd ever heard him utter. "Want some advice from a career public servant? Yes, no, maybe? Good, I don't care. Drop this investigation and stick to safer activities, like snake handling blindfolded or juggling high explosives."

"You're jealous because I'm going to nab an infamous killer and get all the credit."

"Wrong. This mofo don't play. I'm concerned he's going to put your head on a stick."

"That's sweet, Agent B. Although, the dude has to be a gray-bearded pensioner." I laughed to demonstrate bravado I didn't feel.

Bellow joined in. His laugh sounded as fake as mine.

CHAPTER TEN

Before you shoot a man, you have to find him.

In this instance, my task was to track down a murderer, or at least determine the murderer's motive. Perhaps a distinction without a difference. Friends and associates of the subject are always a solid starting point.

Since my exile from Alaska, I'd invested significant resources extending my network of contacts to New York State. Local denizens of the underworld knew me by sight. Between these contacts and Curtis's list, I hoped to dig up a lead or two.

First order of business was to snoop around Harold Lee's home and interview his housemate and colleague, Nic Royal, should he be on hand. I'd glimpsed Royal across a crowded room or two. Tall, dark, and mean. Apache and African American; lousy with cryptic tats from his stint as a Marine grunt on tour in the Middle East. Another former Alaskan by way of Fairbanks. The book on him was typical of men who parlayed ferocious tendencies and military discipline into civilian enterprises. He'd tried his hand at several trades—long-haul trucker, carpentry, night watchman—but a vicious streak inevitably sabotaged his efforts to maintain consistent employment.

Often sighted in the company of businessmen tangentially affiliated with the local underbelly, Royal swerved clear of direct Mafia ties. Debt collection and bodyguard gigs in service of penny-ante loan sharks were his forte. He broke heads at dives in Kingston and New Paltz.

"Oh, you kids have a common interest," Lionel said after I familiarized him with the state of affairs.

"Us? I'm a lowly civilian. Aren't jarheads brothers from different mothers?"

"Some are kinda adopted."

I bought breakfast at the Regal Diner in Kerhonkson. Corned beef hash, four eggs over easy, toast, and a quart of OJ for me. He ordered an everything bagel and a cup of black coffee and laughed heartily when I further detailed my struggle with Mr. Skinhead and Mr. Beardo and the unfortunate revelation that Beardo played ball for Team Curtis.

Afterward, we cruised north along Route 209. Fields and hills spread on either side. The Catskills formed in the enchanted distance. New York State's bucolic panoramas beat the hell out of wandering the frozen Alaskan tundra.

Lionel drove methodically, two or three miles per hour over the limit. He smiled with the corner of his mouth at the traffic jam behind us. Locals treated this stretch of the highway like the Autobahn, and he extracted perverse pleasure from antagonizing drivers who'd cut the morning commute too close. A career of wartime military service had estranged him from the niceties of civilization. After absorbing a skinful, he often lamented the necessity of state-sponsored violence; yet his treks into the Afghan wilderness had brought him a sense of peace. His eyes were faraway in those moments, and glassy like an eagle's, intent upon some small prey it might like to kill.

"The dude's head? Where did that go?"

"Bobbing around on the reservoir until some trout fisherman snags it."

"Related question—what's the motive for chopping off his hands?"

"The killer may have a fetish. Or he's harassing the pathologist. No dental records, no fingerprints, no quick ID."

"He left the victim's wallet in his pants," Lionel said. "Doesn't square with a calculated act of subterfuge. Unless it's next-level clever. Can't decide."

"Are you suggesting the body might not be who the authorities, and my grieving client, think it is? For the sake of my sanity, I'm going to assume the corpse belongs to Harry Lee, until he pops out of a cake or somebody persuades me otherwise."

"I'm spitballing. I ponder the bad and then imagine how it might be even worse. There's always something worse. My bottom dollar is on Curtis guest-starring as the worse thing in this episode."

"Mankind dwells in a wilderness, red of tooth and claw. I tend to classify him as the devil I know."

"It's what the devil knows that should worry us. Curtis is sandbagging. Weigh the evidence: Lee freelanced, which nixes mob vengeance or retaliation on his behalf. Even if retaliation were on the table, Curtis has goons who handle this stuff. Only, he hires a washed-up hitman in secret—"

"*Retired* hitman," I said.

"You're retired the way Brett Favre was retired from 2008 through 2011. I get that you're chummy with Capone Lite. Doesn't mean you have to do business with the dillhole."

"Man, you have a hate-on for Curtis."

"I really don't like anybody. Present company excepted."

"This is entirely a business decision. To date, the local mob suffers my existence. It would be nice to stay in the black. You're right, though. The plot has indeed thickened." I relayed Bellow's brief concerning how an average schmuck named Morris Oestryke might also be an infamous serial killer and an even more infamous hitman.

Lionel digested this information.

"How's Bellow?"

"Cool."

"And he's serious about this Croatoan character?"

"As a heart attack."

He scowled.

"Curtis knows who we're looking for, doesn't he? He's playing coy. Why is the fucker playing coy? Why not tell you what's what and turn you loose?"

"There are numerous possibilities," I said. "One of those possibilities is that we're wrong and he's on the level. We've been wrong before. Another possibility is we're being set up for a fall. I dislike that possibility."

"No shit."

"Sounds far-fetched. The Croatoan theory. Curtis may be asshole buddies with Oestryke, except the more I think on it, the less it matters. Simply doesn't jibe that Oestryke is active. A coincidence or a copycat is the smart money. Oestryke, nah."

"Ask yourself why FBI bosses are derailing the investigation."

"Two problems." Lionel raised three fingers. "First, people don't just walk away from explosions and assume brand-new identities—"

"This won't be much fun unless you try being a tiny bit credulous. Play along—how does Oestryke assume a new identity after faking his death? The Outfit has people who can arrange it, but not easily and not for cheap."

"Inventing a past is within the realm of possibility. I'll grant you that. Especially in the '80s. Being a sneaky SOB was simpler. Bellow said the DoD has an interest? Intelligence agencies whipped up canned identities for their assets at the drop of a hat. More than fake IDs and papers. Spooks designed Cadillac backgrounds. Deep, granular stuff. Plastic surgery, false memories via hypnosis; cloak-and-dagger to the max. I don't buy any of that in this instance. Government redacts his military service for what, black ops hijinks? Guy doesn't have a college degree; he was a raw recruit. Years later, he does mob hits and fakes his own death via a fireball? Then, in his dotage, retires to a quiet life of butchering hookers? And, for an encore, he's icing former colleagues to honor some vendetta we haven't the first idea of what the fuck over. *Riiight.* Nope, here's the reality: he died, somebody liked his style and picked up the reins."

"And problem two?"

"Problem two is the point I made a second ago. Oestryke pulls off the impossible black ops stuff? Black ops cowboys are all twenty-five and gymnasts. Bellow's dude would be in his late sixties. At least."

"You ageist bastard," I said. "My dad can still whip my ass. I've known a hitter or two who kept punching tickets into their golden years. Assassination doesn't require agility, stamina, or black belt reflexes. It requires viciousness. Our very own Harold Lee was fifty-nine and doing the good work."

"Unlikely some glycerin-addicted senior citizen is creeping around the Hudson Valley making like a ninja, cutting off heads with a knife while the victims are alive. Man, that's hard work. Younger man's work." He flapped his hand dismissively. "Harold Lee? Motherfucker broke cue sticks over the heads of two-bit debtors. Let's not compare that action with some world-class massacre artist."

"Over-the-hill baddies are full of surprises," I said. "It pays to assume a snake can and will bite until the day it slithers into the afterlife."

"For the sake of argument, there's a geriatric hitter run amok in Upstate New York. He's stabbing prostitutes and evening up scores with former criminal associates. Superduper far-fetched." He cracked the bottle, took a long swallow, and wiped his mouth on his sleeve. "And for the sake of argument, let's assume Harold Lee and that other bozo, Ray Anderson, were done in by the same person, this Oestryke, this Croatoan motherfucker. Oestryke whacks them because . . . why?"

"Could be for any reason. Pick one you like. They're lowlifes. Falling-outs among lowlifes are often calamitous. The trio had unsettled business together."

"Curtis has an agenda, is all I'm sayin'."

"Evil agendas and Machiavellian plots are in the job description of mob captain." I peeled three bills from my wallet and slipped them into his breast pocket. Driving-around money. "Eyes wide open. This goes pear-shaped, we tuck tail and scamper."

"We always scamper after it's too late."

CHAPTER ELEVEN

Lionel took the Kingston off-ramp and threaded his way across town to a neighborhood characterized by rock-bottom property values. He parked on a wooded street lined with shabby houses. A third of the yards were posted with FOR SALE signs. I tried Nic Royal's number on the off-chance he'd save us the hassle of breaking in. The machine picked up and a man's voice said, *Your dime, leave a message.* I said, "Hi, sorry to miss you, we'll do lunch one day soon."

I pocketed the phone, combed my hair with my fingers, and surveyed the effect in the side mirror. Gray crept through the black. The first hint of snow in the mountains—termination dust, we'd called it in Alaska.

"Coleridge, you handsome devil."

Lionel snorted.

"South end of a northbound mule."

I didn't give him the satisfaction of a response.

He lit a cigarette as a radio analyst lamented the grim contemporary saga of New York professional sports. Dynasties were artifacts of antiquity—an oddsmaker couldn't even trust the Yankees anymore.

"You look like Conan the Barbarian's, um, thicker, angrier cousin stuffed into a Men's Wearhouse special."

"Movie Conan or comic book Conan?"

"The Frazetta version."

"Give me a notched broadsword and a naked princess wrapped around my thigh and I'm the spitting image." I checked the action on my revolver. Today it was the .357. I feigned a double take. "Lionel, you're a closet paperback sword-and-sorcery nerd? Not judging. I had a 1985 to 1991 run of *The Savage Sword of Conan* in my adolescence."

"Closet nothing."

"There's room in your cabinet for writers other than Shakespeare? Color me amazed."

The quickest way to tell if Lionel was three sheets to the wind? He'd quote extensive passages from the Bard's plays on his way to the floor.

"Verily, I dig Bill. Read the complete bibliography, forward and back. The undisputed master of Elizabethan potboilers. I reckon he would've grooved on dime novels and superheroes." He tucked a 9mm under his shirt. "Two of my uncles received a deferment from the Vietnam draft. Thick glasses and flat feet. Both of them read three or four novels a week. Way too smart for cannon fodder."

"More like canon fodder," I said.

"What?"

"Nothing. Bookworm, you say?"

"Bookworm like you ain't ever seen. Winters were long on the ranch . . . Ready?"

"Ready." I paused with my hand on the door lever. "By the way, I'm not Conan or any other Cimmerian. Every Halloween and costume party of my youth, I went as Doc Savage. One shredded dress shirt and I'm done."

"Doc Savage is a white dude."

"Technically, he's a bronze dude."

"White dude, bronze tan. Buzz cut, chiseled jaw, ripped to shit and back. You're . . . swarthy. And your hair is too full and kinky, and you don't have a six-pack."

"This is a fairly conservative haircut—"

"You aren't particularly apt with regard to technology. Or science in general, to be honest."

"Gee, thanks. Who do you go as?"

He didn't miss a beat.

"Race Bannon. Driver, pilot, and bodyguard for the Quest family."

"I know who he is. I watched cartoons when I was a kid. You can't be him."

"Why not?"

"Race Bannon is a good driver."

Lionel made a point of consulting the sun.

"Wow, it's not even 10 and my balls are aching."

"Let's move, Crocodile Dundee wannabe."

WE LOCKED THE CAR and proceeded uphill toward a wooden sign that read CLAYTON PARK VILLAGE, EST 1975. Nobody had retouched the sign since the reign of disco. Shoebox condos clustered among stands of erratically pruned elms and beeches.

Clayton Public Park lay at the bottom of the hillside behind a chain-link fence. In the merry month of May, I'd chased a dealer clear around this mulberry bush. He rode with the Storm Kings Motorcycle Club and kept his homies well stocked with E and other party favors. Woe unto him—a preacher's adolescent daughter OD'd on a bad pill, and the dealer's commensurate pain and suffering were required, in honor of the Old Testament. A sob story and ten grand will buy this Avenging Angel's blade for an afternoon's labor.

My quarry had weaved among the jungle gyms and swing sets while crows screamed murder. Dull-eyed patrons perched upon cement benches observed our flight with disinterest. The switchblade in my fist lent length to the dealer's strides. Each flex of his calf caused a vivid piece of ink to ripple—a chaos symbol, its arrows dripping acid. These days, that dried-and-cured patch of skin served as the bookmark of a King James Bible owned by a grieving dad.

Less than two years in state and I was already making memories.

Lionel and I left the sidewalk and followed a slightly curved drive. The neighborhood resembled a retro-dystopia film set—clogged gutters, broken windows covered with plastic sheets, defunct satellite dishes, and cars on blocks. Clayton Forest stretched north of the ridge, past Esopus Creek, to Highway 87.

"Is that a beehive?" Lionel glared at a lump in the crotch of a birch tree. "That's a fucking yellow jacket's nest, bigger than shit."

"The yellow jackets have vacated, I think." I didn't see any workers buzzing around. Nights had been chilly.

"Children play here! Kingston is supposed to be a nice town."

"Nicer than Newburgh. Way, way nicer."

"*There's* a recommendation to hang your hat on. Should be the chamber of commerce pitch." He made a framing gesture. "Kingston: Nicer than Newburgh."

"Way nicer," I said.

UNIT 215 SAT WELL BACK from the entrance. I scouted the perimeter, peering into windows and trying locks. Lionel took the opposite side. Mainly, I wanted to be sure there weren't any dogs. I've always tried to avoid kicking in doors where dogs abide. Angry wives and girlfriends come in a close second and are arguably more threatening.

Empty carport and no visible movement within the condo suggested we had the place to ourselves.

I wrenched the locked doorknob until it gave and bulled my way into the apartment. Exactly what one might expect of a bachelor pad. ST. PAULI GIRL posters, mismatched furniture, and a huge television. The lone nod to class was a large black-and-white photo of a wolf pack prowling through snowy woods above the fake hearth. The photograph's absolute distillation of predatory spirit gave me a mild thrill. Kitchen trash brimmed with cigarette butts and empty forty-ounce beer bottles sufficient to recoup a small fortune at the recycling depot. Incense diluted the strongest odors of sour beer and cigarette and grass smoke.

Hanging beads had replaced the first bedroom door. Royal's domain, affirmed by a high school portrait and later photos of him in combat fatigues. His portable library included 1970s paperbacks on recreational drugs, occultism, medieval witchcraft, and Arlene Fitzgerald's underappreciated classic, *Satanic Sex*. He'd tried his hand at art. A binder of medium-sized canvases contained rough charcoal sketches of dilapidated structures amid rural landscapes and what I assumed were the Catskills. Several were studies of nude women, their features half done and obscured by shadow. Royal didn't sleep much in his neatly made bed. A blanket and pillow on the floor, on the opposite side near the closet, reinforced my assumption. I discovered a baggie of weed and a roll of twenties stashed in his sock drawer. The tang of incense was almost overwhelming. Ashes caked several dishes and a funky little brazier near the bed. He must've burned it by the bushel.

"Check it," Lionel said from the living room. "Goons scored a kickin' vinyl collection. Got us an *Odd Couple* situation here—one goon prefers metal. Goon two is a golden oldies fan. Inquiring minds want to know who's Klugman and who's Randall."

"Lee was pushing sixty," I said. "No doubt the easy listening type of the duo."

Harold Lee's bedroom was spare. Bed, table, dresser. Nothing but the necessities, ma'am. A signed and framed print of Frank Sinatra in Vegas validated my theory regarding the duo's musical predilections.

I inspected drawers and the closet. Cheap suits, rifle-cleaning kit (but no rifle), a stack of outdoor sports magazines, and a shoebox full of photographs. Some were faded with age; others were recent. I confiscated the box. He'd kept his mail in a tray on the table. I sorted through the stack of envelopes, pocketing numerous receipts, a credit card statement, and brochures for hunting lodges.

The television blared at top volume and I nearly jumped through the wall.

"The goons have cable," Lionel said, lowering the audio. "I repeat, the goons have cable! Full package!"

"Tear yourself away from Skinemax and try the answering machine."

"Oh, c'mon. Nobody uses a landline anymore. Except for troglodytes. Troglodytes groove on landlines and dial-up internet."

"Kitchen counter, next to the cave paintings."

"What are *you* doing?"

"Turning over every stone."

The bathroom didn't provide any obvious clues. Neither of the men took prescription medication. There weren't any signs of a woman's touch—no overnight toothbrushes, feminine products, or makeup.

I returned to the living room. Lionel sprawled on the couch, ESPN football highlights muted. I continued into the kitchen, which was simply an extension of the living room. Economy floor plan.

Semi-legible notes were scrawled on a whiteboard hanging by the calendar. I'd missed this detail on the first pass because somebody had partially erased the marker messages and I had to squint to decipher them. A couple of entries were related to schedules at the Knarr Tavern and Black Stars. Another with today's date listed an address in Phoenicia, a window between 10 a.m. and noon, and a heavily underscored figure of $2,500.

I sat on the opposite end of the couch. Worn springs protested. Floorboards too.

"Let's cruise up to Phoenicia for lunch. It's a nice drive."

My rationale went along the lines that we might get lucky and bump into Royal on his errand, which doubtless involved shaking down some piker for twenty-five hundred bucks. Otherwise, over the next couple of nights he'd be at his post, guarding the Knarr's entrance. Either way, I'd had my fill of that claustrophobic apartment and felt the urge to ramble.

"Okay," Lionel said. "You called the house earlier from the car? Not Royal's cell?"

"He didn't answer his cell either."

"Three whole messages on the machine. Most recent is yours. Royal's boss at the Knarr asked if he wants to cover an extra shift this weekend. I bet he doesn't—the joint is a hellhole. Lastly, a chick named Delia called for Lee an hour ago. Very peevish."

"Peevish?"

"Yeah, man. Annoyed? Bitchy? I dunno. Irritable phone voice. My old man always sounded pissed whenever I got him on the horn. Delia wanted an explanation why Lee didn't return her messages."

"Did she say anything interesting?"

"She said, *Hi, this is Delia. Why won't you take my calls, you rotten sonofabitch?*"

"At least she can forgive him now."

"There were no other messages."

"Deleted?"

"Probably. I'd be looking for a new roomie if he deleted my girlfriend's calls."

"What if she yelled a lot and your roomie just wanted to spare you the grief?"

"Ignoring a woman only leads to *more* grief."

We stared at a series of artfully curated football collisions.

Lionel cracked a forty. Last beer in the fridge. He lit a cigarette from a mostly dead pack of Natives he'd snagged during his sweep of the area. Who smoked Natives? Not anybody I'd want to kiss or engage in a close-range conversation.

"Delia sounded young and hot." He made a face and coughed. "Sweet Jesus, what have I stuck in my mouth?"

I thumbed through my ragged dossier of Lee and the contents of his shoebox until I uncovered a photo of a blonde in a snug mohair sweater posed on a wooden dock against a backdrop of water and distant trees. Early thirties, dark blue eyes. Total knockout. She'd signed *Love, D.* on the reverse.

"Behold, the fair Delia." I handed him the photo.

"Whoa! Might not be her. Might be a Darla. Or a Debby."

"It's her."

"Or a Dianne. A Dorothea. A Dolly."

"I've decided it's Delia. Far simpler."

"Be that way, man."

"Mr. Lee's very, very secret love? She doesn't nest here, from what I've seen."

"Too young, too hot to be bumping uglies with a granddad."

"May–December is a tradition. Don't knock Daddy issues."

"I'm not. If this chick was sparking Lee's ignition, she's probably a hooker or a stripper. Who else besides a working girl is ever gonna tolerate assholes like this pair?"

"Who indeed, my cynical, single white male friend? Who indeed?"

A sparrow landed on the sill. Brown and sleek and blandly malevolent. Tiny, amoral creature with death in its gaze. It watched us in a way that said, *If you were insects, I'd peck you to bits*. I didn't think Lionel noticed.

Then he muttered, without turning from the screen:

"*'Fly down, fly down, you little bird, and alight on my right knee.' . . .*

"'I can't fly down, and I won't fly down, and alight on your right knee / A girl would murder her own true love would kill a little bird like me.'"

ON THE WAY TO THE CAR, I presented Delia's photo to a group of college-aged slackers dressed in sweats and name brand tracksuits. One carried a basketball under his arm. The red, white, and blue Harlem Globetrotters model. He gave a low-key wolf whistle at Delia's image and said, "Sorry, bro." His buddies stepped wide, shaking their heads. Fellow such as myself, strolling through a bad neighborhood while wearing a conservative suit, had to be Five-0, or, worse yet, a Federal.

I intercepted a withered gray man in a bomber jacket checkered with Navy service emblems and American flag pins. He pushed his equally withered gray wife in a wheelchair. The old vet held the picture close to his face. His hand tremored with palsy when he passed the photo to his wife.

The wife didn't recognize Delia either.

"She's nasty. She has a nasty smile."

"Honey . . ." the vet said.

"Well, she's the spitting image of Molly O'Brian. The tramp who used to chase after you at the NCOs' club. Saucy bitch!"

"Honey, honey!"

"Don't 'honey' me!"

The vet smirked and waggled his brows as he got under way again. Lionel gave him a low five in passing.

CHAPTER TWELVE

The road carried us toward the address I'd copied at Royal's place.

"I hope we run into an actor," Lionel said. "Loads of famous peeps slum around Phoenicia and Woodstock."

"Sneden's Landing, is what you mean. Hollywood on the Hudson."

"Yes, except the Tinseltown crowd are spreading north like a fungus. Second homes, summer retreats. In the 1960s, every Tom, Dick, and Harry scrammed to the Catskills for his vacation. The giant hotels and resorts are dying. Whole scene is mostly dead. God knows why the Tinseltown crowd is attracted."

"Easy. Famous actors are just plain folks here in hill people country."

The Lifestyles Section of the paper proclaimed the Mid-Hudson Valley a hotspot for celebrities. A new Cape Cod or Martha's Vineyard. Cheaper too. I'd yet to run into any movie stars. Although most of them looked dif-

ferent out of makeup and out of character, so maybe I
had, unwittingly.

Reading my mind, Lionel said, "Hanging with the
mob, you surely met a celebrity or two."

"I accepted a contract on an actor once."

"For real? Anybody I'd recognize?"

"Bit actor—listed in the small print during the end
credits scroll. 'Loudmouth in Bar' or 'Cop 2.' Hadn't
been on screen for twenty years."

"Oh. That doesn't count."

Highway 28 skirted the north shore of the Ashokan
Reservoir and eventually climbed into the Catskills. Fleets
of vehicles belonging to fishermen and sightseers jammed
the ditches from spring through autumn. Thinned now,
as September tipped toward October, except for an occasional car surrounded by late-season tourists. There was
many a secluded spot along the shoreline. Many a secret
fishing hole screened by bushes. Many a crack in the earth
to drop through. Harold Lee, did you meet your demise
while casting for a record trout?

We passed billboards for the ZEN MOUNTAIN MONAS-
TERY, which Lionel explained was the real deal, and
EMERSON RESORT & SPA, home of the world's largest
kaleidoscope. Devlin might dig touring a giant kaleidoscope. I made a mental note to investigate what Wikipe-
dia had to say about the attraction. Twenty-first-century
elementary school children were entranced by pretty
lights, weren't they?

"I don't know from kaleidoscopes," Lionel said when
I asked him. "My cousin fussed over hers." He waved at

the driver of a minivan who'd tailgated us for several miles. The driver honked. "You should visit the monastery. Get your head screwed on straight. Be at one with the galaxy, or some shit."

"What's wrong with my head?"

"You can't find a hat for a regular human-sized cranium?"

"That's not entirely accurate. Okay. Other than my hat problem."

"Fun factoid—a hard-boiled SOB goes into a monastery, he or she comes through the other side as an action hero. Bona fide."

"Bet it's expensive," I said. "A sojourn at the monastery."

"Peeling spuds and contemplating your navel? How expensive could it be?"

"AmEx Black expensive. Buddhism is trendy in Hollywood. Or is it Taoism?"

"Yes, and yes."

"Suppose any beautiful people hang at Zen Mountain?"

"Doubtless. No A-listers. Mountain comes to them."

PHOENICIA, population three hundred–plus, spread along the banks of Stony Clove and Esopus creeks. I've always been fascinated by the phenomenon of certain communities reknitting in the fashion of a body that recovers from a grievous wound. Some scars barely show.

Blazes of yellow crackled across the dells and hillsides. Lovely as a postcard. A clean autumn breeze blew in through my window. Woodsmoke, freshwater, and damp leaves; a whiff of death to lend the bouquet body. Plenty of raccoons and possums were flattened on the road.

I verified the address against a pocket atlas at the Main Street intersection. Lionel hooked a right, went half a mile, then turned left onto gravel. Our destination was Benson's Auto Parts Depot—a Quonset hut garage and modular office. A three-legged German shepherd sunned himself on the office porch. He licked the back of my hand when I stooped to pat him. My shadow reflected in his rheumy eyes, but I didn't think he saw me. He approved of my scent, though, one killer to another.

Lionel scoped the office. Empty.

We walked past a wrecker and an acre of tire mounds and abandoned vehicles. Inside the garage, a beefy man slumped in a chair near a cooler. He pressed a bottle of soda to his tenderized face. Blood spattered his coveralls and obscured the name tag. His left hand dangled. It had swollen colorfully. He'd lost his right shoe. That foot was squashed.

"Mr. Benson?" I said.

The mechanic's stare reminded me of his dog's. He focused upon another reality beyond the one our bodies occupied.

"Benson been dead since 1987. I'm Vern." He spoke thickly, drugged with shock.

"Ow," Lionel said. "Vern, dude, you got a bone poking through your wrist."

The man slowly turned his head to study the mess.

"Oh, yeah . . ."

Lionel consulted his cell. Presumably to dial 911. War hadn't charred the core of his humanity.

"Hold on," I said. My own humanity might've been singed around the edges. "Anyone else here? The hombre who did this still around?" Taking stock, I observed toppled shelving and scattered tools. Nic Royal had blown through with hurricane force and was probably halfway back to Kingston. Still, always best to dot the i's, et cetera.

"My dog . . ." the mechanic said. He closed his eyes. "Did he hurt my dog?"

"Your dog's okay," I said. "Cops are the only ones who blast them out of hand."

"Gunner's a good boy. Real good boy. Younger days, he woulda ripped that bastard's nuts clean off."

I asked again if anyone else was on the premises and he said no. Took some patience to extract the story, given his condition. Persistence triumphed—the mechanic owed a shark in Kingston three large. Goddamned lousy Jets. Royal dropped in, coldcocked him, and went to town with a pipe wrench until the mechanic caved and revealed the location of his stash. The stash covered half the debt, plus Royal helped himself to a Saturday night special and a set of tires for his rig—promised to return in a few days to collect the balance or else finish what he'd started.

"Royal went at you hard," I said. "He's a pro. Pros usually save the rough treatment for incorrigibles." I studied him and his shaved dome and began to divine the motive for his savage beating. "You made the guy mad. Vern, what did you say?" I had a decent idea.

The man hemmed and hawed and allowed that he

might have, possibly, referred to Royal with an ethnic slur.

"He slapped me and I called him a—"

"Say no more, say no more. Everything becomes clear."

"Place gives me the creeps," Lionel said. "Want to bet we poke around, we'll find a pot helmet and a stack of *White Power Monthly*."

"I'm in Dutch," the mechanic said. "Child support, loan shark support, rent. Ain't no way." He groaned, the pain finally trickling into his consciousness. "Mind callin' for help? I'm hurtin'."

Lionel smiled coldly.

"Better peddle some scrap before Royal comes back or you're gonna have to wipe your ass by rubbing against a tree."

"Sage advice," I said.

LIONEL HAPPILY ACCEPTED a gourmet chicken basket and two lagers on my dime at a restaurant in downtown Phoenicia. The Pine Loft was designed with a homey ambience in order to lull unsuspecting tourists until its menu prices jumped up and induced a coronary. Rustic chic, not rustic cheap, Lionel sanguinely observed between gulps of beer.

I skipped the meal and listened to my friend wax rhapsodic over the historic sites.

He pestered the waitress regarding the frequency of celebrity regulars. Ethan Hawke? Susan Sarandon? Bruce Willis? The waitress rolled her eyes. Sure, they were sitting right here at the Elvis Table ten minutes ago; you must've missed them in the parking lot.

"Don't give her a nickel over fifteen percent," he said behind his hand. "She's really sarcastic."

"That's what I like about her."

On the return trip, Lionel inquired as to our next move.

"Home, James," I said. "Today is a good start. We've got Royal in our sights. I'll brace him tonight or tomorrow at the tavern."

A mile or so passed.

"Ugly stuff, what happened to that salvage guy," I said. "Makes me think."

"Uh-huh." He didn't glance at me, which meant he was paying close attention.

"That dog on the porch; an old killer past his prime. Shameful his life was wasted in service of a punk."

"A regular Greek tragedy. Here's some canine trivia— among dogs, *ass-sniffing* is the magic word."

"I'm serious."

"You can't equate every dog with Buck from *Call of the Wild*."

"Or Old Yeller from *Old Yeller*."

"There can be only one Old Yeller."

"My dog Achilles fits the bill. He was brave and loyal. Minerva is too."

"Minerva's loyal," Lionel said. "She'd legit whine and cry if you died. Whimper and then curl up next to her new owner. Oh, and scratch my butt right there . . . Yeah . . ."

"Cynical bastard. Has to go both ways to work. It's

the compact mankind forged with canine when that first scrawny dog came into the cave to share a fire. Dogs were right there when we conquered this world. They helped us wrest it from all comers. We humans owe a blood debt. It can't be repaid, only honored."

"That's beautiful, amigo. Almost convinces me I should get a mutt. It gets cold in the cabin, those long winter nights, and, well—"

"My point being, Vern's bookie is pitiless and now the poor dog won't get as many pats on the head until the dude's mangled wrist heals. Who's *your* bookie?"

"What's his face," he said. "The Mexican."

"Which one? There are four of them."

"Dan."

"Mexican Dan?"

"Dan, usually. I go with whoever's on deck."

"Ah, so it's more accurate to say you deal with the *Mexicans*, not the Mexican."

"Yeah, it's usually Dan, though. We're tight."

"Bookie by committee is the definition of impersonal. Miss a payment or two, some thug like Royal will be knocking on *your* door with an updated installment plan. Stick with Dan. Keep it friendly."

"*Gracias,* Uncle Dad. Long as they don't hire you to kneecap me, I'm safe."

"Right. Oh, and on a different subject."

"For the love of . . . what?"

"Remember at the restaurant, that man in the ball cap sitting near the far window?"

"Ordered clam soup. Braver than I'll ever be, trusting restaurant clams this far inland."

"Did he seem familiar?"

"No, he did not."

"I recognized him from an '80s TV show. Asked for his autograph while you were in the john."

"No way."

"Don't be petulant. The universe is a cruel mistress."

"Bullshit. Life ain't that on the nose."

I slapped the napkin with its scrawled signature on the dash.

"Read it and weep."

"I might." He rubbed his eye. "Isaiah, do you have any friends from the days of remember when?"

"Outfit buddies or buddy-buddies?"

"*Any* buddies."

"I know a few. *Buddies* might be a stretch. *Individuals who don't wish me dead* would be closer."

"Exactly."

CHAPTER THIRTEEN

It rained overnight, then cleared. Minerva paced me on our dawn jog. We raced through a misty world of shiny puddles, dead leaves, and raccoon crap—a doggy theme park.

Jogging isn't crucial to my physical health. It's a meditation; my time to reflect on what I've done and what I'm going to do. It's serious business, like changing bandages on a permanent wound that will go septic if I neglect the duty. I reflect upon people and dogs who've died on me; and I reflect upon those I've killed. I envision my own demise and the endless variety of how such an end might be accomplished. Gene K never saw the wisdom in dwelling on ineluctable fate, of rolling in misery as a dog rolls in shit, but he hadn't aspired to the Bushi code. Neither did I, in my heart of hearts; although a fool can delude himself to the bitter end.

After the run, I changed clothes, drove into north Kingston, and loitered at the Darabont Business Plaza. I kept a semi-low profile, intent upon monitoring Burt

Plantagenet's granddaughter, Aubrey—and scoping any unfriendly types who might be watching her as well. I didn't spot any.

The attempt at subtlety didn't make a difference. Trouble sticks to my shoes.

"You're the dirty bastard who broke Chuck Bachelor's leg." Aubrey P marched across the lot to confront me. She reached into her oversized purse. A peace sign was stitched on it.

"We've mended fences. We're tight like Reagan and Gorbachev." My arms were spread along the top of the bench from which I'd innocently spied upon her comings and goings. "Say, Aubrey, do you have a firearm in there?" A purse that size, she could've stowed a bazooka.

She didn't answer; merely smiled a cold smile worthy of a spaghetti western gunfighter.

"Well, I come in peace," I said. "You know who I am. The guy who busted Chuck Bachelor's leg and ruined his career as Dino the Ax's errand boy."

"Yeah, you're hard to miss." She took a breath. "Burt says Chuck had it coming. *Chuck* said he had it coming. I haven't decided. You *look* like an asshole."

"Sometimes a cigar is a cigar. In any event, as I said, politics shift—we're bosom buddies."

"Doesn't explain why you're lurking here."

"Lurking is an integral part of my skill set. I was assessing your salon and environs—wanted to ascertain whether anybody might be watching you besides yours truly."

"Chuck said you're a for-hire type."

"Have brass knuckles—will travel."

"Who paid you to follow me around?"

"Interesting question. You haven't spoken with your old friend Chuck recently?"

"Been a while. None of your damned business."

"He obviously talks with Burt. Your grandfather is concerned you might be in trouble. Chuck is too. My investigation leads me to concur."

She finally blinked.

"Investigation? Burt sent you to . . . what?"

"To do what I do."

Aubrey P stood around five-nine, rawboned and fair. Twenty-three, twenty-four. She didn't bear much resemblance to her grandfather except for the set of her jaw and raspy inflection. She wore a hoodie, linen pants, and track shoes. No ring.

I was still calculating whether I could cover the distance between us before she dragged her *pistola* free when she relaxed and removed her hand from the purse.

"Who am I kidding?" she said.

I patted my chest and exhaled.

"For what it's worth, my heart believed you."

"No, I have a gun. I don't think I could pull the trigger."

"Here's to you never being put to the test," I said. "Coffee? I could use some coffee. Directly injected into my right ventricle."

I BOUGHT AUBREY a coffee at a bagel shop. We walked into the park that stretched behind the plaza and stood near a duck pond. Ducks bobbed amongst slicks of green-and-white scum, as advertised.

"The artillery," I said. "Burt didn't mention you were armed and dangerous."

"Because I keep some details to myself. He's got hypertension. Had it since the war. He's gonna stroke out, as it is. You've met him. He's too old to be carrying that kind of weight. My problem isn't helping."

A geezer in all-plaid went past, towed by a glossy black Lab. The dog smiled to let me in on the secret—he had his human on a leash.

"Your stalker problem," I said. "Let's discuss it."

"Whatever Burt told you, it's worse," Aubrey said.

"You call your grandfather by his given name?"

"Again, none of your business . . . What did he say?"

"He told me you're being harassed and that it's getting rough," I said.

"Yeah, that's true."

"Give me your definition of *rough*."

"Anonymous phone threats. Slashed tires. Cars cruising past my house superslow in the dead of night. They killed my cat. I bought a pistol as soon as I could. Bastards. I loved that cat." I expected her to cry, but she didn't.

"What was your cat's name?"

"Ms. July. Found her abandoned in a ditch the last weekend of July, ten years ago. My dad thought it would be funny to call her Ms. July. Like the pinups."

"My condolences," I said. "Here's what your grandfather said—you style hair at the Nitty-Gritty Beauty Salon; you're involved with Walter Connell, a young man who skipped college and went directly into his father's construction firm. Working his way up from the bottom. I respect that. By all accounts, you're both good eggs. Walter's rough around the edges. Drinks too much, runs his mouth at the tavern, gets in scuffles. Nothing serious; he's no tough guy. This is the book on Walter?"

"That's the book on Walt." She lowered her gaze.

"You want to marry him and he wants to marry you?" After she nodded, I said, "Regrettably, there's a major snag. Walter's former lover, one Elvira Trask, objects to the proposed union. She's a criminal from a family of criminals. Small-ball, but mean as a scorpion. The Trasks push pills and steal cars. The boldest and brightest run short cons and commit the odd robbery. Shake down rival dealers. Cunning as rats. They keep below the mob's radar. A nibble here, a nibble there. This is your opposition."

"Yes, that's the picture."

"How did it start between you and Elvira? Face-to-face, phone call, or an intermediary?"

"Phone call at work. A woman introduced herself as Elvira; said she was extra-special friends with Walter and that I'd be sorry for touching him. I didn't take it seriously. Lots of girls chased after Walter before we got together. I figured she was a loony. Except, Walter freaked when I told him, explained she and her family were hard-core."

"He wasn't kidding. You have a concealed carry permit, by any chance?"

"No."

"Get one since you're packing heat in your purse. Cops take a dim view. And if you have to ventilate a bad guy, your paperwork best be in order."

"Okay. I'll do it."

"Good. Next point—you received a blackmail note."

"Day after they killed my cat. Looked like a ransom letter—cut and pasted from magazines. *50k and you won't bleed on your wedding day.*"

"Do either you or Walter have access to that kind of money?"

She laughed; cynical, although not bitter.

"Ha! We're paycheck-to-paycheck. Walt's dad skates on the ragged edge of receivership. He despises me. I called him a cokehead. He hasn't forgotten. Grandpa might be sitting on a nest egg. I'd never ask him. He has expenses . . . the gym, hired goons. I doubt you come cheap either."

I wondered what gave the Trasks the idea they might extort fifty large from poor folk.

"The police have anything to say about your case?"

"The police are goddamned useless."

"It isn't their job to be helpful. What have they passed along?"

"Claim they can't act until something happens. Like, if I get my throat cut, then okay."

"All pretty standard. This next question is worth double points. Have you reached out to anyone?"

"You mean, have I approached Chuck or his uncle?" she said.

"Right. I'm more concerned whether you've enlisted Dino's aid. If you've involved the mob, I can't interfere."

"No. I'm not wild about the Italian crowd. Is that a code of ethics, or what? The noninterference part?"

"One way to put it," I said. "Another way is, it's me avoiding a bullet behind the ear. You think of these people in terms of your family, friends, colleagues. Chuck, Uncle Dino, Uncle Dino's hilarious pals, Mike the Machete and Tommy-Two-in-the-Brain. Incorrect. They aren't human beings, they're creatures from the Black Forest. Wolves."

"Besides Walt and Granddad, you're the only person I've spoken with . . . Jesus."

"Good. I'll see what I can do to put a stop to the harassment and avenge your cat."

"Avenge my cat? Are you serious?" She studied my face. "You are."

"Ms. July clinched it. Animals tend to represent our purest selves. I'll go a long way past the line in the name of an innocent creature."

"Wait, wait. Before this goes any further . . . Would she back off if I paid? Fifty isn't realistic. What if Walter and I raised some of it? Like, if we scraped fifteen or twenty together?"

"Absolutely, it would help," I said. "Until she gets hungry again. Sooner or later, Elvira Trask and her crew will cut the foreplay and move on you. This type of element sticks to a game plan—and the plan is to bleed you. Once they've extracted whatever you'll give, matters will escalate."

"Escalate?" she said. "That's not a reassuring word."

"I don't have a crystal ball, lady. Educated guess? The Trasks increase the pressure in order to extort more cash. Victims will go to terrible lengths to pay off a relentless bad guy. People will sell houses, cars, plunder the kiddies' college savings. She'll wait to see if you crack."

"I won't crack."

"Yes, and it will escalate anyway. You're lucky, it'll be broken bones and a stern warning and she'll be satisfied that her honor is avenged. You're not so lucky, she'll carve her initials into your face. You're *really* unlucky, she and her homies will drop you in a hole with a bag of lime. Any of those outcomes will stress your grandpa's bum ticker."

"All right, I'll wrap my head around this information. What happens next?"

"What happens next is, I chat with your boyfriend, hear his perspective. Then, I'll probably reunite you with your cousin. He and his homies will shadow you during the day shift. Nights, my partner Lionel or I will sleep on the couch. Tonight, I'll have Chuck's crew sit in the driveway for a few hours. I have a pressing errand."

"As in full-time bodyguards?"

"As in, yes. These amateur criminal families aren't organized as the mob. That doesn't make them any less dangerous."

"Gotta admit, Mr. Coleridge, you dudes camped out at the apartment and the salon might cramp my style."

"Pshaw!" I said with forced cheer. "It won't be a big deal. During daylight hours, it's work and errands—you won't even notice us. Kick back, watch Netflix, binge on ice cream, and abstain from noisy sex with your beau. The whole ordeal will be resolved within a few days. A week, tops."

"Ugh," she said.

I had to agree.

CHAPTER FOURTEEN

Harold Lee's profession seldom required gunplay. Men in the enforcement-and-collection racket nonetheless demonstrate an almost pathological obsession with firearms. Lee's receipts were an arrow guiding me to the next point of inquiry—Crawford's Bullet Shack, located on the borderlands of Rosendale.

Incidentally, Lionel and I routinely frequented this store. The genial co-owners appreciated that we purchased buckets of ammo for target shooting. No pussyfooting required—I presented the newspaper article on Harold Lee's demise and explained I'd accepted the investigation.

Thad and Bonner, the brothers who ran the store, were a pair of Carhartt-wearing, whiskey-swilling good ol' boys. They tripped over themselves to assist my investigation. It didn't hurt that as we chatted, I splurged on one hundred dollars' worth of .38 and .308 rounds.

I showed off Delia's photo and another I'd obtained of Ray Anderson (mousy, forty-ish). The brothers didn't recognize either person. Regretfully, in Delia's case.

Bonner locked the door and flipped the OPEN sign to CLOSED. We went into the backyard, which they'd enclosed to create a private shooting range, and sat in lawn chairs in the sandy patio area. Thad poured each of us a tall glass of hard lemonade.

"Harry ran with a tough crowd," Bonner said. "We didn't pry into his affairs, did we, T?"

"Not goddamned likely," Thad said.

"He was mixed up with the mob. I mean, we ain't idiots—obviously, he worked for loan sharks. Smashed hands in filing drawers, and what have you. Everybody knew that."

"He was nice about it, though. Polite."

"Yeah, yeah," Bonner said. "Extra-polite, is what people said. First-class gentleman, is what I say."

When had they last seen Lee and did they notice anything different in his behavior?

"Must've been the last week of August he come in to browse," Bonner said. "He didn't act nervous or out of sorts. Said he'd dropped a heap on the Giants and couldn't afford his layaway until Christmas. Shot the shit and moved on. I didn't believe him about the Giants, by the by. Harry was conservative. I think it was his grandkid—she's got a heart condition. Two or three years ago, she needed surgery. Harry was outta his mind trying to raise the dough. He had a soft heart. I heard the family don't talk to him or nothin'."

"Gents, you've stoked my curiosity," I said. "Is it too indelicate to inquire what Harry was saving his pennies for?"

"Mossberg 590 Tactical," Thad said. "Tri-rail, laser sight. Bear slugs."

"Harry owned a .223 for deer hunting and a .22 pistol," Bonner said. "Surprised me he wanted the Mossberg. Outta character. I mean, it's a beast. His business, though. If he wanted an elephant gun, I'd put the order in. We accept cash or plastic and tend to our own knitting."

"Was he after black bear?" I said. "The Mossberg would certainly do the job."

"Harry only went for animals he could eat. He didn't care for the taste of bear."

I sipped my drink and dwelled upon the ramifications. A tactical shotgun wasn't remotely the sort of tool Harold Lee normally used. Home defense? Nine rounds, alternating between slugs and buckshot, would annihilate nearly anything or anyone not protected by armor plating.

"Ever meet any of Lee's friends?"

"The black guy? Sure, now and then he walked in with Harry. Didn't say a whole lot. Kinda hard to get a read on him, y'know?" Bonner looked at his brother. "What'd you think of the fella? The black dude. Remember? Tats, soft-spoken—"

"Yeah."

"Well, so?"

"Scary mofo," Thad said.

"Scary?" I said.

"Dead eyes," Thad said. "The kid smiles and says the right things, but he's got them dead eyes. Seen a few soldiers come home with those same eyes. Not as bad, maybe. He didn't realize I was watching him ogle the knives in the display. His expression went slack like some-body pulled his plug. Except, he loved them blades. That's the second his eyes came alive. Crazy, sick eyes."

Bonner gave me a shrug, as if to say, *Who knew?*

I made a note and then asked whether the police had put in an appearance at the Shack. The brothers shrugged and Bonner topped off my glass. No cops yet. The gears of bureaucracy grind slowly, yes? This confirmed what I'd suspected at the outset—John Law wasn't in any hurry to solve the Harold Lee equation, even though Curtis had pull at Kingston PD headquarters and at least two detectives in his pocket.

We shook hands and I thanked the brothers for their hospitality. I hesitated at the front counter.

"Suppose I might take a gander at that shotgun?"

"You ain't afraid of bad luck?" Bonner said.

"Nor ancient Indian curses," I said. "Anyhow, one might argue it was bad luck Harry didn't pony up the cash."

Fifteen minutes later, I slid the Mossberg in its case and several boxes of shells behind the seat of my truck. When I was driving home, the cold draft through the window on the passenger side felt like Harold Lee's ghost trying to tell me something.

CHARLES BACHELOR (Chuck to his pals) and Walter Connell walked through my office door around 3 in the afternoon. Best practice required me to interview Walter, fiancé to the fair and frazzled Aubrey Plantagenet.

Chuck's permanent limp seemed negligible—to me, at any rate. Probably not to him. Here stood Dino the Ax's prodigal nephew. He'd shaved his greasy blond hair to stubble, which represented a dramatic change from his former impression of ponytailed Eurotrash. He wore a dress jacket, slacks, and wingtips. The jacket concealed a plethora of bad prison tats emblematic of even worse life choices. Chuck packed a lot of muscle, as many ex-cons do.

"These are your digs, eh?" He surveyed the room with characteristic dispassion.

"A bit of trivia," I said to Chuck. "You are the very first person to visit my humble establishment, outside of a building inspector and a couple of buddies who helped lug some furniture and the safe upstairs." Meg had also helped me christen the office by having wild sex on the desk. "Who's watching Aubrey P?"

"Two of my boys will soon be parked in front of the salon. Nobody gonna fuck with her. Ain't how the Trasks roll. Uh, this is Walter Connell. Walter, Isaiah Coleridge."

Walter appeared as I'd expected—long, tall drink of water, to put it in the vernacular of my Southern kin. Young and sunburned from hours of laboring in the elements. Corduroy jacket and blue jeans. His scowl poorly concealed nervousness. We shook hands. I disliked him on the spot.

"Man, life boomerangs on you," Chuck said. "Me and Burt are tight; always were. He saw me in the clink, y'know? Dino didn't. Wiseguys are allergic to stir. I thought of Aubrey as my kid sister. But I sort of lost touch with her. Now comes the trouble and we're talking again. Sorry it took an emergency; not sorry to see her."

While Chuck spoke, Walter glumly stared at the carpet.

"Walter, I chatted with your girl this morning." I sat on the edge of the reception desk and waited for him to meet my gaze. Took a while. "Would love to meet the other woman. Elvira seems to be in the wind. I asked around and nobody has seen her since last week."

"Lying low to plot Aubrey's doom, eh?" Chuck said with an appreciative smirk.

"Elvira isn't the other woman," Walter said. "We've been quits since high school. We weren't ever really a thing, you know?"

"Allow me to rephrase," I said. "You *used* to sleep with her."

"I fucked her in high school, yeah."

"Fingerbangin' and hand jobs don't count," Chuck said.

"That's ancient history, isn't it?" I said. "High school romances usually have the half-life of a mayfly."

Walter smirked. The conversation lightened his mood.

"What can I say? She covets the D."

My dislike of him intensified.

"Amigo, get that prick of yours patented. Because if she's still begging for it halfway to your ten-year reunion, the thing should be gold-plated."

"Elvira's a crazy bitch who can't let go. She had it bad and I bounced. She don't like it when people walk. None of the Trasks do."

I glanced at Chuck.

"Seem legit to you? Are the Trasks a bunch of sore losers?"

Chuck frowned the way not-so-smart guys do when

the teacher hits them with a pop quiz. He looked at Walter as he answered.

"Elvira was a wild child, know what I mean? She could lose her shit with the best of 'em. Comes to people, she's got no mercy. Have to say, I wouldn't peg her for a cat murderer. She's soft on critters. Loves dogs, adores cats. Says pets are the only redeeming quality of human beings."

"Maybe one of her flunkies felt differently. Maybe she acquired an edge."

"People change, yeah. She was young and I went inside for a while. The meth and the booze ate her fuckin' brains, or somethin'."

I trusted Chuck's insight in this matter. It jibed with what my own research had shown. History played a role as well. Before informally joining the Deluca organization, he'd run with the Trasks; a misspent youth directly contributing to his chronic delinquency and later estrangement from the Family. He knew the Trasks better than anyone and recognized the real threat his erstwhile comrades presented to Burt and Aubrey.

Folks wrote the Trasks off as trailer trash and small-timers. Chuck didn't argue otherwise, except to note that every single member of the clan subscribed to a philosophy of savagery for the sake of savagery. No slight, real or perceived, against Family honor could go unavenged. One couldn't afford to take madmen (or madwomen) lightly.

I took off the metaphorical gloves and laid it on Walter.

"Hate to ruin your fantasy. That note Aubrey received indicates the true motive here. Your superpowered dick aside, this has nothing to do with love, or lust, or jealousy. It's a cash grab. Although, terrorizing your fiancée is likely a bonus."

"Hey, *that* sounds like a Trask ploy." Chuck nodded approvingly. "Muddy the waters and stick in the gaff."

"Are you on speaking terms with Elvira?" I said to Walter.

Walter didn't reply until Chuck and I had stared at him hard enough to change his mind.

"I wouldn't say speaking, exactly."

Chuck shook his head disgustedly.

"The Trasks will move soon. They've heard of you, and it's a concern, but not enough for them to realize it's time to fold their tents. They'll send a crew to the house. Could kidnap Aubrey P on the street, except they're mad-dog motherfuckers. Prefer terror. Home invasion is their jam. Expect four or five guys, ready to unload if you give them any grief. I'll assume you're going to give them grief."

"That's a safe assumption."

CHAPTER FIFTEEN

I lurked behind a bush, waiting for the Knarr Tavern to go dark at 2 a.m.

Murder wasn't on my itinerary. This presented its own set of problems. Chiefly, that kidnapping is fraught with peril. Far safer to pop a target at two hundred yards with a sniper rifle and go crack a beer. The grand hitter emeritus, Gene K, had admonished me to never get into the bodyguard or bounty hunting professions. Take-'em-alive occupations were anathema to a born predator and dangerous to boot.

Stepping into the world of fixing and detection was akin to circling back into my hellish childhood. Incidents of close-quartered battle skyrocketed. Sadly, I'd traded my authority to drop fools in a hole on a whim for a fig leaf of respectability. It meant more lumps, bumps, and broken bones in my future. I kept all my edges sharp anyway.

Which brought me to the subject of Nic Royal, the roving arm breaker.

Snuffing a man is easy. I didn't want to murder or maim

Royal; I wanted to chat with him at a place and under circumstances of my choosing. Restraint often requires overwhelming force or the application of pain. Pain is unreliable.
In my old line, neither great physical strength nor any elite
level of hand-to-hand skill were essential when it came to
clipping guys. The vast majority of people I've dusted were
unaware of my presence as they segued from this world to
the Hereafter. Any five-foot-five waif armed with a sharp
knife can operate from the shadows. I'd met my share.

Royal trudged across the deserted lot. He started his
shitty two-tone Mazda pickup on the third try.

I climbed in beside him and flashed the .357.

"Both hands on the wheel, slick." The cab was cramped;
not built for a full-sized man, much less two. Naked
springs jabbed me in tender places. My knees were practically in my chest, which aggravated the dull ache in my
ribs. The cab reeked of cigarettes, sweat, and soured meat.
Royal lived a truly unglamorous life reserved for the des-
titute. Mice crept into filthy old vehicles like this Mazda
and made nests. Sometimes the critters died and rotted
within a vent or the very frame of the vehicle. Driving
around with desiccated mice in your truck had to be the
start of a country song.

The radio kicked in with a screeching, metallic blast
that stabbed into my eardrums. I cursed. Royal hastily
lowered the volume on Black Sabbath.

"Apologies, sir," he said. Soft as a shy child, or a rat-
tlesnake. "It's a piece of crap. Speakers take a few seconds
to warm up."

"Let's go for a drive," I said as the ringing in my ears

subsided. Cliché or not, the phrase scared people spitless and that's exactly how I wanted him. "By the by—I went through your glovebox and couldn't help but notice it's crammed with traffic tickets."

"DWB."

"Driving while black?"

"Maybe troopers dig my ride."

In a certain light, I received the same treatment.

"Be extra-cautious, then."

He put the truck into gear and stared straight ahead as he drove. Kingston's streetlamps grew farther apart. Highway stripes and fragments of trees floated in the void sculpted by the headlights.

I GAVE DIRECTIONS that steered us down a lonely secondary road.

Royal whistled a dry, disjointed version of *The Twilight Zone* theme until I told him to put a sock in it.

He parked at the edge of a field somewhere between Woodstock and nowhere. There was a moment when he could've tried to bust a move—I heard the tumblers clicking in his brain. Doubtful he carried a piece while bouncing in the tavern. I'd searched the Mazda earlier for a hideout and confiscated a .32 from under the seat. The lack of a gun would severely limit his options.

Still, my pulse thumped as we exited the vehicle. In terms of controlling an adult human, nothing is certain. My due diligence notwithstanding, there might be another hidden weapon; he could decide to make a break for it. After three steps, the night would swallow him whole.

Nothing bad happened. Royal didn't believe in the principle of carpe diem. Regular guys seldom do when it's their ass on the line. He beat people with a pipe, yes, but that didn't make him dangerous to me. I'd reversed the script and penciled myself in as the wolf. He complied like a dutiful sheep.

We stood fifteen feet apart. I held my revolver pointed toward the dirt.

"Sir, permission to smoke?" he said.

"Already? I haven't even given you the blindfold." I chuckled at his sharp inhalation. "Kidding. I didn't bring one. Go ahead, smoke."

He reached with exaggerated care into his jacket, got a cigarette going. The burning match was the only artificial light for miles. His hands trembled. I liked that.

The brief halo of flame confirmed he was a handsome dude. Around my height, decent build. Looked quick and fluid. Leather jacket and leather pants. Exactly as I recalled him, except up close and personal.

The match fizzled and we became silhouettes to each other.

"Did you kill Harry?" He stole my line. Still soft, still ominous.

Intriguing gambit on his part. Were he innocent, his natural assumption *would* be I'd done for his buddy and returned to snip dangling threads. I couldn't determine whether he was cunning or as ingenuous as advertised.

"Someone did." I let it hang. "Clipped Harry and

swiped his head for a souvenir. Who, oh who, is capable of such an atrocity? There's the kind of wild man I'd love to meet." Again, I waited. "Sixty-four-thousand-dollar question is—am I talking to that charmer right now?"

"You're talking to a poor boy who's shitting his pants."

"Are you afraid because you think I killed your partner, or are you afraid because *you* did it and time has come to pay the check?"

"Uh, the first choice."

I buzzed like a game show special effect.

"I'm not a trophy hunter. The powers that be sent me down from heaven to sort this business."

"Who—"

"Far as you're concerned, I'm Archangel Michael. Oversized wings, fiery sword, a yen for avenging injustices perpetrated by idiots. I toil for God. God is extremely interested in solving the mystery of Harold Lee's tragic demise."

"Sir, I—"

"Shut up. *I* didn't kill Harry, and *you* allegedly didn't kill Harry . . ."

He smoked furiously, then realized I was awaiting an answer.

"I didn't. He was a friend. Murder isn't my speed."

"Murder isn't your speed?" I said.

"Negative."

"Okay, double jeopardy—what does the Croatoan mean to you?"

"Negative. I don't know what that is."

"*Who.* Who he is."

"Never heard of him, sir."

"Pinky-swear?"

"Excuse me?"

"The man you maimed at the salvage yard didn't give you a sterling character reference."

Royal hesitated.

"Would you believe me if I said that racist prick got what he deserved?"

"Well, I'd at least acknowledge he was breathing, last I saw him. You're a model of restraint."

"Fucking A." Drowning, he grasped at this bit of flotsam on an ocean of trouble. "I could've jacked his shit permanently. Skinhead was begging to get capped. But I don't roll like that."

"Ray Anderson. Freelance thief. Somebody bumped him too, in fairly recent history. He a friend of you or Harry?"

"I saw the dude around and that's it. Heard he got whacked. Harry took him drinking sometimes. They fished too."

"They do any jobs together?"

"Harry never mentioned."

"Easy for me to verify your story."

"Feel free. I'm not lying."

"It's your lucky night, Nic," I said. "I'm going to extend you the benefit of the doubt. You and Harry rubbed elbows with unsavory sorts. He put the hurt on his share of suckers. One of these acquaintances or victims is probably responsible for the murder."

"Sir, if I had the first clue, I'd sing like a canary. Listen, they zapped Harry and I could be next. I've wracked my brain for a name, a reason."

"Hit me with your best estimate."

"I'll tell you what I told the cops. Problem with our job is everybody and his dog has a hard-on for us. Be easier to make a list of the five people who *didn't* want to stick his head on a pole."

"Who'd you speak with?"

"Dumpy older guy and a blonde chick sniffed around yesterday. Plainclothes detectives. They wanted to come inside the house and poke around. I said, *No warrant, no joy.* And they bugged. Didn't give a rat's ass."

"They *might* give a rat's ass. A small rat. I heard Harry's granddaughter has medical issues. He bailed her family out in a major way not long ago. Is that true?"

"Affirmative. Girl's got a leaky heart valve. Harry called in a marker and paid what the insurance didn't cover. I didn't ask who loaned him the scratch. He only mentioned paying it off. I wonder if he did."

At this point in the conversation I'd reached the unscientific conclusion that Royal was partially on the level—seventy to eighty percent. Criminals hoard the truth like gold even when it has zilch to do with their predicament. Stubbornness is a hallmark of this type. Another strong possibility was PTSD. Some of his mannerisms reminded me of Lionel's tics—particular quirks of speech and posture, gesticulation that were indicative of weariness and wariness.

How hard to press is always a judgment call in these circumstances. Too light a touch, you're a patsy, and

word travels fast in these circles. Too brutal and a guy
will sing any song he thinks you want to hear. I played it
safe and grilled him for easy stuff; info he was practically
begging to divulge. My hammer-and-pliers routine could
wait for another evening, if it came to that.

Where had Harry gone previous to his murder? Was he
on the trip alone? Anybody make extraordinary threats
against him lately? Had he come into sudden money? Who
was Delia?

Royal spilled.

When not smashing kneecaps and seducing showgirls,
Harry enjoyed long nature walks and hunting and fishing
in the Catskills. He often disappeared for weekends away
from the loan-sharking grind. His destinations were vague.
Usually he went alone, although he sometimes mentioned
meeting a buddy en route, or hooking up with a girl.
Around two weeks ago, he'd headed north for such a trip;
the plan was to catch the final days of trout season at several
choice locations. Harry said he'd be back within a week.

I asked Royal if he'd ever ridden along.

"Did all the hiking and foraging I could stand in the
service. No thanks."

He couldn't recollect any recent threats. He and Harry
had been friendly acquaintances for a while and divided
the condo the last year. Rarely, Harry flashed a wad of
money—scores came and went with the tide. As for Delia, Royal met her in the flesh. Smoking-hot. Neither she
nor Harry volunteered her personal info such as a last
name, where she lived, et cetera. She danced somewhere—

Harry had a weakness for showgirls. He frequented the Bird of Paradise, a nightclub that hosted a weekly review.

I privately noted that the Bird of Paradise wasn't among Lee's receipts. Did he receive a pass in return for off-the-books services? Happened a lot, tough guys getting comped that way. Some places, barter was as good as cash.

"Strippers?" I said.

"Negative, sir. Burlesque chicks don't take it all off. Harry liked that those girls leave something to the imagination."

"And Delia? You expect me to buy that he didn't talk about her?"

"Harry was a gentleman. He bought flowers for women, held the door. Wasn't the kind to kiss and tell. He didn't date a lot anyhow. Said a bachelor's life is simpler."

"A gentleman *and* a scholar," I said. "Earlier, before I tossed this fine truck, I snooped around your pad. My observations. First, restock your beer. Second, you're sleeping on the floor. Flashbacks to the military, or what?"

He finished his cigarette and tossed the butt.

"Probably paranoia . . . Feels like I'm being watched in the condo. Woke up the other night in a cold sweat. Weapons instructor of mine in the Corps said it's smart to heed your sixth sense. Your skin crawls like you're under a scope, then you're being scoped. Unless that was you, peeking through my curtains."

"Wish I could ease your mind. Stay frosty, or whatever it is you Marines do in troubled times."

"I'm pissing ice cubes."

I approached and passed him my card. I'd scribbled one of my private numbers on the reverse side.

"Hold on to that. It's tempting to run. Don't succumb to the instinct. You get scared, call me instead. The hills have eyes, the fields have ears. Because if you run, if you hide, well, the optics aren't favorable. Lay low, but like the cops say, don't leave town." I waited for him to confirm his understanding. "Last thing . . . What's a nice boy like you doing with books on witchcraft? Funky collection you got at the *casa*."

"Sex magic," he said.

"No shit?"

"Bitches love sex magic."

I made him drive me back to Kingston, and square one.

PART II

MASKS

CHAPTER SIXTEEN

Do evil deeds by day (or morally questionable deeds) and suffer headaches and nightmares as a reward. I dreamed of a forest, green and black and mysterious. Dad and I were fighting. Dad thrashed me as easily as ever. In this nightmare, he loomed twelve feet tall. He gripped my throat and raised me off the ground. Hellfire crackled in his eyes and whiskey vapor steamed from his nostrils.

Your problem is that you think you escaped. There's no escaping the darkness. Each word was a peal of thunder, a glacier scaping a V into the earth.

Partially hidden within a stand of trees, my dead mentor, Gene K, called to me: *The woman, the boy, your faithful dog. Hold on to them, Isaiah—you're sinking fast.*

Seemed about right.

NEED TO RESURRECT THE DEAD for a brief heart-to-heart? Lace on his or her shoes and take a walk. Over the weekend, I strolled down Memory Lane and past the proverbial graveyard.

First, I tried the electronic route.

Harold Lee's family proved as dysfunctional and obdurate as I'd anticipated. Goons, thieves, and inveterate gamblers share that commonality. His ex-wife and eldest son didn't return my calls. The eldest son had the sick daughter. I finally got the youngest on the horn. He knew *Nothin' 'bout nothin'* and said that his deadbeat dad could rot. No comment on Harry's charitable donations to the child's medical fund. He disconnected and left me to bitterly reflect on my own father and our nonexistent relationship.

Sorting Lee's receipts was my method of consulting the spirits via tea leaves or vying to glean a clear picture of a jigsaw from a mere handful of puzzle pieces. I learned that he slapped expenses on plastic only when necessary; otherwise, he chose cold, hard cash. He frequented upscale bars, gentlemen's clubs, and the neighborhood liquor store near Clayton Park. He dined at a downtown Sicilian restaurant twice a week, minimum, and had approximately nine payments remaining on a Chrysler sedan. Law enforcement hadn't recovered the car. His Esopus Sportsmen's Club membership was good until December, as were his Empire Pass and season ticket to Mohonk Mountain. The man hadn't lived large; however, he'd spent freely on his passions. Typical of rent-a-thugs, gamblers, and assorted ilk. I'd done the same until recently.

He'd scribbled the name and number of Ray Anderson, burglar extraordinaire, inside a matchbook cover.

That pricked up my ears. Nic Royal insisted Lee and Anderson were friendly outside of work. A shady character
telling me the truth? Either pigs were sprouting wings or
he'd seen his life flashing before his eyes.

Ray Anderson's wife managed an office for a water
treatment company. A modicum of research revealed the
company boasted a client list in the thousands, with numerous celebrities among the mundane well-to-do customers.

*Oh, Ray, you rascally cat burglar. Those addresses came in
handy for your nocturnal activities.* Here's a grim reality
check—a preponderance of burglaries are committed either by associates of the victim or by crooks in the employ
of the service industry. Tom and Dick are installing your
new cabinets as Harry (Ray, in this example) makes a key
mold of your back door lock. The crew returns weeks or
months later—say, while the family is on vacation—and
strips the house to its foundation.

I idly wondered whether Mrs. Anderson had been in
on the scheme or was an unwitting pawn. Did she sincerely believe Ray's cover story that he was a professional
gambler? In my experience, spouses (and estranged children) of bad guys prefer to be kept in the dark, and none
of them care to talk.

On a flier, I called the widow anyhow.

Nothing dramatic came of our ten-minute conversation, which I prefaced with the blunt admission that I'd
been hired to investigate the killing of Harold Lee, an
individual her husband might've known professionally, if
not as a friend.

The basics were old hat: She barely glimpsed the stranger who drove away with Ray the night he died: an adult male of indeterminate age and ethnicity in a brown sedan.

She did confirm that Harold Lee was a relatively close acquaintance of Ray's. He came by the house for dinner and the men went fishing together two or three times a year. Where? Day trips to the Ashokan Reservoir, Esopus Creek, and High Falls. She described "Harry" as rather charming; an old-fashioned, courteous man who unfailingly brought her flowers or a bottle of wine—a shame he'd died. Did I suspect a connection between his and Ray's murders?

Truth was, I did. Strongly. By the way, did Lee ever bring anybody else around? Either an older gentleman or a youngish woman? Late twenties to early thirties; attractive, buxom, called herself Delia?

Nope.

Next, I searched online for the Bird of Paradise nightclub and the burlesque review Royal mentioned. There was nothing in Lee's receipts to indicate he'd patronized the joint. That suggested management comped him or Delia got him a sweetheart pass. Interesting.

No matches for Delia, which didn't prove anything— she probably danced under a stage name. Eventually, I struck gold, finding an older advertisement for the Sapphire Review that featured headshots of its performers. Subtracting the raven-black wig and heavy makeup, a woman who went by Midnight Star bore a striking resemblance to the elusive Delia. Midnight Star was the main attraction, although biographical details were sketchy.

I called Curtis and asked if he could persuade management at the White Rock Hotel to hook me up with a VIP table at the next Sapphire Review.

Curtis snickered.

"What do you think, schmuck? Not a problem. We've buried guys under their golf course for years."

MEG INVITED ME OVER for early supper. She said Devlin looked forward to a visit from "Uncle Isaiah." After a rocky beginning, we were pals, the boy and me.

Devlin mumbled "Eyez-zay-yah" for the first six months of our relationship. He'd gradually gotten the pronunciation under control. I missed it. The boy was dark-haired and wiry. Unafraid to use his teeth whenever I got him in the kiddie version of a half nelson. I appreciated that feistiness. He didn't ask after Mac. Children are unsophisticated, not stupid. He knew damned well his dad had flown the coop, in that weird logic peculiar to anybody under the age of sixteen, Mac's departure embarrassed him. Maybe he blamed himself. No age limit governs guilt.

I opted for the coward's route and pretended everything was hunky-dory. Checked out DVDs of the latest Star Wars flicks (a major fixation). Played Darth Vader to his Obi-Wan with plastic light sabers in the yard. Read him a story before bed on the nights I came over. Bloody fairy tales—the unabridged versions full of fornication, cannibalism, and man's inhumanity to man. Minerva usually lay at the foot of the bed, drowsing. He loved Minerva and she loved him right back.

We were dueling in the backyard and I noticed he seemed glum. Took some prying to get the story that he'd caught a ration of crap at school.

"The kids at school made fun of you?" I said.

"Because of my Wonder Woman shirt. Bobby Sweeney says it's a girly shirt." He made a face and explained that his mom got it for him at Target. He owned most of the Justice League—Green Lantern, Batman, and The Flash shirts, and Superman PJs.

"You like Wonder Woman a lot?"

"Yeah." He nodded bashfully.

"Geez, Dev, join the club. She your favorite?"

He squirmed and studied his nicked-and-battered work boots.

I knelt so we were eye to eye and laid my hand on his shoulder.

"Listen, buddy. You wear whatever the fu—the heck— you want. It doesn't matter what Bobby Stinky says, okay?"

Devlin cracked up over *Stinky*.

"Okay."

"He's a fool. Anybody who doesn't know Diana Prince is the greatest, baddest hero in comics is a lost cause."

"Even greater than Superman?"

"Wonder Woman kicks Superman's butt all day long." I glanced over my shoulder. "While we're on the subject, maybe the time has come for me to teach you to throw a punch. Would you like that?" I made a fist and smacked my palm.

"Yeah!"

"Isaiah Coleridge!" Meg yelled from the kitchen.

"Your mom has superhearing," I said.

"Oh, that she does," Devlin said.

Meat loaf, mashed potatoes, and greens. Afterward, Devlin bolted for the living room and a show on the Cartoon Network. His mother and I shared the dregs of the wine.

Normally, Meg declined help in clearing the table—the kitchen was her unassailable domain. Tonight, she sipped wine and watched me rinse the dishes and inexpertly load the washer. She hadn't changed out of her work clothes.

"Can you wrangle a babysitter for Wednesday evening?" I said. "Let's paint the town."

"Ooh, sounds enticing," she said. "Sweep me off my aching feet."

"Dinner and a show?"

"Dinner would be terrific. Honestly, it doesn't have to be swanky. You could hand me a bag of Burger King if it meant escaping the damned kitchen. I haven't been to a show in ages. What kind of show?"

"Cabaret. World-class."

"Cabaret," she said with a hint of suspicion.

"Singing, dancing, glitter. The Moulin Rouge end of the spectrum."

"Moulin Rouge, eh?"

"It won't be that glamorous. Except for the tits. The tits might be pretty posh."

CHAPTER SEVENTEEN

Wednesday evening rolled around.

As I sat on the bed, waiting for Meg to fix her makeup, I told her about a recurring dream. She was aces with symbolism and I'd become increasingly obsessed with the notion that *everything* meant something.

Whiro, the demon of Māori lore, rose from stygian realms to menace me. Whiro assumed a variety of guises when he infiltrated my nightmares. This dream occurred in a deep, dark forest clearing at night. Primeval sequoias loomed, their roots sunk into the brainpan of a sleeping giant. Old naked men circled a bonfire. A *bone fire*, in the mother tongue of the Celts—flames shot from a pyramid of blackened, heat-cracked skulls.

The ancients whooped and sang.

My Māori grandfather, Hone, war club brandished overhead. My father, Mervin, medals hammered into his bare breast. Gene in corked logging boots. Harold Lee, whole and hale, natty tie dangling to his soft belly. Burt P girded by a weight lifter's belt and naught else. Agent

Bellow flashing his G-man shades. The Croatoan, knurled as a petrified tree, his features slick with scar tissue.

Whiro, the horned Māori death god, presided as a two-story-tall effigy. Carved from primordial rock, the statue glistened, black as creosote from eons of blood spatter. It absorbed red fire glow and spat back the tectonic roar of a subterranean river, a demonic Mississippi or Amazon or Nile down, down below.

I don't have much attachment to the Māori aspect of my heritage and yet it seemed that ghosts swam in my blood. The men, caricatures produced by my overheated subconscious, gazed into my eyes and performed a haka.

"Why the males?" I said, watching with appreciation as Meg wriggled into her dress. "Why not the women? Burt P, Bellow, my father . . . they have wives or lovers, mothers. What about my own mother? Why only the men?"

"Women are the nurturers," she said. "Men are the destroyers. Especially the men in your world. You don't dream of women because you don't think you can be loved. Or saved. How is it you recognized a Māori god of evil and darkness?"

"I'm a fan of world mythology."

"The Mid-Hudson library system has excellent resources. We could research your genealogy on your mother's side—"

"*Mythology*. Books on mythology are fine."

"How are you feeling?" She laid her cool hand on my forehead. "You seem a bit off."

"What gave me away? The bags under my eyes?"

"Sleep more. That'll help with the bad dreams. You're burning out."

I gulped a handful of aspirin to blunt an oncoming headache and the minor pains in my hand and ribs. To be fair, my battered condition was the new normal, and had been since my latter twenties.

"A double date," Meg said a few minutes later when Lionel made the scene in his fabulous and sweetly detailed Monte Carlo. Impossible to detect whether she was genuinely excited or being sarcastic.

Lionel introduced his date—a woman in a HELLO KITTY T-shirt, acid-wash jeans, and cowboy boots. She wore a purple bob and a fistful of rhinestone rings. Whale of a shiner under her eye. I recognized her as the Saturday night bartender from the Golden Eel. Punching and getting punched came with the territory in that worthy establishment.

"This is Robin, my wingman—uh, wingwoman," Lionel said. His buckskins matched Robin's boots. I yearned to inquire after his choice of duds. He anticipated my gambit and swiftly changed the subject. "Coleridge, *moderation* is your watchword tonight. You'll be driving the chariot home, because I mean to get crocked. After that, I'll start drinking." A whiff of his breath suggested the first phase of his plan was well under way.

I'd optimistically chosen an outfit from the classier, less violent portion of my wardrobe. One of the suits minus bullet holes, in other words. Meg wore a sheer white dress, backless. Watching her glow like a diamond made me acutely aware of her lack of an engagement ring.

Early on during our courtship, she'd explained kindly, and relentlessly, that I wasn't marriage material.

On the way to the car, she said into my ear, "It must be tough, Mr. Private Eye, toiling in a line that requires frequent sorties to watch nubile chicks strip to the bare essentials."

"Hellish," I said.

"The last time we went to a joint this swanky, it was a mob den, and someone got their leg broken."

"How is it that Chuck forgives me while the rest of you harbor a grudge?"

"He's afraid you'll snap the other one."

"Point taken. Some clodhopper gets rowdy, hold me back."

"I carry bear mace in my purse."

"Pepper spray for bears? The heavy-duty stuff?"

"Yes. A two-second blast in the eyes should do the trick."

"Good grief, lady. I'll try to behave."

"It's more for the other women who get out of hand when they see you in that suit."

"Might take a three-second blast," I said.

WHITE ROCK HOTEL represented one of the last great family resorts built during the early 1960s. Survivor of near bankruptcies, seven or eight changes of ownership, and a Frankenstein's chart of half-completed renovations, WRH resembled every inch the palace that had hosted presidents, kingpins, and the entire Rat Pack.

Olympic-length pools, beauty salons, ice-cream par-
lors, golf courses, swanky restaurants, and an upscale
nightclub—the hotel persisted as a small pocket of reality
where vests and ties were the staff uniform, monied la-
dies still wore ballroom gowns, and gentlemen wore fe-
doras and Brooks Brothers ensembles.

The WRH should've done more custom as a one-stop
family vacation. Regrettably, the tourist model had
changed radically since the turn of the twenty-first century.
Scuttlebutt indicated the property (three hundred acres
near Accord in a forested nook among the Shawangunk
Mountains) would soon be assimilated by foreign inves-
tors, modernized, and converted to a conference center.

Sorry, middle-class working folks on the make for a
semi-affordable family getaway; the pool was about to
close forever.

The Bird of Paradise Lounge emanated more Flower
Power/ Disco–era San Francisco than faux-1960s Catskills.
Lots of velvet and brass; scoop-shaped chairs and dimly
volcanic LED lighting that was all the rage back when
America still fantasized about flying cars, unisex bathrooms, and returning to the moon. The hostess (in a Vegas
showgirl feather bonnet, powder-blue flight suit, and
three-inch heels) seated us near the stage. Drinks were gratis, compliments of management. Curtis had certainly
come through.

Lionel slapped my arm.

"Meg mentioned you're having nightmares. Lemme
tell you mine."

"Oh no," I said.

"This spring, while you were off on that thing in the city, I took Minerva camping off the Silver Lode Trail. Remember, I told you a dog ain't a dog 'til she's gone on a camping trip."

"Did you?"

"Made a honkin' bonfire and slept in the portable hammock the Walkers bought me for Christmas. Minerva climbed in there and whined. I told her everything was cool. I fell asleep as the fire died to coals. Man, I don't know what it is about the mountain air, but I always have technicolor dreams. A gorgeous, naked blonde woman materialized amid the shadows of the trees and walked toward the camp. She raised her arms and embraced me, but we started wrestling, and not in a good way. She squeezed my throat and clawed my eyes. So, I tripped the bitch and hauled ass along the trail, and here she came flying like a Claymation harpy. I woke as her talons grazed the back of my neck.

"Minerva was on my chest, growling at the bushes. The campfire had blazed to life—flames were shooting into the lower branches. Freaked me the hell out. I suddenly recalled those Catskills stories about Bigfoot and witches and shit. Broke camp in fifteen minutes flat and hightailed for the car. The main thing that sticks in my mind? It's damned difficult to run with a boner."

Booze arrived in enormous goblets of blown glass. The girls ordered something blue and frothy as chemicals reacting in a beaker. I nursed a double bourbon. Lionel quietly settled in to drink Nail Ale like a boxer working the heavy bag.

My companions seemed content for a while.

The opening acts were a magician who did erotic card tricks, a comedienne, and a cellist. An emcee in a pinstriped suit introduced the performers and kept the crowd warmed up with canned patter.

House lights dimmed. Midnight Star sashayed to her mark in a raven wig, domino mask, and a silk wrap. My girl for certain. She sang a medley of classic jazz and blues tunes in a smooth contralto, capped by a rendition of "Where Did You Sleep Last Night?" that resonated as an inauspicious augury. I'm a wary believer in signs and portents. The universe is always muttering threats.

"Chicks in domino masks are so hot." Meg pressed a sweating goblet to her cheek.

"Yeah, totally bangin'," Lionel said, although I don't think he'd even noticed the mask until she mentioned it.

A striptease artist in the finest sense of the tradition, Midnight Star's clothing melted, article by article, reducing to gemstone-studded tassels and matching panties. She half absorbed, half reflected the arctic beam of the spotlight. Its remnants spilled over her shoulders and formed a crescent moon backdrop. She could've made do inside a phone booth with that mesmerizing shimmy and shake.

The manager paid us a courtesy call between numbers. A bland, professionally unctuous man, who probably had Curtis on his mind as he inquired whether we were enjoying the show and complimentary liquor. I assured him all was well, especially for Lionel, who'd amassed a serious graveyard of beer bottles.

I then mentioned that we'd love ever so much to meet

Ms. Star and score an autograph. I knew the dancers were strictly off-limits; such is the rule in upscale clubs. The manager didn't blink. Of course, our group was warmly invited to an exclusive after-party. VIPs only. Before he could escape, I caught his arm and showed him Harold Lee's photo. The suit gave a tight nod and said yes, he'd seen the gentleman. He wriggled free and skedaddled.

Midnight Star returned for an encore, clad in a slinky black dress and pink boa. She'd stripped gloriously naked (or almost) by the time she danced her way over to our table and serenaded Lionel with A-ha's seminal '80s number, "Take On Me," her slipper planted on the chair near his crotch. He drooled while his date sipped her cocktail and glared murderously.

Up close, Midnight Star was a heart-stopper. She flaunted a timeless, voluptuous figure reminiscent of Rita Hayworth and Betty Brosmer—a strutting, crooning Varga Girl in living color. Sex and malice crackled in her eyes. The woman belted the high notes too—when she cut loose, ice rattled in cups.

Midnight Star segued to Michael Jackson's "Smooth Criminal."

I've been around the block and seen it all. What happened next caused me to reconsider my skeptical position on witchcraft and voodoo. Lionel shook free of his drunken stupor, bounded semi-gracefully to his feet, and danced with all the rubbery loose-limbed agility of the King of Pop himself, if the King had downed half a gallon of malt liquor and hard whiskey. There is every possibility my friend won her heart when he executed a brief moonwalk that ended with him collapsing into his chair to scattered applause. He undeniably won mine.

She gave him a playful slap with her boa and sauntered back to the dais to conclude the show. And when I say *sauntered*, I mean slow-motion, smash close-up; every man and woman in that club was mesmerized by the motion of the ocean, so to speak.

My three-quarters-full glass of bourbon had gone inexplicably dry.

CHAPTER EIGHTEEN

Staff escorted us to a rise overlooking the deserted golf course. Strings of paper lanterns illuminated our path. At the summit, upon a plaza of irregular paving stones, twin firepits blazed against the darkness and veined the rising mist with red. Guests clustered, their conversations indecipherable as the chirr of insects infesting the nearby swamp.

I mildly relished watching rich folks huddle with instinctive dread of nature. Laughter, high and thin, drifted past me, toward the forest. Combinations of mating calls and utterances of nervous frivolity. The dancers accompanied a cadre of stiff-backed gentlemen in suits. Midnight Star stood aloof in her own circle of adoring patrons.

Meg hooked her arm through mine.

"Midnight Star is Delia Labrador, daughter of Jonathan Labrador. Mr. Labrador is the superindustrialist, chairman of the board and majority shareholder of Zircon Corporation. Delia's grandfather Matthias founded the corporation right after World War Two. Zircon is headquartered in Albany. Defense and communications systems are the core interests; it also strongly pursues medical, security, and aerospace fabrication tech. Two of its largest affiliates develop pharmaceuticals. Internationally, the company and its subsidiaries employ a quarter of a million people at factories and research facilities. Government contracts galore—no surprise."

"Wow. Where did you—?"

"Wage slave at the library, dear."

"Clearly, I should have shown you the photo," I said.

"But then you would've had less of an excuse to ogle the dames." She flicked my tie. "Delia frequents the library two or three times a month. Heavy reader. She digs ornithology and regional history. Volumes of neglected verse."

"What's your read on her?"

"My 'read' on her? Is that a librarian joke?"

"Maybe."

"Watch that razor wit, Coleridge. She's sweet as pie; demure. Doesn't advertise she's a society-page heiress. Wears a kerchief and shades. Sometimes she travels with security."

Currently, Delia wore cat eye glasses, a bullet bra, and a metallic skirt. She basked in the firelight while suppliants mingled in the shadow of her radiance. These suppliants were fellow performers, slavering men, and the wives and girlfriends of the slavering men. Her bodyguards waited, conspicuous as a pair of misplaced Stonehenge slabs.

"Tonight, she's Midnight Star," I said. "By day, she's Delia Labrador. Interesting."

"Delia-by-Day is another mask. I doubt anyone has seen the real her, except for her victims." Meg acknowledged my raised brow. "Broken hearts. Notches on her bedpost. Love 'em and leave 'em. She's a destroyer of worlds."

"Isn't that a femme fatale's purpose?"

"I've heard rumors to that effect. Women talk, especially about other women."

A yard to my left, Lionel and his date were in the midst of conversation or the nascent stages of an argument.

"What do you call 'em?" Lionel pointed indecorously at Delia Labrador.

"Bullet bra," Robin said.

"They still make those things? Thank Baby Jesus anyway."

"It's *vintage*, Lionel. Vintage." The *you lout* was implied.

A server plied us with pink champagne. So armed, we approached Delia and her circle. She observed our group imperiously as an ice queen noting an incursion of filthy peasants in the throne room. Her bodyguards edged forward. They watched me and I smiled jauntily. Their posture indicated military training. Both were strapped.

"Delia!" Meg said, and the women side-hugged and did the air-kiss deal. She went around our party and introduced me last. "This is my boyfriend, Isaiah Coleridge. He's an investigator."

"How nice for him," Delia said, whiskey-rough. "What does he investigate? Car accidents? Insurance fraud?"

"He investigates lying, cheating, murdering scum," I

said. "He's particularly interested to discover why your boyfriend, Harold Lee, got it in the neck."

"Meg, he's bored me to tears in under five seconds. Who said it could be done? Bravo."

An enigmatic expression flashed across Meg's face. I *did* recognize her death grip on the champagne flute.

Delia had already moved on. She gazed past both of us, fastening upon Lionel.

"Ooh la la. You're rather sexy. Isn't he just, girls?" The girls were in accordance that he was *definitely just*.

His neck flushed as he kissed her hand. Mr. Gallant.

"Oh, baby," Delia said. "You could be an actor. I'm not even teasing. What did you think of the show? Hot, right?" She thrust her hip at him.

Lionel blurted, "Hot? Honey, you're so hot, you should be painted on the fuselage of a B-52!"

She graced him with a huge smile and scribbled on a napkin, embossed it with a lipstick smooch, and tucked it into his belt. Classic. Then she patted his cheek and walked away to rejoin her kind.

The powers giveth and the powers taketh away. Robin slapped him not too long after that. Full windup, dramatic as a whipcrack. He fell on his ass and sat there with a look of tragicomical bewilderment common to drunken louts the world over. She didn't stick around to explain the error of his ways.

"But, I thought she was his wingwoman," I stage-whispered to Meg.

"Yes, congratulations. You're both idiots."

I MAY HAVE SULKED A TINY BIT driving home from the party.

"Get anything useful?" Meg said to break the mood.

"Jack shit," I said.

"For a moment there, I thought you might try the Columbo routine with Delia. 'Oh, yeah, I'm an idiot, but one more thing . . .' You know the routine."

"That lady is bulletproof. Immune to my charms, at any rate. In short, no."

"Worked for Peter Falk."

"Round one. I'll regroup and come at her from another angle."

"Will it help?" Meg turned to partially conceal her smile.

"Ms. Star is smitten with Romeo." I jerked my thumb toward Lionel, snoring in the backseat. Moments prior to collapsing, he'd muttered deliriously that this evening had gone far better than the last time I introduced him to a stripper.

"Even if she's not head over heels, maybe she's willing to bat him around like a mouse. We can hope."

"Oh, dear," she said.

I dropped her and Lionel at their respective homes and slumped into the easy chair in my cabin. I dreamed of Fred Astaire in a suit and tap shoes dancing in ethereal refinement with Ginger Rogers. Fred and Ginger morphed into Lionel and Delia; him in his outlandish buckskins and she in the altogether.

CHAPTER NINETEEN

Lionel and I were in the main barn at Hawk Mountain Farm; ostensibly, repairing the tractor, but really we were bullshitting while Lionel got hammered. I asked if he had had a nice time at the burlesque show.

He removed his hat and crumpled it in both hands. That morning, my friend had, in a demonstration of grit that would've made Rasputin blanche, dragged himself out of bed at an ungodly hour to repair fences. His knuckles were scraped bloody. Filth blackened his nails. He bowed his head.

"The other day, last week? Yeah, last week, I didn't walk the hill. Usually, most of the time, I walk that hill every day. Except, not that day. That day, I stayed in and finished a half rack of beer. I drank a dozen beers, a third of a bottle of vodka, and a swallow of Jim Beam. I watched a football doubleheader and the news, and then whatever was on. I didn't shower, didn't eat, didn't do anything but drink and watch TV until I fell asleep. The next afternoon, hungover and fucked-up, I found a turtle on the hill. Squashed flatter than a flapjack in my path. Little sucker made it to the edge where the weeds are before a car got him."

He set aside his hat and popped the top on a bottle of beer. The cheap stuff, since it was his tab today. The light through the window and the hay dust in the light lent him a halo. Then he belched and leaned into darkness again.

"I've helped turtles before. Picked them up and carried them into the bushes where it's safer. Suckers cross there like pilgrims on the road to Damascus. He was just trying to make it to the creek in the gully on the other side. It's a long crawl for a turtle. I didn't walk the hill and so I wasn't there, didn't see him to get him out of the road." He looked at me then, his eyes bright as nailheads. "That's everything, isn't it? Everything in the universe? You're struggling on your belly to cross some fucking road and the one person who could help you is somewhere, not where you are, drunk off his wretched ass. And you're dead. That's it. That's all there is."

I massaged my temples, yet throbbing from last night's smoke, loud music, and too much booze, and studied him.

"Are you . . . Lionel, are you a turtle? Is this a metaphor? Do you want me to give you a lift somewhere? I'm here, man. Tell me where you want to go. Jump on."

"I want you to answer a question."

"Sounds serious. What sort of question?"

"It will determine your moral character. Suppose—"

"The matter of my moral character stands resolved."

"Suppose you could travel backward in time—"

"Theoretically or in an actual time machine?"

"Time machine."

"Okay."

"If you could go back . . ."

"I can't. I don't have a time machine. Besides, as a man loved to tell me, *There's no future and there's no past, only the eternal now.* Time is a ring; no beginning, no end, just a big hole."

". . . would you have become a hitter?"

"I don't know."

"No?"

"I don't have a magical machine. I choose not to torture myself with *What if?* bullshit. I recommend it." We stared at one another. "Gene and I were Keesh and Son of Keesh."

Lionel shrugged. It was impossible to slip anything lit-related past him.

"Jack London? I read him as a teen."

"Jack London. Gene was a devoted fan. He favored the weird, bloody works to the famous ones. 'The Red One,' and 'The Story of Keesh,' and *Children of the Frost*: 'Keesh, Son of Keesh.' The Keesh stories are nebulous, morally ambiguous. Especially the latter. It's a paean to savagery and vengeance."

"Two of my favorite things," he said.

"Delia gave you her number," I said.

"Aha! We arrive at last. I framed the napkin and hung it over my dresser."

"Avail yourself of that number and ask her out on a date."

"Can't do it, Hoss." He sipped his beer. The spooky part was, except for this melancholy bent, he didn't seem the worse for the wear after his epic evening while I was dying in slow misery.

"Okay. Why can't you?"

"I'm playing hard to get."

"But you aren't hard to get. You're completely the opposite."

"She doesn't know that."

"Yes . . . Yes, she does. Every woman knows that about every guy." I glanced at the garbage can. Three empty bottles nestled atop the detritus. My watch read a quarter past noon. "This is important. Pick up the phone, arrange a tryst, and let nature take its course."

"A tryst? You poaching my Shakespeare collection again?"

"Young love inspires my poetic mood. Call her."

"The rule is, uh, three days."

"Today, and before you're too drunk."

Lionel killed the bottle. Flicked the dead soldier to rest with its brothers. He reached down behind the toolbox and produced brew number five.

"I'm guessing there's a reason you're so pushy. Something's happened." He closed his eyes and touched his temple. "Oh-oh, there's a message from the void . . . Curtis has fucked us, or I don't know what." He opened his eyes. "That it? Curtis show his colors?"

"Let's develop our leads. For the moment, several days at the outside, we keep our lips sealed and gather clues like obedient lackeys. Safest course. I'm going to personally evaluate Oestryke's background in Michigan. You hang tight and watch the home front. Fair?"

"Fair," he said. "Whole scenario is fucked, but yeah. You can't walk away, can you? It's the hookers. You've got that, I don't know what to call it—a gleam, a fever glow—in your eyes."

"Girls. They're girls and women. I don't think of them as hookers."

"You can't save them in any meaningful sense. It's the nature of their business. Wolves cut the weak from the herd, same as it ever was."

"They're fated?" I said. "That's my out, eh? Concede to the inevitable and hit the showers."

"Absolutely, they're fated."

"There are times in a man's life when he must make the grand gesture."

"Is the gesture you have in mind throwing a double bird at the cosmos? The cosmos will gesture back and you won't like it." He paused. I thought he was egging himself into mentioning our failure with Reba Walker as my prime motivator toward kamikaze behavior—and he would've been on the money. Instead, he changed course. "The man trusts you."

"Who? Curtis?"

"No, Bellow. I'm positive that intel is classified. Damned sure not meant to be bandied about the underworld."

"Trust is less a factor than opportunity," I said. "Bellow considers me a potentially important connection, an asset. And vice versa."

"What are we—I mean, what are *you* supposed to do?"

"Dig and dig some more. That's why I want to inter-view Delia. She and Harry were an item—"

"Those two were cozy, okay," he said. "Jury's out on *how* cozy."

"Whatever strokes your ego, son. Depending upon how long the affair lasted, she likely met some of his pals and associates besides Royal."

He regarded the innards of the tractor with the air of a man contemplating the unpleasant side of divinity.

"Suppose your future ex-girlfriend unwittingly en-countered Oestryke?" I said, since he wasn't going to bite.

"*Grasping at Straws* for five hundred, Alex."

"Such is the essence of detection. Look, man. Bellow sent me a couple of file photos. All I want is for Delia to take a peek. Then you lovebirds can go canoodle to your hearts' content, and God bless your unholy union."

"There *won't* be any canoodling after you infuriate her. Cockblocked by my best friend. What a deal."

"I'm not blocking you." I made a kung fu chopping motion. "More like deflecting."

He turned from me and walked through the door. Looped back a moment later to snag the last bottle. He glared sullenly.

"You win, I'll call her."

"Attaboy. Bros before crazy-hot heiresses."

"Laugh it up, pal. I'm not going to tell her about you until the third date."

CHAPTER TWENTY

Late-afternoon sunlight seeped over the mountains and illuminated my office desk, where I sat wrestling with a choice and my third or fourth nasty headache of late.

My weekly progress report to Curtis was due, and though I wanted to grill him about Morris Oestryke, or whatever the Croatoan called himself these days, it was safer to gather more intelligence. The quandary—tell Curtis an abbreviated version of what I'd learned or stall him for a bit longer? I defaulted to the traditional wiseguy method and went with light obfuscation when I reported in—*Early days, nobody admits nothin'. Might have a promising lead, stay tuned*—that sort of jazz. He didn't press; said to keep him informed, *ciao*. Mobster capos have plenty on their plates without double-checking on the spear-carriers at every turn.

I stared out the window at the sunset and crushed a handball. Twenty-five reps with the left, twenty-five with the right. Repeat and repeat. Hand strength is crucial;

life-or-death struggles come down to grip more often than one might suppose. My left still lacked in power since getting smashed.

A strong breeze pushed the treetops around. Leaves shook loose and whirled down the empty street. Velvet bats and lace cobwebs adorned the windows of shops and homes. Pumpkin spice wafted from the art gallery below. The American version of the Day of the Dead loomed in the near distance. Superstition isn't my bag; on the other hand, I tend to respect the notion of synchronicity. Butterfly wings, prophetic dreams, and so forth. The atmosphere and the Americanized, commercialized tokens of death and devilry collaborated to reinforce my sense of impending doom.

I'd perused the files Bellow sent and pinned a handful of photographs to the virginal corkboard wall. Morris Oestryke as a baby-faced Army private and again as a smiling, clean-cut salesman, father of three. Other pics of sheet-covered bodies and chalk outlines alongside photocopied newspaper articles detailing the unsolved murders of transient women; the New York tri-state version of the Highway of Tears in British Columbia.

A pair of intensely macabre crime scene pics warranted closer examination. These photos were representative of the vast majority of victims—one of a mobster (male) whacked by the Croatoan in 1996 and retrieved shortly after death; the other of a hapless drifter (female), aged twenty-six, who'd disappeared in 2007 and was discovered in 2010 in a shallow grave and presumed to be a random victim of the Croatoan's hooker-slaying hobby.

According to a file summary, both victims struggled prior to decapitation. Both had been bound and tortured. Neither was sexually assaulted. Cause of death was attributed to the decapitation event, conducted with a heavy, serrated blade. Besides elements relating to their murders, nothing else linked the pair. They'd never met, didn't associate with the same crowd, hadn't attended school together, et cetera. Nonetheless, the ritual nature of the killings was nearly identical. Another constant—the missing murdered women were generally young and attractive. Caucasian blondes of medium- to full-figured builds.

Eyeing the photos didn't spark any leaps of deduction. I'd made a few calls to contacts who might have heard something. My preliminary takeaway after several phone interviews? Agent Bellow was on the money in terms of his dreary assessment of the Croatoan/tri-state murder cases and their lack of progress.

Few within law enforcement dwelled upon the Croatoan's mob activities—there was a sense that an era had passed. Even fewer cared about the possibility he'd taken to bagging civilians in his dotage. As Bellow had reported, the tri-state murders primarily targeted hookers and indigents. Infamous manhunts for the Green River and Zodiac killers notwithstanding, this type of crime wasn't sexy enough to draw significant resources as it concerned populations that authorities weren't particularly motivated to protect or avenge. *Save the hookers!* isn't a popular cop rallying cry.

Digging through the files left me with several basic questions, which I committed to my notes:

Where had Oestryke gone from 1974 to 1978?

Who had "Morris Oestryke" become after he faked his death in the factory inferno in '87?

Why had he decided to kill at least two fellow criminals?

Where is he hiding? Though he'd ranged the length of the Atlantic seaboard plying his trade, documents confirmed the vast majority of his activities occurred all over New York. Home sweet home?

Why have FBI bigwigs stonewalled the investigation? I had no reason to doubt Bellow's interpretation of events. The intricacies of government politics lay well afield of my own expertise, so I could only hypothesize that Oestryke was, or had been, under protection. The FBI is infamous for cutting deals with small fry in order to land bigger fish. The involvement of the Department of Defense was the ringer. What did they want with a mob assassin and why had they redacted his military records?

A tangential query—*What is Marion Curtis's angle?* Sooner or later, I'd be forced to confront the question head-on. Discretion contested with pride. I'd hate for Lionel to be right about this one. He gloated, without fail.

Another avenue of inquiry pointed toward Delia Labrador and her daddy's corporation, Zircon. This could prove difficult. Billionaire tycoons and international businesses were hard nuts to crack. They employed armies of suits with guns to dissuade snoopers and armies of suits with fancy law degrees to guarantee the accounts balanced, fair or foul.

Delightful as the sound of skulls smacking together might be, I stuck with socially acceptable tactics. Getting the goods on Delia Labrador and her family wasn't difficult; our lives are compiled online here in the twenty-first century, with the real dirty dirt hidden behind a paywall. I paid and added the expenses to Curtis's bill.

Raising the curtain on Zircon and its myriad subsidiaries presented a stiffer challenge. Database research catalogues were my initial line of attack—resources such as Dun & Bradstreet. My second line? Because it is essentially a corporation unto itself, the mob knows everything worth knowing in the arena of business. The Outfit acquires vast stores of information covering a spectrum of companies, large and small. Some of the intel collection occurs via dubious means; the majority derives from entirely legal but esoteric sources not available to John Q. Public.

I contacted somebody who knew somebody and put in a request for Zircon's corporate history, as well as documents on the official background of Morris Oestryke's civilian employers. Might as well go whole hog. A few dollars into the right pockets and several cartons of material were en route to my humble office.

Sifting a mountain of papers hews too close to law enforcement drudgery. Being a man of action, I delegate monotonous tasks as much as is feasible. In that spirit, I got on the horn to bring in a data specialist from a local accounting firm. I'd provide a cheat sheet of key words and specific info pertinent to my investigation. This specialist would burn the midnight oil whittling the information to a manageable size, then collating and cross-referencing it for my approval.

Banal, and counter to my career of investigation conducted via strong-arm tactics. In the meantime, I'd play it close to the vest and give Lionel a few days to work his magic and see where "canoodling" Ms. Labrador might lead.

Yes, I'm a cynic.

CHAPTER TWENTY-ONE

The accountant camped at my office, gobbling billable hours like candy as he and an assistant combed through stacks of files related to the Harold Lee investigation. There wasn't anything to do except wait for data to crunch.

Not one to twiddle my thumbs, I booked a round-trip plane ticket to Michigan; red-eye out of Stewart Airport. Rearranging Aubrey P's protective detail was a small circus. In the end, Chuck Bachelor tagged a couple of his ne'er-do-well buddies to scope the salon during business hours while he camped in her living room at night. He had Lionel on speed dial if it hit the fan. I promised to return asap.

Would a tour of Morris Oestryke's childhood stomping grounds yield anything fruitful? Odds were long. Intuition, hard work, and luck are the fundamentals of tracking. Additionally, there's the practical matter of osmosis. My powers of deduction aren't worthy of Holmes, but my subconscious is a diesel thresher. The secret is to give it something to chew on. And so I set forth.

I've traveled to far-flung locales to soak up the atmosphere, breathe in the smoke of strange bars, listen to the ebb and flow of conversation, and open myself to the background hum of humans doing their ant thing. It's the hunter's trick of observing a meadow from a blind—you watch nothing and everything at once.

Occasionally, the cogwheels click into place of their own accord.

The Feds had questioned Oestryke's relatives and friends and presumably came away empty. A list of names, addresses, and phone numbers went, folded, into my pocket. No reason for me not to make a run at them as well. I budgeted seventy-two hours for the trip. Sounds reasonable, yes? Reasonable or not, I'd decided to stretch my legs and call it due diligence.

Right before hitting the road, I dialed a number in Detroit and briefly explained to the brusque individual who answered where I intended to go and why. I reiterated that I wasn't on the job. Wouldn't want someone to glimpse me on the street and leap to errant conclusions. Technically, only Alaska and Chicago were off-limits following my breakup with the Outfit. Men frequently get it in the neck due to technicalities, so I exercised discretion.

He requested basic details of my itinerary, which I gamely provided. He said, "Okay," and disconnected. Did that qualify as permission? This exchange did not fill

me with confidence. I squared my shoulders and sol-
diered on.

A TAILWIND PUSHED MY JET into Detroit twenty minutes
ahead of schedule. I rented a luxury car and escaped the
city limits before rush hour. I tuned the radio to an oldies
station and sank back into plush leather while the black-
and-blue panorama morphed from urban blight to mile
after mile of rural scarification.

I motored northward into the sticks.

It didn't get any prettier when the sun rose, shivering
cold. Crumbling secondary roads wove like clogged arteries into the poisoned backwoods. Industry had voided
its bowels over the course of a prolonged death rattle,
leaving behind a hollowed scene. Unless one could get a
manufacturing job in Detroit, Lansing, or Grand Rap-
ids, the forecast was for "hard times." No presidential
messiah was likely to resurrect this rusted-out carcass of
a fallen empire anytime soon.

I PITTED AT A REST AREA/TRUCK STOP. Sipped a cup
of not-too-bad coffee and watched punchy travelers mill
around the food court. I gave whatever might be in
motion ten minutes to develop.

A midnight-blue Cadillac nosed into a parking space
near the huge glass façade of the court. It had tailed me
from the airport. The five men who unloaded from the
Caddy wore sunglasses and better-than-average suits, ex-

cept for the fifth man in a crème-colored number—his tailoring tipped the scales in excess of a grand.

I rose, stretched elaborately, bought a second, larger cup of coffee, and headed for the men's room. Public bathrooms are excellent stages for murder and mayhem, second only to dark alleys. I faced a urinal, pretending to piss, coffee balanced atop, next to the flusher. A migraine stabbed into my eye like a bolt from the blue.

The man in the fancy suit assumed the position at the next urinal. Civilians puttered around us obliviously. I wished for my guns and knives. I don't carry any of those items for short hauls. Too dicey in this age of hyper-paranoid airline travel.

"Where ya headin', Mr. Coleridge?" The wiseguy didn't introduce himself. We both knew he represented Detroit, and, by extension, the Chicago plexus. He rotated slightly and his jacket fell open, revealing the butt of a pistol.

Blackness ate inward from the corners of my vision. Reality crumpled and bloomed like a cigarette burn on a movie screen. The hole let into an alternate universe, where the scene unfolded bloodily. No, in Universe B, Mr. Fancy Suit had no intention of conducting a peaceful exchange. He'd spoken to cover the stealthy approach of two of his goon buddies. I snatched the supersized cup and smashed it into his eyes. Hot coffee scalded my hand. He shrieked and clawed at his face—done for the day, at least. Fair trade. I elbowed a goon in the jaw and got my left forearm raised to protect my head and neck as the second goon tomahawk-chopped a switchblade into my forearm.

The blade lodged in bone, and I pulled him close and scooped his eyeball with my thumb. He struggled wildly, and I used his momentum to drive his forehead into the urinal pipe. Bones crunched, and what was inside slopped on the wall and into the drain. The guy I'd smashed in the jaw gargled blood as he rolled on the dirty floor. A common symptom of chomping one's tongue in half. I escaped the bathroom and ran like hell most of the way down the hall to the cafeteria. One of the reserve thugs stepped from behind a vending machine and let me have a full magazine from his automatic pistol. GAME OVER, as the video game screen says.

Waves of agony and migraine-spawned dizziness receded.

The cigarette burns reversed and I was in the regular space-time continuum once again, my future yet undecided. Mr. Fancy Suit studied me with a trace of a puzzled frown.

Smiling with every iota of geniality I could muster, I explained my itinerary in a few words and passed him my card.

"Thanks for calling ahead. The big guys appreciate your courtesy." He glanced at the coffee and back to me. He washed his hands and walked out.

I exhaled. Sometimes the elk is lucky and the wolves are only cruising.

THE PANORAMA WASN'T as friendly or colorful as New York's postcard autumn. The atmosphere had a death metal ambiance as winter approached Deering, Michigan. It would be the brutish type of winter that features ash in the snowflakes and black ice on playground slides. In the interim, everything was gray and bloody rust splashed with plague yellow.

Deering was a quintessential blue-collar town gone to seed: shuttered factories and Main Street businesses with SPACE FOR RENT signs plastered everywhere; sullen men in ball caps and denim jackets at the wheel of late-1990s pickup trucks; pregnant teen girls, bright-lipped and exhausted, sucking diet sodas, toddlers attached at the thighs. The Christian Reformed Church looked sharp with a relatively new coat of paint, though. A jaunty placard advertised an upcoming penny social.

I'd observed a bushel of Deering clones in my travels. Mobster capos eagerly recruit foot soldiers from the wastelands' warring tribes. Whenever a life of not-so-organized crime goes sideways, the saps always beeline for home miserable home, where unemployment, alcoholism, and delinquency crest every year.

Here lay the kind of town where wives wore sunglasses to hide black eyes, kids regularly missed school or came to school hungry in tattered shoes, and locals shot at each other, or brained each other with pool cues and bottles, on the regular. Such is the stultifying madness born of desperate poverty and hopelessness.

One and all pledged his or her soul to the Deering Bucks High School football team. Because, of course, the peasants pay obeisance to their gods. Hometown sports were the nearest thing these modern-day Roman citizens had to bread and circuses. Recessions and state legislative malfeasance stifled financial resources to push the Deering Bucks into the upper echelon of high school powerhouses. This wasn't Texas where even the poorest community collected its loose change for shiny new uniforms and a state-of-the-art coliseum. Deering High's football field doubled as a baseball diamond; dirt and rocks instead of artificial turf. A history teacher and his brother coached both squads.

Bucks forever!—the boys lost last season in the championship on a field goal missed wide right. The kicker and his family wisely fled town. A cashier at the gas station informed me of this, as did a waitress at the diner, and the clerk at the motel when he handed me a key to room 16.

In the span of an hour and a half, I could already detect the will to live siphoning from my veins, replaced by an icy desire to sleep forever and ever. Entropy is a hell of a drug.

I would've liked to interview Morris Oestryke's family, but none were local; nor were his teachers, except for a lady who'd slipped into dementia and now resided at the Deering Golden Era Rest Home. I settled for the scattering of grade school and high school classmates who remained in the area. Deering would be a tough place to escape. Small, eternally moribund towns possess outsized gravity wells.

People talked willingly; regular folks usually do. A three-piece suit and granite scowl sets a certain expectation that I undermine with courtesy and a touch of humor. I call it my *See, that wasn't so bad* technique. It's the opening salvo in every Coleridge charm offensive. *Oh, I thought you were going to kick my ass. You want my help with a matter of life and death?* Let a homemaker or a construction laborer believe he or she might hold the key to solving a mystery and after a minute or two you can't get them to shut up.

There are exceptions to every rule.

A retiree slammed the door in my face with ire generally reserved for Jehovah's Witnesses and traveling salesmen. The proprietor of a tire shop stared wordlessly over his newspaper until I conceded defeat and exited his establishment. An aged fellow who wrangled concessions at the movie theater pretended to be deaf. *Nope . . . What? . . . Nope, nope,* is all I gleaned from our brief encounter.

In a moment of weakness, I yearned for the days of kneecapping people and dangling them from windows. Somebody's face offends you? Rearrange it. Some dope giving you the runaround? Bounce his head off a countertop.

Nostalgia overwhelmed me.

Other folks were eager to help, albeit useless. *Morris Oestryke? My parents say he was a nice boy. Nice, real nice kid. Great kid—the best! Football star. Or baseball. I was a baby. You should talk to his old teachers, if any are still aboveground—hehe.*

A scaly-eyed duffer sorting shoes at the bowling alley bucked the trend. *Yep, yep, he'd gone to school a couple of grades behind Morris Oestryke.* Dare he hope I was an attorney sent to deliver a surprise inheritance windfall? No? Another day at the alley, then.

The Big O had proved a fair-to-middling back on the football team and a decent fellow, not swellheaded, or anything, the way jocks can be in a community where they were demigods. A decent, hardworking kid who cared for his sickly mother; after school and football, he mowed yards and took shifts at Valero Technologies. He ran off to volunteer for 'Nam like a damned fool and nobody saw hide nor hair of him after that.

I asked for directions to Valero and what, exactly, it created.

The duffer spat tobacco into a beer can. The laboratory had been the subsidiary of a defense contractor based in California, don't ask which one. Armed guards patrolled the grounds. Employees wore plastic picture ID cards, color-coded according to multiple levels of clearance. They signed nondisclosure contracts. Most of them were out-of-state drones. The company had hired a few locals for janitorial and labor services. Valero shut its doors in 1981. It lived again as a furniture warehouse store, northeast of town a stone's throw from Slocum Field. The end.

Shortly, I parked in an empty lot next to the aforementioned furniture store. Finger-width cracks split the asphalt. Opposite where the highway cut through fields of dead grass, a storm fence girded the far perimeter of the property from a marsh and copses of mossy-gray trees. Shadows of birds rose and floated and fell against the pale sky. Here lay purgatory.

The store was a tall, shit-colored metal block; rooted in the earth, invasive as a tumor. I estimated a thousand of those wizened trees were plowed under to make room for the lot and its altar to American commerce. A Day-Glo banner strung along dirty-glass frontage proclaimed FURNITURE! Inside lay a soaring vault, wherein the atmosphere was stale and hushed as a mausoleum. Unsmiling, stooped attendants shuffled to and fro across the tacky showroom floor and between racks of off-brand furniture. Fluorescent lights twitched and spilled their ghastly bluish-greenish glow.

I counted three clerks under thirty and a manager in her forties. Their ages and expressions of chronic disaffection advised me to save my breath. The likelihood of any of these folks being willing or able to answer questions regarding a company dead these past thirty-plus years was nonexistent. Nobody made eye contact. I ambled past the EMPLOYEES ONLY warning and into the bowels of the warehouse.

Architecture in this section harkened to an older period and hadn't benefited from much renovation during its existence. Here, the ceiling drastically lowered, and a series of intermittently lighted bulbs did little to dispel the gloom along a network of corridors. More concrete flooring, except with painted alternating bands of black, then crimson, and worn to a slight concavity. Doorplates designated bathrooms, offices, and storage. Muzak droning in the showroom did not persist here in the warren.

Meandering through the store was probably a futile exercise. As I've stated, in the absence of solid evidence, I'll settle for indulging my instincts. My personal theory of osmosis and the subconscious mind prodded me to sniff around, to breathe it in, if for no other purpose than to have broken the rules of a corporate slave pit. I expected to be challenged and sent away with an admonishment. Frankly, I half hoped such a confrontation would occur. The place disturbed me for reasons that defied explanation. Its claustrophobic murk and the subterranean monotony of the passages were repellant.

Hush prevailed as I moved inward and reached a set of doors marked RECEIVING. Old, old metal doors with metal handles. The left door was painted crimson, the right black, and, to either side, brick walls pallid as a dirty eggshell. The doors had been frequently repainted; a detail that inexplicably heightened my disquiet. Whatever had transpired in this area in the '60s and '70s lingered as a dim, psychic taint. I tamped down the urge to growl. When a wild animal encounters something outside its natural routine, primordial instincts surface.

Chipped almost beyond recognition, a logo emblazoned the wall to the left of the doors. Possibly a black crescent moon, its horns angled toward the bend sinister as aficionados of heraldry would describe its orientation. I snapped several cell phone pics for future reference.

Gazing upon this faded symbol reinforced my rising unease.

My heart rate accelerated as I seized the handles and pushed into a large area cluttered with crates and loose furniture. A hard-hat-wearing driver on a forklift and his clipboard-toting supervisor stared at me diffidently. Nothing to see, I waved to them and nonchalantly fled the scene.

I slumped in the car and took several deep breaths while my nerves settled. You wouldn't believe I was a big, scary dude who'd seen twenty men's share of trouble. Adrenaline squirted through my veins as if I'd escaped certain death in a house of blood while a horror movie score swelled at my back. Gene called the effect *genius loci*. It's the genesis for the mythology of haunted locales— houses, swamps, caves, bodies of water, and so on. Some places don't react well to the presence of humans.

Defeated, I resumed knocking on doors in town. The list wasn't long; nonetheless, chasing false leads, cornering people, and the interminable junctures in waiting rooms, lobbies, and on doorsteps, eats daylight fast. Two nights in a row, I returned to my dingy room, crashed on the hard-as-marble single, and fell asleep to black-and-white cinema mayhem. Some guys binge porn on the road. Me, it's cartoons, westerns, and samurai epics.

Pounding the pavement and bashing my head against doors instigated migraines. I nabbed a bottle of aspirin at the drugstore and popped them regularly. This eased the thudding headaches, but did nothing to alleviate my nightmares.

On the second evening, I forestalled sleep to phone Meg while Kurosawa played. She asked me what was happening in my motel room. I explained that a matter of grave personal honor was being resolved by thousands of men stabbing one another with swords.

Matters of grave personal honor can be resolved no other way, she said, and then she said good night.

True love? I had a hunch it might be.

CHAPTER TWENTY-TWO

Denis Swenson played varsity fullback on the Deering Bucks football team, '67 through '69. He'd blocked for Morris Oestryke, the first-string running back, and missed the fun in Vietnam thanks to a college deferment and bum knees. Got early retirement from the International Brotherhood of Electrical Workers, Local 600—and whatever—after a cherry picker malfunctioned and dumped him three stories onto asphalt. The accident shattered his spine. He now divided his golden years between his home and the Antler Taproom.

Swenson's name resided near the bottom of my list. The signs weren't promising. Bald and thick. His heavy-lidded eyes narrowed in suspicion; his mouth curled in a habitual sneer. A beer-swilling troglodyte parked in a cheap folding wheelchair with a U.S. flag on an antenna. He'd doubtless resembled a moldy carving of a potbellied Scandinavian troll since junior high. Not a chance this sourpuss would give me the time of day, much less discuss a comrade from an era when golden rays of prosperity irradiated the town.

I bought him a round, regardless, and made my pitch.

Two p.m. and three barflies squabbled as they nursed cans of Pabst. The soundless TV monitor flickered unintelligibly. The customers paid it not a lick of heed.

"Dick is dick, but pussy absorbs DNA," Drunk A said to Drunks B and C. The trio wore coveralls issued by different, inevitably defunct, companies. "You fuck some sleazy broad, you fucked every dipstick she ever had in her honeytrap."

"Where you hear that?"

"*Good Morning America*. Science segment."

"Bullshit."

"It ain't bullshit. Why you say that?"

"It's *Good Morning America*, is why. You ain't rollin' outta bed to watch the science segment on a morning show."

"Well, it's what I heard, is all I'm sayin'."

Swenson hefted his drink. His eyes were pink as flayed meat.

"A shame the fucknuts in the Capitol banned cigs. Man hangs around the bar in daylight for one reason. He wants to die. They banned cigs, they removed one of the best methods of suicide. Anymore, the whole shitaree takes twice, three times as long. Except, you gotta factor in respiratory infections on account these knob jobs go outside, rain or shine, to smoke. It's Deering, so more rain than shine. Ain't Miller Time, it's Pneumonia Time." His was a smoker's rasp. "I suppose shitheads croaking due to pneumonia evens the score."

"That's a unique perspective," I said. "Are *you* committing slow suicide? Moving to a warmer clime might be a less permanent solution to a temporary problem."

"Yeah. Yeah, I am. Beer does half, gravity handles the rest . . . You a cop? I get a feeling you're something along those lines."

I explained I wasn't a cop or a Fed, but basically a ronin on the make.

He cracked a smile. His diminished complement of teeth was a jumble.

"The Feds locked my pop away on a bullshit charge. Total shitshow. Won't talk to a Fed. Might stab him in the throat. Won't talk with him."

"What did your dad do?"

"Kidnapped some asshole swindler, drove him into Wisconsin and nailed him to a sheet of plywood and left him there."

"Sounds as if it might've been a raw deal." I didn't specify for whom.

"Dad kicked in Ionia, doin' twenty-five-to-forever. Yeah, I guess you could say it was a raw deal. You don't hold yourself the way a cop does. I like it. You're a mean sonofabitch. Not cop mean, the real deal. Rabid-dog-tearing-into-the-balls mean."

"Denny, you okay over there? That asshole botherin' you?" The pencil-neck behind the counter must've packed a scattergun to speak with such boldness.

"Fuck off," Swenson said. And to me, "The hicks have worn tinfoil bandannas since 9/11. If you ain't lily-white, you might be an Arab." His attention drifted to the snowy TV. The image crystallized to reveal a famous actor in uniform giving a perp the third degree. "Cop shows are such a load of garbage. Yellin' threats and slappin' suspects around."

I managed not to roll my eyes.

"They aren't called dramas for nothing."

"Investigators tend to be polite," he said. "Especially the Feds, and especially when interviewing a subject who without a doubt executed a fellow human. There's no percentage in playin' rough until the hard-nosed approach is necessary. Have a smoke, have a Coke. Relax, we're all friends here, we're just guys shootin' the breeze. You can tell us whatever's on your mind. We're here to listen. We don't judge. We're here for you, man. Personally, I dig why you did what you did. More of us had the balls, we'd do the same. Et cetera, like that."

"They ran that game on your old man?" I said.

"Hell yeah, they did. I knew what was what when the Feds came down here four years ago, curious to learn all they could about my friend Morris Oestryke. Tried to be cagey; it became obvious they wanted Morris for something real serious. I spit in their faces and they went away mad."

"I'm not cagey, but I could use some help."

"Give me a lift home? Sidewalk doesn't make it to my house."

I slapped two twenties on the table and dangled my keys.

"Ready to ride."

"Okay, my new best friend." He polished off his brew. Then he unlocked his wheels and headed toward the exit.

"Whoa! Where you takin' our buddy?" said Pencil-neck.

"Where you goin' with this guy?" Drunk A said to Swenson. Drunk A's cronies grumbled their support.

"Piss up a rope, boys," Swenson said. "See ya tomorrow."

"Not if we see you first!" the barflies cried in unison.

I HELPED HIM INTO THE CAR, folded his chair, and put it in the trunk. Five minutes later, in front of a seedy split-level house in an equally neglected neighborhood, we reversed the procedure. This time, I let the chair slide backward as he shifted his weight. Easy as pie; he'd begun to trust me. He toppled forward and landed on his face.

"Fuck," he said when he rolled over and blinked dazedly at the sky. A muzzy sunbeam through clouds caused his bloody mouth and nose to glisten. "You're a sonofabitch, aren't you?"

"A *clumsy* sonofabitch," I said.

"Why'd you do that?"

I didn't know. Sometimes I make snap judgments about people. Sorting the marks from the hard cases is a talent.

"Sorry, pal."

"Oh yeah? I'm thinking this was a mistake." He pawed at his lips.

"No take-backsies." I squeezed the meat of his bicep to give him the idea he should go along to get along. There'd be a bruise in the morning. To reinforce the threat, I lifted him bodily at arm's length into his wheelchair. My ribs had finally knitted together over the past week; lingering aches had subsided to twinges. I was, as the televangelists proclaim, healed. "Shall we?"

I wheeled him up a makeshift ramp into the house.

It's against my nature to beat an animal without cause, but it's also a morbid fact that certain creatures respond solely to force. An unsettling number of humans share this brand of masochism. He adored me now.

"Meet my wife, Norma. Norma, this son of a b is Coleridge. He's a detective." He introduced a heavyset matron in a bathrobe and a bright green shower cap who'd appeared from the back of the house.

Norma eyed us dourly.

"A detective. Yeah. Mister, wanna Faygo? Glass of water?" She touched her husband's swollen, streaming nose and clucked wearily. Some variation of this scene had played out a hundred times before. I declined and she nodded and left us alone.

Swenson's house featured wood paneling, shag rugs, and linoleum floors. I whiffed dead flowers in the spacious living room. He'd covered the furniture in plastic. The dozen or so prints of famous vamp Anita Ekberg, in various stages of undress, almost distracted me from noticing a bolt-action hunting rifle leaned against the wall near a sliding glass door that let onto the balcony.

"You're preoccupied with pinups."

"Only have eyes for Anita."

"Cute rifle." I inspected the rifle, detached the magazine, and tossed it into a newspaper basket.

"A man is sensible to keep a longarm in easy reach. We're in the wild. Got to take special care." He rolled into the kitchen and returned with a towel pressed to his face.

I carefully set the rifle down.

He watched me with a soft light in his eyes. One predator ceding right-of-way to a larger, more dangerous animal. Anger and pride pale beside self-preservation.

"The suburban lights aren't foolin' anybody who's lived here a week, forget about their entire life. A pack of coyotes stalked me right here in town. I was twelve, so that made it autumn of 1963. My family lived on Redburn and Darkman's. Mile, mile and a half east a here. Wild and woolly, lemme tell you. The burbs had a black problem— no offense—and not enough cops then. Real rough in our neighborhood; you wanted to be in by dark, because that's when the gangs would come outta the woodwork. Folks used to joke that Charles Bronson should drop by our town and clean up the trash. It was only a joke. You got strapped in Deering. For all the good it's done.

"The streetlamps were far apart and some had burned out. I glimpsed the pack in a yard across the way. Seven or eight coyotes sniffing in the grass. Then I scuffed the sidewalk, or whatever. The coyotes spotted me and trotted in my direction. Sprinted like Jesse Owens for our back door. Man, could I run. Gotta be why God took my legs. Sky Daddy is a joker."

"You should narrate a Rust Belt documentary for *National Geographic*," I said.

"Wanna pop? Got some Faygo in the icebox. All the flavors. Redpop, Root Beer, Creme, Grape, Cotton Candy. All of 'em."

"I didn't want one when Norma asked. Morris Oestryke was your pal in high school. Dazzle me with some
insight into the man." The truth was, my headache had
returned, hammer and tongs. I palmed some aspirin and
swallowed them dry.

"We weren't pals," he said. "We were *teammates*. Ever
been on a team? No? There's a difference."

"Comrades under fire. I respect that. Family, friends,
lovers; nobody is closer than a man who's walked through
hell with you, shoulder to shoulder. Old-timers say Oestryke worked at Valero," I said. "Did he talk about his job?"

"Sharp, aren't you?" Swenson said. "Hang tight." He
disappeared down the hall. I entertained several scenarios should he come back with a weapon. He came back
with a high school yearbook instead. "This is us, Class of
1969. We'd just finished a practice. Flattops and farmer's
tans. In pads, I was a god. There's Morris O." Morris
draped an arm over Swenson's shoulders in the photo.
Both were young and flushed. "Where are those pictures
you had?" He accepted Oestryke's military and company
headshots and laid them near the yearbook for comparison, and repeated this with the official class photos. "See?
Close, but no cigar."

I glanced at him and back to the photos.

"Okay, what?"

"It's not the same person in your pics," Swenson said.
He sounded petulant; a child insisting to an adult that
he'd seen a ghost. "Same hair, similar build. Close, yeah.
Cheekbones are real close too. Like brothers, or cousins. I
rolled around in the mud with Morris for three years.

This isn't him in an Army uniform. Sure as shit isn't him in the suit."

"Interesting. Half of Deering has seen these pics. You're the first person to claim this isn't Oestryke. What makes you so sure?"

"I am positive because I visited the man in 1987."

"You command my rapt attention, Mr. Swenson," I said.

"Mo didn't go into Witness Protection when he left Deering. He wasn't hard to find. I heard through the grapevine he'd settled back east. Called the operator with a number request and there he was, shittin' in high cotton in a tidy suburb. My wife has relatives near Albany and we were in town for a family reunion. I slipped away and dropped in at the Oestryke residence at suppertime. I didn't call ahead, just walked up and knocked on the door. This kid answers. I ask for the man of the house. The kid yells for his dad. Mo is sitting twenty feet away on the couch. I get a long, hard look at him. It ain't Mo. No, it ain't him."

"Who was it, then?" I tried to ignore the blood leaking from under his towel. Ooze gathered into a fat droplet and splatted his sweatshirt.

"John Doe. What gave me the heebie-jeebies was, the resemblance is uncanny. Actors can change their posture, how they hold their jaw. Some makeup, an accent, and the magical transformation is complete. That's how it felt—the man on the couch was starring in a reenactment. An actor who's played a role for so long, he almost believes he's become this whole other person. He don't recognize me either. Thank fuckin' God. If I woulda copped to knowing he wasn't the real Mo Oestryke, blown his secret, I'd wager my bottom dollar Denis Swenson would've vanished from the face of the earth one night soon after.

"There's somethin' in his expression that trips a few alarms, you see. Malice? Evil? I dunno what. *You* got the same coldness in your eyes. It's what a deer sees if it comes upon a hunter in the woods. And speakin' of that . . . one thing I noticed straight off was this poster-sized black-and-white print of a leopard, or a jaguar—one of those jungle cats—draggin' a baboon by the neck. Didn't seem like an appropriate piece of art for a family home. Dude was sittin' directly under the fuckin' thing, and, I don't know, it was kinda surreal and creepy, almost posed. I apologized for the mistake, said I was lookin' for Bill Smith—first bullshit name off the top of my head—and scrammed."

"You sound convinced," I said. His mention of the wildlife photo rang a distant bell. "Me, *I'm* less convinced. Couldn't it have been a misunderstanding? A coincidence? Has to be more than one Morris Oestryke in the world. You ran into a doppelgänger. We each have one."

Swenson's eyebrows furrowed as I punched holes in his theory.

"Doppelgänger? What's that? The guy followed me. Fucker appeared in my rearview as I got on the freeway. He must've been speedin' because I saw cop lights flash and a cruiser pulled him over. Only reason I spotted him, to be honest. Why would a normal person jump into his car and come after me like that? Answer is, they wouldn't."

His words possessed a screw-you authenticity I couldn't dismiss. I'm fairly unflappable. Swenson's account spooked me when I put myself in his shoes.

"Tell me about Valero," I said.

"Mo kept his mouth shut. Valero's nondisclosure contract was ironclad. I heard rumors. The one I buy is, they tortured small animals to test weapons tech for a defense contractor."

"Bioweapons? Electronics? Military R and D covers a lot of territory."

"Yeah, man. Laser technology and sonic weapons. Blind the enemy, fuck with his mind, or make his brain hemorrhage out his ears. Nobody knows dick except the pudknockers on the inside. In those days, the woods were darker and the entire property was locked tight as a gnat's ass behind an electric fence. Valero was part of Deering the way your old drooling cousin Ned in the attic is 'part' of the family. Blended right in. Weren't here even a winter; people drove right past without lookin'."

I'd reached the final hours of my heartland tour and couldn't estimate whether the trip had merited the effort. Surely there was more, some nugget I might tease forth with dogged effort. Isn't there always? The damp, musty earth of Deering seemed the kind of place to harbor a substratum of rotten secrets.

Swenson said, "Here's why them photos don't match his graduation portrait. Morris Oestryke died in 1969, is my guess. I last saw him a week after graduation. They killed him before he ever got on that bus and headed for basic."

"Your theory is that somebody iced Oestryke to assume his identity. Which makes no kind of sense. Who?"

"Couldn't tell you. He hung with people inside Valero Tech. Big-cheese types. I told him somethin' was hinky— rich fucks don't associate with their inferiors unless there's something in it for them. They inducted him into their circle. No names. Except I saw him once at Jack Rubie's— it closed in 2000—hanging with two university-aged guys. My first take? One of them had to be a half brother or a cousin. The resemblance was uncanny. I didn't give it a lick of thought until twenty years went by and I saw the phony sonofabitch pretending to be my friend."

"Did you encounter the Oestryke impostor after that occasion in Albany?" It was the last question I had right then, born of the strangely affecting logo at the back of the furniture warehouse. A screwball.

"You asking if my friend's stunt double ever come home to Deering? Creep in through my window one night for a reunion?"

"Sure. Or slithered down the chimney, whatever."

He lowered the towel and grinned as if I'd finally gotten a painfully obvious joke. His teeth were red.

CHAPTER TWENTY-THREE

Upon flying home to Rosendale, I went straight to my girl and my dog. Dinner, drinks, and mindless comedy on the tube unkinked the knots my muscles had formed over the past three days. It was like crawling from beneath an anvil. I spent the night wrapped in Meg's arms. Borrowing her warmth helped. We'd grown attuned to our respective moods. I didn't ask what latest domestic disaster had occurred in my absence and she didn't ask what had happened during the foray to Michigan.

The next morning, I booked an appointment with Marion Curtis. I requested an in-person meet to accept the weekly retainer fee. Time had finally come for the dreaded face-to-face. Curtis was, in his words, busier than a one-legged man in an ass-kicking contest. Since he suspected I had juicy intel for him, he granted me a fifteen-minute audience.

We rendezvoused at the abandoned YMCA near the river in Poughkeepsie. While the YMCA logo had been removed and much of the sprawling, ancient structure shuttered since the latter aughts, sections remained lighted and in operating order. Somebody somewhere evidently forked over installments to avoid the bulldozers and wrecking balls. Private parties were welcome to rent the facilities—the mob used it as a clubhouse.

A wiseguy rocking a pompadour buzzed me through the security entrance and said Mr. Curtis awaited in the gymnasium. The wiseguy patted me down. He dropped my gun, knife, and brass knuckles into a plastic container like the type used at airports. He pointed. I followed red LED signs along dim corridors, down short flights of stairs, up short flights of stairs, and from light to darkness and into light again. Easy place to get lost despite the signage. The building was a cavernous maze and I hadn't thought to bring a spindle of twine.

Muffled shouts and the harsh squeal of rubber soles on parquet flooring guided me to my destination. I scented the alluring tang of blood and adrenaline before I got there. A dozen rough men gathered near the far free throw line. The busted-nose and cauliflower-ear set. They wore T-shirts and sweats and were divided into teams of red and blue. Some of them leaned forward, hands on knees. One guy lay prone, his arm flung over his head. Nary a basket-ball in sight.

I'd seen this exhibition at the "classier" backwaters—a no-holds-barred mixed martial arts format popular in Russia and the former Eastern Bloc countries. Two teams of men faced each other in parallel lines and charged at the whistle in a semi-organized gang rumble. I winced at the barbarity of performing these antics, even with shoes on, on an unyielding surface.

Blood sport isn't my bag, although I'll make an exception for humans.

Three stern gentlemen in striped shirts and black pants circulated among the fighters, checking for broken bones and concussions. Off to the side, an amateur crew fiddled with a bank of lights and a Panaflex 35mm. The crew bitched and argued and exchanged idle threats. None of them were certain how to operate the circa 1970s camera.

Curtis reposed in the bleachers, flanked by a trio of no-neck flunkies. Albany boys; otherwise, I would've met them before today. He gave me the *Come along* gesture.

"Yowza! This ape here to rumble?" One of the thugs appraised me, hand poised near his pistol butt.

"He'd *be* the entire blue team," Curtis said. "Scram, boys."

His guards cast reproachful glances as they relocated to another row.

"You win points for originality." I sat next to him so we were both staring at the court. "Beats a nightclub, titty bar, racetrack, or warehouse. Or a church. Gangsters love to palaver in a church."

"Aquariums and art galleries are cliché too." Curtis dressed in steel-gray: big, heavy peacoat, unbuttoned, and a fedora pulled low over his eyes. "Should come get a load of this joint next week. I have it on good authority that the White Manitou are playing Aztec basketball."

The White Manitou were a major gang; ostensibly,

Native American, but in reality multiethnic, and currently engaged in a cold war with the mob. The gang warily ignored my existence—maybe I'd be of use one day. Providing I didn't step on too many moccasins in the interim.

"If I catch the guy who bumped Ray and Harry, he could be the star attraction," I said. "Sacrifice him right there at center court."

He set another of those thick envelopes on the bench and nudged it toward me with the back of his hand.

"Whole lotta dough. I could afford a down payment on a Lexus, what I'm forking over to you. Braces for my godson. Fancy new pistols for the boys here."

"A year's supply of Viagra."

"Two years'. Wanda put me in the doghouse, so I'm on half rations. My gut tells me what you've learned will be worth every dime."

"Uh, let's not hype this like Geraldo Rivera opening Capone's vault."

The red and blue teams straggled off, stage left. A dozen young men, evenly divided between yellow and green outfits, replaced them. The banter was Slavic.

"Those morons haven't a clue how to run that camera." Curtis clapped loudly to get the crew's attention. "Hey, jerks! Two minutes and that camera is rolling, or I'll know why not. I paid these apes to bash each other's brains in, not stand around with their thumbs up their asses."

The techs' argument escalated. If they kept going, those old boys would be the ones rolling around punching and gouging. Nobody wants Caesar to grow restless on his watch.

"That's a classic setup," I said of the Panaflex. "Where'd you score one of those models?"

"It fell off a truck." He braced his arms behind his neck. "You went sniffing around the Bird of Paradise the other night, as I recall. I hope you had a swell evening on the company dime. Harry was like a bad penny around there, wasn't he?"

"He and the girls got along famously. Thought I'd ask for their opinions."

"Whatcha got for me, Coleridge?"

"Okay, don't get mad."

I inhaled and dove in headfirst. Potentially mortal enemies surround me, but I was cool and measured. I related precisely what my patron needed to know and nothing more. For example, I detailed what I'd uncovered about the Croatoan, including the distinct possibility he'd murdered the original Morris Oestryke and assumed his identity in 1969.

Conversely, I elided the existence of my source inside the FBI. Nor did Delia Labrador's name escape my lips, although I guessed he must be aware she'd been Harry's paramour. Then again, life is messy and rife with loose ends.

Did I hedge on Delia's involvement because of chivalry? Nah; I hadn't determined the extent of her value. Every instinct warned me to keep Curtis at least slightly in the dark until I got a handle on the situation. A strategy not without risk. Mobsters are touchy dudes. It was not beyond the realm of possibility that an annoyed Curtis could snap his fingers and have me ventilated on the spot. I fervently hoped that his motive for setting me on the trail was sincere.

"I wish you would've told me about Oestryke from the beginning," I said in conclusion. "Why the runaround?" Offense might unbalance him and prevent him from zeroing in with questions I wasn't prepared to answer.

Curtis didn't gesture to his soldiers to have me dragged away and capped. He smiled wryly, reached into his pocket, and got a cigarette. He lit the cigarette and puffed. Then he turned his head slightly to regard me.

"My friend, I have an inkling as to why your boss was so eager to boot you outta Alaska. You're lippy."

"Lippy . . . uppity? Tomato . . . tomahto?"

"Hey! Whoa, there, Coleridge. I didn't mean anything racial."

The camera crew signaled to the refs and the refs organized the brawlers, six on a side. The whistle blew and the men rushed in, swinging. At first, the fighters engaged their opposite number. Head-butting, rabbit punches, dropkicks to the groin—anything seemed to go. The single-combat phase didn't last long. As soon as somebody fell, the victor assisted his nearest teammate. Then it was two-on-one, and finally a dogpile atop the last fighter on the losing side. I'm uncertain what purpose the refs served, except to blow the whistle after the vanquished were immobilized or unconscious.

Green triumphed, more or less.

CHAPTER TWENTY-FOUR

The Family lives by a set of rules," Curtis said. "You are well aware of our traditions or you wouldn't be aboveground. I kid about your Alaska exile. Apollo woulda made you a member, if such were possible."

"Mr. Apollo treated me well," I said. "He saved my life and I'm grateful."

"Respect will carry you far. The street taught me that. I started with nothing, knowing nothing. Main thing I learned since becoming a capo? The smart play is, keep everything nice and simple. This Morris Oestryke you investigated? Forget him. He's a goner. Six feet under. Sleepin' with the fishes. Dirt nap. Wooden kimono. I wasn't trying to deceive you—I don't fuckin' know who dusted Lee and Anderson. It ain't the Croatoan. That I can vouch for."

I began calculating the implications, reconfiguring my prior theories and suppositions. I made an intuitive leap. Or, perhaps, a hop.

"You dusted him."

He nodded, pleased I was following the bouncing ball. "That's right. Very good. Give the man a Kewpie."

"If the Croatoan is dead, who's doing your associates? Because it feels like payback."

"People in this line got our share of enemies." He puffed his cigarette and assumed the expression of a man rapidly adding numbers and not liking the sum. "Granted, this is damned specific. A copycat. Has to be a copycat in possession of the dirty details. I thought maybe Nic Royal, say they had a fallin'-out, or what have you. Reasonably sure it ain't him. No motive, and murder ain't in his résumé. Royal's a nobody; keeps his nose clean and his mouth shut. It'd be safer to clip the kid, though. I'm all about safety. I decided to wait and see what you think."

"I assume 'wait and see' means Royal has skipped town since our chat."

"Ask me no questions and I'll not tell you my guys swung by his condo last night and found it empty. He hasn't shown for his shift at the Knarr. None of the usual riffraff have seen him lately. He must've run for the hills after your 'talk.' It's all good. We'll look high and low. Meatheads like Royal never run far."

To say this was an ominous sign for Royal would be coy. Unless matters corrected themselves, he'd soon join Morris Oestryke in the Great Hereafter. On the flip side of the coin, I worried—and not for the first time—if I'd erred in letting the guy walk without pressing a lot harder.

"Do me a favor," I said. "Don't ice the kid until I get a chance to speak with him one more time. Good heavy, bad heavy, might be our play."

"Long as you don't let the fucker take a powder, if you happen to find him first. Chat him up and then turn him over. Deal?"

"Deal. Another thing. The mutilation of Harry's corpse feels wrong. Why take the hands?"

"Why take the head? The Croatoan is a trophy collector, is why."

"Yes, but this feels too pat. Any word from your contacts in the police department? Autopsy results, a DNA match? Without dental records or fingerprints, a body could belong to anybody."

"Hurry up and wait," he said. "There's always a backlog of stiffs at the ME's office. I'm tellin' you—no way Harry faked his death and picked up the Croatoan's knife. That's what you're implying—Harry iced a patsy in order to pull off a scheme."

"It occurred to me."

"I got a talent for judging what's inside a man. He didn't have the stomach for this. Believe me, no way is it possible. All I can say is, even fifteen, twenty years ago Harry had already made a lot of connections. People liked him, so they told him stuff. He heard I needed a mechanic for a tricky contract. Came to me and said he could put me in touch with the best of the best; a hitter who went by the name the Croatoan. For a retainer, natch. Thus began a beautiful partnership. Until the treachery and murder."

"Okay, the basics, then," I said. "What did the Croatoan do to incur your wrath? The Outfit is normally excited to have highly skilled psychopaths on the payroll."

"Sure, we love our madmen. Too bad he was also a rat."

The Family policy on squealing is nonnegotiable. Snitch to the cops and the mob happens to find out half a century later? Grandkids of the offended mafiosos would track you to your rest home and snuff you on your deathbed.

"The Family heard rumors for many years the Feds planted a rat in the organization. We had not a fuckin' clue as to the dirty bastard's identity. Coulda been anybody. An unfortunate circumstance for the fellas I ordered whacked to be on the safe side."

I smiled to be polite. Preventative culling is the mob's standard operating procedure. Related maxims—dead men tell no tales, never talk, better safe than sorry, don't sit with your back to the door at an Italian restaurant.

He went on.

"Outta the blue, a piece of vital information landed in my lap. One of our street-level associates confessed to tipping the Feds to a deal. He'd gotten pinched and made the fatal mistake of squealing in exchange for a reduced sentence. Or should I put it, he made the mistake of getting caught—twice."

"Liability with a capital *L*," I said. "How did you catch him?"

"The prick wore a wire. Too bad for him it was Random Stop-and-Frisk Day at Goodfellas HQ. Feds weren't even getting sound. The transceiver was on the fritz. Ha! Better believe he babbled like a baby in hopes of savin' his skin. *Please don't solder my toes together! Please don't give me a Sicilian necktie!* Pathetic. His bargaining chip? Punk was cozy with a broad who pushed paper for the

FBI. Would you believe they met while he snitched for the Feds? He'd primed the bitch for eighteen months, pumping her for inside dope. She got drunk and blabbed about a 'weird' case that had popped up on her supervisor's radar. Something to do with an old, retired contract killer who'd occasionally informed on the Family in the past. The hitter's name was Morris Oestryke and he'd faked his death in the '80s. The Fed boss wanted the report deep-sixed, no reason given."

"That's some heavy pillow talk," I said.

"Real hush-hush deal too. Top secret, eyes-only shit. Almost nobody heard a whisper in the department. Probably embarrassed to be runnin' such a lowdown dirty scam. Fidelity, bravery, integrity—my ass."

I could see where this was going. I let him have his moment.

"See," he said, "the fearless G-men gave the hitter free rein to run amok so long as he tossed them actionable intelligence now and again. This Oestryke character could torture and slaughter all the lowlifes he wanted. If a few capos went to jail, it was worth the trade."

"Did he actually make any cases? He was merely a hired gun, right?"

"In retrospect, Oestryke made Machiavelli look like a rube. He exerted a weird influence over certain types; collected down-on-their-luck hard cases and put 'em to work. The exact details are sketchy. What I've heard is, he used a variety of methods to cultivate his own informants inside the Family. Some he bribed, others he threatened. Disguise and deception were his bread and butter. None of these idiots realized who they were talking to, or that they'd been taken in. For Christ's sake, he posed as an undercover cop and 'flipped' a couple of made guys. Arranged for an accomplice to pose as their counsel and everything. It was a master-level con. Those shitheads were ready to give up their mothers before he got done with them.

"Over fifteen, twenty years, the FBI received detailed info regarding who, what, when, and where in connection with a number of major jobs. Capos in New York and Jersey took a long fall. I won't mention names. You read the paper, I'm sure you can guess."

"And for that the Feds ignored his extracurriculars."

"Sick bastards, our government, huh? The name Oestryke meant nothing to me at first. Then my source spelled it out. He fingered the Croatoan, aka Morris Oestryke, aka take your pick of a dozen noms de plume. He was the spy we'd heard rumors of for years. My jaw hit the floor."

"Your informant made a compelling argument. It isn't every day that two and two equals five."

"Sure did. I had faith in his story since I held a blowtorch idling near the jerk's toes during our powwow."

"That must have been a fascinating conversation," I said. "How is it you weren't aware that Oestryke and the Croatoan were one and the same prior to this revelation?"

"He'd retired the Oestryke identity when he presumably 'died' in '87 and I didn't make the connection until I interrogated the stool pigeon. Like I said, Oestryke went by a whole Rolodex of aliases. Frank Smith, Joe

Jones, Bob Brown, Donnie Duster, and on and on. Regardless, I'd thought of him as the Croatoan—or Mr. C, to keep it simple. Now you're tellin' me whoever this fucker *really* was, he stole the Oestryke identity too; that he got married and raised a family for deep cover purposes, like a commie mole. There's no bottom to this pit. Doesn't surprise me. Shady fuck."

He lit another cigarette. Below us, the fighters shuffled off the court and a custodian trudged in with a mop and bucket.

"Since the ass end of the '90s, I hired him for seven or eight jobs. He wasn't always available, and, in the last decade, he'd disappear for months and years at a stretch. Went off the rails and whacked some transients, is what I heard. Very bad, very sick. Guy had screws loose, no question."

"You ever have a real conversation?" I said. "Any impressions? Did he mention a partner? A protégé?"

"Heard he used to be a party animal. Times change. We got together twice. Meeting in the flesh wasn't remotely in his comfort zone. He conducted business through an intermediary or a dead letter drop. Y'know—cloak-and-dagger. Don't know if he had an understudy or a partner. Never saw him with anybody, for whatever that's worth. As I said, I didn't learn his real identity, where he lived, nothin' useful for hunting him to ground. As for all those wild stories? People say he wore a mask, he whistled his victims to sleep, the exotic torture methods, and the rest . . . some of that is one hundred percent, Hand to God the truth. Other parts, I don't wanna know."

"Allow me to test my psychic powers," I said. "The

Croatoan goes into quasi-retirement. However, when you received news that your favorite contract hitter smelled of Odor La Rat, you squeezed your mutual pal Harry to set a meet, for old times' sake, and x'd out the premiere button man of our era."

He nodded, evidently savoring the recollection.

"Laid an ambush that went off smooth as shit through a goose. Boy, was I nervous, considerin' who the target was. I capped him with a .22." Curtis cocked his thumb and forefinger to demonstrate. "*Pop-pop* to the back of the head. Drove the schmuck to a spot in the Pines and tucked him in. So much for the dreaded Croatoan. I owe Harry. Couldn't have done it without him."

"Harry's wiles were not to be underestimated," I said. "Oestryke must've trusted him implicitly to come out of hiding."

"Ironic, yeah? Secretive sonofabitch like the Croatoan had friends too. That's the weak link in the chain for everybody in the life. It's always a buddy or a broad that does you in. Although, *friend* is a weak word for the relationship Harry shared with the Croatoan. *Lion tamer* might be more precise."

"You have to assume there's a story in there somewhere; how they met and became amigos."

"I don't give a flyin' fuck at a rollin' doughnut," he said. "Harry was his handler and that's all I needed to know."

It hit me then, that I'd gotten it backwards. Harold Lee's special relationship with the Croatoan, not Delia, had opened the doors and afforded him VIP access to pretty girls and exclusive gin joints across the Hudson Valley.

"No chance Harry was Oestryke's only liaison to the mob," I said. "He had other connections—low-level criminals with access to the right people. He could've switched to suit his aliases and to divert suspicion."

Curtis nodded.

"Inquiries are under way."

"He wouldn't have willingly given up his extremely dangerous friend," I said. "Except, he didn't have much choice. He could either play ball or get whacked himself."

"The sad sack got screwed by fate. He didn't want to go down as an accomplice to the Croatoan's rat-fink ways."

"That's not what motivated him into selling out Oestryke. There's loose talk regarding debts."

"True. His granddaughter was very ill. A chronic condition. The dumb lug personally covered what insurance didn't. Medical expenses in the USA are fuckin' obscene."

"Harry took out a big fat loan from the bank of Marion Curtis." I swallowed my disgust. Nic Royal had alluded to this very detail during our chat. "I hope you cleared his marker."

"Well, well, look at the bleedin' heart on the Māori Menace. Let your heart not be troubled. Harry's pluckin' a harp among the angels, and I maintain a fund for his granddaughter's health and welfare. He earned the consideration. Didn't cost me nothin' upfront either. I just told the hospital administrator he was gonna go for a swim in concrete boots if he didn't play ball. 'Course,

Harry wasn't privy to the details. All he needed to know is that he owed me big."

"Why would Harry borrow from you and not his bosom buddy?"

"He was desperate, not fuckin' insane. And anyhow, the Croatoan was a hoarder. It was against that cat's very nature to part with a red cent of his moola."

"Oestryke must've had a fortune socked away. Any likelihood that Harry had access to the loot after Oestryke's demise?"

"Fuck yeah, Oestryke was worth a bundle. No way he revealed its location to Harry or any other patsies he had on the string. Some jackass will uncover the dough in a bank vault or a hole in the ground years from now when we're tits-up. Rubs me raw."

"As you say"—I nodded toward the goons—"this has been enlightening. Leaves us where we started—somebody who's read the Croatoan's playbook is picking up the slack. Worried?"

"Worried enough to bring you in. You understand why this has to stay quiet. Why I'm keeping this a circle of two."

His secrecy made increasing sense. He'd potentially compromised himself by using the Croatoan's services on behalf of the Family. Learning of the hitman's cooperation with the Feds doubtless came as a shock. It mattered not one iota that Curtis would merely relay bad news. The Family had an unpleasant tendency to kill the messenger. Just to be on the safe side.

I tried to organize the puzzle pieces and they kept sliding through my fingers. Solving a mystery is exponentially more difficult when you don't trust anyone involved, including your own patron.

"There's a certain amount of kismet involved," he said.

"Let me stop you right there," I said. "*Kismet* doesn't belong in a capo's dictionary. Visions of you bumming around California beaches are dancing in my head."

He smiled a tight smile and the tension loosened a notch.

"I dated a surfer girl when I was a young stud. But what I'm tryin' to say is, there's a sense of dark fate intertwined with this Croatoan deal. Sure, Harry made the introductions. Truth is, I inherited the psycho killer. Mr. C did business with the Family long before I entered the picture. The Croatoan was a weird trade secret—the old capos wouldn't say fuck all about him, except the bogeyman tales; how he did in his victims, and whatnot."

"Try not to take this the wrong way," I said. "Are you absolutely, positively sure you finished Oestryke?"

"Sheesh! We may not all be world-famous hitmen, but I know how to cap a guy."

"Right on. Thanks for the talk." I stood. "I'll report when there's more to say."

"Yeah? Got a plan?"

"To keep hunting, to keep digging. My best leads are Oestryke, Harry Lee, and Ray Anderson. Who they knew, who they hated, or loved." There was the lie by omission I alluded to earlier. Delia Labrador and Zircon Corporation flitted on the periphery of this investigation and I meant to bring them into focus.

Curtis let me walk a few steps before he called my name.

"You're gutsy to saunter in here," he said. "Unarmed among lions, no less. Climb right up in my grille and call me a liar. Don't do it again, okay? I'd hate to forget my admiration for your work ethic."

I smiled.

"I'm not unarmed. Your man at the door missed one."

Thankfully, he laughed.

"He ain't made. Break his arm or somethin' before you leave, will you?"

"Christmas is coming," I said.

CHAPTER TWENTY-FIVE

Leaves continued to brighten and fall. Hillsides evolved through shades of gold and maple. The north breeze tasted of late autumn in Alaska; brittle as an icicle, except greener and less cruel. I inhaled the wilderness during my dawn jogs. Late mornings, I punched a striking post, or fired a few rounds through my guns. Sighting in the Mossberg and configuring its choke to shape blast patterns was pleasurable. So was the shotgun's kick.

The agency line buzzed with increasing frequency. Cheating spouses, defrauded business partners, lost lambs—the typical woes of modern society. Some pleas for assistance revolved around slightly more exotic difficulties, such as terrified debtors, gangbangers gone straight and looking to clear their names, and moguls desperate to beef up security due to credible death threats. I took a rain check on several and declined the remainder.

My dance card was full.

Days, I encamped at the office. Aided by my consultants, I located Morris Oestryke's widow and three kids.

Mrs. Oestryke lived in San Francisco at a group home. She hadn't been compos mentis since the 1990 car accident that killed her eldest son and severed her spinal cord in three places. The middle son died a few years later while laboring at a construction site in Denver. Heart attack.

The youngest son drove a bus in Reno. He told me to piss up a rope. *Dad died when I was nine months old. Way too young to remember anything useful. Maybe that's to the good. Maybe it's best he passed on before I got to know him.* He didn't answer the multiple follow-up messages I left. Did the FBI find it odd—or, dare we say, suspicious— that Oestryke's family fell like dominoes within a few short years of his own presumably faked demise? Who could say?

The horrible, yet inescapable, conclusion I bumped into no matter which direction I turned was that Morris Oestryke had coldly and ruthlessly engineered this dead end from the corpses of his own loved ones.

I yearned to clamp my hands around his neck, whether or not he was a moldering corpse.

AS I'D TOLD CURTIS, all I could do was put my head down and keep digging. I nurtured the faint hope that if I talked to enough people, somebody somewhere would divulge a scrap of information and blow the case wide open. Legwork meant going over the same ground time and again, squinting at the same clues from varying angles and praying for a bolt of insight, or plain old luck.

The existence of the Croatoan was bad enough. That

he'd been removed from the board and a copycat had assumed his mantle pushed us into deeper darkness. The universe had cracked open to reveal a panoply of new and unpleasant possibilities. She likes to keep us on our toes, Mother Nature. The idea that psychopathy and evil can vector and corrupt in the manner of a disease is among the most heinous propositions my imagination could conceive.

When I informed Lionel of recent developments, his response was to shrug and crack another beer. He'd told me so and didn't have to remind me of the fact.

I built the crime collage on the wall and sifted through a voluminous list of people who'd even remotely associated with Lee and Anderson. Anderson was known at the local clubs, but in the casual sense and not as a major partygoer. Bookies reported that he'd done most of his gambling (just enough to maintain appearances) from the comfort of his living room and a sports bar in New Paltz. Anderson's real job involved breaking into places and robbing them blind, so his nights were generally committed.

Harold Lee cut a completely different figure. The wannabe Sinatra got around in a major way. To stretch my legs and give my aching eyeballs a rest, I visited several of his favorite places. Mainly Kingston joints—Tom Thumb's, The Stocks, and a slick new watering hole called Falling Eagle. Lee also frequented Sable & Chic, a gentleman's club out on the rough on Route 32. He'd done collection work for the management of The Stocks and acquitted himself well. A waitress at Sable & Chic recalled Harry in the company of a woman who closely matched Delia Labrador's description.

The list of Harry's friends, associates, and favorite locations shrank by the hour. Nary a discouraging word was uttered in regard to the departed. Nary an enlightening word either. He'd tipped adequately and kept his hands to himself. Women liked him; he evinced a sweet, paternal air and a sense of humor. Men liked him because he was easygoing, the polar opposite of run-of-the-mill thugs. Unlike most goons, a nickel in the pen for battery (what else?) imbued him with an aura of genteel danger that caused men to grin in camaraderie and women to get hot and bothered.

Folks who should've been wiser didn't believe this urbane, mild-mannered gent actually cracked heads to make rent—no evil sneer, no knuckle scars. I didn't bother to explain that Harry fancied a pipe over his bare hands. I certainly didn't explain that Saint Harold had buddied up with a twisted psychopath and, eventually, under duress, participated in said psycho's execution.

I STOLE MOMENTS HERE AND THERE to monitor the Trask crew. Elvira Trask slunk out of the woodwork and was seen at her usual hangouts, albeit far from Aubrey Plantagenet's salon. Elvira sported a shiner and a new purple dye job. Rough girl. Under other circumstances, I might feel empathy for her.

There's no rest for the ambitious private eye. I spent every other nightshift at Aubrey P's apartment, planted in a recliner, marathoning old black-and-white samurai flicks and westerns. Kurosawa and Hawks are faithful amigos in the wastelands of boredom. Sometimes I brought Minerva for extra company, and as an early-warning system in case I nodded off and bad guys sneaked up on us. Clint Eastwood's Toshiro Mifune could've used a loyal hound.

As I said, dull as dirt, albeit not without several annoying incidents, befitting the mentality of the shitheads perpetrating the terror campaign.

The phone rang at 1 a.m. four nights running. Heavy breathing on the other end before disconnection. Vehicles rolled by or parked across the street. The cars always left before daylight. I could've alerted the police or burned some of my capital to roust Elvira's thugs. That would've merely kicked the can down the road. Trouble delayed is still trouble.

There are three primary impulses to journey into the darkness. To investigate and rectify. To seek knowledge. To hunt and bring down prey. I'm the third kind—a hunter. The hawk, the wolf, the spider. Other men gather clues and follow trails their own way. I observe as an animal does. I dream with the scent of prey in my nostrils; I plot trajectories and paths of flight. I bide my time, but my hindbrain is always working, chewing at the problem.

Therefore, I hung tough and waited for the Trasks to show their hand. The moment they did, I'd hack it off at the wrist. *Domo arigato*, Mr. Kurosawa, for your timeless inspiration.

———

WE ARE WALKING BLACK HOLES, Gene said. He'd resorted to wildly paraphrasing Itzhak Bentov while loaded. *Our brains are receivers made of meat. Consciousness is a quantum field that trickles in from someplace else and interacts with our gray matter. Anyways, that's my guess.*

My subconscious sends angels to roost upon my shoulders. With increasing frequency, Gene K had winged back from the Other Side and taken up residence where the better angel normally sets up shop.

You can't sleep on the troubles we see, killer. Keep your head on a swivel or it will wind up at the end of a pole.

Well past midnight found me dozing in Aubrey P's recliner. I came to, startled by furtive movement. A shadow pressed against the window.

The would-be home invader was a skinny little bastard. He lifted the window inch by inch. Stealthy as could be. I let him get an arm, a leg, and his head through the opening before I struck. Put my back into it, starting from the floor, right between his bulging eyes that were reflecting the night-light in the hall.

Practically speaking, my concrete lump of a fist walloping his forehead had the same effect as a hammer stroke against the skull of a cow in the slaughterhouse gate. His bones gave. He flew backward as if sucked through a sudden hull rupture into deep space. Took the window frame, curtains, and a chunk of the wall along for the ride. I laughed because it felt good, and because I thought I might've killed him, which also felt good.

The front door smashed inward. I sobered up fast, grabbed the couch, lifted it chest-high, and hurled it in that general direction like a hammer thrower going for gold. The resultant crash and the scream were encouraging.

I bent my knees and got the .357 ready and slid sideways until my shoulder pressed against an interior wall. Glass broke in the kitchen. That would be the side door. I partially shielded my eyes, swung my arm, and fired twice—you can't win if you don't play—and immediately scuttled forward to avoid return fire directed at the muzzle flashes.

My vision quickly returned like a print developing in its acid bath; blots and floating stars, as opposed to a void of fiery darkness. I might've drooled, yes. It happens when my blood is up.

Several moments of quiet passed before I realized the attackers were either incapacitated or fleeing. Slamming car doors and a revving engine confirmed that at least a couple were alive and making their getaway.

I reached the front porch as a late-model Cadillac peeled rubber and barreled across the neighbor's lawn. The driver crashed through a picket fence and roared around the corner.

"Jesus! Fuck!" Aubrey P shouted from her bedroom. Walter had worked a double at his dad's latest project and wasn't present. Did the Trasks plan their assault with knowledge of Walter's schedule taken into account? The plot thickened.

Lights flickered on in the adjacent houses. Aubrey joined me on the steps.

"Oh God. Who's that?" She pointed at a body lying motionless in the grass, cattycorner to where we stood.

I walked over and examined the skinny dude who'd tried to sneak in through the window. Shards of glass glittered around his head; drapes covered him. I kicked his thigh, hard. He was too far gone to complain, but his limbs twitched. The butt of a small, cheapo automatic protruded from his waistband. That was fortuitous.

"Oh God. Oh Jesus. Oh fuck. Did you kill him?"

"Nope," I said, slightly disappointed in myself. Nor did I find any corpses on the opposite side of the house where I'd directed a couple of bullets.

The cops arrived promptly after the excitement. I disarmed myself and made certain to raise my hands during the initial confusion. Private investigator performing legitimate security work thwarts home invasion. Shots fired put a slight damper on the report, although multiple attackers breaking in at night all but guaranteed I'd be cleared by the D.A.'s office. An ambulance team scraped the unconscious dude off the lawn and whisked him to a date with a trauma surgeon. His near future included a spinal halo, intravenous tubes, and traction.

Aubrey P was less than grateful.

"You goddamned gorilla," she said once the cops finished debriefing me. "You could've killed that kid. You could've killed one of the neighbors." Her eyes shimmered with rage and tears. "That's it. I don't care. You're fired. You and Chuck and your drunk Army buddy can stay the fuck out of my house."

Technically, she couldn't fire me since I worked for

her grandfather. Still, her wrath caused me to take a strategic step back.

"We'll replace the windows," I said. "Uh, and the sofa. Insurance company will be here in the morning; take care of the whole schmear."

"Fuck the windows! Fuck you!"

Anybody with an ounce of self-preservation declines to argue with a woman in that kind of mood. I escaped while I was behind and went home and slept.

The accountant woke me a quarter after 9 a.m. to confirm he'd finished his task and had left the report on my desk. I skipped breakfast and headed directly to the office.

CHAPTER TWENTY-SIX

There's a passage in *The Prince* wherein Machiavelli discusses the capricious nature of fortune and its propensity to screw with a ruler's best intentions. He says something to the effect that while a man can't control fortune's flow, he can damned well dig a channel and shore up the dikes. Amen, Niccolò.

I'd dug a channel and shored the dikes. Now, synchronicity followed the path of least resistance. Wonders never cease.

In addition to several manila folders of potential goodies, I checked the machine. Delia Labrador had left a message. She offered to meet at a café in Stone Ridge and save me the drive. Call it a lunch date. I combed my hair and everything.

Since it was still early, I spent two hours poring over the files and taking notes. A certain pattern emerged. I required more time to study and internalize the data before drawing any conclusions. Suffice to say, I began to seriously ponder the mysterious intersection of coincidence and fate. Not for the first time either.

THE STONE ROOSTER was one of those restaurants that served breakfast, closed during the afternoon, and reopened for the dinner crowd. Bay windows splashed sunlight on a checkerboard marble floor, granite bar, and a scattering of iron tables painted white. A gold-and-green wooden rooster stood watch near the front door. The carving's detail had worn away beneath flaking paint. I'd read somewhere that certain cultures believed wooden roosters protected buildings from fire.

I arrived early and ordered the chicken, of course, and the house ale. I had the meal on the ropes and started on the second beer when Delia waltzed into the room. Her bodyguards remained on the front steps like a couple of vampires who hadn't been invited inside. I waved. The less surly one of the duo waved back.

Delia wore a dark jacket, slacks, and sandals. She'd piled her hair and wrapped it in a shawl. Her natural blonde self today. Hollywood shades with bright red frames, brighter red lipstick, and a shiny red clutch completed her flawless ensemble.

"I have decided to assist you," she said. "Lucky duck."

Immediately suspicious, I smiled winningly.

"Against your better judgment."

"Against my *worse* judgment, dear. Misgivings notwithstanding, I truly am excited to help."

"You want to help bring Harold Lee's killer to justice? Commendable."

"Screw justice. I want sweet, sweet revenge." She ordered a glass of white wine. She tasted the wine and dabbed her lips on a napkin she removed from her clutch. Her nails were also red. She leaned forward and said in a stage whisper, "Before we proceed, I must ask—will it be a problem? My dating your best friend?"

"I'm confident it will be a problem for somebody. Not necessarily me." I nodded toward her manservants on the porch. "Jekyll and Hyde won't be overjoyed."

"Jekyll and . . . Ha-ha, how clever. They're not jealous."

"They *should* be worried. Lionel has terrible luck and is a magnet for trouble. You being a likely example."

"Of course, dear Lionel is plagued by misfortune. Poor farm boys flock to the military for a reason. My guards might not love your friend, but he's a true-blue patriot. They absolutely loathe you."

"Hyde has such a friendly smile. Thank you for holding them at bay so we can have our chummy talk."

"You're welcome. *Hyde* really is ready to shoot you through the window should I require rescuing."

I tried to read her expression. Her big dark glasses thwarted that—by design. The pupils and the lashes, the corners and crinkles, tell a story. I watched her nostrils and the muscles around her mouth instead. Her mannerisms were faintly reminiscent of elite gangster molls I'd met, divided by what one might logically expect from a ruthlessly spoiled heiress.

"Is Lionel aware that you're meeting me?" I said.

"Hmm. We've had one inconclusive date. Unless he slipped a tracking bug into my purse . . ."

"Taking that as a no."

"Sergeant Robard is oblivious."

"Lady, truer words were never spoken."

"This is more fun anyway." She abruptly reached across the 38th Parallel that divided our place settings and clasped my hands. Stronger than she appeared. "Secrecy is the special sauce of a whirlwind romance." She settled back, dug into her purse, and passed me a full-color brochure with ZIRCON CORPORATION printed on the front cover above a fanciful starburst zircon stone. "Have a souvenir. It's not available to the general public. Every time the Feds investigate Father, or some P.I. with delusions of grandeur comes sniffing around, I give them a door prize."

"Zircon receives its share of attention, no argument. What, a dozen Federal inquiries since the Reagan presidency?"

"Closer to two dozen. Zero indictments." She made the zero with her thumb and forefinger.

"The government twice investigated your granddad for industrial espionage. Two of your uncles seem like chips off the old block. Uncle Zebulon is liable to run out the clock in Federal prison for corporate espionage and arms trading; Uncle Ephraim was probably also bound for infamy. As a kid, he had numerous encounters with the law. A juvenile delinquent, some say. Except, he died young—car accident, wasn't it? No insider trading or corrupt politicking for him."

"Uncle Ephraim was allegedly antisocial," she said. "He passed through the Pearly Gates before my time. Uncle Zeb, he's sweet. Prison is treating him well. We converse once a year around Christmas. Every family has its scoundrel. Surely you can relate."

"No shortage of scoundrels in your family. Daddy's been probed by law enforcement agencies so often, he's a major investor in petroleum jelly futures."

"The price of success. Zircon suffers a fair bit of scrutiny. My family too. It's a farce. Whenever a Labrador sneezes, somewhere a politician reaches for the phone to assemble a congressional oversight committee." She watched me riffle the pages of the pamphlet. "Let's talk about me. You *are* pretending to be an authentic detective, aren't you?"

My contacts had come through nicely. I'd gotten my mitts on her transcripts, among a slew of other documents. Collating the information would be a bear, as old mountain men of my acquaintance would say.

I cleared my throat.

"Thirty-three, graduated from Vassar, majored in film. Trained at the Arrington School of Performing Arts— voice and dance. You travel. Italian ski resorts are your weakness. Engaged briefly to a Sicilian magnate. It ended poorly."

"He couldn't ski," she said.

"Neither can Lionel. Be forewarned."

"Fortunately, I'm not interested in skiing with him." Volley to the lady.

"You sit on several department committees within Zircon and are assistant chair to the Arts and Sciences Council. All this to keep your claws sharp. It's not as if you have to lift a finger to make rent. Your net worth is considerable and will compound once Mommy and Daddy shuffle off."

Delia clapped politely with the tips of her fingers.

"Bravo, my dear. It's for show, alas. I'm the prodigal daughter. The powers that be assign token roles to keep me from underfoot. Assistant chair sounds important. It's nothing of the sort."

"Daddy isn't keen about your dirty dancing," I said. "Or your cavorting with thugs such as Harry. Or ex-soldiers."

"He isn't keen on a great many of my hobbies. We are both old enough to realize nothing will change. My idols are incorrigible women. I do as I please. Or as much as I can get away with."

"How did you and Harry become acquainted?"

"Someone introduced me to Harry in the flower of my youth. A year or so after college. Impressionable me versus a dashing older guy with an edge. We frequented the same clubs—"

"A millionaire chick and an arm breaker patronized the same nightclubs?"

"He had connections and I slum. We met in the middle. Flirted for years. I was chasing industrialists, remember? Nothing romantic until recently. Bad, bad scene at a party. A coked-up D-list celebrity put his hands on me. Harry knocked the man's teeth down his throat. You would never in a million years guess from looking at him that he was capable of such an act."

"Turn-ons include brutality," I said.

"Sweetie, you haven't any idea." She signaled for a fresh wine, though her first glass remained nearly full. "*I* have a question. Who hired you? Surely not his estranged wife or children."

"Ms. Labrador, your dead boyfriend is hardly a sympathetic character in this drama. This isn't news to you. Whatever their faults, Harry's family deserved better, and I'm not interested in hashing out their infelicity to his memory."

A hint of color bloomed in her cheeks.

"Ouch! Over to you, then. Coleridge CV highlights? You contracted for the Mafia and now you don't. Well, as far as we know, you don't. You weren't a common hitman. Your file indicates a significantly higher class of assassin. One with social graces and specialized training to smooth over those rough edges. The Chicago mob invested time and resources in your tutelage. Not a hooker, but a courtesan."

"Some would say a whore is a whore."

"They'd be correct, wouldn't they?"

I laid a manila folder on the table and spread the four known photographs of Oestryke in a crescent. I placed her photo at the center; the romantic one Harry had taken.

"Ever see this guy? His name is Morris Oestryke. These were taken in the '70s. He'd be a senior citizen today."

"Your suspect is a senior citizen?"

"Some old men have lead in their pencil, don't they?" Zing!

Delia rested her chin in her hand and regarded the spread. Her lips wrinkled in distaste.

"I don't know this person. I wouldn't let him get within a hundred yards. His eyes are fishy."

"Fishy? Fishy how?"

Her hesitation lasted a millisecond longer than it should've.

"Cold, dead. Fishy." She dismissed the Oestryke pics and plucked the photo of herself, turning it side to side. "My affair with Harry lasted for eighteen blissful months. An Olympic record for me. This one is from last autumn at the cabin. A lovely honeymoon minus the bureaucratic entanglements. We were on the rocks when he died. I regret the quarreling, most of it my fault."

She got under my skin; I adopted a bland expression to compensate.

"Ever meet Ray Anderson? He and Harry were tight. Anderson got bumped on a previous episode. Smart money says the same person did them both."

"Ray?" she said. "Yes. I fucked him."

"Say what?"

"Are you a prude? We had a lost weekend. Nothing memorable or extraordinary."

"Lady, you slept with two men who were later murdered. We have varying definitions of *extraordinary*."

"Worrying is your department. My assessment is that Ray was another borderline criminal. Birds of a feather, and so forth. I don't find it a tremendous surprise he and Harry might've shared a similar fate."

Her reasoning wasn't implausible. She'd consorted with a group of criminals who lived under the shadow of trouble.

"Ray Anderson stepped way across the border. What can you tell me about him?"

"We slept together. I didn't take notes, sorry. I admit, the fling had an unforeseeable effect. The experience was an awakening. It caused me to entertain vivid fantasies of older men. *Sexier* older men, that is. Under the surface, Ray was tapioca. Satisfied my curiosity and never looked back. I don't want to discuss it further."

"Fine. Next item. Considering your tremendous resources, you must have hired someone to investigate Harry's murder. Any word?"

"I *haven't* retained a detective," she said. "It's unnecessary. Curious you should ask, however. Father assigned personnel to the case. We have access to excellent security services."

I gestured toward the guards.

"Daddy's worried for his princess?"

"Black Dog is cheaper than a ransom, dear."

"Father knows best, sometimes. You decided to help me. Before we get to how, I have to ask why. Is Lionel that persuasive?"

She laughed, lovely and sensual and unaffected. My collar tightened.

"Your *girlfriend* certainly has a silver tongue."

I'd related the bare bones of the investigation to Meg—a sketch of Oestryke and his alter ego, the Croatoan, carefully omitting the gruesome details. Meg wasn't squeamish. She *did* worry.

"Wonderful," I said.

"Totally serious. Meg is terrific. A wise man holds on to a woman like her."

"I endeavor to do the smart thing occasionally. Tell me about this cabin you mentioned. Is Jonathan Labrador a hunter? A Catskills bolt-hole for a New York industrialist seems fitting."

"Father owns a rare-gun collection. Swords, battle-axes, and bows. The butler is the only person who ever touches the displays. Pathetic as it feels to acknowledge this, the only thing Father shoots are clay pigeons. He's no hunter. Wouldn't stay in a cabin in the filthy woods for love or money. None of the contemporary Labrador men are comfortable in the outdoors. The tradition died with Grandfather. My father was the baby. He focused on expanding the family business while his brothers reveled in the princely lifestyle."

I nodded compassionately without feeling any.

"Line up portraits of successive generations of nobility and the foreheads bulge and the chins recede and nobody wants to play Cowboys and Indians or slaughter hapless woodland critters for kicks. Tragic. Whose cabin is it?"

"Harry's."

"Oh?" None of my research had turned up deeds to property in Harold Lee's name.

Delia quickly solved this particular mystery.

"Allow me to rephrase. It belongs to a friend of Harry's. He didn't say who. North of here, on a lake near West Kill. Are you familiar with the area?"

"I'm familiar with the idea of maps and finding things on them."

"Presumably, you're visiting his old stomping grounds, chatting up his loved ones and miscellaneous relations. Wouldn't you appreciate a look at his private getaway? Do your bloodhound routine?"

"On the button, Ms. Labrador," I said. There might be evidence at the location. Photographs, papers, and who knew what else. "Did you mention the cabin to your father?" I hated the idea that somebody might search the place before I had the chance.

"I do believe it slipped my mind."

"Point me the way and I'll be out of your hair forever."

"Agreeable notion, yet highly doubtful. You're a professional nuisance."

"Thanks, lady. I don't expect you to lead me by the hand into the sticks. Could get your sandals muddy. An address will suffice."

"You've pumped me for information and now you're done. News flash—I'm not done with you. I take after Grandfather—I'm the adventurous one in the family. Plan on Friday. We'll make a holiday of it, muddy sandals and whatnot. You, Lionel, and me."

"We?" The best I could manage.

"More enthusiasm, Mr. Coleridge. Wheee!"

She picked up the tab, so there was that.

CHAPTER TWENTY-SEVEN

The excursion to Harold Lee's country bolt-hole entailed agency housekeeping on my part. Thursday, I configured the schedule to accommodate my impending absence. I rang Chuck Bachelor and gave him the rundown of the previous evening's fireworks and how Aubrey P had disowned us.

Chuck said he'd try to smooth her ruffled feathers. We concurred that after the dustup at her house, and the subsequent increased police patrols, the Trasks were likely to maintain a low profile, at least temporarily.

"The lady's shaken up," I said. "With good reason. So, don't antagonize her. Lay back and continue surveillance of the salon. Cruise past her house randomly—that should be enough coverage for the moment. I'll catch you Monday morning."

That left a hole in my afternoon.

I picked up Devlin around lunchtime at school and took him on a field trip to the Wild Acres Animal Sanctuary in High Falls. I'm not fond of zoos—animals should inhabit the wild, fighting—root, hog, or die—not exist in a cage for the pleasure of slack-jawed looky-loos.

Thankfully, Wild Acres wasn't a zoo, but rather a preserve. Its owners leveraged grant money and private donations to carve a series of rambling enclosures among heavy timber. The fence line wound into the hills, which afforded the sanctuary's population of large predators miles of territory to roam.

The sanctuary housed black bears, golden eagles, foxes, raccoons, coyotes, and a pack of gray wolves. Staff trolled pathways on electric golf carts. Animals and guests were monitored by discreetly placed cameras.

A guide, dressed in drab olive-and-brown khakis with WAAS stitched on a badge over her heart, led our group of twenty on a walking tour. She recited the natural history of the region, and the history of the sanctuary and its denizens, in detail. I watched Devlin's face light up when he glimpsed the foxes and raccoons. Farther in, we crossed a small bridge. Three wolves separated from the underbrush and trotted parallel with the fence, pacing us. The guide called a halt and invited guests to take photos.

"Whoa!" Devlin said in a tone of hushed awe. He wore a denim jacket and sneakers. He snapped pictures with one of the disposable cameras I'd brought. "Do you like wolves, Isaiah? Have you seen lots of them? I love them!" These questions were on an infinite loop since I'd asked him about visiting the sanctuary earlier in the week.

"I've met a few in my wanderings," I said.

"Scary, like these?" he said.

"Oh, yes. Grays are common in Alaska. But I once saw a pack of black wolves rip the guts out of a bull moose."

"Black wolves!"

"Black wolves. The pack hunted that moose for days. They cornered him near a river, and then—"

"They ripped his guts out!" Devlin bounced in place, smacking his lips.

"Ripped 'em right out."

Parents tend to be overprotective of their offspring, worried the sensitive dears will blow over at the first breeze. Children are monsters. You could persuade most of them to chew moose guts too. That said, I didn't mention the biologist who was eaten by wolves near Coldfoot.

Made me reflect upon the father figures who'd influenced me—my Māori grandfather, Hone; my father, Mervin; Mr. Apollo, don of Anchorage; and Gene K. A troupe of crusty, malevolent old sonsofbitches.

Gene K mused on children with less contempt and keener insight than I might have assumed for a confirmed bachelor. We'd discussed nature versus nurture as it applied to a career of violence. Gene K had strongly believed in both qualities.

You don't teach a child to become a killer by rote lectures related to physics—trajectory, velocity, impact, penetration— nor by morality, nor ethics, nor correlation. To create a predatory machine, you foster an appreciation of the natural world and our minuteness upon its canvas. You create an association between scents of gun oil and blood with pleasure. The sound of a breaking bone is pleasurable. The grip of a knife hilt is pleasurable. The taste of cold steel is pleasurable. You begin by altering his or her view—first of their self, and later the world. We are as nothing and that permits us to do anything.

A horrifying and objectifying philosophy, no argument. I'd heard as bad or worse. Dad claimed my peculiar intuition originated with my mother, Tepora, and her New Zealand kin. He asserted that my appetite for violence was an inherited trait, genetic memory passed down through generations of savages. Yeah, he referred to Mom and her people as savages. Coming from him, that passed for a compliment. No acknowledgment of his own Saxon tribal ancestry, of course.

"Can I have a wolf?" Devlin said. The tour had ended with pamphlets, buttons, and programmatic requests for donations. We were walking to the truck.

"For a pet?"

"Yeah!"

"What about Minerva? She loves to play."

"But Minerva's not a wolf. She's a dog. She's a canine. Wolves are lupine."

"Who taught you the difference between canine and lupine?"

"Mom did. I wanna wolf puppy."

"You can't have a wolf puppy."

"Why?"

"What would your mother say? I'll give you three guesses, and the first two don't count."

"She'd say no!"

"Sorry, big guy."

He tucked his chin into his chest. I visualized a tiny thundercloud forming overhead. He made a sly, dark expression kids do to remind you that a chunk of their brain isn't fully developed. The chunk that contains germinating seeds of morality and compassion.

"You're bigger than Mommy. You could make her."

Talk about the very definition of an uncomfortable pause. Several rhetorical tactics presented themselves. None seemed adequate to the task. Devlin had knocked most of the wind out of me. I helped him into the booster seat and stalled some more adjusting the straps. I allowed the swelling silence to indicate my disapproval; let that disapproval gain solidity and weight. Yes, I decided to intimidate a little kid.

Finally, I locked eyes with him.

"Nobody, but nobody, makes your mother do anything. Got it?"

His lip trembled as he nodded.

"Good." I wanted to tell him that a real man didn't bully women, but I couldn't muster the hypocrisy. "When you get older, you'll have to make choices. Do you understand? You'll have to decide if you're going to push people around, if you're going to hurt them to get what you want. You decide to push, you decide to hurt? The world reacts. It will push back and it will hurt you." I waited to see if he grasped any of it, and damned if I could tell.

Devlin remained stoic on the way home. Arms crossed and rigid. Once I parked and got him free of the booster, he ran up the walk to his front door. He hugged Meg around the waist and excitedly related the earth-shattering events of our trip to the Wild Acres Animal Sanctuary. Storm clouds had retreated for the moment.

I leaned against my truck, sweating, nerves in tatters. Was this what real-deal fathers experienced on a routine basis—the sense of being giant walking assholes? Probably the decent ones. A small and inhumane sliver of my mind acknowledged an instant of pure empathy with Mac, who'd fled the whole scene for the safety of a perilous, backbreaking job in an underdeveloped Central American nation administered by a tin-pot dictatorship. Less stressful.

That made me feel worse. Maybe what my soul required was to go break something or wade into a fight. The beneficial side effects of the most recent brawl were already dissipating.

CHAPTER TWENTY-EIGHT

Manual labor is allegedly good for the soul. Meg handed me a rake and pointed at the yard. Conveniently for *my* no-good soul, there were plenty of leaves. As a reward, she ordered Chinese from a joint in Rosendale. After chivvying Devlin to bed, Meg and I stood on her porch and watched the neighborhood lights.

"I have a craving for a cigarette," she said. She'd smoked in college, and for a long while after. She quit the day she went to the clinic and learned that the rabbit died. The occasional toke was her concession to wilder, carefree days. It wasn't the same. "I think my nerves are fried. Dev's school performed an active-shooter drill today. Teachers direct the children where to hide if a 'bad person' enters the school. They try not to scare them, but how can the kids not be afraid? The world we live in. You know?"

I said that I did, and thought, *Hadn't it always been a tough row to hoe?* Ask the Christians in the Colosseum; ask the Australian indigenous tribes, the Aztecs, the Native Americans, African Americans, or a few million Jews. Ask the ones who weren't around to ask and they'd say there's never been a necessity for perdition when we have this existence.

Melancholy gripped her. Curse of the sensitive mind. Not a curse I suffered, although I empathized. Each of us has his or her own brand of Kryptonite.

"I don't want to feel guilty for bringing Dev into it, but I do, on some level. It's a nagging sensation. A minor toothache that doesn't let up. You ever feel the same? How do you cope?"

"Violence," I said.

My daddy hurt me. Your daddy hurt you. Now we hurt people because it feels good. Because it quenches our anger. Gene's words, echoing across the void, or my mind, at least.

"A writer came into the library last week for a reading. Small event; she used to be a best seller in true crime. Been a while; maybe fifteen regular patrons and a handful of the author's friends."

I asked who and whistled when she told me the writer's name.

Meg leaned on the rail, partially turned in my direction.

"She said something that caught my attention—serial killings peaked in the 1980s and '90s. The killers were so popular they had trading cards. I vaguely remember how scandalized the media was when the cards appeared. Over the last couple of decades, that popularity has waned. Those types of killings are less common. Her theory is . . . Well, care to guess?"

"Oklahoma City," I said. "Columbine. The Twin Towers. Virginia Tech. Crime, a broad spectrum of crime, is a response to the state of the world. What's happening and what's coming down the pike. Slashers ceded to shock and awe, and to mass murder."

"Yes, that's essentially what the author said. Evil mutates. Vestigial tendrils bury themselves deep while the main body adapts to a new environment."

"The traditional killers are still doing their thing. With less press coverage."

"Tough to compete with bombs and assault rifles. Society has become numb to terror. She described dreadful possibilities and I couldn't shake the chill. My child already faces an entirely new continuum of danger. An unprecedented threat . . . The writer described the latest breed of psychopaths as being akin to an antibiotic-resistant strain of virus. A bunch of people will die before we discover a cure."

I hugged her. The scalpel of grim epiphany sliced into my consciousness. I held my breath and waited for her to regard me in the fuzzy dimness and say, *You're so much like them, Isaiah. The serial killers. You carry the virus and you need to leave me and my son before it's too late.* She spoke in my dad's voice at the end.

Meg didn't say it, though. She pushed her forehead into my chest. Her breath was warm.

"That's why I contacted Delia Labrador and explained how the man you're hunting is probably a butcher of women. A Ted Bundy, a Richard Speck, a monster among monsters."

"Whatever you said made an impression."

"This is the Reba Walker tragedy all over again. Reba was a black girl with a past and nobody but her family cared about her. These women . . . Nobody gives a damn about hitchhikers or prostitutes on the highway. Go get the creep."

Replaying the afternoon with Devlin and absorbing secondhand what Meg endured on a daily basis, contemplating her anxiety and exhaustion, I acknowledged she was diamond hard compared to me and my relatively soft life.

After a while, we retired indoors for cups of cocoa laced with brandy. She looked in on Devlin and returned to the living room in a brighter mood. Moms possess that ineffable power; the ability to set aside grief and misery, to stabilize and set anchor against the vicissitudes of mortal existence.

"Much as I applaud the mission—and I do—you *are* gallivanting into the Catskills with the hottest babe in New York." She said this, half teasing, half not. "I've only myself to blame."

"Second hottest." I put my arms around her and squeezed. "She and Lionel are gallivanting, and probably worse. I'm the driver."

"Second hottest?"

"Distant second. Eating dust."

"What a woman wants to hear. We should go get you out of those pants."

"What a man wants to hear."

NIGHTMARES ROUSTED ME AT 3:30 A.M.

I was a boy again, and naked and injured. Wolves stalked me in the forest and among the ruins of large, elaborate buildings. The buildings were familiar; lodges and hotels rotting to their foundations. A park ranger in a tattered, blood-stained uniform joined the wolves. We raced through the ruins and across a meadow strung with loops of barbed wire and rusted mesh fencing. These were the wolves of the Wild Acres Animal Sanctuary, except in their red-eyed nightmare incarnation. The park ranger drew close, eating the gap between us with terrible strides. He wore a stocking mask that grotesquely twisted his features out of joint. He raised his knife and I woke.

Minerva crawled into bed as I rose. She stretched into the warm depression I'd left. I limped into Meg's kitchen and made a ham sandwich and poured a glass of milk. My reflection blurred in the window as I unsnapped a briefcase containing file folders and hunched over a ream of notes the accountant had compiled. It wasn't me for a second or two; instead, an ancient iteration of myself, wrapped in rancid pelts, squatted in a dimly lit cave, savaging deer entrails. The atavistic me glared in fear.

Sanctuary. Preserve. Refuge. I highlighted these words among the documents. *Valero Technologies. Rowden Refrigeration. Anvil Mountain Refuge. Morris Oestryke.*

Interesting words. Potentially crucial words. How a wildlife refuge fit into the greater web of intrigue remained to be seen; but there it was in ten-point type.

Scanning methodically, I selected another pair of words that tied these disparate elements together, yet left the core mystery unresolved.

Zircon Corporation. Threads linked the corporation to each important designation on my list.

Either the universe continued to expand every day or earth and its flea circus shrank further into minuteness.

CHAPTER TWENTY-NINE

Since learning that Morris Oestryke might be the culprit behind a heap of misery, I'd sent feelers into the criminal underworld, searching for intelligence on his Croatoan alias, actionable or otherwise.

The fact that Marion Curtis swore to snuffing Oestryke added a wrinkle without altering the basic premise of my investigation. Accepting Curtis at face value meant someone sympathetic to the Croatoan was at large. The only way I'd get any closer to solving the problem would be to learn everything possible about Oestryke's circle—which mainly included wiseguys and wiseguy wannabes.

I clutched at any straw, precisely as Lionel had intimated in his sardonic fashion. Rumors, hearsay, tall tales—I prepared to entertain, and evaluate, whatever far-fetched crap came down the pike. Similar to panning for gold; a man has to sort through a lot of sand to find the merest glint of color.

It's not as if we have a club, Hitmen "R" Us. Technically, I remained persona non grata with the Outfit. But there were a couple of guys from my Outfit days who'd risk talking to me. I phoned an independent contractor in Chicago; a former colleague. I asked what he remembered about the Croatoan, or if he could pretty please steer me in the right direction. The guy in Chicago knew zilch; however, he promised to broach the subject with his northeastern associates who might be better placed.

That's how I got in touch with the only person who'd talk to me—a hitter who'd worked up north in Buffalo and owed my Chicago associate the courtesy. Mr. Buffalo also knew Curtis and Curtis's word counted for plenty. Buffalo reached out on Friday morning. His ID and location were masked. We exchanged passwords provided by our mutual friend in Chicago. The hitter quizzed me about Curtis to satisfy any lingering misgivings.

The anecdote he relayed didn't assuage my mounting sense of worry and misgivings.

"I ain't in the life no more." Mr. Buffalo's voice crackled and distorted. I got the impression he'd called from a windy beach. "Coleridge, I heard of you. MC vouches for you, you're okay by me. You know Gene K? Gene moved to Alaska. Maybe you met him? Fuck Alaska. Too cold for my bones. I retired and put Buffalo in the rearview. Froze my nuts every winter. Maybe worse than Alaska, I can't say. Did you run across Gene K up there? Hell of a guy. The absolute best. Shoot your fuckin' eye out at a hundred paces, no problem. Shoot your eye right fuckin' out."

I explained that by some miracle I retained both eyes. Could he relay any firsthand knowledge about the Croatoan or his methods?

"Oh, I saw him around at parties in . . . Fuck, Reagan was president. Parties and the clubs. Went by Donnie Duster. Donnie Duster. What's that? Advertising you're a cleaner? Fuckin' porn handle, or what? The guys got a laugh outta that. Congenial fella, although he didn't really mix, kinda kept to himself. You couldn't get him talking. He didn't do too many jobs for the Outfit. His territory was farther south in Albany, and Philly and Pittsburgh. He contracted with the Five Families and their friends. Everybody knew he was a serious dude. We didn't know how serious. He wasn't the Croatoan then; he was just Donnie D.

"I got a personal glimpse into his dark side on account of a coke deal that went wrong. Superfucking cluster-fuck, lemme tell you. Three weeks after the deal, every-thing supposedly died down. I was at a card game with some of those guys who'd fucked the deal so bad. I stepped out to grab some booze and when I came back they were all dead, with their brains and their guts splat-tered every-fucking-where in that apartment. Okay, all except two guys who'd actually run the coke deal. Those two were on their knees, pleading for mercy.

"One of the capos and Donnie Duster stood over them, having a discussion about who was gonna live and who was gonna get whacked. Donnie D was, like, 'This one?' and the capo said, 'Yeah,' and Donnie sliced the guy's throat with a knife, and the other guy got it in the neck too. I'll never forget Donnie staring at me while I'm in the doorway, holding a half rack of suds in one hand and my pecker in the other. He says, 'Him?' and the capo shook his head and says, 'Nah, he's okay,' and I set the beer on the table and fucked right off. The cocksucker iced a roomful of seven or eight armed men, and he didn't have no whites in his eyes. Weren't regular fuckin' eyes. Just a couple pieces of black ice stuck in the sockets.

"Last thing I saw was Donnie D in a leather coat and leather pants and a big hunting knife in his hand and somehow not a fuckin' speck a blood on him. He set the knife down and pulled a nylon stocking outta his pocket. He was sliding that stocking over his head as I beat feet. Got to ask myself, who the fuck puts on a fucking mask *after* they've whacked everybody?"

I agreed it was an excellent question.

"You are welcome, fella," Buffalo said. "You've got no worries. The Croatoan ain't around. He's dead. Surely dead, or dying like the rest of us. And I gotta go to the whorehouse because it is high time for me to get my pecker wet. Have a day." He hung up.

DELIA LABRADOR couldn't escape the family mansion in Rhinebeck until midafternoon. We planned to rendezvous at a Kingston art gallery, where she had pressing last-minute business, and proceed from there. Delia instructed me to pull into the alley at 4:30 p.m. precisely. I did and she ducked out of the service door and into the car. She giggled, and that's when I realized her ubiquitous body-guards had been thoroughly ditched.

"Those oafs would be a real anchor on our fun." She snapped a selfie. "I'll text Father that I've run away for the weekend. Otherwise, he'll inform the National Guard I'm being held for ransom."

Lionel entrusted me with the keys to the Monte Carlo. He and Delia snuggled in the backseat, smitten as a pair of teenagers. Periodically, one of them momentarily surfaced to criticize my driving. It was great.

I am a believer in karma. Obviously, I had a truckload to work off.

Our destination lay an hour northwest of Kingston. One of Harold Lee's brochures expounded upon the virtues of West Kill Lodge and its magnificent environs, which encompassed thousands of acres of game trails, winding streams, and timber.

Delia had insisted that we spend the night at the lodge and venture into the boonies at first light, or at least by brunch. Since deer hunting season was under way, I said there'd be no room at the inn. Lodges typically book to capacity months in advance. She'd vowed her Palladium Visa would find a way. Ten minutes later, she secured a bungalow for Lionel and herself and a woodshed for me.

I'd churned Lee's history with the West Kill Lodge.

Lee's papers provided passwords to his online bank account. The account languished at four hundred bucks and had seldom contained more than fifteen hundred. Scrolling back in time, I ascertained that he'd patronized the lodge regularly for a decade. He never rented a room or purchased any of the guided packages. Just dinners and bar tabs exclusively. No need for a pricey room if he had a place to bunk nearby.

Lionel extricated himself from Delia's embrace, popped

the top on his second or maybe third beer, and cursed as it foamed over. He chugged, inhaled, and gulped the rest.

"Anybody from your death board kick it near this lodge?" he said.

"No confirmed murders."

"How many *unconfirmed* murders?"

"Three disappearances in 2006 and 2008. College girls. A couple and a lone hiker. The cops don't have them listed in the tri-state murders profile. I'm more suspicious."

"Game wardens and forest rangers are realists," he said.

"The purported innate pragmatism of forestry experts seems to be at odds with the inherent romanticism of capering around the great outdoors and insisting it's a career."

"Scoff all you like. They know from bitter experience that idiot greenhorns wander into the woods and disappear without help from serial killers. Plus, there's a shit-load of wilderness to be searched. Ain't nobody got time for that."

"'Ain't nobody got time for that,'" I said under my breath.

Lionel toasted me and had another slug of beer.

I met Delia's eyes in the rearview.

"Not to stick my oar in, or anything—"

"Preamble to your butting in," she said, freshening her lipstick. She'd dressed in an eye-popping designer T-shirt and fashionably torn jeans.

My intuition forecast this weekend would feature more costume changes than a Broadway musical.

"Yes to butting in. Isn't he kind of young for you? Aren't you happier if they've got one foot in the grave?"

"He's broken down," she said.

"This Marine is fully functional," Lionel said. He sounded borderline sober and on the road to drunk.

"Got a mint tin chock-full of Viagra," she said.

"When I say 'fully functional,' I promise you—"

"Dudes *always* say one thing."

"Ms. Labrador is a Girl Scout," I said to Lionel.

"*Be prepared* is a great motto," he said. "Don't say it like it's a bad thing. It's good."

"That's the Boy Scout motto," she said. "I adhere to the Girl Scout Law, which I've rewritten as *To thine own self be true; do unto others as they do unto you*, in honor of Anton LaVey . . . How's your heart? Will it tolerate heavy stimulants?"

"Lionel, you're gonna die," I said. "Mind if I keep the car?"

CHAPTER THIRTY

Greene County is lonely. Flat in the north and east; thickly forested and mountainous to the south and west.

Two miles of winding lane off the main road, the lodge occupied a low hill. The lodge and a collection of smaller wooden structures overlooked a dinky lake. Not the lake I'd come to see. Pretty, though; slashed purple and red by the falling sun. Fields of brown grass marched into the foothills south of the lake. Evergreens and cottonwood demarcated mountain slopes.

Combines rustic charm with modern convenience was how my former client the realtor would've pitched West Kill Lodge. Huge bay windows aglow with soft interior light; logs planed on two sides and buffed and stained for that distinctive faux-Colonial appearance; a clay-shingle roof; and a gravel courtyard. Sparrows flitted around the cedar hedges. I counted twenty vehicles in the adjoining lot. My fears were unfounded—the inn wasn't completely full; three-quarters capacity, perhaps.

When the front doors swung wide, warmth and the scent of baked sourdough wafted forth.

The lobby ceiling rose to a peak buttressed by timber joists. Deer-antler chandeliers hung from the center beam. Dead animal heads adorned the walls. Bearskins spread before the hearth. The furniture was wooden and heavy. Underfoot, a muted diamond pattern in slate was broken by throw rugs.

Delia checked our party in with an unaffected breeziness. The staff responded warmly and sincerely. She'd brought a valise and her purse. For a snooty heiress, the woman conducted herself with flawless grace when circumstances demanded. I reminded myself that it's best not to underestimate a beautiful person of incalculable means who doesn't mind chatting with the plebs. Such an individual represents a triple threat.

She and Lionel clasped hands and vamoosed to their bungalow. I was shown to a "cozy" room at the rear of the longhouse—a single bed, sink, and closet. The closet door jammed into the bed if I swung it all the way open. One of the ubiquitous hedges crowded outside the window and blocked it completely.

"Fantastic," I said to my favorite duffel bag.

Nobody had batted an eyelash when I waltzed into the lobby carrying the Mossberg in its soft case. The odds of using the shotgun were low to nonexistent. It seldom hurt to blend in. The people here fully expected the clientele to mosey to and fro armed for bear.

I secured my weapons in a cabinet, except for a jawbone hunting knife, which hung from my belt, concealed by the tail of my untucked shirt. The legal-sized briefcase containing the investigation notes went into the closet. Bedtime reading, albeit largely moot. Delia and her father, going forward, were the keys to the mystery. My challenge was the best method to pry this information free.

I detest hunting lodges almost as much as I hate zoos; encircled by trophies to the vilest form of narcissism, with strutting creeps whose weaponry couldn't scream overcompensation any louder. A man kills a wild animal by necessity—food, fur, or self-defense. A man does not hunt an animal for the joy, nor to acquire a trophy, nor to demonstrate his dominance. The latter breed of *Homo sapiens* is almost invariably a coward and a boor. It sorely tests my fortitude to abide either.

SUPPER HAD BEGUN in the dining hall. More scents of warm bread; also stew and roasted chicken. A wolf's head over the entrance stopped me cold; a bolt of déjà vu—the black wolf's glassy yellow eyes fixed upon my own.

I trembled as a wormhole dilated, connecting this moment to the foggy past. I instantly recalled the wolf's snarling countenance from the Alaska roadhouse Gene K and I visited. This might have been the selfsame beast, inhabited by an identical savagery that neither time, nor death, nor taxidermy could exorcise. Beneath its ever-shifting surface, beneath its changeable moods, dark-hearted nature is implacable and unforgiving.

In a gesture of bravado, I cocked my thumb and forefinger at the wolf before retreating to gather my composure. The recent nightmares and my compulsion to divine specific patterns within the greater mystery was a sign of delusion, or my intuition kicking in hard. Invariably, left to its own devices, my subconscious will detect the murky fin of doom cutting through the water. I'm stubborn, not stupid. A man ignores his instincts at his own peril. Currently, those instincts counseled me to stay alert to sudden danger, and, more important, to be patient.

Patience comes at a premium for a man of my temperament, and I've shed much blood and many tears along the path to enlightenment. Patience contributes to a fighting man's longevity with a reliability that few other qualities will. Sun Tzu's venerable quote about waiting beside the river long enough for one's enemies to float past is one of my golden rules. There are related applications. Insomuch as I regarded Delia Labrador as a vital lead, my gritted teeth and foot-dragging already paid dividends compared to the time-honored Mafia foot soldier tradition of running around with one's hair on fire.

Up to this juncture in the Croatoan investigation, I'd proceeded systematically, favoring incremental steps. I determined to tread lightly until my enemies appeared and their machinations were revealed. Or until somebody pushed back. Another golden rule in the *Coleridge Survival Manual*—I assume the default existence of enemies. My very existence is liable to run at cross-purposes to someone, somewhere, sooner or later.

Several guests lounged near the parlor hearth; another handful played poker at a card table. I find it expedient to categorize such groups. These people didn't fit into a niche, besides the incidental detail they fetishized the great outdoors and expensive weaponry. This was a higher-end resort, although hardly exclusive, which guaranteed rich assholes would bump elbows with blue-collar assholes. Some dressed the part in plaids and big boots; some dressed for a ski lodge vacation in cardigans and turtlenecks. Whatever their class differences, these boys pretending to be grown men bonded garrulously over booze, cards, and machismo.

Arguably, it was hypocritical to harshly judge insurance salesmen, middle-management office drones, machinists, off-duty soldiers, and small-business owners playing Daniel Boone for the weekend. Had I too not come to hunt? They were merely men—I was a wolf. It takes one to hunt one. Wolves were my spirit guides of the moment. Lone wolf, specifically. Yes, lone-wolf behavior was the key.

The bar slotted against the wall; a shiny oak countertop and stools designed to approximate hewn stumps. Slim pickings in regard to the variety of liquor in stock, although it featured an acceptable selection of bourbon.

The man behind the counter had twenty-five pounds on me, and about as many years. His uniform was a blue wool shirt and corduroy pants. He poured me a tall glass of Booker's. His knobby hands bespoke a lifetime of setting chokers and swinging an ax. I asked if he'd happened to lop a few heads in his day, because every well-preserved senior tripped my radar, so why not inquire? The bartender scowled as he turned his back on me. Too burly, too tall, to match Oestryke's profile.

The Croatoan would be average height and not so broad of shoulder. I chided myself—as if we'd bump into each other by random chance in the Catskills.

A pine post bracketed the terminus of the bar. Maps and postcards decorated the post. Visitors had carved their initials and dates into the stained wood. I scrutinized a framed map of the immediate region—West Kill Mountain and the Devil's Path caught my eye. I made a note.

Presently, Lionel and Delia appeared. Smug, flushed, and hastily put-together. Still holding hands with the covetous fierceness of new lovers. They fetched me to join them for supper, and this time around I steeled myself and made it past Fenris, or the long-lost head of Cerberus, or whatever mythological monster guarded the entrance to the dining hall.

The meal was fine. I demolished a T-bone steak, bloody. My companions ordered salmon and picked at it while swapping moony glances. Once Lionel recovered from whatever ordeal he'd endured in the bungalow, he resumed hitting the booze. That loosened him up. My friend became jocular after three or four rounds, and, counting whatever he'd downed in the car, he was well past that stage.

He soon explained, in a booming voice, why his last relationship had deteriorated despite a promising start.

"It fell apart after she got a tattoo of her geriatric cat," he said. "The cat was okay; kinda decrepit, and had that funky smell ancient, half-dead cats get. He was practically ossified. Deaf, half-blind, toothless. Nice kitty anyhow. The chick's losing her mind over the cat's imminent demise and, *wham,* she does some ink to commemorate his life or some such shit. I mentioned that it distracted me when we were, uh, you know. She took offense. Majorly."

"Very insensitive, Sergeant Robard," Delia said. "Clearly, the woman was distraught. You couldn't overlook a little tattoo? Tolerate pussy for the sake of pussy?"

"I tried, man. Truly I did. The tat was enormous and lifelike. Goddamned Michelangelo didn't put any finer detail work into the Sistine Chapel. The ink covered her whole back like a yakuza body sleeve. She's up to a thousand career hits, easy." He shuddered. "I'm getting my freak on and trying not to make eye contact with Chairman Meow. Mission failed."

"Horribly traumatic, I'm sure." Delia stroked his shoulder and tilted her head to regard me. "You're remarkably quiet. Feeling neglected?" Before I could answer, she said in a confidential tone, "I am absolutely dying to know two things, Mr. Coleridge. How did you become a 'hitter'? And, what's your high score?"

Asking a professional how many people he's dusted is discourteous. On par with asking him to tell you the worst thing he's ever done. Contract killers have feelings. Fewer than most, but feelings nonetheless.

I smiled and imagined fitting her for concrete shoes.

"Men should do what they are designed to do. Dharma."

"A lion should be a lion, not a zebra," she said. "Such a cute way of justifying execrable behavior."

"There the first immortal spirits were at the beginning of time, sitting around in the golden haze, choosing their roles for the next few eons. I wanna be a god! I'll be a demiurge! A fox! An elephant! A sequoia! A shit-lobbing chimpanzee! A man! Et cetera. The ancestors of these individuals followed in the tracks of divinely in-spired provenance."

"Quaint," she said. "I don't get it."

"I gotta see a man about a horse." Lionel understood, but elected to avoid conflict. He heaved to his feet and walked unsteadily toward the men's room.

"Got to go powder my nose," I said to Delia and left her alone at the edge of the wilderness.

CHAPTER THIRTY-ONE

Lionel and I ventured behind the lodge and stood on the lawn where it began its slope toward the water. A lamp shone an eerie greenish glow over the dock. A couple of skiffs, an outboard motorboat, and a canoe bobbed in the murk.

"We may have been tailed," I said.

"You spot someone?"

"I would've given you the high sign. It's a feeling."

"Black Dog?"

"They'll be along presently. Different feeling."

He lit a cigarette.

"Has it occurred to you that solving this case isn't in your best interest? Finding the Croatoan might be unhealthy. Digging around in the mob basement . . . what if you turn something up everybody wishes you hadn't?"

"We'll all have a good laugh?"

The stars glittered with menace over the black slope of the mountains. I couldn't make out the Death Heads like Gene might've. An ill wind whipped the lake and caused me to shield my eyes against a sudden sting of twigs and dust. Gone in an instant. The chill remained.

"About Delia," I said.

"We're going to try tantric sex!" He licked his thumb and stroked his eyebrows. His movements were exaggerated and he almost missed his face.

"Nic Royal might give you some pointers in that department," I said.

"I'll try to handle it on my own."

"Keep your wits, amigo. I agreed to let her tag along on this trip—"

"Because she knows where the cabin is and we don't?"

I considered informing him that my research painted an increasingly strange picture of the Labrador family's peripheral involvement with the death of Harold Lee. Zircon Corporation had controlled Valero Technologies back in Deering, Michigan; equally curious, Zircon essentially owned, through a chain of subsidiaries, the Albany refrigeration company—Rowden Refrigeration—where Morris Oestryke worked during the 1980s.

Further, there was a privately funded expedition to Anvil Mountain in 1976, which resulted in a prime chunk of land getting designated a bat preserve. The preserve was administered by a nonprofit foundation related to Zircon Corporation and sanctioned by the Federal government. None other than Morris Oestryke had accompanied the original research expedition. This particular detail escaped the almighty redacting brush of the DoD by virtue of a typographical error. A clerk had inadvertently altered Oestryke to read "Ostrike."

I loved and hated it simultaneously. Progress was welcome. The bore of a rich family's cannon orienting on my person, less so. Why do the bad guys usually possess an abundance of power and wealth? I suppose the question answers itself.

The signs indicated that this investigation was approaching critical mass. My blood weighed heavily in my chest, and a clean, pale light burned through the clouds. How many of my collected facts amounted to mere coincidence? Coincidence happens and it doesn't necessarily portend weal or woe. That's my stance on the phenomenon. Contrariwise, Gene K had insisted that *coincidence* was a cowardly skeptic's word for *fate*.

Gene's cynicism felt undeniably apropos right then.

The cherry on top? Zircon also owned interest in a certain mercenary company that Lionel hated from personal experience. Black Dog operated in war-torn regions around the globe, skirting international law and human rights protocols with the adroitness of spy-thriller villains. The two bodyguards assigned to Delia were Black Dog agents, sent from the company's personal Security Solutions division. Lionel had done a brief tour with Black Dog and gotten a bitter taste of their extrajudicial routine. He departed under a cloud.

Weighing the history of bad blood between him and the organization, I estimated my friend was too drunk and too emotionally unstable to trust with that kind of news.

I opted to ruin his tomorrow instead of his tonight.

"She may have lied when I put Oestryke's photos in front of her. Said she didn't recognize him. Seemed nervous."

"Isaiah, you're suspicious of everyone—always. You might intimidate her. That mug of yours would make a grizzly nervous."

"Delia isn't afraid of men. Good, bad, or ugly."

"Are you supposed to be bad or ugly?"

"Men are her playthings. She's—how do I say this without giving offense?—the living embodiment of evil."

"A *femme fatale*? That's the phrase you were going for."

"A femme fatale. I fear you're in trouble."

"Sign me the hell up for a recurring subscription."

"Delia's the kind of woman who moons around with a shiner and, next thing you know, you're digging a hole for her husband. She's the kind who shoots you and smokes a cigarette after."

"You're projecting," he said.

"Do tell."

"How do *I* say this without giving offense? Your description fits Meg to a T. Miss Library has a hard-case-gone-straight wrapped around her finger. Tell me true—has your unsavory past gone from a curse to a blessing? Has she joked about hiring you to off the estranged hubby yet? Has she cried over the mounting bills, unpaid child support, and his wicked ways in general?"

I doubt he noticed I'd walked away until he turned and called for me. The slamming door muffled his voice.

MY ROOM SMELLED STRANGE. I didn't notice the odor until I'd stripped and rolled back the bedcovers. It lingered in my nostrils and clung to the roof of my mouth—a cloying whiff of decay, ripe as a hunk of green meat. I searched the room for dead mice or discarded material missed by the housekeeping sweep. By the time I'd finished, the odor had dissipated.

Another night, another dream. Gene stood at the foot of the bed, his face hidden in the shadows. My muscles were paralyzed and I couldn't open my mouth to call his name. His eyes were red pinpricks that brightened.

I loved it. Big-game hunting, except instead of hapless beasts, I'm filtering the dregs of humanity. You wondered if I liked my job subtracting assholes from the populace? I whistled on my way to the office. His voice was different, flatter, metallic.

Then I awakened. In daylight, nothing is ever as ominous as it seems in the dark. The dream latched onto me, though, and I reflected upon Gene and what he'd make of my case.

As my apprenticeship wound down that one winter in Alaska, he'd pinched my ear and sat me down for a tête-à-tête. He disliked my attitude and where it might lead. He professed a reluctant fondness for my health and general welfare.

He conducted a minor intervention.

Bellicose youth that I was, I seriously contemplated reaching for the knife at my belt. Gene K had whacked more people than I'd shaken hands with, so I reconsidered any impulsive movement and endured his rough manners. He was loaded, although coherent. His features were hard and dead as a totem, except for the deadly glint in his eyes.

He sipped from a bottle of single-malt and said unto me:

Isaiah, evil is a real force. Now, we don't get a free pass to commit our devilry—evil is an influence, a shadow that man gives form through supplication, veneration, and deeds. It's a partnership between the impermanent and the immortal.

Over the succeeding years, I've cut back on drinking and drugging. Gene's words still percolate. "Hoodoo nonsense," my dad would say. Nonsense? Anything that breaks off like an arrowhead and rattles around inside your brain . . . Well, skepticism hath its limits.

Long after the witching hour, I've lain awake, hand over my heart, measuring the intervals between beats, wondering how much blackness has oozed into the hollow spaces where a large portion of my conscience and morality should theoretically reside.

I testify that despite ongoing renovations, it's dark in there.

CHAPTER THIRTY-TWO

Breakfast proved interesting.

Lionel slouched, messy, stubbly, and unwashed, his presumably bloodshot eyes obscured behind amber-tinted aviator glasses. By contrast, Delia smirked and preened, fresh as Muhammad Ali and ready for the middle rounds. She missed no opportunity to ruffle his unkempt hair or touch his arm or hand with the familiarity of a longtime paramour.

I bemusedly drank coffee and watched the lovebirds interact. I couldn't recall many instances when I'd witnessed my comrade share breakfast with another human being this early in the morning. In the wake of his increasingly epic debaucheries, he preferred solitude until the agony subsided. The whiteness of his lips and clenched fists told me he wasn't ready for domestic bliss and might not be built for it in the first place.

Jekyll and Hyde, the Black Dog security detail Delia had left in the dust, walked in and threw a literal shadow over the already tense proceedings. Their customarily grim expressions were extra-sour. I fantasized they'd received a royal ass-chewing for allowing the heiress to give them the slip.

"Hello, boys." Delia briefly raised her hands with a droll smile. "You've found me."

These were attack dogs disguised by snappy clothes. Murder glinted in their eyes. I scooted my chair backward in order to free myself from the table if it became necessary to move with alacrity. I draped a cloth napkin over a steak knife and held it against my thigh.

Lionel gave me an exaggerated look of amazement.

"You're a goddamned prophet."

My well-honed paranoia had predicted the result. It didn't tell me how the duo accomplished the feat. I ticked the possibilities. Had they tailed us? Was Lionel's car bugged? Had a nefarious type slipped a tracking device into Delia's purse? Could it be that Mr. Jonathan Labrador ran a credit card check and pinged Delia's reservation? With Black Dog at one's disposal, extrajudicial remedies were on the menu. Or, someone tipped them to our location; perhaps inadvertently, perhaps not.

That's the solution the cynical half of my brain lent the most credence. I flashed back to Delia texting her father as we departed Kingston. Oh, yes, we were well into the game. The "fun" lay in apprehending its objective.

Another question nagged me—had anyone else sneaked into West Kill on our back trail?

The bodyguards escorted Delia to the veranda, where an animated discussion ensued. I crunched a piece of toast and studied Lionel. He removed a cigarette from its pack, frowned, and stuck it back into the pack and shoved the pack into his shirt pocket.

"Today is going to suck with passion," he said in a rusty voice. "I'm calling it right here, right now."

We weren't going to touch last night's argument with a ten-foot pole. Fine by me if it remained buried forever.

"Those dudes wear nice suits," I said. "Their ensembles exude authority. Handsome, but rugged. Ready for a tussle in the dirt and confident they'll look great. Slicker than that trash the Feds buy at fire sales, more utilitarian than mobster-wear."

"Sweet Jesus, why?"

"Psychology plays an important role. From the Nero haircuts to their snazzy wingtips, it's a uniform designed to address a spectrum of goals. Chiefly, intimidation."

"Allow me to repeat—why are you doing this? Someone, possibly a power slugger for the Mets, is pounding on my dome."

"You do realize those two lunks are Black Dog muscle?" I'd sat on the news for several days. No better time to break it to him than when he was in the throes of a skull-busting hangover. No *funnier* time.

His response defied my expectations of a *China Syndrome* meltdown.

"Old news. I sussed that out at the burlesque show."

"Oh," I said.

"Give me an ounce of credit, would you? I served with jokers like these two. Smell 'em from half a klick. Fuck 'em. I'm too tired; you fuck 'em."

"That's another thing," I said. "They smell great. Their aftershave is subtle and masculine. It makes getting put in a headlock almost worth the pain. It's impressive they maintain that professional aura since they must get worn to the bone traipsing after your girlfriend day and night."

"You're a terrible influence. Thanks to you, she refers to her nightshift detail as Humpty and Dumpty. I got a glimpse of those jokers. She's not lying. Black Dog standards of physical fitness aren't entirely uniform, to put not too fine a point on it."

"So, there is another item. I was going to suggest Black Dog unionize for improved working conditions."

"And the short haircuts you admire? Jekyll and Hyde are getting thin up top. Look how the morning sun reflects off their domes."

"I'll concede, a close haircut is the last refuge of the balding man. Want to know what bothers me most about Black Dog?"

"The raping or the murdering?"

"Dogs are ferocious, brave, and loyal," I said. "The best dogs are. This Outfit should call itself Black Curs."

"Can't argue."

"Black Dog began as something else. Zircon Security Solutions was the first iteration and its remit merely covered defense of corporate interests and personnel."

"Gonna be a chapter on merc companies when you publish your memoirs?" he said.

"In the 1980s, BD became larger and split off into a subsidiary. That sweet, sweet windfall of overseas terrorism, the Soviet occupation in Afghanistan, the endless conflicts in the Middle East and Africa. BD didn't really come into its own until around the time of Desert Storm, and blew it up—pardon the pun—during the Iraq War. No stopping them once we invaded Afghanistan. Ironically, agendas such as 'peacekeeping' and 'nation-building' gave those who lusted for war and chaos all the license they'd ever need to perpetrate crimes against humanity."

"Your dad consults with them, doesn't he?"

"Another reason we don't exchange Christmas cards."

Delia returned to us while her men-at-arms conferred on the veranda. She appeared radiantly unfazed.

"My, oh my, they are beside themselves. Father is displeased and, as is his custom, blaming them for his impending stroke. He's flying in from a trip to Switzerland. I can expect a phone-lashing soonest."

"I assume 'displeased' is an understatement," I said.

"Vesuvius erupting would be an understatement. Shall we get going before he sends a platoon of Marines?"

"Got all the Marine you need, honey," Lionel said.

She stroked his hand sympathetically.

CHAPTER THIRTY-THREE

Six miles along the secondary highway, then right onto an unmarked dirt lane hidden in the saddle of two steep hills. Jekyll and Hyde cruised in a black SUV. They tailgated me for a bit, then fell back when we made the turn, and I lost sight of them. Earlier, as we'd loaded into our separate vehicles, I had the distinct impression they would have happily shot Lionel and me, as they'd likely done unto defenseless citizens in Iraq where American law didn't reach.

Lionel went dark, as I termed this among his variable moods. Every move was deliberate; calmness notwithstanding, the set of his jaw and the fever in his gaze bespoke a profound depth of loathing. He smiled, yet his eyes could've nailed a man to the cross. I regarded him as my buddy, Lionel Robard. The reality? Getting on his wrong side wasn't a keen idea.

I inched the Monte Carlo forward as branches scraped its sweet paint job. The road hadn't been graded in years.

A hard rain would render it an impassible quagmire for anything less sturdy than a tank.

Twice, the road forked and Delia gestured left, then left again, and thus I steered. We stopped at a padlocked chain gate. I knelt and studied the ruts, hoping to ascertain approximately when the last vehicle had passed. Impossible. She unlocked the gate and on we went. Her possession of the key might be another subject to discuss presently.

Fifteen minutes and another fork, then I rounded a bend into a clearing. The "cabin" rested on a knoll. Over its shoulder and down, I glimpsed water shining through a notch in the dense stands of pine, cottonwood, and willow.

I'd anticipated a humble wooden shack or a homey log cabin. What awaited was a medium-sized Cubist house of metal and glass resting atop a foundation encased in rock slabs. The house ticked all the boxes of the weird, avant-garde constructivist homes dreamed up by eccentrics in the early twentieth century and further mutated during the psychedelic '60s. Vines climbed downspouts and metal trellises. Mold and moss and verdigris proclaimed this an oft-neglected structure. It withstood the worst elements thanks to the imperviousness of its base materials and not to the diligence of its owner.

We got out and surveyed the property. The rotting woodshed and generator shack were more traditional wooden outbuildings. Nothing special. I estimated someone hacked the encroaching bushes and weeds every few years, in a holding pattern. A worn path led to a narrow stretch of muddy beach and a ramshackle dock. The lake stretched for a half mile into pervasive mist. Sunlight flashed from the windows of other weekend cabins perched on a ridge directly across the water. Birds twittered in the woods all around us; our voices were the only other sounds.

Incongruously, the house and surrounding acreage reminded me of the furniture warehouse in Michigan. I whiffed an indefinable sense of wrongness. Abandoned slaughterhouses and asylums radiate a similar, palpable afterglow of malignance and death.

"Hey, Lionel," I said. "What do you suppose? Two or three acres, and the house, nets you a quarter of a mil? Half a mil?"

"Easy."

I went into the generator shack and examined the diesel rig bolted to a concrete footing. These beasts were built to survive nuclear winter; nonetheless, someone had maintained it properly, kept it greased and gleaming. I topped the fuel and oil and pushed the button. The engine chugged and power flowed.

"Hurray!" Lionel called down from the terrace entrance. "My beer will stay frosty."

"What's left of it," Delia said.

Jekyll and Hyde reversed their SUV in and parked beside our car. Jekyll wore an earpiece with a slender Bluetooth mic. He spoke into the mic—doubtless, contacting Papa Labrador. I noted the time and wondered how long before that platoon of Marines—or, given the circumstances, Black Dog mercs—arrived to retrieve Ms. Labrador. Lionel and I might even be the lucky recipients of a bonus ass-kicking, depending upon her old man's mood. Neither her descriptions nor the snippets of gossip I'd procured suggested superindustrialist Jonathan Labrador ever made the short ballot for the Nobel Peace Prize.

THE INTERIOR OF THE HOUSE enhanced the Russian-cum-1960s-mad-architect aesthetic. I counted two bedrooms, a bathroom, modest kitchen, living room, and a storage closet. More storage under the house and in an attic crawl space. Formica, iron railings, thick rugs, patterned sheetrock, and that general aesthetic, merged with unusual angles, Art Deco furniture, crystal lighting fixtures, and paintings torn from pulp science-fiction covers—bubble-helmeted astronauts strode across barren moonscapes in one series while dashing men armed with ray guns and buxom women clad in strategically torn uniforms fought horrible alien brutes in jungles and the calderas of active volcanoes. Prints of the Rat Pack were prominent in the hallway and bedrooms. Harold Lee's contribution to the décor.

Starker were numerous black-and-white photos of forbidding landscapes and animals. The animal scenes exclusively featured predators in action. Lion prides pursuing zebras amid dust clouds; charging brown bears; crocodiles preying upon wildebeests in a muddy river; and a great white shark breached, its jaws agape. The one that arrested my attention was of a huge golden eagle tearing the brains out of a young, starved wolf on the taiga. The photographer's signature devolved over the life of the sequence. From the earliest, I derived "X. M. Vance."

I took pics of each to add to my burgeoning album.

We'd come to the right place, the place we needed to be. In the back of my mind, a lizard stirred, a blood moon beamed through a scrim of black clouds, and a revolver cylinder rotated until a bullet lined up under the hammer, the hammer cocked. It gladdened the killer in me to feel the rightness of it, the inevitability of an onrushing mass of fur and claw. But it also terrified me every bit as much.

"Isn't it absolutely marvelous?" Delia performed an expert twirl with her arms outstretched. "You almost expect Andy Warhol and a bevy of his girls to waltz in wearing jumpsuits and crack a magnum of pink champagne to celebrate our arrival." She swept into the kitchen and rummaged in cupboards.

Lionel sidled close to me, scowling. He grabbed my elbow and guided me to one side.

"Warhol and dancing girls, my ass. Corpses dangling from meat hooks is more realistic," he said. "It doesn't feel like a house. A cave—"

"The lair of a man-eater," I said. "Round a corner and find a half-mad black bear lying on a mound of bones. It smells like somebody tried to bleach away bloodstains."

"A lair, yeah. The Croatoan was here?"

"It wasn't Kilroy. I'm of a mind this served as Oestryke's HQ after he did a French leave from the mob and took up stamp collecting and casual murder."

"What makes you certain?"

"The animal photos." I'd told Lionel about Denis Swenson's surprise visit to Morris Oestryke. "Swenson mentioned that he saw one similar to these hanging on the wall. When we cased Harry's place, there was a photograph of wolves in a forest. Be damned if it isn't the same photographer. This is the den of the beast."

"Because friends share interests?"

"Don't they? Lee and Anderson were thugs and outdoorsmen. Oestryke obviously liked that about them."

"Well." He took in our surroundings. "Expensive clubhouse."

"The sheer amount of dough Oestryke hauled in for those hits, he could've afforded this pad a dozen times over. Say he bought it way back when as a getaway from the wife and kids. It has to be registered under an alias. Later on, it would've made a terrific hideout and staging area. Sufficient quantities of fuel and supplies, a desperado could fortify here indefinitely. Secluded . . . the neighbors are usually absent. String victims in the storage room or the shed, and take your time. Who cares how much they scream; nobody will hear them. If I'm right—and I'm right—there might be a few nasty surprises on the property."

"We're on the same page, man. I've swept for obvious traps. Clean. Doesn't mean there aren't any, depending on the sophistication. The Croatoan isn't known for explosives, is he? Tell me he's not."

"No, but I'd watch for trip wires and pressure plates. I'm hoping that since Harry stayed here and didn't get blown to smithereens by a booby trap, there aren't any."

"You sound like a pair of conspirators." Delia hung her coat on a rack. "Do you tear this house apart next? I hope not. Perhaps a mild ransacking?"

"Lionel, the lady says we should ransack the joint."

"By all means, then. A gentleman never refuses a lady."

"Mild," she said. "A *mild* ransacking. What are we searching for? Property deeds? A bloody knife? A signed confession?"

"*We're* not searching for anything," Lionel said. "Brew a pot of coffee and plant your sweet ass on that recliner while the men sort out this business." He laughed at her dangerous frown and kissed her cheek. "But seriously, stay put and don't touch anything. There might be booby traps, and I love you just the way you are."

"You're joking." Her tone made it clear that a *smidgeon* of sexism is sexy. More than a pinch is plain old sexism.

"About you staying put or the possibility of traps? Neither."

Her smile flickered as she tried to decide if this had progressed from fun and games to something less wholesome. Discretion won the day. She flopped onto the chair and messed around with her cell phone.

"Won't be two shakes of a lamb's tail," he said.

"The scientists who developed the Manhattan Project were fond of that idiom." She didn't glance up from her phone. "Quite appropriate if you're worried about triggering high explosives. Life comes at you fast."

We tossed the house with brisk efficiency. I was aware of a ticking clock in the form of the Black Dog mercs. As was Lionel; he frequently peeked through the blinds to monitor their positions.

Soon, we made our way to the storage room, which lay at the bottom of a flight of stairs. I entertained the notion that Oestryke once used this room to torture and kill his prey. The faint residue of bleach and the haphazard arrangement of cheapo shelving were giveaways that they were props. He might have built a separate kill chamber elsewhere on the property. A serial killer wouldn't want to risk legitimate guests, such as Harold Lee, stumbling over half-dead victims. The weekend cabins on the other side of the lake were contemporary construction. That meant more weekenders, and more potential interlopers. A man needed complete privacy for a hobby this involved.

Left to my own devices, I would've flailed around and come away empty-handed. Lionel scanned the room for a few seconds and zeroed in on the trapdoor. His tours in Afghanistan had taught him the fine art of locating (and hiding) contraband. A section of tile flooring shone ever so slightly brighter than its surroundings. He sliced the linoleum apart with a box cutter and revealed an inset pull ring.

"Think it's wired?" I said.

He waggled his hand to signify a fifty-fifty chance.

I grunted and heaved until the hatch sprang open. We

weren't blown to smithereens. He clicked on a penlight and shone the beam into the hole.

The hidden crawl space was festooned with dust bunnies and spiderwebs. It hadn't seen light for three or four years. The crawl space proved to be a treasure trove—jammed into its confines were a foul, musty ghillie suit that Special Forces snipers were partial to; a stained nylon stocking; a set of skinning knives—serrated, hooked, and filleting models—and bone saws wrapped in a canvas tarp; and an Army ammo box stuffed with hand-drawn diagrams and heavily annotated maps of the greater Catskills region, plus four passports and multiple driver's licenses issued with Oestryke's photo, but with various aliases, the most recent of which was dated August 1985. I would've given a quart of blood to have seen a more recent headshot.

There were also two plastic sealable bins. The smaller bin contained several VCR tapes. The second bin was packed with bundles of weathered C-notes. Unexpectedly encountering so much cash—or coke, or diamonds—has a bracing effect on a man akin to getting slapped hard or socked in the gut.

We crouched in the storeroom, examining our evidence; speechless for a few moments as the implications sank in and took root. My thoughts spun wildly, pinging from exhilaration to worry and back again. Which direction should I jump? Any choice, such as keeping this find to myself, was freighted with unknowable pitfalls and consequences. Should I call in the cavalry? Bellow, or Curtis, or neither of them?

What of my own "sweet" dad? Mervin had parlayed his military intelligence service into post-retirement consultation with mysterious government entities. He was at least tangentially affiliated with Black Dog. Weighing these factors, I concluded I'd roast alive on a spit rather than beseech his aid.

If my admittedly vague theories regarding Oestryke's true identity were on the mark, then the presence of a Zircon heiress and her Black Dog retainers complicated the imminent peril by magnitudes. Matters of life and death are often more fluid, more volatile, than people understand.

I've long believed that human existence is a story tree, a branching series of decisions, large and small. The catch? You don't always recognize which is which from a distance. Life indeed comes at you like a train. Blow the wrong call and it's curtains, my friend.

"Oh, Harry Lee, you poor sad-sack bastard," Lionel said in a musing tone. "He screws over his hitman pal to repay a loan, co-opts the dead man's weekend shack, and, the whole time, he's sitting on a fortune."

I was thoroughly impressed Harry had managed to keep the existence of his home away from home a secret from Curtis and the rest of the Mafia. Harry had possessed his own version of protective coloring—bumbling, apologetic, heart-on-his-sleeve, aging thug with a pathetic fetish for out-of-date pop music and burlesque dancers. A man nobody took seriously until his murder caused a stir.

"This is the tip of the iceberg," I said, thinking back

to the conversation with Curtis wherein he'd reached the exact same conclusion. "There are millions out there, scattered across the state, moldering in caches and safe-deposit boxes rented under false identities."

Hyde leaned his oversized upper body into the entryway. He appraised the knives, ammo box, and our guilty demeanors. Fortunately, Lionel had covered the cash with the ghillie suit. Hyde ducked around the corner, his footsteps rapidly receding.

"Fuck me running," Lionel said. And that summed it up.

CHAPTER THIRTY-FOUR

We sealed the trapdoor with the flap of tile, dragged a shelf over it, and adjourned to the living room to plot our next move. The mercenaries were conferring with Delia. Tense scene. In retrospect, the strategic play would've been to jump them preemptively. A split-second opportunity that came and went. I poured a glass of water. Lionel cracked a beer. We men all stood around, feigning coolness.

Evidently, the Black Dogs tattled to their boss.

"Ms. Labrador, your father requests that you contact him immediately." Jekyll's gaze fixed on Lionel as he delivered the message in a marginally elevated tone. "*Immediately*, ma'am. Without delay."

Delia didn't sting the merc with a snappy retort or roll her eyes dramatically. She pressed her phone to her ear and stepped into the master bedroom and shut the door. *Immediately* was code for "Daddy means business," it seemed.

The mercs stood near Lionel where he'd settled into a funky iron-and-vinyl chair.

"Mr. Labrador has a message for you, Robard," Jekyll said. "He strongly feels it would be better for all concerned if you became scarce. Further, he advocates traveling light. You aren't walking out that door with anything you didn't bring here in your pockets."

"Scarce as hen's teeth?" Lionel said. "Honest car salesmen? Virgins on prom night?"

"You should've been in the wind thirty seconds before we knew you were gone. *That* scarce."

"Or?"

"Mr. Labrador anticipated your smart lip. Jarheads are notorious assholes. Nonetheless, he hopes you will accept his suggestion. Your continued presence may result in health complications. Personally, I'm fine if you refuse his advice."

"Aha! You're gonna fuck my shit up?"

Jekyll smiled broadly.

"Whatever you do, not in the face," Lionel said.

"For God's sake," Delia said to me. She'd returned at an opportune moment to gather the gist of the conversation. "Aren't you going to do something?"

"Yes. I'm going to watch Lionel get his ass beaten . . . Couldn't reach your dad?"

The glare she hit me with was loaded with shrapnel.

"Un-fucking-believable," she said. "My father is sending a helicopter for me. He wasn't in a talkative mood."

"Perhaps you could call off your dogs before you go," I said.

"Actually, we answer to Mr. Labrador," Jekyll said.

"Coleridge, as far as our boss is concerned, you're with Stupid here."

"'I am a pretty piece of flesh.'" Lionel had propped his Stetsons on the coffee table. He rested the bottle against his knee.

"*Romeo and Juliet*?" Jekyll unbuttoned his cuffs. "I was in the chorus in our senior-class performance." He rolled up one sleeve, then the other. A detailed tattoo of the Black Dog corporate logo scored his forearm.

"'I strike quickly, being moved.'"

The big men traded glances.

"All right, punk—"

Lionel became still.

"Say 'move.'"

Hyde reached into his jacket for what I knew to be a large handgun. That gesture escalated the confrontation from pedestrian trash talk to rocket velocity. It didn't exactly surprise me, given the nature of Black Dog thug culture, but it *did* narrow my options.

People were bound to die.

I say that with authority because I fully intended to ventilate both goons if they laid a finger on my friend. Coarse jokes and petty bickering aside, Lionel was more of a brother than any of my legal kin. Also, I hadn't capped anybody in a while. Sad to admit, it's something a man can grow to miss.

"Gentlemen and lady, this portion of our program is over," I said.

Jekyll noticed the revolver in my fist. He nudged his

partner. They faced me at an angle, hands raised to shoulder height. Hyde slid his left foot back an inch or two, attempting to separate from Jekyll. I nixed that with a slight motion of the gun barrel.

"You won't take both of us," Jekyll said. He might've been right. He and Hyde were muscular and composed—stood to reason they'd be fast too. I'd murdered, maimed, and mutilated plenty of men like these two and reckoned it could be a messy proposition.

"No need. After I shoot Ms. Labrador, her infuriated dad will shred you into fish flakes and save me the trouble." I nodded at Delia. Her flat mien betrayed contempt rather than fear. Kudos to her. "That said, after Ms. Labrador's brains hit yonder window, I *will* plug you, then the other Bobbsey Twin. Then, I'll find an anchor and dump the three of you in the lake. I'll hum a show tune while disposing of your carcasses. Later, I'll eat an expensive dinner and sleep like a baby. Assuming that Mr. Labrador takes it hard, he'll send some guys. They'll suffer lead poisoning as well. Days or months afterward, I'll pop out of a cake or a laundry hamper and put several rounds into the old tycoon himself."

The men remained silent. Nervous, but not panicking. Former soldiers, they'd obviously survived perilous situations. Nonetheless, I very much wished for them to experience doubt as to the wisdom of defying my commands.

"My father—" Delia said.

"Hey, sweetie." Lionel swigged. "Please, please, please stifle yourself."

"Have you done your homework?" I said to Jekyll. "Do you understand my capabilities?"

"Yeah."

"Wonderful. So, when I direct you to remove your holster rigs and place them on the table, it will happen smooth and easy and nobody will miraculously receive an extra hole in his or her body."

It went smoothly and easily.

After the duo sullenly positioned themselves lotus style on the floor, Jekyll seized the opportunity to remark Mr. Labrador wasn't a man to provoke and that Lionel and I were digging a hole. Lionel interjected and told him to shut up too. He fished cable ties from his jacket pocket and secured their hands and feet.

I beckoned Delia to sit on the couch.

"Kindly get your dad on the horn." I holstered my revolver and waited.

"Daddy?" Her demeanor remained cool as she summarized our current pass, including my sincere threat of violence. She made eye contact without flinching. I almost felt a pang of guilt for ruining Lionel's red-hot romance. "Coleridge wants to talk to you. Yes, Coleridge. Yes, the big guy. No, Dad. Dad . . . you'd better talk to him."

I accepted the phone and said hi.

"Swine," a cultured, and thunderously enraged, voice said. "You have committed a serious error in judgment."

"Mr. Labrador? Isaiah Coleridge. We were enjoying a swell vacation until your bullyboys crashed the party. At your behest, I'm certain. Two reasons it was an ill-advised strategy. One, everybody here is a consenting adult. Delia accompanied us of her own volition. Second, sending a pair of lunks to do the job of a whole squadron of lunks is always ill advised."

"Fret not, you'll be up to your ears in 'lunks' at any moment." Mr. Labrador wheezed every third breath. Stress can aggravate asthma.

I lowered the phone and raised my eyebrows at Jekyll and Hyde.

"Black Dog is organized; that's the rep. Can the boss really snap his fingers and summon a paramilitary death squad to this location in a matter of minutes? Lie and my friend will smash your kneecap."

"Fat chance," Jekyll said without hesitation. "He can dial in maybe two or three professionals and a carload of yahoos. We have yahoos by the bushel. A *real* strike team takes forty-eight hours to a week, depending."

"Depending on whether they're busy pillaging a village in a developing country when the call comes in?" Lionel said. "Three-to-one you're fired, by the way."

"Sorry, Mr. Labrador," I said into the phone. "Where were we?"

"What do you want, besides a reprieve from execution by sniper fire today? Did you force Delia to call in order to negotiate terms of surrender?"

I'd seen pictures of Jonathan Labrador—silver-haired, patrician, impeccable dresser. His features were deeply grooved and stern. I doubted he smiled unless grinding someone under the heel of his prohibitively expensive Italian shoe. A conceited winner and a sore loser. In essence, a generic ultrarich shithead.

"Sir, allow me to explain the situation."

"I understand the situation perfectly. Your objections notwithstanding, the material facts are plain. You've kidnapped my daughter and are holding her at gunpoint."

"Nobody is pointing a gun at anybody. However, if a helicopter with mercenaries hanging off the stanchions shows up, bullets will inevitably fly. In that scenario, her safety isn't guaranteed."

"More threats!"

"Hear me out before we cross the Rubicon."

"Fine. Twenty-five words or fewer."

"Valero Technologies. Rowden Refrigeration." I enunciated each word. "Anvil Mountain Refuge. The Croatoan. Tri-state murders. Morris Oestryke." He didn't interrupt. I'd seldom actually witnessed a pause so very pregnant.

He finally said, "Go on."

I drily recited the relevant details, highlighting Zircon's elaborate yet critical relationship to Morris Oestryke in the form of two intermediary employers, one of which seemed to maintain an unwholesome arrangement with the Federal government and another whose main factory exploded, killing several people; and the corporation's indirect funding of an expedition into the Catskills that Oestryke accompanied for reasons unknown after a long period of absence from the public eye.

"Utterly compelling and utterly opaque," Mr. Labrador said. "Should this Oestryke person be relevant to me? If you have a thesis, do make the argument."

"Relevant? My hunch is he's a long-lost Labrador who changed his name and entered Zircon's Witness Protection Program catering to guilty scumbags; thus, yep, relevant. I recall your older brother Ephraim bought the farm in an accident. Right around the time Morris Oestryke's bizarre, post–high school career took flight. Ephraim's funeral wasn't closed-casket, by any chance? What a coincidence. Oestryke—and I'll refer to him as Oestryke rather than Uncle Ephraim, as a courtesy—is a notorious murderer.

"I may not yet be able to prove in a court of law that Zircon abetted his criminal activities, starting with the murder or otherwise dastardly disposition of the original Morris Oestryke, but I'm putting the pieces together." I didn't confuse the issue by noting that Morris—or Ephraim, depending on one's inclination—was likely dead for real. There'd be time for further complications if I escaped this predicament intact.

"Your accusations and threats are duly noted. I've listened to enough of this—"

I cut in with my flattest tone.

"There will be time to sort the dirty laundry. For the moment, focus on what's in front of you, okay? Once the Feds get involved, I'm willing to wager a bundle you're up the creek with no paddle in sight. Or, perhaps you think the authorities will lay off in perpetuity—could be the DoD still has an interest in protecting 'Oestryke' for reasons unclear. Hate to break it to you, but not everybody is willing to play footsie with your organization. You and your daughter are cognizant of who employed me before I came east and hung my shingle?"

His wheezing encouraged me to carry on.

"Make no mistake, the New York branch of the Family is distraught over the deaths of Harold Lee and his dear pal, Ray Anderson. If you are unfamiliar with those names, your daughter can fill in the blanks. Highly placed members of the New York Family are understandably concerned that a trend has developed.

"They ask themselves who might be next. They ask themselves who's responsible and what horrible punishment should be meted upon that person or persons. What I'm trying to explain, Mr. Labrador, is that I'm only the opening salvo in a private war. I'm reconnaissance. An army of Mafia foot soldiers is on standby—piano wire, machine guns, car bombs, and the rest of those fun toys. You're a powerful man, and Black Dog has firepower galore. But you don't want to go to the next level with these guys. Neither does Delia, unless she plans to get plastic surgery and go into hiding in South America."

"What do you want?" he said. I'm confident he hoped this was a problem that could be remedied with a bag of cash. Most problems are.

"As it stands, I'm inclined to hand over my files to a certain vengeful criminal boss and let nature take its course. Do you know any reason why I should do otherwise?" Again, I played fast and loose with the truth by not explaining that an imitator or acolyte of the Croatoan was the real culprit in Harold Lee's killing. I wanted to tighten the screws while I had the opportunity.

Another long, icy pause.

"Please permit me to speak with my daughter." He sounded as if a pair of large, muscular hands were lightly squeezing his neck.

Concentrating on stoicism, I passed Delia the phone. She muttered affirmations. Then she looked at me.

"I think it best if you two leave."

And that, friends and neighbors, is how my Catskills weekend ended with a whimper instead of an orgy of blood. I wasn't totally disappointed. The way this shit-show was headed, there'd be plenty of mayhem before I closed the account.

Delia quietly informed us that her father had forestalled his plans for retribution and we'd receive an RSVP to discuss the incident in a civilized setting. I said thanks. Meanwhile, my thinking ran along the lines of *Whatever, lady. I'm bringing an assault rifle with a grenade launcher to our next tea party.*

Lionel and I gathered the materials from the crawl space and hustled for the exit. As we bailed, he made a phone of the cradle of his hand, gazed mournfully at her, and mouthed, *Call me.*

I wondered if she would.

PART III

BLACK SUNSET

Lionel bombed that Monte Carlo back to the farm. He chain-smoked, and I stared at the countryside whizzing past under an overcast sky. Accoutrements of murder and a cool $1.5 million in the backseat. A film noir afternoon in New York State.

Neither of us spoke the entire drive.

"Apologies for how it went down today," I said once we arrived. "You were chill and I appreciate that."

"'Chill'?"

"While I was menacing your girlfriend, you were a trouper."

"Oh, man, *that*. Why wouldn't I be cool? You've got the 'no women or children' policy. I just played along." He checked his phone for texts. Ninth or tenth time since we'd made it home.

"I don't have"—I cleared my throat and reversed course—"any idea what I did to deserve a pal like you."

"Were you on the level about Delia's uncle? You like him as the Croatoan?"

"As the Croatoan, yes. Somebody else whacked Harry. History indicates Ephraim Labrador was a budding psychopath. Then he dies suddenly. Zircon has the resources to pull off a caper; change his identity and set him up with the DoD doing cloak-and-dagger bullshit. No college, which would be a disadvantage for a government agent, although the Labrador kids attended private schools and were instructed by world-class tutors from kindergarten on."

"Sounds wild."

"Got Labrador's attention."

"Surely there's photographic evidence," he said. "Compare some pictures of Ephraim Labrador and Oestryke. If the pics match, case closed."

"I checked the old photos of Ephraim. There aren't many available—not publicly and not through my back channels. The ones I examined are grainy newspaper clippings. He and Morris Oestryke were within a year or two. The men in the shots resembled each other. I don't know; not with any certainty."

"Well, something I *do* know. We made ourselves a bona fide motherfucker of an enemy today in Jonathan Labrador. How far would a man in his shoes go to cover up the truth about his killer brother?"

"A question to keep a man awake at night," I said.

WE UNPACKED, barred the door, and drew the curtains. How to proceed?

"Shitcan this and this." He tossed the ghillie suit and

knives onto a chair. "Hide this." He lifted the bin of cash onto the table. "I'm not watching those."

I unboxed the VCR cassettes and inserted one into the ancient machine he'd given me as a cabin-warming present.

He watched anyway, mouth curled into a half snarl. He whistled, dry and tuneless.

"Mother of Christ. What I thought. We are hip-deep in shit and the tide is rising."

"Get your snorkel." I wasn't smiling.

Nothing remotely amusing about a murky video shot in a cave where a guy, probably a mobster, lay bound and helpless on the ground, his eyes bulging as he tried to scream against a gag. Rats crawled over him, gnawing flesh here and there. The cassette was labeled 1985: SQUEALER. The other videos weren't any more enlightening—locations were unknown, so too the victims, although I could discern each was an adult male. Screams interspersed the few garbled words. Some gray-haired capo probably would've recognized the dying men, as it stood to reason these were wiseguys, or close associates of wiseguys, based on the dates.

The videos were filmed via camera and tripod. The Croatoan, when he appeared, wore indistinct clothing of the era, and a stocking mask. In this instance, I refer to him by his nom de guerre because he wasn't in character as Ephraim Labrador, Morris Oestryke, or Donnie Duster. He was a demon with a name of power who had traveled from the lower circles of hell to manifest in the world of men.

Lionel and I had witnessed and done terrible deeds in our professional capacity. *This* cracked our armor as if it were papier-mâché. Wordlessly, I poured bourbon and we drank. He poured and we drank. And for at least twenty minutes, that is all we could do.

While the violence enshrined on the tapes lacked inventiveness, it excelled in barbaric cruelty. The torture itself may or may not have served a larger purpose—the audio was partially degraded and I couldn't make it fully intelligible. Whatever the motive, it was terrifying.

How many related snuff films existed in the wider world and was Agent Bellow cognizant of them? I'd heard the catch in his voice during our phone conversation and now I knew why he'd been evasive. He'd seen a version, and in proclaiming the tapes to be a hoax, attempted to spare me the horror. I flinched at a vision of him grilling in his apron and hat while innocent children raised hell nearby, and how his even temperament disguised monumental suffering. No one should witness such vileness, least of all a retirement-age family man.

Cassettes 4 and 5 were odd departures, primarily due to their subject matter and because an accomplice operated the camera, tracking the Croatoan as he walked into vistas of ever-unfolding gloom. Labeled BLACK MOUNTAIN 2011, these tapes were recorded in several locations: grand, deserted structures fallen into ruin against woodland backdrops; deep, forested mountains; and the interior of a cavern illuminated by the spotty flash of a miner's lamp or the light from the camera. Each segment of film was presented without audio except for the infrequent sigh of wind or clatter of loose stones. The cave sequences hinted at coldness and the presence of moving water.

The sixth cassette wobbled my universe on its axis.

The label read 1988: I'M BACK, BABY! I recognized the storeroom at the house in West Kill. Someone slumped in a chair. The figure was caked in gore, thick as a layer of tar. The Croatoan entered the frame and leaned close to the camera, blocking out everything with his upper body.

His visage shone pale and stiff in the glare of an industrial lamp. Victims who've suffered burns have waxen, drum-tight flesh around the eyes and mouth. That's what it reminded me of as I watched the recording flicker through microloops. He didn't resemble the man in earlier photographs. That's the moment I realized he'd actually gotten torched in the factory explosion and a surgeon must've put him together again to uncanny effect. There are a limited range of miracles modern science can pull off, judging from the imperfect results.

Nice theory, except the longer I studied him, the eyes and lips were wrong.

"It's a mask," I said.

"No mask. He's wearing someone's face," Lionel said, nailing the horrid truth, first swing on deck.

The video stuttered the way a *Max Headroom* bit would've in the latter 1980s when that show and MTV were popular. The Croatoan dug his fingers into his cheeks and peeled aside latex, cured human flesh, or whatever material it was, and revealed his traditional stocking mask as the next layer. He laughed and pulled the stocking upward, inch by inch. His grinning teeth dripped black. I flashed to Denis Swenson baring his fangs at me in Deering.

Before we saw what came next, the image cut to static.

I poured another round and savored mine this time around and told myself what I'd seen was an optical illusion; low-budget special effects and clever editing. Lionel stared at the dead screen. His features were wooden. I dared not ask his opinion because I feared he might disagree with my own assessment. He might tell me there'd been no trick photography, that the images were all too real.

Battling the compulsion to dump gasoline on the tapes and set the collection ablaze, I returned them to the container and sealed it in duct tape and shoved the mess into the closet until such time as I decided their ultimate dispensation. Swore I felt their vile radiation under the door gap.

That wasn't going to fly.

YET ANOTHER GLASS OF BOOZE; the most I'd drunk since Reba Walker died. Lionel and I loosened enough in our skins to mull the events of the day. We discussed the strands linking Zircon and the Department of Defense to the Croatoan and what it portended. We two ants were trapped in no-man's-land while the government, the Mafia, a clan of industrialists and their globe-spanning corporation lumbered around the field like elephants. To say nothing of a serial killer and a mercenary company with a history of mayhem.

"Which strands us in the middle of . . . where?" Lionel said, intercepting my very thought. We were already an old married couple. "Where are we stranded, Isaiah?"

"We're not stranded." What else was I going to say? I swallowed my bourbon, thankful for the bite in the back of my throat and how the buzz took the edge off my nerves. I opened the ammo box containing Oestryke's maps and spread them over the table. "Temple Hill, Granite Hall, Baranowski's Hiatus, The Bonaventure, Wasser's house, Goldstein Hotel."

I tapped my index finger on red marker dots sprinkled throughout the Catskills. Each dot represented a former luxury vacation site akin to the White Rock Hotel. Each had fallen by the wayside, reclaimed by the forces of nature.

"Bellow called it. He theorized Oestryke used the abandoned resorts as hubs. Oestryke's cabin was fine and dandy as a spot to bring friends, associates, and the occasional victim. Not enough by itself. To do it right and expand his reach, he required multiple safe houses. There are over a dozen of these defunct resorts along the range. Stands to reason Oestryke's successor moves around them as well."

Lionel pinned the corner of the map with his glass. He traced a line along the red dots.

"You might be onto something. It'll be of interest to the authorities. I mention the authorities because what needs to happen with a fucking quickness is those tapes and weapons get sealed and anonymously delivered like a baby in a basket to the nearest cop shop." He didn't say the rest of what he was surely thinking: *Dump the info in*

Curtis's lap and hit the showers. Let the mob fight Zircon Corporation. The winner can deal with the Croatoan or his copycat. Or not.

There was a reason he didn't say it aloud. Attractive as the notion might be, we'd committed ourselves a while ago and then sealed it with a bloody kiss at Oestryke's house in the woods when we absconded with the dirty money. In the words of somebody wiser than either of us, *If you're going through hell, keep going.*

"The box of cash should be high on our list of priorities. It's a fat stack, amigo." He watched my expression. "Been a rotten day, yeah. But, my God, the dough. Life-changing dough. Why don't you look happier?"

"Did you check the serial numbers?" I said. "Those bills date from the '60s and '70s. Could be hard to wash. Another problem is that you're right—it's a fat stack. Might as well be a suitcase nuke so far as it represents a clear and present danger to our health. Life-changing? Nah, life-ending if we make the wrong move. Half of our 'friends' would slice our throats ear to ear for a taste."

"You're harshing my buzz."

"And I say unto thee—we've drop-kicked a hornet's nest. I don't even trust the cops or the Feds after some of the insanity I've seen. Watch your six. I'd even go further and counsel taking steps."

"But, the loot, Isaiah. All that sweet, wrinkly folding green. Please don't say we've gotta burn it, or something."

"That's crazy talk. We have to be careful and we have to be smart. We don't do anything hasty. Sock it away and formulate a plan for how we'll get it back into circulation. I've hunted down numerous low-rent guys who all committed the same fatal error—they absconded with a heap of loot and became conspicuous consumers. The morons thought a new car, a fancy watch, a modest hacienda, or a few big-spender nights at the strip club would fly under the radar. Every last one of those suckers walked around a corner and bumped into me."

"Right, point taken. We're keeping the cash."

"We're keeping the cash."

"Hear! Hear!" He topped off my glass. He killed the bottle by gulping straight from the neck. His eyes were red-rimmed and metallic. A man's eyes harden to metal when he breaches a certain threshold and everything reduces to a weight or a calculation; when his thoughts linger increasingly on the gun at his waist, the knife in his pocket.

The drink wasn't celebratory or in honor of some small victory amidst the never-stopping carnage of the universe. The booze had scalded and then numbed my throat. I wanted to keep that numbness going, help it spread. We sealed the money bin inside an industrial garbage bag and buried it in the woods. The wind rose like a black-gilded tempest in a fairy tale. Branches slashed our shoulders and sleet pelted us. The last of the leaves cascaded to join their fallen brothers.

Definitely a warning.

CHAPTER THIRTY-SIX

When we'd finished acting the part of pirates burying treasure on a nameless island, I parted ways
with Lionel and changed into dry clothes. My cell rang.

"How's it hangin'?" Curtis said. He sounded too
cheerful. Never ever an auspicious sign when mob bosses
are sunshine and roses. "Got us a problem. Noon today,
a little birdy told me Nic Royal ducked into the Knarr to
collect his pay. Same little birdy next saw him sneakin'
around over in Clayton Park. Packin' his bags for Tim-
buktu, if he's got a brain. Sent a couple guys over to keep
an eye on him."

"Keep an eye on him or roll him up in a carpet?" I
said.

"Six of one, half a dozen of the other. Didn't hear
from them, so I grabbed more guys and paid him a personal visit. No sign a my men or Royal. My crew's car is
gone too. I'm assumin' the worst."

"Okay. Thanks for the news bulletin."

"Save your thanks. This is on you, Coleridge. You had

the cocksucker in your grasp and let him walk." He pulled away to yell at a subordinate. He sighed into the receiver to demonstrate the burden of his forbearance. "Forgive my temper. It's a delicate problem. We'll straighten this out at a later date, yeah? You see that peckerhead in the meantime? My advice is shoot first. *Ciao.*"

I'd always acknowledged the possibility that Royal was somehow involved. This development with Curtis's missing soldiers didn't necessarily confirm the worst, although it was far from cheering news. Honestly, Royal had every reason to be paranoid, and maybe he'd gotten the jump on the mob brutes.

The angel on my left shoulder—he with the nub horns and larcenous grin—muttered into my ear that it was equally fair to venture that Royal had lain in wait for the goombahs. The dragnet was closing in; why not take some mobsters with him on the way to thug Valhalla? I tossed this speculation onto the mounting pile of worrisome unknowns.

It felt intolerable to store evidence from Oestryke's house anywhere near where I ate and slept. I gathered the materials, stowed them in the truck, wrapped the Mossberg in a blanket and laid it beside me on the seat, and drove over to the office.

I slid into my space behind the Elton Cooper Building several minutes past sunset. My neighbors had already closed shop for the day. Oestryke's papers, knives, and films went into the safe. I hung the ghillie suit from the coatrack. Light from the solitary desk lamp I'd switched on didn't reach the corners of the office. The suit, with its tangle of burlap strips and hanks of twine, resembled a tall man hunched, his misshapen shadow creeping across the wall and ceiling.

Messages blinked on the machine. Two were telemarketing pitches; another was left by the building manager advising of a power interruption for repairs on the first of the month; Burt P requested a return call in regard to his granddaughter's problem. She put a bug in his ear after the brouhaha at her house the other night. I understood his anxiousness. He'd given me a decent amount of money with next to nothing to show for it, except a wildly antagonized granddaughter.

Headlights bounced off the ceiling. I went to the window and spied a pair of Ulster County Sheriff's patrol cars bracketing my truck. I locked up. Full dark had stolen over the world. It was an interminable and strangely unpleasant walk downstairs, across the dim lobby, and through the security doors.

The deputies were edgy until I produced ID and detective credentials. One of the neighbors had reported a prowler about twenty minutes ago. A vague description, except the caller noted the prowler absolutely didn't belong, whatever that meant. Trooper A figured the citizen had mistaken me for an intruder because of my skin tone, like as not. Thanks, buddy. The timing felt off. I didn't mention it, though; I nodded to him and his partner and watched them drive away.

In the truck, I dialed Meg and apologized because I wouldn't be available in the near future. Hard to do, because I missed her fiercely. She knew something was amiss, but cheerfully suggested we touch base when my schedule permitted and let it lie.

The investigation had swerved ninety degrees and all bets were off. Anybody could be tracking my movements: the mob, Black Dog, law enforcement, or a serial killer. Last thing I wanted was to lead a bad guy straight to her doorstep.

An image of the black wolf materialized in my imagination. It crouched a dozen paces away and gazed down at its kill. I couldn't discern what kind of animal lay in the red snow, but I could guess. The wolf yawned, pleased with the death it had completed and the death to come.

Gene K whispered from its gory muzzle, *Prick up your ears, killer. Didn't you smell the odor of death in your office? Faint, oh so very faint.* It turned in profile and raised its head to inhale deeply of the breeze. *The universe has noticed you.*

Where else had I encountered the rank odor? Nic Royal's truck, and, later, in my room at the West Kill Lodge. A sensation of doom rolled over me, like I was lying in an open grave. I didn't spare a moment to snatch the shotgun as I exited the truck, took three huge bounds, and flattened against the side of the building.

Gene the Wolf chuckled, a blot in my peripheral vision.

That's the way. It won't happen at close quarters. A smart enemy will snipe you from a distance. You'll never feel your melon blast apart. You'll cruise unto Kingdom Come with that sappy look on your face.

Intuition told me that Gene's theory didn't fit this scenario. A sniper's bullet wouldn't be my fate. The Croatoan had reveled in intimate violence. He'd enjoyed the tactile and auditory sensations of murder within blood-splash distance. Odds were, his imitator felt the same. Odds were, if the imitator had indeed been here, he longed to plunge a knife into my heart and watch my eyes go dark.

Praying that the nosy neighbor wouldn't spot me and summon the *gendarmes* for round two, I sneaked to the rear entrance, punched the key code, and moved inside. Next came the stairs, carpeted and solid. They muffled my steps as I ascended, hugging the wall, revolver in hand.

No direct light in the second-story corridor, nor my office. I froze, a shadow within shadows, for five minutes or an eon. A clock ticked. The boiler kicked on and ducts thumped and rattled. My entire performance was tactically unsound. Gene, Lionel, and my dear old dad would've unanimously excoriated me for my recklessness. Clearing a structure that size requires a team of trained personnel with overlapping fields of fire moving in tandem. Lacking such a team, the odds of neutralizing an entrenched opponent before he got the drop were prohibitive.

I tried my office door. The dead bolt was disengaged. No denying the evidence; someone had lurked while I bumbled around the room. I stepped through and immediately crouched and held my breath. Nobody took a shot, nobody rushed me.

I flicked on the lights and took stock. Everything seemed undisturbed except for one detail. The ghillie suit was missing from its hook. My reflection warped in the tall, black window that overlooked Atwood Street. I almost put a hole through my own distorted face.

The drive home to Hawk Mountain Farm was winding and intricate. Dad and Gene K had instructed me in the basics of evasive driving and the lessons had stuck. I put those skills through the paces. I peeled my eyes for a tail; detected only crimson shadows trailing in the truck's wake.

BACK AT THE FARM, I reclined in my favorite chair, selfishly wishing Minerva were at my feet instead of camping at Meg's house. The dog would've hated my mood anyway. She and I were entirely too sensitive to amorphous peril.

Fire crackled in the hearth and two generous glasses of bourbon warmed my gut. The shotgun lay across a small table near my right hand. I hadn't bothered to attach the laser sight or the tactical grip. I *had* loaded it with four rounds of double-aught buckshot and three bear slugs. Another slug nestled in the chamber, ready.

The phone I kept on hand for dubious contacts and informants buzzed one minute after midnight. Unknown name, unknown number. I held it to my ear and waited for the caller to speak.

Both of us breathed for a few seconds. A third someone whimpered in the background. Gurgled, really. There are several injuries that can cause a man to make those sorts of noises. Each possibility was worse than the last. That would be one of Curtis's vanished minions.

The caller set down his handset with an audible clack of metal on metal. Footsteps receded. The background whimpers transformed into frenzied screams. They were somewhere private with no chance of interruption. It went on and on and finally stopped.

Sweat trickled down my cheeks. I sipped another bourbon through gritted teeth. Heavy footsteps scuffed and scraped. The caller breathed into the phone the way a man does after a sprint, or sex.

"Nic?" I said. A reasonable guess, considering recent events. "Abducting Curtis's soldiers wasn't smart. Bad, bad men are looking for you. Shoot to kill."

His chuckle, when it came, was low and malicious.

"The darkness isn't killable."

I couldn't decide whether or not I recognized the voice. Could've been Nic Royal; could've been anybody.

"Historically, a hail of gunfire is reliable," I said. "Man, you snowed me. You were the Croatoan's sidekick all along. You killed Harry because he betrayed your mentor. Classic motive."

He didn't respond.

"The time line is confusing," I said. "You inserted yourself into Harry's world at least two years ago, roomed with him for nine months with the express intent to end him at some point. How did you know Harry sold out Oestryke? Did Harry let it slip? He wasn't an idiot. He would've taken that secret straight to hell. Had to be someone else. Who?"

"Maybe a spying bird lit down," he said. His breath-

ing roughened. "Ask the right person the right questions, all will be revealed."

"And Ray Anderson? You opened him like a sack of
rice. Why?"

He chuckled again.

The realization that got to me? Royal had likely parked
near my office with a couple of wiseguys in the trunk of a
stolen car. Which further confirmed I had a certifiable
maniac by the tail.

What malignant set of circumstances originally brought
Nic Royal and Morris Oestryke together? My gut insisted
that Oestryke, a collector of men, as Curtis had stated in
not so many words, scooped Royal off the street. He'd
swooped down shortly after the younger man cashiered
out of the Marine Corps—penniless, friendless, rudder-
less. The Croatoan had introduced the soldier into a more
rigorous methodology of violence. Groomed him for the
inevitable day when the butcher's blade would be passed
to the new generation.

Gene K half formed in the shadows. He nodded and I
averted my gaze until he evaporated.

"Nic, you there?"

"I could have taken you before."

"At the office?"

"Yes."

"Why didn't you?"

"I'm the messenger, so listen. Your life and death belong to another. Take a walk. Onetime offer. At the end
of this conversation, it's gone."

Whatever else is true of a man, if he makes an offer, he's usually in a bind. This bolstered my morale.

"Who does my life belong to?" I listened to him breathe. "Scared, Nic? You sound scared. Oestryke possessed a license to murder, courtesy of the rich and powerful. That day is over, pal. The Family will hunt you until the stars burn to ash. You pop up anywhere on the planet and a little egg timer starts ticking. The mob doesn't find your sorry ass, I will. No one like me has ever come after you before."

"Phony heart of gold," he said. "Hypocrite. Pretend rescuer of lost lambs. You want to be a guard dog, but you've bitten too many of the wrong people. Slink away."

"I can't."

His reply wasn't what I expected.

"Good."

"Good?"

"Mexico City was named Tenochtitlán in the golden days," he said. "The city squatted in the middle of a lake. The Conquistadors came along and jacked the Aztecs' shit." He swallowed audibly. When he resumed, his voice had subtly altered. It traveled a great distance, perhaps through time.

"Today, the city is modern on the surface; a Third World labyrinth of steel and glass and neon. Millions of people tramp about their daily routine, and the underworld yawns all around and beneath their feet. Municipal laborers dig up ziggurats in back alleys and a piece of the greater universe is revealed. Cartel armies slaughter citizens and police en masse. Soldiers take the heads of the sacrifices. Mexico City opens into the underworld, but the underworld is everywhere and has many openings for a man to fall into. The old death gods still require blood. You understand about the death gods, don't you, Isaiah?"

I understood, all right.

"Do you remember the night we took a drive in the country?"

"Yes," I said. "A lovely drive on a lovely evening. I remember your fear. It occurred to me to shoot you then. That's on me."

"Who do you suppose you were with that night?"

"I was with *you*, Nic."

"Were you with me? Were you?"

"I distinctly recall screwing my revolver into your ear."

"Nic Royal existed briefly and now he doesn't. I have one of *those* faces."

The connection clicked off.

I FIGURED CURTIS was awake and burning the midnight oil. Unlike solitary me, my Mafia captain associate would've surrounded himself with foot soldiers and machine guns.

I knocked back another shot to fortify myself and then hit the speed dial. I informed him that his men were goners. Also, my lingering doubts had evaporated: Nic Royal was the odds-on favorite as the new Croatoan. The question of who *Royal* was before he became Royal seemed a topic safely ignored for another time and place.

Curtis implied, in his laconic fashion, that a minor manhunt would ensue. I shouldn't concern myself with

Meg and Devlin or my hosts, the Walkers; his crew would patrol the places where Royal could be expected to make a move.

What would he say to his henchmen? Would he reveal the truth or continue to keep a lid on? Had events begun to slip from his control? Mafia thugs don't typically ask penetrating questions of their captains; he might yet right the ship without alerting the bigwigs.

"Curtis," I said toward the end.

"Yeah, what?"

"You're absolutely, positively sure you killed Oestryke?"

"What, you want I should drive out to the Pine Barrens with a pick and a shovel and dig up the bones? Would that make you happy?"

"It's not the worst idea."

"Coleridge? Kiss my ass."

We said our good nights. I doubt he slept much either.

CHAPTER THIRTY-SEVEN

Gene K routinely exhorted me that so long as I worked as a hitter, I'd be well advised to keep a passport and a wad of bills stashed for an emergency exit. Thanks to his nagging, I'd heeded the advice since before I could grow a full beard. Lately, in my dreams, he uttered the mantra like a broken record.

You can't fall in love. Love is a major fucking no-no. You say your dog died? Good! One less attachment. You have to be able to cut ties and disappear. If you love something, your enemies will destroy it to reach you. Harden your heart.

But I'm out! Such was my protest.

Sometimes, Gene K evaporated and Dad took up the gauntlet: *Are you, son? Are you out? You're a fool.* Awake or dreaming, when the bastard is right, he's right.

PREVAILING MYTHS notwithstanding, serial killers aren't usually geniuses. Even the sneakier, smarter alpha specimens are merely animals, and, like animals, are enslaved by their baser instincts. If the sadistic sonsofbitches had impulse control, they wouldn't act out their miserable fantasies and end their days confined to a concrete pen or riding Old Sparky into the sunset. I wasn't on the trail of a mastermind; I wasn't on the trail of a *man*, but a wolf too clever and too vicious for its own good. A wolf, in its native environment, possesses nascent advantages.

Yet for all this, its chief disadvantage lies in the fact that it *is* a wolf. Nonetheless, recognizing the nature and limitations of one's quarry isn't tantamount to dismissing the perils involved. Lacking support, intelligence, or appropriate infrastructure, a hunter can find himself overmatched.

Into every life some rain must fall. In *my* life, rain is a metaphor for men with guns or knives intent upon perforating my precious hide. Staying in the plus column has boiled down to a simple premise. There are bigger and better killers roaming the earth and I endeavor to behave accordingly.

None of my physical and psychological attributes have contributed to my continued survival half so much as well-honed pragmatism. There are people who exceed my abilities. Should we ever go head-to-head, I'll lose. I can think of five or six guys off-the-cuff who qualify. The specifics aren't important. What's important is, I'm aware of my vulnerabilities and enact measures to mitigate them.

I didn't *know* whether the Croatoan—or his imitator—was my superior. The Croatoan had slaughtered hundreds of victims, the majority of those being well-armed wiseguys. A king snake preying upon rattlers. I could've racked up hits for the rest of my natural span and not made a dent in his body count. That alone hinted at the likely disparity in our talent levels.

Yeah, on second and third thought, I was relieved Curtis had smoked the guy. Competition doesn't motivate me. Testing one's mettle in a life-or-death struggle is a child's fantasy. Continuing to breathe is all the affirmation I require. To that humble goal, I fervently hoped to acquire information that would help Curtis do unto Royal as well.

SUNDAY DISINTEGRATED in a barrage of phone calls— three to Delia without reply—and internet research. I had to laugh. Lionel and I were in the same boat, hoping for a callback from the inimitable Ms. Labrador.

In domestic affairs, Chuck Bachelor confirmed all was quiet on the Western Front. Aubrey P remained a bubbling cauldron of fury, and the Trask gang hadn't ventured from their stomping grounds on the other side of Kingston. I decided to let it ride and continued my preparations for Monday; a whirlwind trip to Rhode Island to visit wildlife photographer Xerxes Vance, apparent favorite of the Croatoan.

Providence is a three-hour drive from Kingston. I rented a car and applied a lead foot to the pedal, zooming north before dawn.

The former, excessively rancorous version of myself rattled his chains. Angry, hostile version of Isaiah Coleridge

estimated the most efficient method of extricating himself
from this debacle would be to locate Nic Royal, blow his
head off, and present the corpse to Marion Curtis. That
would settle accounts and even scores and life could sub-
side to a semblance of normality.

Yes, Nic Royal had become my new priority, although
he wasn't in Providence. The man I went to interview
wouldn't know Royal from Adam either. An oblique
angle isn't necessarily more direct than a straight line; in
this instance, it might've represented the only path.

Oestryke's cryptic maps would be helpful if I wished to
spend weeks, or months, tramping around the Catskills
poking into ruined hotels in search of hidey-holes where
Royal might flee now that the heat was well and truly on.
I didn't relish the idea of counting on Curtis nailing Royal
before Royal decided to forgo an intimate murder and
ended the game with an ambush, a car bomb, or a rifle.
My loved ones and associates were also potentially at risk.

Possibly Vance knew something that would lead me in
the right direction, and faster.

I didn't spot any Black Dog operatives on my six. Either things were unfolding too quickly for them to organize a surveillance detail or their people were doing a
crack job avoiding detection.

Upon crossing into Providence, I left the car in a park-
ing garage and walked three blocks to the Westminster
Arcade. I'd dressed to blend—windbreaker over a heavy
T-shirt, dark pants, and a pair of scuffed tennis shoes.

Cloudless midmorning, less than a week before Halloween; the mall was hopping. I mingled with the

throngs, ducked into a bistro on the promenade, and slipped out a service door. I hustled several blocks, zigzagging through alleys, watching over my shoulder for pursuers. On the corner near the historic home where H. P. Lovecraft lived and died in the 1930s, I summoned a cab and directed the driver to ferry me south and east of downtown.

XERXES VANCE GRADUATED FROM Suny New Paltz in 1977 with a degree in English lit. He went on to achieve cult fame due to his wildlife photography, a nascent and untutored skill honed in far-flung locales such as Siberia, Mongolia, the Amazon Basin, and Bangladesh. Ascetic dedication to his craft led to an isolated existence and a reputation as an eccentric hermit. Mainstream success and major awards eluded him; he'd survived on royalties derived from his sequences of wildlife photography and the beneficence of a handful of doting patrons.

Currently, he resided at a big, decaying apartment complex called Willow Heights. My background sweep unearthed multiple residences over the past decade; he moved frequently, and seldom to anyplace nice. Willow Heights was no exception to his migratory patterns. It loomed over a shabby neighborhood of sparsely occupied shops and cramped houses with pointy roofs. Surrounding lots were hemmed by rusted fences and potholed streets.

The keypad on the heavy, graffiti-marred entrance was defunct, and I walked right into a stale foyer that might've been grandiose between the First and Second wars. A rattletrap elevator emitted a yellow sulfurous light when it disgorged a couple of drunks. I noted the dings in the brass-plated doors, the maroon blotches on the carpet, and how the interior lamp flickered, and said, *No thanks.*

I ascended the broad stairs to the fourth floor. A hallway ran east to west, illuminated by a series of recessed lamps. Washed-out-gray carpeting lolled like the tongue of a dead animal. I didn't see or hear any of the residents, although classical music drifted in from somewhere.

Vance occupied a corner apartment on the alley-facing side of the building. Nobody answered my knock. After a conservative interval, I used a credit card and the tip of a knife to jimmy the not-up-to-code lock and let myself in. Lackadaisical security, considering the high rate of crime in Providence.

The loft was a narrow rectangle and brutally austere. I inventoried a cot, couch, bench, and three long tables loaded with arcane parts of equipment, stacks of photography and travel magazines, and not much else. He kept a transistor radio tuned to National Public Radio and had a 1990s Apple computer powered by a car battery. The lone concession to décor was an oversized print of a leopard carrying a limp baboon in its jaws. Had to be the original version of the photograph Swenson described viewing at Oestryke's home in 1987. It compared perfectly with the chilling photographs I'd seen at Oestryke's Catskills retreat.

I settled in to wait.

CHAPTER THIRTY-EIGHT

Vance returned two hours later. Conveniently alone. Handsome and athletic, for an older man; he sported a buzz cut and was clean-shaven. I saw right through the façade. His grooming was typified by vagrants who'd lucked into a night or two at a good shelter where razors and aftershave are doled out gratis. In fairness, I hadn't turned up any liquor around the apartment, just the meagerest quantity of grass and three bottles of meds with unpronounceable names. Years of hiking in the wilderness imbued him with a sinewy toughness that disguised his ailment—cancer abetted by malnutrition, if I knew anything about anything. He dressed in a wrinkled T-shirt, khakis, and hiking boots.

He noticed me standing near a window and froze like a deer. First thing he asked was, had I come to put out his lights. I said no and he relaxed. He boiled a pot of coffee and we had cups, seated at the corner of a worktable.

As we spoke, more tension drained from his shoulders

and he finally smiled the smile of a prisoner who'd won a reprieve from the gallows. Reflexive, certainly. At this proximity, I smelled the taint of decay. The odor on his breath and emitting from his pores reeked of burnt copper. His shiny skin stretched tightly over his bones. He was nearly translucent—I almost expected to see his beating heart and the slosh and churn of his intestines as the shadows of goldfish swam past like his chest was an aquarium. The Big C, for certain.

Once we'd moved past the preamble, getting-to-know-you segment of the date, I cut to the chase and inquired why Morris Oestryke owned a collection of personally signed Xerxes Vance masterpieces. Did he realize Oestryke was a mass murderer who also was most likely not even actually "Oestryke" but rather the black-sheep scion of a wealthy family by the name of Ephraim Labrador?

"The man contained multitudes, as the poet once said. He called himself Morris Oestryke and that's it. I became acquainted with him on a project in the '70s. We've kept in touch since. His idea, not mine, believe me. Yes, I possess an inkling of his proclivities. Morris brags. He can be loquacious, if he takes a shine to you. I turned a blind eye, out of an instinct for self-preservation. But I knew. Here, in the twilight's last gleaming, I'll accept that much culpability."

His statement gave me pause.

"The 'project' . . . Are you referring to the Anvil Mountain expedition?"

"We were dispatched to assess the impact of development and recreational activity on a species of bats that lives in that region of the northern Catskills. Ridiculous. Our fearless leaders went through the motions nonetheless on behalf of . . . well, someone."

"Zircon Corporation. I've heard the name around."

"Well, then. As I learned in the fullness of time, our expedition leaders received a hefty cash advance from Zircon operatives and promises of fully funded research projects in years to come. Any inclination to ask questions was mitigated by pure greed. Anyway, our findings were complete fabrications, and, later, a corporate ally within the government rubber-stamped the scam. I initially regarded it as a harmless boondoggle to protect some inconsequential wildlife. Or so I thought until it was too late."

"I've read the report. You aren't listed."

"My participation was off the books. Two professors organized the trip. Six students—three grads and three undergrads—came along as flunkies. Morris was assigned as a nonstudent by administrative fiat. Someone designated him the official photographer, although he couldn't tell one end of a camera from the other. The younger professor and I were friendly off campus. I was his weed-and-pills connection. And—key point—I was handy with a camera.

"He paid me under the table to tag along and supply dope and backup photographic documentation. The head man didn't care—one more peasant to schlep baggage was agreeable to him. I may as well have been a ghost, as far as the official account is concerned. The devil protects children and fools. I'd be dead too if they'd handed me an application and a tax form."

"Oestryke was a plant," I said. "By Zircon, right? For what purpose?"

"Dust off the records, you'll see Anvil Mountain has existed as a forestry stewardship since the Reconstruction era. Some folks—natives and European settlers—referred to it as the Black Mountain because its caves are haunted by the spirits of tribes who were around prior to the known indigenous cultures. The first official stewards were a committee of fabulously wealthy pricks—railroad barons and tycoons who amused themselves as hunters and naturalists. Men who manipulated State and Federal government by proxy; Zircon and its subsidiaries being the latest in the long, long procession. The Labradors sat at the head of the table then, and they sit there today."

His comments matched my own research, although I maintained a poker face.

"Big bad companies usually want to clear-cut and strip-mine natural resources, not preserve their scenic wonders," I said.

"That's how scams work. Sleight of hand and misdirection, my friend. There's an unsurveyed cavern complex inside Anvil Mountain; main entrance is on the eastern slopes. Our expedition stumbled across it in the process of tracking and recording a huge colony of bats. Yes, the scientists did put in a bit of work. Had to make it appear legitimate, you see. We camped at the base of the mountain for a week. The professors, two of the grad students, and Morris descended each day. It was dangerous, stupid, and unauthorized. We'd received clear instructions from on high to not venture within a mile of the actual foothills. For once, though, our team leaders were genuinely enthused."

"Zircon was aware of the caves. Gold vein?"

"Gold isn't a bad guess. They're protecting something else, likely a hominid graveyard. It may be similar to Sima de los Huesos in the mountains in Spain. The Pit of Bones. The *important* thing they're hiding is an anomalous substance; a fungus with potent medicinal properties. My money is on the fungus as the proprietary motive to close the area off and conceal any evidence of the hominid fossils. Should the world at large get wind of a historical archaeological site, Zircon would lose their drug mill in a hurry."

"Science and progress are the ultimate in eminent domain," I said. "How did you put it all together?"

"I got one of the grads wasted and pumped him for all he was worth. Which wasn't as much as I'd hoped. He'd witnessed a gallery and evidence of fossilized artifacts— he couldn't determine what they were. Morris filled me in on the fungus angle a bit later. Zircon hadn't planned for their fake expedition to discover the caves. They'd arranged this elaborate scheme to help shield the region from interlopers, not have its minions expose a secret the corporation had hidden for decades. The team's precipitous action triggered a precipitous response."

"Corporate skullduggery ensued. Tears flowed. Then blood."

"Why do you think I hunkered in this shithole and

hoped to run down the clock? Zircon and members of the government are in cahoots. Ask everybody else who went on that trip. Oh, you can't because they're dead."

I'd perused the obituaries of the Anvil Mountain team. Without context, *accident, misadventure*, and *natural causes* read innocently enough.

Vance calmly recited the facts as he perceived them—within six months of completing the impact study and filing it with the relevant authorities, both professors were deceased. The older man died of a heart attack, while his junior associate committed suicide by leaping from the roof of an apartment building. The younger prof got engaged the week prior. A year later, two of the grad students were tragically killed in Mexico—hit and run, no arrests. An undergrad fell victim to a fatal robbery in Philadelphia; another went missing and was presumed drowned while kayaking in the Pacific Northwest.

"When the last grad student choked to death in his Birmingham flat, two and a half years after our expedition, I couldn't ignore what had unfolded," Vance said. "Somebody was snipping loose ends; making certain we'd never tell tales about the expedition, never testify at a congressional hearing, never contradict the official designation of Anvil Mountain as a wildlife refuge."

"Did this 'somebody' come after you?" I said.

"Morris and I remained friendly after 1976. My photography caught fire with several small-time magazines and I traveled extensively. Whenever I got back into town, which was New Paltz, Morris materialized and we'd hit the bars and catch up. He loved my work, especially the red-of-fang-and-claw material. Got off on dangerous animals and desolate landscapes the way other men stroke it to porn. He'd gotten hitched and had a baby on the way. Landed a job with a refrigeration company. Drove a wide route across the state. Said he envied my footloose and fancy-free lifestyle. I was flattered.

"We were drunk as lords one night and I confided in him my theory that our companions from the Anvil Mountain trip didn't expire due to natural causes, that I suspected they were murdered. Morris had appeared slobbery drunk for half the night. Totally plastered. He straightened on his stool and his face changed, became cold and sterile. Hard to describe unless you looked at the visage of a wolf or a leopard with zero compunction about its biting your throat. I wasn't nose to nose with a human anymore. He laughed and said I should be a detective because I was right, they'd been murdered. He'd snuffed them himself on behalf of people in high places.

"In his opinion, he'd done his victims a kindness. Particularly the ones who'd descended into the caves. Spared them what he termed a living death. He confirmed Zircon coveted the fungus's 'exceptional' medicinal properties. Dedicated chemists could surely develop applications to give the DoD a raging hard-on. Drawback? Unfiltered exposure to its spores is as lethal as a high dose of radiation. Might kill you in a month, might kill you in a decade. Claimed that the death gods slowed his demise because of his devoted service. Morris presented a pattern of weird sores on his shoulders. Whole time I knew him, he kept shriveling. Stank of decay and a persistent infection. In other words, I have no reason to doubt he was telling some version of the truth."

"If anybody ever needed a drink, it's us," I said, parched and lamenting the distinct lack of booze in his loft.

"That night at the bar when Morris O confessed himself to me was the last time I ever got drunk. I toke to manage the pain. Pop a pill here and there. Same reason—pain. Late-stage pancreatic cancer. Considering how it all shook out, I stupidly neglected a sea of vodka. While we're on the subject, would you mind if I spark a jay?" He proceeded to roll a joint. Got it lit and took a drag.

"Oestryke killed your colleagues and spared you. Your square jaw and charm win the day, or what?"

"Wasn't due to my clean living, not back then. Morris said he couldn't kill me because I wasn't on the list. Promised I'd be okay for a while if I kept doing my thing. He liked me doing my thing." He made a camera-clicking motion. "Morris is a collector. Art, people. Especially people. Sociopaths have a knack for attracting flies into their web."

"You'd be okay for a while?"

"He had bizarre ideas, bizarre stories. He field-tested experimental weaponry in Southeast Asia. Zircon subsidiaries—Valero and others developed the hardware and he ran trials on behalf of the Department of Defense. Zircon has tentacles everywhere."

"Someone else mentioned unorthodox weaponry. Give me an example."

"Lasers—you can burn or blind with focused light; induce seizures or hallucinations. That's old hat. Infra-

sound. The military is enamored with the offensive potential of psychoacoustics. Boil a man's brains, make him
shit himself, or become delusional. Weirdest, though? He
claimed to have undergone chemical and psychological
experiments related to Cold War programs like MKUltra.

"Said he could slow his pulse and breathing down to
almost nothing. I personally observed him hold his breath
for nine minutes on a dare. It's impossible. He did it
anyway."

"He allegedly died in an explosion in 1987. How did
he seem after that? Did his appearance change; his demeanor?"

"Morris suffered burns to the majority of his body. A
plastic surgeon did a stellar job patching him up again. His
face was doll-like, if you stood next to him, but small price
to pay. The accident altered his brain for the worse. Either
that or exposure to the spores. Whatever. He became
sneakier. And radically paranoid. Like, tinfoil-bandanna-
level craziness. Yet inflected with a horrible, conniving
rationality that scared me shitless. He carried false papers,
wore disguises—the whole bit. I didn't comment, for obvious reasons."

"His home videos fell into my possession," I said.
"One was called Black Mountain, filmed in 2011. Did
you run the camera?"

Vance nodded unhappily.

"Yes, he dragged me along to revisit the caves. He said
it was dangerous, but possibly a pilgrimage would cancel
out the cancer in my cells. I didn't have cancer then—the
diagnosis came well afterward. Sometimes I lie awake

wondering what came first, the chicken or the egg? Did he foresee my affliction or is there some type of background radiation in the caverns? That system is a labyrinth. I was upside down and backwards after thirty seconds."

"He cared for you."

"I've come to accept that despite his asocial tendencies, Morris valued me. There's a valid correlation. Animals can form attachments with humans and remain fundamentally wild, amoral. He told me, *It's later than you think. Time has come for you to behold a terrible wonder before we sink into the wall of sleep.* I didn't want to accompany him anywhere, but was afraid to refuse."

Terrible wonder sounded too close for comfort to some mystical bullshit Gene K would spout while we were skinning a moose or diagramming the best method to sever a man's arteries.

"Your camera work leaves something to be desired," I said. "What did he show you in the caverns? Was it terrible? Was it wonderful?"

"He wanted to show me the Garden of Night. The sacred gallery of Those Who Came Before Men. A site of worship, of sacrifice. My memory is Swiss cheese. Fumes, electromagnetic currents. Claustrophobia, perhaps. I was positive he meant to leave me down there in the dark. Fear scrambled my senses. I recall dizziness before I fainted. He carried me to the surface and brought me home without a word."

"Okay. The caves held an irresistible attraction for him. I wonder if that's where he took all those heads he chopped off."

"Morris was pathologically fascinated by the idea of death. His and others'. Insisted the black ops programs and his forays into the caves changed him on a molecular level; opened doorways of the mind. He believed he could intermittently predict the future. Gripped my shoulder, looked me dead bang in the eye, and said that by the time I betray him, it won't matter anymore. We'd both be as good as dead."

"A reliable source assures me Oestryke is already *dead* dead."

"With any luck, your source is correct. I'd have to see it myself before I popped a champagne cork."

"Why do you say that?"

Vance rose and went to one of his cabinets of tools. He moved gingerly, his body already stiff from remaining motionless for just this brief interval. He retrieved a bundle of cloth and unwrapped it. Inside lay a chunk of amber, almost as lustrous as his flesh. An elongated fragment of some larger blackness hung suspended at the milky core.

"It's a spearhead fashioned by a Paleolithic hominid."

Archaeology intrigues me; I've skimmed *Scientific American* in a few waiting rooms. The fossil would be tens, perhaps hundreds of thousands of years old.

"That arrived in a package this summer. Postmarked Kingston, bogus return address."

I was thinking that while fascinating as an artifact, it didn't prove anything conclusive. He unfolded the stained and blotted note that accompanied the spearhead. The note read *Dear X, greetings and farewell from the Garden*

*of Night; blackest heart of the Black Mountain. Carry this
with you into the underworld. Yrs. truly, MO, 6/5.*

"Morris's handwriting," Vance said.

I'd seen examples of that script on a collection of vid-
eotape labels and multiple documents. Absurd as the
proposition appeared, as of June the Croatoan was aboveground. Gene, wherever he was, had to be laughing at the
look on my face.

CHAPTER THIRTY-NINE

I assayed a circuitous path back to the rented car. Climbed in and turned the key. The ignition didn't fire. I almost tried again before an alarm bell rang in the primordial depths of my subconscious. That damned lizard stirred again. I stepped out of the car and performed a walk-around, inspecting the undercarriage where a bomb might be easily placed. No bomb. However, snazzy wingtips and the cuffs of expensive pants were visible on the passenger side of the car. A hammer cocked, cold and metallic, in the vicinity of the back of my head. I glanced over my shoulder and Hyde smiled. A rare expression for him.

Jekyll stepped from behind a pillar. He strolled over to relieve me of my revolver and sundry implements of violence while Hyde continued to train the bore of his hand cannon at me.

"Happy Halloween, Coleridge. Check it. Are you aware Black Dog has a nifty, proprietary app that alerts us when a flagged credit card is put into play?" Jekyll dropped the .357 into his pocket. It off-balanced his jacket. He didn't seem to care. "Here's another trade secret—we have a separate, equally handy app that permits us to tap antitheft devices or onboard GPS of any rental vehicle in the registry. Very cool. Scary, if you're twitchy about Big Brother. But cool."

"What a time to be alive," I said. The Black Dogs need not have tailed me; they'd merely had to track an icon on a screen until they found my car and then bided their time like patient little mutts. "Too bad you dumb bastards haven't dedicated more man-hours to tailing the actual bad guy."

"Can I get you to come along quietly?"

I said I would, mentally crossing my fingers. They escorted me across the lot and up a level. Delia Labrador awaited in the fancy black SUV her bodyguards drove everywhere. This was her idea of returning my phone calls.

"He's disarmed and clean," Jekyll said as Hyde prodded me to get in facing Delia.

She'd dressed down for the occasion—a light overcoat, slacks, boots with fur trim, and a snow-white handbag lacking diamonds or gold embroidery. Her makeup did its level best to provide the illusion it didn't exist. I had a fiery, all-consuming passion for Meg, but, merciful God, you couldn't linger that close to Delia Labrador and not get heart palpitations. Her barely there fragrance hinted of top-shelf brandy.

Jekyll shut the door harder than necessary. He and Hyde seated themselves in front. Hyde started the engine as a tinted partition whirred upward and divided the compartment. Moments later, the vehicle rolled forward and onto the street. I didn't inquire where we were bound. Stubbornness is a virtue.

I affected a stoic demeanor and visualized waiting by the river for the bodies of my enemies to bob past.

"I apologize if they were rough. Father terminated their contracts. They're piqued." She produced a lovely, and elaborately engraved, flask from her purse, unscrewed the cap, and took a dainty swig.

I laughed.

"Black Dog will find something for them to do."

"They're already doing it."

"You're paying them out of pocket?"

"Yes."

"Daddy excommunicated you."

"Father and I had a major . . . disagreement. The summerhouse is my new abode." Another swig.

"About Lionel."

"About many issues. Personal security is my own concern, for the moment. Father will calm down."

"Will he?"

"Mom's on my side. She'll exert her wifely influence."

"Pleasant forecast for you, lady. I wonder what the weather has in store for me."

"He's a right sonofabitch. It depends upon his cost–benefit analysis. Your Mafia ties unnerve him. Executives abhor subjecting themselves to the vagaries of the unknown. He isn't certain what will happen if he tries to put you in check."

"Rather curious to find out myself."

"It could be useful to have a spare hitman lying around. I'd prefer you alive for the present."

"Don't forget the man of your dreams," I said. "Wouldn't do for that pretty face of Lionel's to be tenderized. Or notched with bullet holes. Not until you get whatever it is you're after. You didn't maneuver us to Oestryke's clubhouse for fun. I'm sure the honeymoon weekend was incidental."

"On the contrary, it was a pleasant vacation until you waved a gun around."

"I hope you don't expect an apology."

"Damn."

"Damn what? Who? Me?"

"You're cold. I've enjoyed the company of criminals and brutes who were gentlemanly, or at least civil."

"It's a hard knock life. I'm not rich—faking civility isn't integral to my skill set."

"No, don't cop out. Don't pretend it's the nature of the business. Your problem is, you can't imagine anyone loving Harry or Lionel—any woman who gets close to them must be running a con. Try showing your friend a modicum of respect."

"I respect *him* plenty." Her words stung more than a few of the punches I'd ever taken. Funny how that works.

"Lionel is sweet. Alas, you're the one calling the tune. I wanted to impress upon you the resources that my family has at its disposal. May this knowledge advise your decisions going forward."

"You wanted to impress upon me that I'm an ant under your family's boot?"

"In essence."

"Alas, you've got this whole scene backward."

Her smile flickered between uncertainty and contempt.

"Do I?"

"*You* didn't catch *me*, Delia. The reason your valets aren't lying shot full of holes back there in the parking garage is because I very much wish to speak with you."

Her smile faded. I would say she belatedly remembered who was seated across from her.

"Before you do anything rash, bear in mind there are two large, heavily armed men two feet behind you. Your weapons have been confiscated and—"

"Not all of my weapons. These dopes always miss something."

"Oh, I see." She composed herself. "Please, continue."

"Last week, I showed you a photograph of Morris Oestryke—or, as he's fondly known around the plantation, Uncle Ephraim. You recognized his face."

"I recognized his eyes. Hardly the same thing. A man visited my shows in the early aughts. Infrequently, perhaps five or six times, but his presence left an impression. Like a stain." Her hand trembled as she lifted the flask to her lips.

"Come on. Blood knows blood."

"He was a creepy, nameless old man who watched from the back of the room. Creepy old men are a ubiquitous hazard in the song-and-dance industry. Like sand traps on a golf course. Anyway, he hadn't come around for a while and it slipped my mind."

"Nic Royal murdered Harry and Ray. Tall, ornery fellow. Roomies with Harry. I'm sure you've met."

"Your theory regarding his motive?"

"Ray's death is a mystery. Harry and your uncle were tight. Then Harry got himself in a bind and betrayed Ephraim to the bad guys. The bad guys took Ephraim into the woods and shot him dead. Or left him for dead. Distinction without a difference—Royal is Ephraim's protégé and he took exception. Getting even became his mission in life."

"This is a shock. Nic seemed decent. For a thug, at least. Harry treated him like a kid brother."

"By 'decent,' you mean not the type to decapitate someone."

"I suppose that's what I mean."

The SUV escaped surface street traffic and merged onto the highway south.

"You're the common denominator," I said.

"I'm anything but common. Nic only hung around us because Harry took him under his wing. Nic was a wallflower."

"Some wallflower."

"I wasn't stonewalling you—not entirely. Harry's death stunned me. I initially assumed his past had caught up to him: a jealous lover, a vindictive hustler, the mob. He'd alluded to the possibility."

I waited.

She sipped. She'd had a skinful, yet maintained control and was probably more formidable than ever. I'd begun to think maybe she and Lionel were compatible on a more meaningful level.

"Every wee Labrador grows up hearing that Uncle Ephraim is the devil. Some claim he murdered a boy his own age whose family worked on the estate and that he trafficked in the occult. Grandfather staged a car accident and Ephraim was eventually shipped away under a different name."

"We're both up to speed on your uncle's crazy adventures since then," I said. "Hitman, serial killer, lurker at striptease shows. Alas, there's one last, nasty wrinkle."

"I'll brace myself."

"Obviously, the guys who shot your uncle are totally convinced he's dead. I've also labored under that theory. Until recently. In light of new information, I've come to believe he's alive and kicking."

She waited.

"More important, I think you know his current whereabouts." I watched with minor satisfaction as her soft, gloating expression went rigid. "Your uncle must be a physical wreck. At his age, a man doesn't easily recover from chronic illnesses or bullet wounds. While Royal may do his bidding on the Murder, Inc., front, the old man likely requires regular care. A private clinic or hospital, say?"

She could've done with her all-concealing movie-starlet glasses at that moment. Fear, anger, and a peculiar hint of relief shone in her eyes, in the set of her lovely jaw. For an instant, her affected diffidence, her meticulously cultivated disdain, wavered.

"Trouble is, you're an amateur," I said. "How far can I be trusted? Well, my dear—how far can you throw me? Worse—for you, at least—you've already dived into the deep end."

"Your agency motto should state *Better to be lucky and persistent than good*."

"Win is a win. Now, tell me what I've won."

"Bravo, Inspector Clouseau. 'The Croatoan' is among us, albeit in a moribund condition." Her contempt resurfaced. "After you lumbered onto the scene and we spoke, it occurred to me that Father might not be totally invested in capturing Harry's murderer."

"You pulled back the carpet to see the dirt."

"Exactly. I sniffed about, putting together years of partially overheard conversations and rumors. I snooped into Father's secret papers, which are hardly as secret as he'd hoped. Lo and behold, I realized the man you're hunting is a Labrador. 'Realized' is a dodge. I admitted to myself who it had to be. When I confronted Father with what I knew, he unburdened himself."

"Did this 'unburdening' involve a gun barrel fixed between his eyes?"

"No. It involved my knowledge of a trip he took to Moscow to secure a clandestine business loan. He sincerely believes the less my mother knows of his fetish for prostitutes and water sports, the better."

"Assuming Mom's as ruthless as you are, I'd have to agree," I said.

"Your suspicions are in line with the ugly truth. Father and Ephraim have been in touch, off and on, since

1969. Three years ago, somebody—a 'vengeful criminal boss,' perhaps—shot Ephraim and buried him in a shallow grave in the Pine Barrens. Ephraim clawed free and dragged himself to a road. A Good Samaritan took him to the hospital as a John Doe. My uncle managed to call in the cavalry, and Father spirited him away before the authorities arrived."

"Daddy couldn't very well refuse a brother in need. Especially not this brother."

"Father did what Labrador protocol demands—he squirreled his brother away at a private facility. Alas, my uncle didn't perish of his wounds and thus spare everyone subsequent troubles. He persists in a semi-catatonic state. Long periods of unconsciousness punctuated by brief intervals of lucidity." She passed me a scrap of paper with an address scribbled on it.

Contemplating the case in its entirety, I wondered if in addition to "brief intervals of lucidity," her uncle also enjoyed brief intervals of mobility. An unsettling thought.

We traveled in silence for a while. She with her flask, me itchy under the collar and vulnerable despite my size, experience, and skill. Reality currently manifested as a vast body of dark water. Bottomless, trackless.

"I'm curious what you think will happen next," I said; and I was.

"You're an attack dog. My dearest hope is that you'll behave true to type and commit acts of reckless and extreme violence. Sic 'em, boy."

"I don't 'sic 'em' anymore."

"Nonsense. Isaiah, you'll never be a detective. You

are, however, singularly qualified to deal with this problem."

"Murdering an invalid?"

"Putting down a feral beast that would rip you apart, if given an opportunity. Isn't it a mistake to underestimate a foe? Just when you think the monster is dead, it opens its eyes."

"Get it straight—*Royal* is my foe. Your uncle is a world-class asshole whom everybody wants to make my problem."

"The victims deserve justice."

"Some of them," I said. "Have you considered putting this on Jekyll and Hyde? Those two passed the BD psych eval? They aren't averse to a spot of wetwork. My main man Hyde; he wouldn't flinch to cap a man on a gurney."

"I asked."

"Paid-by-the-hour goons said no to the spectacular Delia Labrador?"

"These men aren't like you," she said with a great deal of acid. "Not underneath where it counts. They're paid to appear menacing and disperse the rabble."

"They're too smart to go against your dad, is what you're saying."

"It seems so," she said.

"You think I have a less developed survival instinct than your goons?"

"That remains to be seen, doesn't it? If you act, act quickly. With all this excitement, Father may decide to relocate my uncle soon. It may already be in the works."

The day we'd met at the Stone Rooster, Delia matter-of-factly proclaimed an interest in vengeance on behalf of her lover. I was starting to believe her.

"The Labrador family closet is full of skeletons," she said. "Two weeks ago, I could choose to ignore the rumors. Harry and I weren't in love at the end, although we cared deeply for each other. Even you should understand that idea."

"Yes."

I held out my hand. She passed the flask and I drank. I didn't recognize the variety of brandy, except that it was of a caliber well beyond what I could casually afford.

"Harry and Ray were killed for the exact same reason," she said. "In Harry's case, his betrayal of Uncle Ephraim was a significant factor. However, I think in your line, they call it a secondary motive."

"And the primary?"

"I slept with Ray and Harry. There's the real reason they're dead."

"Okay, let me process this a moment," I said.

"Ephraim is in a state of rapid decline. Barely capable of speech. I had to put my ear too close to his lips. The reek would turn your stomach. He whispered I resemble my mother. My gorgeous, blonde mother. I defiled myself rutting with filthy old men, so he'd sent an Angel of Death to watch over me."

My breath caught in my chest as the yellow, bestial eye of the universe opened and beamed forth a torrent of frigid light. Those girls and young women slaughtered by the Tri-State Killer were blondes of a similar size, form, and physiognomy; although none compared to Delia Labrador. Who could? Here was the Madonna–whore complex taken to its furthest logical extreme. I grappled with what to say. My arsenal of quips and homey observations was inadequate. So, I bit my tongue.

"I intended to end his wretched life," she said. "Murder doesn't seem to be in my repertoire. I couldn't bring myself to end him. And so, we come to your role in this tragicomedy."

A tear trickled down her cheek, silvery and pure in the light that filtered through the window tint. Maybe genuine, maybe not. She brushed it aside and took a full-on gulp from the rapidly diminishing flask. *That* gesture I bought completely.

"I don't care whether Ephraim rose like Lazarus from his deathbed and personally stuck the knife in Harry. I don't care if a psycho disciple acted in his name. I don't care whether my grandfather or my father, or both of the sonsofbitches dressed in matching onesies, yanked the marionette strings." She spoke through clenched teeth with the painstaking enunciation that incipient drunkenness induces. Her body tremored, as if she were recreating an act of horrific mayhem in her mind. "I don't care. I don't fucking care. Harry didn't deserve that horrible death or to be desecrated. Somebody has to pay."

"You're in luck, Ms. Labrador. Somebody always does."

CHAPTER FORTY

Delia's boys dropped me at the Hudson Valley Mall. Lionel leaned against the frame of his car, smoking a cigarette. He and Delia may have made eye contact before she rolled up her window and the SUV sped away.

We headed in the opposite direction.

"Be dark in forty-five minutes." Lionel sounded like a hero in an old horror film preparing to storm the evil count's gothic stronghold. For all I knew, that's exactly what we were doing. Who could say what awaited us at the Labradors' secret hospice?

"Curtis in the picture?" he said. He wore driving gloves.

"This is a need-to-know situation. I haven't decided if I need him to know." I followed his cue and donned a set he'd left on the floorboard for me to borrow.

"*I'd* love to know the plan."

"I want to look at . . . him. We'll go from there." Despite my conflict, despite my protestations, nothing was going to stop me from seeing the Croatoan up close and personal. What then? That's as many moves ahead as my mind could process.

"Right." He lit a cigarette from the dash knob and cracked his window. "Delia must be supermax TNT furious with her dad to cross him like this."

"She's carrying a torch for you, and Daddy is interfering."

"Yeah? Think so?"

"Whatever you do, when this is over, sleep with her every chance you get. Our lives might depend upon it."

Lionel gave me a two-finger salute and a crooked smile.

"I'll do my best to save you, buddy."

EVENING COAGULATED along the horizon. A phalanx of black-and-purple thunderheads shrouded the emerging stars. The immensity of night and darkness pressed against the rim of the world and trickled into my heart. My hand rested against the butt of my .357. The pistol was a steely comfort even as the solidity of physics and reason threatened to dissolve around me.

My neck tightened and pain knifed into the back of my skull. I closed my eyes and focused. I reflected on what Xerxes Vance told me minutes before I'd bid him farewell.

I've photographed many animals. Predator observation is my forte. Consider an animal in South Africa called the pelican spider. Its jaws and neck are longer than usual—grotesquely so. Nature designed it to hunt other spiders. It's only my pet theory—but I propose there are people like that. I'm not referring to run-of-the-mill serial killers; nor people who lack empathy or are addicted to sadism. I'm not referring to people afflicted by a brain disorder, or people lacking a gene. This is rarer. Humans evolved to catch other humans. These predators don't possess elongated necks or gaff hooks for fangs. The horrible machinery is hidden on the inside. You won't see it before they come very close. They can come very close because they've an inherent ability to mimic unaffected emotion, and because they successfully mimic a spectrum of phenotypes.

Do you think the handlers at Zircon comprehend that Oestryke is more than a hitter? I'm a jaded guy. Even so, it's uncomfortable to believe a corporation would tolerate such a creature set loose upon the world.

Do they comprehend his alien psychology? Vance rolled another joint. *Whoever was involved from the beginning of his transformation? Certainly, they do. His essential inhumanity, his derangement, is the primary reason the patriarchs walked through fire to keep him in the fold. Those who control Zircon are wealthy and influential thanks to their affinity for envisioning the full scope of available opportunities. R and D is the lifeblood of their enterprise, if not the final purpose, my friend.*

I suggest the truth is far worse. Our own protectors have sanctioned this corruption. Morris's wartime exploits and the mob hits were convenient testing grounds. But consider the raw intelligence aberrant psych teams could glean from a war-hardened serial killer. You'll never find proof the Feds were monitoring his murders; charting and analyz-

ing how to weaponize his predilection to hunt fellow pri-
mates. Guaranteed they were. Oh, yes, they were.

BLESSED WITH THE WEALTH of kings and pharaohs, the
Labradors could've hidden their prodigal son anywhere.
Had the decision been mine, I would've chosen the caldera
of a dead volcano on an uncharted island in the South
Pacific; or I would've stuffed the wretch into a burlap bag
and tossed it off the Tappan Zee Bridge.

Eschewing such exotic measures, Jonathan Labrador
opted to conceal his murderous sibling the last place anyone would look—had they been looking—which was in
plain sight.

The nameless hospice occupied a plot of erstwhile
farmland, southeast of Olivebridge and the Ashokan Reservoir. The main structure was a large single-level field-
stone cylinder crowned by a conical roof of overlapping
brown tiles. Thick glass-block windows warped the red
blob of sun and the pastures of tall, pale grass. An A-frame
barn crumbled against the nearest fence line.

Lionel parked at the entrance to a long, unpaved driveway. The yard lay empty but for a white van. The van had
an extended body and ceiling, designed for transporting
patients.

He mashed his cigarette in the ashtray.

"I vote we turn the car around and help the Italian
posse hunt for Royal."

"You're outvoted."

"Breathe it in, amigo. My mom smelled snow from a

blue sky and, next day, here came a blizzard. Granddad's trick knee pained him when bad weather was on the way. My nose doesn't work quite the same, but it's just as reliable. Fuck walking into that building. We should get the hell outta here."

"The person laid up in there can't hurt anybody," I said. It sounded brave.

"That so? Why did you request the Mossberg?"

I glanced over my shoulder. Yes, there she was on the backseat, draped in a Norwegian blanket. The worse of my two angels counseled that I should walk inside and cut the Croatoan in half to prove Chekhov right.

"Reasonable precautions. Have to assume Royal pays homage to the king. Hate to cross paths unprepared."

"To hell with being reasonable. Rather not hang with the Italians? Fine. We can pack an overnight kit and tramp up to Anvil Mountain. I'm a decent spelunker. There might be a jackpot waiting for us to claim it. Kooks love to hide shit in caves. Guns. Millions of dollars. Gold."

"We'll invest in hazmat suits and hit the caves. After we sort this business. Delia mentioned that her uncle might be whisked away in the dead of night. She may have something there."

"Labrador won't do jack," he said. "I'll stake the farm he's sick of this crap. They're counting on you to do the dirty work. We're too deep to tag the cops. Anyway, once a hitter, always a hitter. Bad breeding will out, is how they're betting. Papa washes his hands like Pilate; Delia can tell herself she's clean. Or maybe you *have* turned over a new leaf and take a walk. Status quo is maintained and they ponder the next move. It's not perfect. It's what they've got."

"The die has been cast," I said.

But I did seriously consider his proposal that we scamper like rabbits. Surf crashed against my consciousness with each heartbeat. Another incipient migraine.

An alternate reality seeped into my own, similar to the black hole that had dilated momentarily in the Michigan rest stop and the West Kill Lodge. In this other baby, half-shaped mirror universe, a nondescript sedan screeched into the yard. The make and model most frequently found at the bottom of a lake or torched in a parking lot. Curtis and four of his men unloaded from the car. The foot soldiers were armed with Uzis on waist slings. I recalled these guys from our meeting at the Poughkeepsie YMCA.

Our confrontation unfolded with the hazy logic of a vivid dream.

Shoe, meet the other foot, I said.

Whaddya mean? Curtis lit a cigarette and squinted at the property.

This time last year, you were extricating me from a thorny predicament. Tables have turned.

He exhaled. His eyes were dead. He was ready to whack somebody, anybody.

Coleridge, for both our sakes, I pray this is worth the drive. Wanda promised me a steak dinner and some light role play for dessert. She'd already poured the wine when you interrupted us. That fuckin' ship has sailed.

It'll sail back. I gestured toward the hospice. *The Cro-*

atoan is inside. Alive. Or half dead. Nic Royal serves as his eyes, his ears, his red right hand.

Sonofabitch. Nic fuckin' Royal is the Croatoan's soldier?

March in and put the guy out of our collective misery. Should be easy. He's on death's doorstep. I smiled sardonically. Hasn't been the same since you double-tapped him.

Don't bust my balls.

Wouldn't dream of it. Vengeance is yours, my friend. I'm done. We're done.

Curtis stared with an expression of wonderment.

Wake the fuck up. This news changes everything. I don't care about settlin' the score. I care about the goddamned money. Y'know, those fabulous sums the Croatoan socked away for retirement. Millions. It's always been about the money. Before I shot the prick, I tortured him six ways from Sunday and got zip.

Huh? I think you omitted the torture part from your story.

Did I? Could be I told you what was necessary and left it at that.

What now?

Now I stake out this shithole and catch Royal when he pays a visit.

Be careful. He could already be inside. Plan to torture him too?

Yeah. Maybe the cocksucker has an idea where the Croatoan hid his loot.

Ah, those universal constants, I said. Greed and treachery.

Save your judgment. I slew a terror. A terror! Buried it alive. What was his is mine. No sense letting a fortune rot, eh?

Buried alive, you say. How is it he's returned from the grave?

He sighed and dropped his cigarette butt.

It was a cold night. You got no clue. Frozen dirt and one lousy shovel. I did the best I could, considerin' the circumstances.

I'm sure you did. We're good? Our slate is clean?

Yeah. It's clean. You and your partner need to get gone.

He nodded to his men. One of them drove the sedan down the road. Curtis and the rest of his crew trooped into the house. The front door flew shut behind them.

I snapped back to reality. My reality, at any rate.

The sun finished its plunge behind the mountains; an ice pick stabbing to the hilt into the dark.

CHAPTER FORTY-ONE

I exited the Monte Carlo. My shoes crunched dead leaves and gravel. I fetched the shotgun from the backseat and tucked it under my arm. Admittedly, not a gesture compatible with the protocols of polite society. I doubted members of polite society operated this shady facility.

A rising breeze whistled around my ears. It had an edge. I straightened my jacket and listened to the sighing grass and the creak of limbs in the woods behind the house. Ten, perhaps fifteen minutes along pastoral roads to a busy highway and yet, at the moment, we were as isolated as if we'd parachuted into the Brooks Range in Alaska.

I strode toward the entrance. Lionel's disapproving gaze burned a hole between my shoulders. He couldn't know I'd come to a crossroads while riding with Delia Labrador—obey the righteous prescriptions of my new straight-and-narrow code and spill everything to Agent Bellow; turn over the tapes, weapons, and cash. Or resort to my old familiar patterns and fulfill Curtis's wishes—

which entailed keeping the loot and whacking Ephraim Labrador or turning him over to the mob. Dad knew I'd never escape. My brain concurred; the message hadn't reached my heart.

Gloom cloaked the interior of the old building. Brown wooden walls, threadbare carpets, and blocky thrift store furniture circa a golden era skin-deep beauty pageant America shot through with cancer and institutional malaise like the painting of Dorian Gray. Passages let into cramped recesses. Angles were skewed, proportions off by a few inches. Lilac air fresheners weakly diffused odors of musk and mildew. And it was hot.

No one manned the reception desk.

To the right, pots clattered behind a set of swinging doors. Bacon and eggs were on the griddle, judging by the scents wafting forth to mix with the less pleasant odors permeating the area. Left, cable news muttered from a flat-screen TV mounted in the commons. There were several card tables, metal folding chairs, and a treadmill. Three big full-color Ronald Reagan campaign posters circa 1979 were tacked on a wall near the TV. Everything— style, color, era—was mismatched. The setup could've been a derelict bingo parlor.

A burly man in a tight yellowish hospital coat, khakis, and tennis shoes reposed on a couch, idly clicking his remote. He settled upon a hard-core porn video.

"Excellent choice, sir," I said.

"Visiting hours are posted." The orderly appraised me with a microglance, then intently scrutinized the on-screen action. My shotgun failed to impress. "Come back when we're open for business."

"I apologize for the inconvenience. This is important. We won't be five minutes."

"Get bent until visiting hours." He pointedly increased the volume. When he raised his arm, his sleeve pulled down, revealing the contours of a skull-and-crossbones prison tat. So, the Labradors had stocked this terrarium with disposable individuals who feared no man and answered solely to envelopes of cash. Another former brother-in-arms.

I made a fist. Lionel smiled. I sighed and unclenched.

"Brady Labrador. This is my, uh, cousin Sven."

"Oh." The man flinched, but he didn't set aside the remote or look away from the screen. "Sunset Suite. Go through that archway. Down the hall, straight ahead to the last door."

"Thanks, pal."

"You know what?" Lionel drew his pistol and clubbed the guy with its butt. Two savage blows to the crown of his head and night night. "If these convicts have any complaints, they can take it up with management. They won't." He proceeded briskly into the kitchen. Bemused, I watched him go. He was right—Jonathan Labrador would slap an extra Benjamin in this stooge's pay envelope and consider the matter resolved. The person in the kitchen uttered a challenge. Something crashed. Ten seconds later, Lionel stepped out and nodded the all-clear.

We followed the orderly's directions. There were doors along the way. We didn't meet anyone or hear any sounds of human habitation within the sealed rooms. Dusty ceiling lamps gave off poor light. The hall seemed to telescope and my head swam with nausea.

A door at the far end of the hall was bisected red and black in thick, haphazard brushstrokes I'd seen somewhere else. Where the other doors were numbered, this one had a placard that actually read SUNSET SUITE. It swung inward with a faint protest of warped hinges.

I entered a stiflingly hot room. Ready for anything and nothing remotely like what I found waiting.

An iron brazier, lifted directly from a monk's cell in a Himalayan monastery, fumed with pungent cherry blossom incense. The stink of green rot pervaded, regardless. Thick, black floor-to-ceiling drapes were drawn. A mirror ball provided a circle of illumination that glowed and reflected from chipped tiles. The room was otherwise devoid of furniture. It emitted a weird energy, as if the house custodian had moments ago hastily mopped up a pentagram.

A figure lay upon a reed mat in the center of the room. It resembled a mummified corpse; fragile and gray as a bundle of twigs and partially covered by a red blanket. Morris Oestryke; Ephraim Labrador; the Croatoan. He'd wasted beyond the ken of mere mortals and yet lived. Cysts and boils suppurated on his exposed arms and torso; his lips peeled wide in a permanent grin or snarl. This was the Devil in his ultimate form.

Nic Royal knelt at the Croatoan's side in the posture of a petitioner. He'd worn dark clothing, suitable for sneaking around in the woods. A stocking snugged above his eyes; like a bank robber in the final stages of preparation. I didn't immediately see a weapon, which meant nothing.

We moved several feet apart to best cover Royal in a cross fire. I racked the slide of the Mossberg.

"Hear that, Nic? That's Saint Pete's secretary typing your death certificate."

Royal watched us dispassionately. He slipped the stocking downward, squashing his features into grotesque proportions. It darkened to match his clothes. The stocking wasn't nylon; equally sheer, though. I guessed I was observing firsthand a piece of special military equipment. Shape-forming fibers that elite forces are rumored to carry in their bags of esoteric tricks.

"An infamous murderer once characterized his existence as a 'violent distance between realities.' How would you characterize yours?" His voice distorted slightly. The mirror ball brightened and dimmed with his words. It rotated, beaming rays of alternating white and black.

I ignored the shadows crawling toward me on the walls and the floor, and flying across the ceiling. In my adolescence, Dad took us kids to a carnival where I gaped in awe at a magician's magic lantern. Now I was trapped inside one.

Coincidence had nothing to do with this tableau—Royal had known we, or someone else with bad intentions, would eventually converge upon this unholy sanctuary. Today, tomorrow, a hundred years from that moment; time and distance are illusory. He must have also accepted the reality that he couldn't prevail. The demolition and heat death of the universe are ever in motion; the ouroboros swallows itself whole and takes us along for the ride.

"Hands on your head. Fingers interlaced." Lionel possibly had some notion about capturing our man alive and depositing him with Curtis; as if the captain were the local magistrate offering a bounty. I didn't see it going that way; not even close.

Royal slowly gained his feet. He raised his hands to shoulder height, away from his body. He gently weaved his head to and fro, grooving to nonexistent music. With predators, everything is indicative of a threat, overt or subtle. He wanted to lull us, to acclimate us to his movements. I applied a few ounces of pressure to the trigger.

"The balls on astronauts," he said. "Absolute clanking steel balls. Test pilots and the men who dove the first submarines into the deep. *Mysterium tremendum et fascinans,* brother. Fear and attraction in the face of the tremendous mystery. We're surrounded by majesties and horrors."

The lights whirled faster and the shadows blurred and snatched at my eyes.

"Any second, we could fracture this thin shell and fall into an abyss." His right hand chopped downward and the knife practically teleported from his hand and clanged against Lionel's pistol. Lionel sent a round high and off target. Royal stepped back with easy grace and melted through the drapes as though sinking into a black pool.

I squeezed the trigger in the frozen instant that his

arms and torso were still visible. The hammer clicked. His torso sank into the blackness of the drapes, and then his arms went. One heartbeat, and another. The shotgun barrel ignited with a thundering boom and the shock wave traveled backward along the stock and into my shoulder, the black drapes hanging in tatters, and I ejected the shell and gave it hell again, and time sped up, caught up, and I almost vomited because the mirror ball strobed hot jagged strokes of fiery light past my eyes and into my brain. I chambered another round.

Lionel rushed forward in frame-by-frame stop-motion. He tore aside the shredded curtains. Behind the curtains, a set of French doors hung ajar, and past the framed threshold lay a starless void. Three herky-jerky cartoon iterations of my friend vaulted into the darkness—white limned in black, black limned in white, and a split of both—daisy-chained together, gone.

Forever and a minute to reach the doors. Blood spattered the frame and splotched two wooden steps and the beginning of a stone pathway. The light reached no farther.

I breathed in crisp sweetness. My knees buckled or the world tilted, and I slid away from the portal on slick tiles, back into the chamber of rot and ruin, and took a knee beside the Croatoan. I'd whiffed the green stench before; in my hotel room at the West Kill Lodge and in my office. The mirror ball stopped; a small eclipse with white fires trailing at its rim.

The Croatoan sat upright with horrible alacrity, blanket gathered around his waist. His teeth clenched upon a glossy disc that protruded slightly past his lips. In those abbreviated moments when I should've clapped my hands over my ears, jumped up, and ran, I futilely tried to place the object; closest I came was an elk caller. Clabbered saliva bubbled at the corners of his mouth and oozed over the device. His cheeks expanded and he whistled shrilly.

During one of my not-infrequent periods spent convalescing from some injury or other, I'd caught a program on musical instruments of ancient cultures. The Aztec death whistle is one that made an impression. An archaeologist had trilled the whistle, which emitted a note like a human scream. Though filtered by television, the resulting wails evoked within me a brief taste of primal horror. The Croatoan's toy keened in a manner reminiscent of the death whistle, but far worse in its rawness and immediacy.

A spike of ice shattered my consciousness.

SWEET OBLIVION didn't last long. Five or six seconds, tops.

My subconscious fastened onto Meg, a brilliant point of light suspended against a backdrop of infinite blackness. I flew toward her at tremendous velocity. My thoughts were an open wound, stitching together at eight times on the fast-forward button.

Oh, Meg. Sultry, bluesy. Smoldering lust, fearsome, anger—these are your colors. You love Homer, Odysseus, and mean old Hercules. These are your colors.

Barefoot dancer to Led Zeppelin and Johnny Cash. These are your colors. You're too good, too smart, too much for the likes of me. Pure soul.

She held out her hand and I lunged the last million miles or so and opened my eyes. I lay sprawled at the foot of the Croatoan's mat. My body was leaden and unresponsive, my cheek pressed hard to the floor. I'd lost the Mossberg.

The Croatoan forcibly straightened his bent and twisted legs. Right, now left. His bones and joints and sinews cracked loudly. Forget atrophy, forget immobility, forget dementia and decrepitude. His corroded nails were long from neglect. He dug them under his chin and rolled what I'd taken as flesh upward. Another mask, the same material as Royal's, welded to his face. It cost him to remove the mask; black blood welled from the pores and rawness beneath.

Wait, wait, wait, he said, singsong cruel; or perhaps his words originated within my imagination. *I'll be with you soon.* Gene's voice, somehow.

I may be a fool, but I'm no damned fool. I twitched my fingers, my hands. My legs jerked and kicked feebly, willed to life, and it hurt, pinpricks and darning needles, the way muscles do after you've slept on them wrong. I began to crawl past him and out the way we'd entered the room a thousand years ago.

Wait, wait, now in my grandfather's pleading voice. The mirror ball dimmed. The Croatoan's silhouette wavered and darkened at its center like a black hole. *I've wanted to kill you for years.* Mr. Apollo.

He shucked the stocking and cast aside the sodden lump. I looked away, valiantly tamping down a scream.

In the future where I murder you in ninety seconds or so, I will find forty-seven dollars and an Alaska driver's license in your wallet. The ID is three years old and tucked under your New York State card. Dad's voice, perhaps Dad's not-so-secret desire.

He may have been correct about the contents of my wallet, or not. Half the time, I don't recall what I've stashed in there. I kicked, clawed, swam through the doorway. The hall lights blinked and I heard him coming, nails clattering, moist flesh scudding on tile. He too crawled, hand over hand. Faster, though.

I stared through a fish-eye lens. The hall stretched and expanded into the moonlit wilds of the Catskills—

Water roars down off the black mountain. The black river sweeps you aside as it pours through rock. A bottomless pit where the bones and prehistoric souls dwell in frigid stench. Sheol *of the troglodytes. Even Satan and Whiro want nothing to do with this miserable abscess—*

My hearing came and went, crackling intermittently like a fried speaker. I struggled with the revolver, drew it from the holster, attempted to lurch to my knees, and failed.

The Croatoan grasped my ankle and calf and sank his talons into the meat. He slowly laddered his way atop me. I bucked and tried to roll, desperate to bring the .357 into play. Anvil Mountain may as well have sat upon my back.

Isaiah Coleridge, the man who didn't know his place. Gene again. *The pet savage. A tribal with a slick haircut*

and thousand-dollar suit who speaks English real good. Mr.
Apollo liked parading his tame beast around on a leash.

He plucked the useless gun from my fist and sent it
skating. A loop of hemp, perhaps the mat's drawstring,
made a slipknot around my neck. I managed to insert a
couple of fingers before the cord tightened, which merely
forestalled the inevitable.

His stench suffocated me. My thoughts burned to ash
and the ashes scattered. Oh, I'd definitely had it. There's
no comeback for an expertly applied strangulation. I
couldn't summon the hideous red light of primordial
fury, or tap into my reservoir of enormous strength.

Film and literature usually get garroting wrong. It's a
pet peeve of mine. My dad jeered whenever war flicks
screwed up the details, and this is in the same category
of annoyance having throttled a few guys. Right way to
do it is with wire or cord braided into a pair of handles.
I prefer large-grained wood. You don't strangle the victim facing in the same direction. Why not? Because unless you're my size, your arms don't possess enough
power to ensure a quick, certain kill. Proper execution:
cross the handles in an X and snap-pivot so you and the
target are back to back, ass to ass, and drop your weight
like you're performing a judo throw. Gravity will do the
dirty work. Piano wire slices right through the carotid,
the windpipe, and his fingers if he sticks them in there
before the snare draws tight. I'm a piano-wire guy, although I've used a knitted scarf, jump rope, and neckties
in a pinch. I've resorted to my bare hands, although
that's the caveman method.

The Croatoan made a sloppy effort, but it was working for the sonofabitch anyway. Black stars danced in my peripheral vision. The one tiny saving grace? He was enthusiastic, but not physically powerful. I had a few extra moments to calm myself and struggle with a purpose. Instinct took over. My free arm—the right one—didn't want to die. It remembered the jawbone knife on my hip. My right hand concurred and it gripped the knife and yanked it free. My arm lifted and swept over and behind in a scything gesture. The knife sliced cord, and flesh and small bones.

His weight shifted and I convulsed and threw him off me. I torqued sideways, my face near his own festering mass of ossified fibers and gaping sores, my left shoulder pinning him against the wall. I plunged the blade repeatedly into his chest. Rapid-fire as a prison yard execution. In vain, he attempted to blow his damnable whistle. Bloody froth wheezed from his mouth; a pitiful sob that amounted to nothing. I stabbed until my sleeve was drenched to the elbow. I stabbed until my knuckles broke through his rib cage. Finally, my arm went numb and my lungs convulsed and called it quits.

Afterward, I went on my hands and knees and collapsed at a safe distance. Fending off a gangrenous, decrepit old man wasn't a high-water mark among my exploits. Didn't stop me from congratulating myself on living to fight again.

Footsteps clicked and drew near. Delia Labrador stepped from the shadows and paused directly beneath a lamp. Mistress of the dramatic entrance, illuminated as a

Queen of Ice. She hefted my revolver. Jekyll and Hyde flanked her.

"I had a change of heart," she said. Which probably meant she'd always planned to show up after the fact. "Where's Lionel?"

"Aw, I thought you were worried about me." I had difficulty speaking. Dizziness and nausea came at me in ever larger and meaner waves.

She went to the Croatoan and leaned over him. They exchanged murmurs. She straightened and gripped the revolver with both hands the way it's taught in the law enforcement academy of your choice. She aimed the barrel at his head and fired twice. The reports were muted, as if traveling a great distance underwater. What would Lionel make of this surprising facet of our dear Ms. Labrador? He'd be terrified and aroused, if I knew my buddy.

When she walked back and placed the gun on my lap, I asked what her uncle said as his last words.

"He said to tell you 'She snuffed the cat.' That's it."

Like the gunshots, her words traveled slowly, and it was full dark by the time they arrived.

CHAPTER FORTY-TWO

O f course, there was a hospital stint.

The doc showed me an X-ray of a hairline fracture toward the rear of my skull, somewhere in the neighborhood of a month old. This aligned with my struggle at the trailer when Mr. Skinhead knocked my head on the floor. Subsequent swelling had likely contributed to my recent bouts of disorientation, nausea, and migraines. He asked if I'd experienced hallucinations or related symptoms. His concern stemmed from the fact that I'd suffered a brain bleed within the previous twenty-four hours. Additionally, several older lesions were in the process of healing. The prognosis was optimistic, albeit he would've greatly desired to understand the cause.

I told him he wouldn't believe the cause. Then I went under for a long stretch.

On the sixth or seventh day, my system recovered a little and I lay in bed, staring out the window at a fenced courtyard lawn and the distant outline of the Catskills. Lionel had dropped in earlier to say that I'd definitely winged Royal. He'd tracked the blood trail into the woods until he lost it on account of darkness. He wagered from the staggering amount of blood, Royal's corpse wound up at the bottom of a ravine. A hunter or hiker would trip over the bones.

Sure.

Someone scoured the mess at the hospice. Delia had informed him there'd be no corpses, no official report, and no scandal. Jekyll and Hyde located a car belonging to Curtis's men hidden elsewhere on the property. Lionel made the executive decision to relay an extremely abbreviated account of the incident to Curtis—he excluded any reference to the Croatoan, money, or Zircon. He simply reported that we'd managed to corner Royal and inflict life-threatening injuries upon him before the man escaped. Curtis wasn't happy. Nonetheless, I'd fulfilled my end of the bargain. He consented to pay up and wipe my slate. Although, *for now* was strongly implied.

Lionel inquired what to do with the tapes and other evidence. I instructed him to hide everything in a secure location as leverage in case Zircon or the Labradors tried to get cute down the line. Jonathan Labrador cared for his brother; conversely, he was surely relieved the chapter had closed.

I put a finger to my lips, indicating the possibility of surveillance, and then sketched a note explaining how Black Dog had tracked me to Providence and told him not to give any specific details on the off-chance someone had bugged the hospital room. He was to contact a friend of a friend in Albany who ran a surveillance-gadget shop.

This friend would hook us up with black market toys to sweep for bugs, detect phone taps, and so forth. As for the money we'd buried? A problem for another day when I could plan long-range stratagems.

In other news, Burt Plantagenet called to say our contract was terminated. He'd gone over to console Aubrey and discovered her in the arms of Elvira Trask. Drunk and tearful, Aubrey confessed that she and Elvira were secretly in love and intended to leave their respective partners. Sorry, Walter. Aubrey knew Burt kept a wad of cash for rainy days and cooked up a scheme to acquire it via a fake extortion plot. Neither she nor Elvira—or, most notably, Elvira's boys—counted on homicidally violent me to ruin the scheme.

Outside of that, all was peaceful.

We agreed to not mention Anvil Mountain or its alleged trove of magical shrooms ever again. Not for love or money would we set foot on those slopes—Zircon could do as they pleased. We forged this pact loudly, again for the benefit of eavesdroppers. I meant every syllable.

Lionel squeezed my arm and said a hot date beckoned—he meant to save my life or die trying. I thanked him for his service and missed him the minute he walked out the door.

Over the last month of madcap adventures in the name of clearing my marker with Curtis, I'd likely acquired corporate enemies in Black Dog and Zircon. I'd also made another foe, Nic Royal, who, like Schrödinger's cat, would represent an unknown variable until his corpse surfaced or he returned from the "dead" to exact vengeance. Possibly worst of all, I'd seen and learned of things I could've happily gone a lifetime without encountering.

Which side of the win/loss column should I mark? Considering that I yet drew breath and had "subtracted" a monster from the equation, I knew what Gene K would've said.

Halloween came and went without me to squire Devlin on his trick-or-treat rampage. Meg and the boy visited my bedside prior to the main event. Loopy from drugs and exhaustion, I settled for holding their hands, rather than witty conversation. Meg assured me that Minerva had kept them terrific company; she pined in my absence, lamenting our morning jogs.

The calendar rolled over into the early days of November.

I BROODED ABOUT what we might've discovered within Anvil Mountain had we mustered the guts to explore its depths. When I closed my eyes and drifted on the current of the latest dose of feel-good medicine, my astral self warped there instantly. I shrank to a gnat in God's ear.

No number of guns or amount of training or meanness could stand against real evil grown mammoth over time. Conspiracies crushed men and swept the obliterated remains into a starless abyss. In my fantasy, we brought the untraceable guns. Dad—God alone knows why—Lionel, and me.

We trekked along an overgrown path in the heart of a dark forest. The trail led us to a cave in the foothills where the Black Mountain proper heaved up through stands of pine into a peak like an old, wicked shard of flint. The cave mouth opened before us, its rim overhung with drippings of moss. Prevailing breezes and the bright musk of the evergreens masked the fetidness until we actually crossed over. A cold, damp breeze plastered my hair. We descended and descended and came at last to the Garden of Night.

Struck dumb with awe, we may as well have been prehistoric hunters in the cave of a man-eating tiger or bear, pitiful torches raised to repel the darkness. Our lights played across a tableau of carnage that had unfolded for eons. Broken shapes peeped through amber and flowstone, suggestive of the cryptozoic and the pea soup fog that cloaks all we humans don't readily comprehend.

It was the contemporary embellishments that arrested me and chilled my marrow. The Croatoan had dedicated an altar to murder here in the dripping recesses of the earth. Pickets of severed heads on stakes crisscrossed the uneven floor and adorned rock terraces. Several were fresh enough to draw flies; others were stripped down to yellow skulls. Still others lay embedded within curtains of quartz and flowstone; fossils of an ancient massacre. There would be countless layers beneath these, the earliest predating man. Dad shone his light upon petroglyphs chipped into limestone and contemporary scrawls of gibberish graffiti.

Lionel broke the silence.

Satan's Trophy Room.

That's as far as I got. That's as far as I'd go.

THE BONES IN MY SKULL reknit. I felt restored, if not completely renewed. The experience had dislodged something deep within me. That "something" now tumbled like a splintered bullet through the void that lurks within us all. It manifested as a brief, sharp pang, a stray, violent memory, a cold breath on the nape of my neck. What did it mean? What would become of me? What becomes of anyone?

I took Meg and Devlin roller-skating at the Wooden Wheel on family night. Devlin zipped around gleefully. He wasn't any more coordinated than we adults, but kids have the advantage of bouncing when they fall. He and I wore our matching WONDER WOMAN T-shirts. Mine was a skootch tight in the shoulders, so I flexed shamelessly for Meg and whoever among the congregation of hot cougar moms might appreciate the show.

Days were fine; nights were passable. It didn't get bad until I slept.

IN DREAMS I RETURN TO ALASKA and that frozen plateau where Gene and I stalked the caribou hunters so many years ago. Gene stands in the fire. He rants at the dead and dying stars. Red flames engulf his legs, then all of him, and he laughs.

Ex-mob enforcer turned private investigator Isaiah Coleridge pits himself against a rich and powerful foe when he digs into a possible murder and a sketchy real-estate deal worth billions. Badja Adeyemi, ex-majordomo and bodyguard to an industrial tycoon-cum-U.S. senator, is in hiding and shortly on his way to either a jail cell or a grave, depending on who finds him first. In his final days as a free man, he hires Isaiah Coleridge to tie up a loose end: the suspicious death of his nephew four years earlier. At the time, police declared it an accident, and Adeyemi isn't sure it wasn't, but one final look may bring his sister peace.

So it is that Coleridge and his investigative partner, Lionel Robard, find themselves in the upper reaches of New York State, in a tiny town that is home to outsized secrets and an unnerving cabal of locals who are protecting them. The epicenter of it all is the site of a stalled supercollider project, an immense subterranean construction that may have an even deeper, more insidious purpose. . . .

CHAPTER ONE

A blood moon glowered over the Catskills as I climbed out of the hole. I glowered back, imagining claws and fangs and muscles bursting through my clothes the way it happened for Lon Chaney Jr. on moldy old *Wolf Man* posters. Nothing doing. I remained plain old Isaiah Coleridge, but that was probably bad enough. Werewolf movies were on my mind, for various reasons. Earlier that evening, I'd commented on the topic to my girl, Meg.

Freudian as all get-out, she'd said. *Good guy on the surface; woman-and-sheep-ravishing beast on the inside. Those faux romantic posters where the werewolf—in pants!—carries an unconscious gothic heroine in his arms? Not like that. He—it—dragged the woman by her hair. Blood drooled from where the roots tore free. Her shinbones gleamed in the moonlight. . . .*

You're ruining everything, I'd said. *Why do horror movies always preface the main story with a curse that began years, if not decades or centuries, in the past? Does evil*

need to steep like a tea bag before it can manifest? Didn't
get an answer, but one of Meg's enigmatic smiles, as if to
say I needed to pay more attention.

"Every rock in the state of New York is in this goddamned hole." Lionel Robard tipped back his safari hat.
He leaned on a pickax. It was chilly; steam rose from the
sweat on his brow and his matted hair. Rawboned and
sinewy, he was built for marathon bouts of hard labor.
His Monte Carlo's headlights were on so we could see
what we were doing like a pair of resurrection men in a
graveyard after the world had gone to sleep. He needn't
have bothered, what with all that nickel-plated moonlight spilling through the mist and the trees.

I wiped my face and popped the top of a beer.

"The wages of sin are digging rocks when you go to
bury your ill-gotten treasure." I eyed the inky shadow of a
man crouched near an Austrian pine. The longer I peered,
the more closely the shadow-man resembled a stump.

Last year, we'd snatched a bunch of money from the
secret cache of a notorious murderer romantically dubbed
the Croatoan, since deceased. North of one and a half
million dollars. Held it and waited. First, to see who
might creep from the woodwork searching for the loot,
and for us. Second, the bills were minted in the 1960s
and '70s. Changing that filthy lucre into contemporary
currency without tipping the authorities, or other Wrong
People, presented a challenge. Our best bet was to laun-
der the trove via one of my underworld connections at a
substantial cost and risk of alerting the aforementioned
Wrong People; in this case, the Albany mob.

I kept other items from the Croatoan's cache. Tools of murder, documents, and videocassettes, chiefly. These were buried too, although closer to home in my own backyard. I was tempted to destroy these evil mementos. Yet, what if I needed them one fine day? *That* possibility stayed my hand.

Sinister home videos and killing knives weren't the issue right then. One and a half mil was the issue. Lionel had proven a good sport so far. He wouldn't, couldn't, stay cool forever. Prudence and temperance weren't his watchwords. The Marines taught him other skills, other bellicose virtues.

Thus, here we were in the sneaking hours, burying the money once again (we'd originally stashed it near home and then decided a lonely plot in the hills was wiser) with an eye toward a more permanent solution and only the gods knew when that might be. I set aside a portion for a sample, should a sample become necessary. We sweated a hunter or hiker stumbling across our hand-iwork and leaving an empty pit for us to find later. Far-fetched, yet eminently reasonable to our minds—which spoke volumes about the state of those minds, I suppose.

"I vote we quit pussyfooting around and cash in our chips," Lionel said as we made ready to lower the sealed containers. "The German? He could handle this weight."

"The German isn't safe. His partners were pinched in a sting. The Feds will have him under a magnifying glass."

"I hadn't heard. Who then?"

"Japanese liaison to the U.S. government might be our ticket. Former liaison. Sonny loves America and

Elvis. Three years stateside near Graceland as a teen. I stayed with him in Tokyo when the Outfit sent me over on business. Elvis memorabilia out the wazoo."

"Rhinestone suit?"

"Rhinestone suit."

"Isn't he with the yakuza?" Lionel said.

"Sonny provides equal opportunities to all criminal gangs. I have to be careful. He likes me, but we aren't bosom buddies. He makes one call and we're boned. These ex-diplomats aren't loyal to anybody."

"Man, whatever gets us paid."

"The loot isn't going to evaporate."

"*We* might."

Touché. My left hand trembled. In the dim, and not so dim, past I'd broken it, had muscles torn, the fingers dislocated. Healed, all healed, yet the nerves were weakening, the rubber bands of sinew and tendon losing their snap-back, and no matter how many racquet balls I crushed daily, or spade-loads of dirt I shoveled, the status quo slipped and my hand quivered when it grew tired and it grew tired ever more quickly.

"Hold tight a bit longer. I'll ask Meg for help."

"You ready to take it there?" he said. "You loop her in, this gets real."

"She's a research genius. Be peachy to know what we're dealing with." Detective license in my wallet notwithstanding, my girlfriend was the brains in the relationship.

"Kinda your job."

"I'm too busy getting punched in the face."

He hefted a stone and chucked it onto the pile.

"Does the origin matter? Gotta figure it's blood money, pure filth, the veritable root of evil. Get it laundered, problem solved. Who cares where it came from as long as we know where it's going?"

Any counter I threw at him would be weak.

"Blood money tends to carry a curse. I don't want to get bitten in the ass down the road."

"Brother, we were screwed the moment we walked into the madman's lair." He dropped his cigarette butt and commenced digging again. "Go read one of your books on mythology. Any of them. Curses get stronger with time. Dumping it for whatever we can get is the smart play."

"The smart play is to douse it in gasoline and strike a match."

He laughed as if I were making a joke.

Increasingly, there were moments when I wished heartily that we *were* capable of making the smart play. Just once.

NATURE HAS EVERYTHING PLOTTED to a gnat's ass. Her vast blueprint overwhelms our ability to fully comprehend the true shape of reality. We glimpse points of intersection, we hear phantom notes on a cool autumn breeze, but seldom apprehend the greater symphony at play.

The day after we relocated the money, I sparred a few rounds with the regulars at the Deadfall Gym in Kingston. The Deadfall didn't help me improve my skills; it slowed their degradation. I'm strong and have fought enough to acquire an arsenal of nasty techniques. Fighting isn't a static art; it mutates rapidly, endlessly, and for every offensive tactic, there's a defense or a counter. I gave better than I got and while sparring isn't really combat, to put it bluntly, I'd slowed. Somebody drilled me with a flying knee, applied a guillotine choke, and cranked my neck; somebody else hooked me behind the ankle and flung me headfirst onto the mat. The crash rattled the gym's metal garage door. Also got a complimentary dented nose in the bargain. Rub-some-dirt-on-it-and-walk-it-off type of damage.

Food for thought, these sessions, coupled with the aforementioned weakness in my left arm. Proof positive my problems weren't localized; they were systemic. I'd withstood copious measures of physical punishment in my days with the mob. The physical abuse quotient only got worse since I began sticking my nose into folks' business as a detective. Hospital visits and medical bills accrued. MDs tsked and clucked over my collection of injuries and chronic ailments. They passed around X-rays and CAT scans with the enthusiasm of kids trading baseball cards. The upshot being, my bones and muscles ached in the morning; neither hand was quite so steady at the range, and I squinted to read fine print. I did my level best to outwit and out-grapple Father Time; in ad-

dition to sparring at the Deadfall, I religiously committed to physical and mental exercise, which included
jogging, swimming, and weights. Daily I completed
crossword puzzles and played chess matches against the
computer and valiantly argued philosophy with Lionel
and Meg. I read a book a week.

Regardless, the slippage couldn't be ignored, only endured.

HOMEWARD BOUND, downtown rush hour, I waited at
a red light. A couple of frat bros in the oncoming lane
jumped out of a Saab to harangue a guy in a rattletrap
Chevy. The frat bros jeered abuse and pounded on the
Chevy's door; its driver slowly emerged. He required
some time because there was a lot of him to unfold from
the cab. Six-six and two-fifty, easy. He wore grungy work
clothes and an orange safety vest. His hairy arms dangled
near his knees. I didn't get a clear look at his expression
and didn't need to. His posture spoke volumes. Reminded
me of the deceptive laziness of a grizzly several heartbeats
before it decides to charge.

Obviously, the punks had never seen an angry bear or
heard death call them by name. The bright orange vest
was a pretty clear metaphor. DANGER. KEEP OUT. BEWARE
OF DOG. MINEFIELD. They weren't reading the signs of
impending doom.

More yelling ensued, coupled with threats of a beating. When this didn't resolve the matter, one of the bros

decided to raise the stakes. He poked the construction worker's chest. The big guy palmed the kid's face and slammed him into the pavement. The other bro wisely beat feet toward his own car. My light turned green and I didn't catch the end of the melodrama. Or perhaps that *was* the end. The dude pronated in the intersection was bound for somewhere on a stretcher.

Once I'd gotten home and sipped a tall whiskey, I considered the implications. It's no evolutionary mistake that men default to stupidity and aggression. No accident that they overestimate their capabilities, recklessly court danger, and are reliably delusional regarding the hazards involved. Nature greases the gears of progress with blood. I'm a believer in omens and auguries, except by different names—pattern recognition and quantum entanglement. Reality is a frequency, time is a ring, and gravity bleeds through a membrane that cocoons this universe from its neighbors; cells gently colliding within an infinite superstructure.

Which is to say, I'd scaled a mountain summit and instead of finding a wise man in a cave, Death looked me in the eye and winked. Guru Death compelled me to consider my allotted span in less than romantic terms— the phases of an animal's life cycle. Maybe that's the reason I'd recently obsessed over werewolf movies. The popular legend of the lycanthrope featured a surcease of mortal weakness. Werewolves shrugged off disease and lead. They shunned personal responsibility, and that might've represented their most attractive quality.

Loping through a night forest, howling in bloodlust, and doing what comes naturally without remorse.

SINCE MY OUSTER FROM Alaska, home was a cabin on a sprawling farm-slash-commune near the rural outskirts of New Paltz. I enjoyed the abiding quiet of Hawk Mountain Farm at night, when the tourists who came for the sweat lodge, or the meditation circles, or the folksy seminars drifted away and the animals were dreaming in the barn. I yearned for the scent of green bark after a hard rain and the rush of wind in the trees. Darkness was truly dark on the edge of the forest—a security lamp hanging from the barn center beam and the porch light of the main house up the hill floated in a void. On those occasions when a storm knocked out the power, we were instantly transported to an epoch of peasants who took shelter behind barred doors, praying for sunrise when all the beasts withdrew into the forest.

I savored it because I knew change was inevitable. Much sooner than later, Meg would demand a gesture of commitment and that gesture would entail wholesale changes by yours truly. She and her son, Devlin, wanted me to move in. Or, I assumed they did. They loved me and my faithful hound, Minerva. We'd edged around the subject and watched it grow into the proverbial elephant in the room. Even I couldn't feign obliviousness forever.

Lionel inhabited a shack not far from mine through the woods. He acted as farm roustabout for Virgil and

Jade Walker, the elderly New Age hippie gurus who
owned the property and dazzled clients from around the
globe with their peppy mysticism. Evenings, he bunkered with a case of cheap beer, or, if feeling sociable,
went hell-raising in town. In the manner of the ancient
Greeks confronted with an epic dilemma, I knocked on
his door to seek his wise, albeit booze-soaked counsel. I
explained my worries—physical and spiritual.

He shrugged and said my chickens were coming home
to roost. Quote, unquote. I grumbled about the enigma
of cornpone aphorisms.

"Consult the foolproof Getting Old Checklist," he
said. "Has your dick stopped responding to commands?
Do you moan when leaning over to fetch a beer from the
fridge? *Cluck-cluck-cluck,* amigo."

"The goths and the decadents had it one hundred percent correct," I said. We sat on the porch, watching
snowflakes gather in the dusk. A storm was coming; a
storm was always coming.

"Which ones?" He sipped a beer and patted my dog,
Minerva, who sat between us, panting contentedly. She
was blanketed in pine needles and dead leaves from
romping after rabbits in the nearby woods.

"Poe, Baudelaire, Camus. The usual suspects."

"They think we should spend that dough too?"

"They think a man is going to suffer no matter which
way he jumps."

When I thought of the treasure, all I could picture
was the Croatoan's gangrenous features welded to the
mask he'd worn while slaughtering all those mobsters,

prostitutes, and hapless jerks who'd stumbled across his path.

"Are you okay?" He studied me intently.

"Meg stopped what she was doing and stared at me, like you're staring. She said, 'You've changed.'"

"Was it a compliment?"

I didn't know.

CHAPTER TWO

Seventy-two hours before the Feds brought the hammer down on Badja Adeyemi, a right bastard of an ex-NYPD cop, he summoned me to his cabin on Elkhorn Lake. He offered my day rate and some Glenrothes 18 to hear his spiel, so I cleared the decks and made the hour drive upstate from my residence in the hinterlands of New Paltz and Rosendale.

The call intrigued me on its face; the offer of scotch and money didn't hurt. A man with his clout had access to every detective in the book. We weren't acquainted and my agency was in the Catskills bush league. Yet it was doubtful that he picked my name out of a hat. What I said about nature having a plan counts here too. The machinery of the universe is always grinding. Now and again, we fleas intersect with the gears' teeth.

Normal people hadn't heard of Adeyemi; however, if you were a criminal, politics junkie, or partial to tri-state high society, the name likely rang alarm bells. Hop a time machine back a couple decades on the mean streets of New York where Adeyemi toiled as a patrol cop, detective and, lieutenant, respectively, and you happened to operate on the wrong side of the law, his size thirteen jackboot might well have trod your face in the name of justice. His latest résumé highlights included ex-bodyguard and majordomo to a world-renowned business mogul turned politician. U.S. Senator Gerald Redlick, aka Mr. Charisma, CEO and owner of Redlick Group. Him, everybody knew.

Adeyemi had been holed up in the sticks since August. That summer, he'd participated in the epic public foreign corruption trial of the former Redlick Group CFO. RG specialized in real estate. As with any other heavyweight corporation, its subsidiaries and affiliates extended the mother ship's reach into dozens of techs on multiple continents. Laundering filthy, filthy Russian dough was the key indictment against the CFO. Due to his history with the organization, Adeyemi got tagged as a minor player, although everybody figured he knew more than he'd proven willing to divulge. His cooperation hadn't extended past invoking the Fifth Amendment.

The spectacle ended in a hung jury. News analysts predicted the Southern District of New York would reload and try, try again, this time armed with new information and more pressure on potential witnesses. Redlick was the big fish they wanted; this was known. It beggared credulity to assume anything had transpired at the corporation without his say-so. Problem for the DOJ was, the senator had cunningly insulated himself as a matter of course; he'd placed the majority of his holdings in a blind trust upon assuming office. Critics alleged that he'd orchestrated certain aspects of his business with a wink and a nod, as a mafia don might. Redlick's former CFO declined to flip on the senator, immunity deal notwithstanding. Apparently, the exec was more terrified of vengeful Russian oligarchs (and likely Redlick himself) than doing five to ten in a federal prison.

Adeyemi was likely to be the player without a chair when the organ stopped playing. His prize? An unlucky recipient of the government's full attention. The Feds reasoned that a longtime bodyguard, driver, and confidant would possess mucho dirt on Redlick. Surely said bodyguard, driver, and confidant had been corrupted by proximity. Surely he possessed a weak spot that the Southern District of New York could exploit to force his testimony.

Redlick, a rumored deviant and scofflaw long before this current scandal, had cause to be mightily worried. He was the first New York Republican elected to the U.S. Senate since the 1990s and the odds were stacked against another term. Whatever his legal and political jeopardy might entail, and amid a chorus of fellow GOP senators calling for him to quit his office, Redlick exuded trademark smugness at every press conference. He was either a man with nothing to fear, or a man who feared nothing.

I got on the road.